About the Author

A former teacher who specialised in English and History. Married with two sons. Brought up in Worcestershire and now living in Yorkshire. An avid reader who always had an ambition to write. Other interests include travelling and antiques.

Other books by Felicity Knight:

Carenza's Journey
ISBN: 9781849634472
Austin Macauley Publishers (2013)

Carenza's Heirs
ISBN: 9781849638715
Austin Macauley Publishers (2014)

To my granddaughter Amber, with love.

Felicity Knight

THE SECRETS OF WESTBOROUGH HALL

AUSTIN MACAULEY
PUBLISHERS LTD.

A CIP catalogue record for this title is available from the British Library.

ISBN 9781785546167 (Paperback)
ISBN 9781785546174 (Hardback)

www.austinmacauley.com

First Published (2015)
Austin Macauley Publishers Ltd.
25 Canada Square
Canary Wharf
London
E14 5LQ

Printed and bound in Great Britain

Acknowledgments

I would like to thank my husband for his IT support and research for the historical aspects of this novel, also my family Jamie, Jonathan and Wei for their IT support when the computer goes wrong. Also to thank my sister Judith Milne for the creation of the front cover.

Prologue

Viscount James Devine, who had been born in the second to last decade of the nineteenth century, was the heir to the Earl of Westborough, who owned vast lands across the Midlands in the counties of Worcestershire, Herefordshire and Gloucestershire. The family had farmed these acres for centuries dating back to the fourteen hundreds when England's wealth had been found on the backs of the nation's sheep. Wool had been traded with the Continent and the Westborough family had acquired riches like many other prominent families in the land. The next century saw a further rise in prosperity for the Westboroughs when a member of the family was knighted. As century followed century Henry VIII created the then baronet an earl for services rendered to the monarchy during the dissolution of the monasteries and their place in history had been assured.

The family seat had been rebuilt during the reign of the Great Harry's daughter, the indomitable Elizabeth. Its Tudor architecture took the form of an E as many great buildings did at that time as a mark of respect to Her Majesty. The fine building, aptly named Westborough Hall, was situated on the Worcester and Hereford borders overlooking the Malvern Hills. It had been an enviable place to live.

The history of the family still continued to be entwined with royal causes and during the English Civil War saw the Westboroughs taking up arms on the side of their royal masters. Exile had even been known but the family always returned to their home strengthened by their experiences and the causes that they had upheld. Down the centuries as such crises had come and gone, their role in history had not lessened but had changed as the Earl sat in the House of Lords and helped to forge the future with his peers.

James Devine, heir to the ageing Earl, had been raised to be proud of the family heritage. He was a much treasured and precious only son. Therefore, it was not surprising that he had become indulged and spoilt. His parents had been late in producing an heir which they had truly believed might never happen after his mother had suffered numerous miscarriages and the premature death of a male heir at six months old. James' subsequent birth had heralded new hope for their dynasty. His mother had never been pregnant again; now nearing her middle forties nature had smiled sweetly on them and they were eternally grateful for this final blessing that they had received so late in life. James had been a lusty baby from the first, frustrating the cousin who was licking his lips at the possibility of inheriting the title and the lands and wealth that went with it.

The old Earl died leaving a fifteen-year-old son to inherit the title and begin a lifelong feud with the new dowager Countess Cecily who was not prepared to release the reins of parental control even when her son should eventually reach his majority. Cecily had been an heiress in her own right and often used disinheritance as a way to keep her errant son under control, but he would scoff in her face and used his father's millions to quell her ever increasing hold over him. But James could not have it all his own way for, legally, he was a minor, but he vowed that as soon as he attained his majority he would rid himself of his mother's tight hold. He would then be master of his own destiny and she would know her place. Eventually as time went on he had attained a good degree from Oxford in History and Politics in order to give him a greater knowledge of the world that would one day be his when he took up his seat in the House of Lords. However, his greatest passion was for the land that he had inherited. From being a young child he had enjoyed the freedom that the land gave him, riding here and there to discover more about it and the people who lived upon it. His mother was ever fearful that he would be killed through his wildness but his father had been much the same during his youth. They were very alike in such matters and would have been a force to be reckoned with had the old Earl lived a much longer life.

'Leave the boy alone,' the old Earl would say to his wife, 'let him get this phase of freedom and wildness out of his system. He will learn eventually to settle down to what is expected of him.' But the Earl had died soon after the words had been uttered and Cecily drew the reins ever tighter. James, with little personal freedom, grew ever more rebellious and strong headed. He stayed away from the main house often residing in the smaller properties on the estate, working the land with the tenant farmers so that he did not have to spend time in his mother's orbit. Once James left Oxford he came into his inheritance and now totally renounced his mother's hold over him, knowing that the only way that he could do so was by marrying, thus removing his mother physically from the main house into the dower property which would be hers for the duration of her life. It was at this time that he first set eyes on Lady Clarissa Jenkins at a dinner party in London given by mutual friends of both families. She was a beautiful young woman who was the younger daughter of the impoverished Earl of Dunhaven. She and her family had lived a life which could only be described as a frugal and struggling existence; it had been difficult to maintain appearances in the aristocratic world without the wherewithal to finance such a lifestyle. Their estate had been sold to a captain of industry whose fortunes were in the ascendancy, but the town house in London had been retained to keep some semblance of normality in their life, to still hold their heads up in their social world. James was not bothered that the woman he was attracted to came from such circumstances. She still had the breeding and status that he was used to and would be regarded as a good match. There was enough money within his family to not have concerns about a prospective bride bringing few coffers of wealth to his table in the form of a dowry. He knew that he was smitten with the young woman, not necessarily in love in a passionate sense but he knew that he needed an heir and marriage would remove him from his mother's clutches. It was a decision that was hastily made. The nuptials of the young couple were to be sooner rather than later and, after a short courtship of only three months, the wedding took place in the Church of Saint Peter set in the village of Durston on the Westborough estate. Cecily, however, was not as pleased as she might have been for her influence on her son and his choice of a future bride had been taken out of her hands and there was nothing that she could do about it, other than utter the most vociferous of protests which were duly ignored by her son and his bride. Thus began the feud which was to last until Cecily drew her last breath. She had become an outcast, a social pariah even within the Westborough community and her withdrawal into a small world left her lonely and bereft. James had naively felt that his troubles were over only to find that his new wife was not quite as docile as he had once thought. The trouble began nearly as soon as he had placed the marriage band on her wedding finger. She had taken well to being the lady of the house, running it with great precision but at the same time alienating the servants who began to look for employment elsewhere. Even those of long standing could not stomach her rudeness or criticisms about their work.

'Standards have to be raised,' she had spat at them as they stood before her in the entrance hall as she railed about the lack of dedication to the cleanliness of the place or the way they addressed herself or the Earl. In the lower precincts of the downstairs world complaints were rife. The butler Perkins was asked to intervene with the young Earl but James was enjoying his status of a married man too much to interfere in what he considered to be his wife's domain, but eventually her venom began to be directed at himself and the novelty of his position as husband began to wear very thin. The words 'marry in haste and rue the day' echoed through the chambers of his mind and he began to regret the hasty decision he had made. But that was now history and life had to move forward to embrace any failures and successes that might lie in their path. James needed an heir and felt that if there was a child soon it might soften her emotionally and she could focus her energies elsewhere. Was he about to force on a child what had been his own experiences? He hoped not but he knew that his wife would never own him body and soul as she hoped to do. He decided that a quick succession of children would keep her occupied while his own life followed another direction. He was most definitely his own man and it was time that his harridan of a wife learned that he was in charge and she had to toe the line.

Part 1

Chapter 1

The whole country had been buzzing with the news of the King's friend for months. It was a liaison of some magnitude which did not seem to be going away. He had had many friendships with other women over the years but Wallis Simpson seemed to have captured his heart. However, conjecture was mixed in the public domain. The older generation thought she was a gold digger and the young enjoyed the romance of the whole affair while politicians, particularly the old school, were concerned for the monarchy while it rested in Edward's hands, some thinking that they were unsafe in his very emotional state of mind. He had accepted little advice on the matter of his love affair and suddenly everything had come to a head. Now he had made the most momentous decision of his life to give up the throne that he had only occupied for a few months for the sake of a woman, an American at that. The nation held its breath wondering what would happen next. It had been a night to remember, Thea Cavendish thought to herself, as she took a long look at her reflection in the mirror. She ran a comb through her unruly mass of short, blonde curls which had a will of their own. She shook her head and the curls bounced into place and then she smiled. But the smile vanished as she remembered last night's wireless transmission to the British people. Like many the previous night, December 10th 1936, would be etched on memories up and down the nation for possibly all time. He had abdicated the throne for the woman he loved leaving a nation feeling bereft, tearful and angry. This was the first time in a modern era that this had happened. The historians said that you had to go back before the Conquest to draw parallels. So what next, Thea wondered for the former King and his future wife and the British people? Thea had specifically risen early to fetch the newspapers from the vendor at the end of the street and she was going to devour every single word that had been written on the subject. She wanted to know all about the King and the woman who had captured his heart. There were also likely to be titbits about the new, shy king and his lovely young family. Her heart went out to them. They were reserved, not groomed for the limelight that had been thrust upon them. How must they be feeling now that a new reign had begun and, as for the delightful princesses, their destiny had changed too, particularly for Princess Elizabeth?

The house was quiet as Thea closed her bedroom door silently behind her. Her sister, Sabine, would be still be asleep as would her mother Beatrice. Both would be equally emotionally drained as herself over last night's broadcast. Thea held her shoes in her hand as she tiptoed down the stairs. At the bottom of the staircase she placed a hand on the newel post to steady herself before slipping her feet into her shoes and then opened the front door wide. A blast of cold air hit her and she closed the door against the elements before going to find her coat and scarf from the tall cupboard at the end of the hall which was usually reserved for the outer garments of visitors. Now wrapped up against the cold she opened the front door again and noted the brightness of the morning. Drawing her coat more closely around her slender frame, she walked briskly towards the end of the road where she would find the newspaper vendor's kiosk. It was George who stood in the cold at this early hour, as he did most mornings of the year

'Read all about it!' he shouted wafting a paper above his head to attract the attention of passers-by. Thea smiled. He had no need to do that as people stopped regularly to buy their newspaper from him, but today they would want to know more about the Abdication Crisis, as it was known, which was dominating the headlines.

'The usual Miss Cavendish?' George asked as he regarded Thea who was hesitating in her decision.

'Yes please George and I will have these two as well.' She collected her purchases and placed them under her arm as she fumbled in her pocket for the correct change.

'Thanks miss,' George said touching his cap in appreciation of her custom. 'There is plenty of reading for you today then, Miss Thea.'

'Yes,' she said smiling at him as she turned to retrace her steps along the street, her head bent against the bitter wind. It was too cold to linger so she hurried to return to the warmth of the house. By now Hetty would have the range in the basement kitchen functioning; a cup of hot tea was always welcome. She entered the house discarding her outer garments and thrust them onto a hall chair. Tidiness had never been her greatest attribute. Descending the basement stairs she heard Hetty hard at work and the heat from the kitchen met her like a wall of flame. Already Thea could hear the kettle whistle cheerfully on the range and the noise of china being placed on the table.

'Morning miss,' Hetty said cheerfully. 'It's a cold one out there today.'

'Yes,' Thea answered in an abstracted fashion as her eyes were riveted on the headlines of one of the papers.

'Cup of tea miss?' Hetty continued with her diatribe. She was not used to having company in her domain so early in the morning. Even Mrs Platt, the cook, would not arrive for another half hour or so. Usually breakfast was served between eight thirty and nine thirty in the dining room unless Mr. Cavendish was at home when he usually rose early and ate his breakfast at eight o'clock before spending most of his day in his study. That was a holy of holies she thought. Nobody was allowed in there without permission except when it wanted cleaning or he had a visitor. She disliked the fact that it always smelt of his Havana cigars. She did not approve of people smoking but it was the fashion these days, particularly amongst the young. Hetty placed Thea's cup of tea in front of her young mistress. Thea continued with her reading so absorbed that she could barely remove her eyes from the page.

Suddenly she looked up. 'Is the fire lit in the drawing room, Hetty?' she asked.

'Yes miss. It should be warm now, miss.'

'I think that I will take these there then and my cup of tea.'

'Shall I tell you when breakfast is ready, Miss?'

'I don't think that will be necessary. Mrs Platt should have everything arranged as normal, but thank you.' She smiled at Hetty before climbing the steep stairs to the floor above.

Settled in the warmth of the drawing room, Thea continued her perusal of the papers. *The Times* and the *Telegraph* had not yielded anything new on the business of the Abdication although most of the pages appeared to be filled with the news of the crisis as it had become known. She picked up the newspaper that she read every day, *The Daily Gazette*, the local London newspaper, which offered gossip about the court or people who were part of London Society. She loved to read about such things although she did not mix in such circles. Again the headlines shrieked out at her about the Abdication. She was bored now so she flicked casually through the pages to see what the reaction from London Society would be. As she reached page six her hand flew to her face, half concealing it and a cry emanated from her lips as she read on. There in front of her was a picture of her father but it could not be. The headline said 'Death of Earl.' Her father was not an earl but the likeness between the two men was uncanny. The paragraph concluded that the Earl of Westborough had been survived by the countess and their three children. He had died in his sleep from a heart attack. Thea continued to thumb through the rest of the pages but with little interest. She was unable to erase the photograph of the Earl from her mind. She felt restless and distracted, wanting to show other members of her family the picture so that they could still her fears, but she just knew that she was being ridiculous for her father was not an earl but plain Mr. James Cavendish. But strangely the Earl shared the same first name as her father.

In the distance she could hear the dining room door opening and closing which was an indication that breakfast was nearly ready. Upstairs a door closed noisily followed by the sound of feet padding along the landing and down the stairs going in the general direction of the dining room. Picking up the newspapers Thea walked into the hallway and followed her mother into breakfast. It could only be her mother for Sabine often missed the first meal of the day, particularly after a late night with a new beau. Thea's assumption was correct. Her mother stood at the sideboard filling her breakfast plate from the hotplates which Mrs Platt had placed there earlier. Beatrice turned at the sound of her daughter. 'Hello darling. Did you sleep well?' She smiled, displaying the love for her children which was always near the surface.

'No, not really, Mummy. I think that my mind was too full of the King and what he has done.'

Beatrice sat at the head of the table, placing her dish onto the stiff white tablecloth. Flamboyantly she shook out her napkin and placed it over her knees. Thea seated herself to her mother's right and placed her small portion of bacon and tomatoes in front of her.

'Mummy where is Daddy?'

The question had been asked before she realized what she was saying.

'He's away on business. You know that darling. It is part of the downside of being married to a politician.'

Thea bent her head over her food but just stirred it around her plate, unable to eat. She felt that she would choke if she tried. Her mother watched her for a moment puzzled by her daughter's behaviour.

'What is it Thea? Tell me.'

'Is Daddy an earl Mummy?'

Beatrice turned pale as the question hit its target. 'What a silly thing even to suggest. Where did you get such a fanciful idea from?' Thea looked at her mother and then produced the *The Daily Gazette* from beside her chair. She unfolded the unwieldy newspaper and found the page where she had seen the photograph of the dead Earl which she proceeded to show to her mother. Beatrice took the paper and perused the article before turning to her daughter. Just at that moment the telephone rang in the hall and then it stopped. Hetty's voice was just audible. The dull sounds of the conversation ceased, to be followed by the maid's head appearing around the door of the dining room.

'Excuse me madam but your solicitor would like to speak to you. He says it is of some urgency.'

'Thank you Hetty,' Beatrice said, having already risen from the table, her face a picture of concern and her napkin abandoned in her haste to take the telephone call. Her face was as white as a sheet as she seemed to anticipate what the urgency was about.

'Please excuse me Thea; I must take this telephone call,' Beatrice added. Her half-eaten breakfast was abandoned as she hurried from the room. Thea's eyes followed her mother's swift departure. She was perplexed by the whole situation. Her mother had picked up the telephone in the hall but Thea could not hear what was being said; only the intoning of her voice was audible. Hetty entered the dining room to see if the family had finished breakfast.

'Can I clear away, miss?' she asked.

'Yes of course you can,' Thea agreed but she was straining to hear if her mother was still using the telephone. 'Is Mrs Cavendish still using the telephone Hetty?'

'No miss. She finished her conversation and went upstairs. If you don't mind me saying Miss, she looked a bit upset.'

'Thank you Hetty I will go to her. I fear she might have had some bad news.' Thea had abandoned her breakfast and left the dining room to go to her mother in her hour of need, suspecting that their recent conversation had not been quite truthful. She tapped on her mother's bedroom door and opened it a little. The anguish which she heard emanating from her parent nearly broke her heart.

'Can I come in Mummy?' she said, opening the door a fraction wider, but there was no answer; only raw grief met her ears. Thea went to her Mother who lay on the bed in a foetal position and began to cradle her parent in her arms; she rocked her like she would a child allowing her mother to keen in her intense grief.

'What is it?' she asked suddenly feeling frightened by her mother's distress. 'Is it about Daddy? You must tell us. Sabine and I are entitled to know.' Her mother turned her ravaged face towards her daughter and nodded her head. 'You were entitled to know a long time ago but we decided the fewer who knew our circumstances the better, even our own children.' Thea sat up looking puzzled; her secure world was beginning to turn and spiral out of control. Nothing was as it seemed any more. All news of the King's abdication was long gone for there was a crisis here within their four walls.

'Is my father this Earl of Westborough?' she asked; her demeanour was sober and anxious. Beatrice nodded her head while the tears flowed in rivulets down her cheeks. 'He is no longer ours to love,' she said enigmatically drying her eyes on her lacy handkerchief. 'In fact he has only been ours on the rare occasions he spends with us. Spent with us,' she corrected herself.

Thea was confused but what she did now realize was that her father had another family. She and Sabine had half siblings somewhere. Was her father a bigamist or were her own parents not married making herself and Sabine…? She could not contemplate what it all must mean. But she knew that it was time that the truth was told. The news headlines about the King were forgotten now that they had sorrows of their own.

Chapter 2

Thea looked at her mother's tear-stained face and her heart went out to her, but what she was failing to understand was the secrecy over her parents' union. But having thought that, it was deeply frowned upon to have a child out of wedlock let alone two if Sabine was included in this. Her father had obviously tried to protect his second family from gossip as he had used the name Cavendish like they all had. It had been Beatrice's family name that had been adopted by her parents she now realized. It made her understand the reasons why her parents had only a small circle of friends: otherwise they kept very much to themselves. There were no aristocrats in this inner circle of friends or even politicians that she knew of and that kept the reality of the situation at bay. There were too many things to wonder about and as it was she had not heard the full story. There was just too much to absorb but it was something that they just had to get used to. Their world had changed; crumpled into oblivion at their feet. Her mother's bedroom door opened and Sabine's tousled head appeared. She had heard the anguish and the muffled voices as their father's story had unfolded.

'What's the matter?' She levelled the question at her sister. Thea smoothed her mother's damp hair from her forehead and covered her with the crisp white sheet which was freshly laundered.

'Try and sleep Mummy,' she advised, 'you will feel better in a while. I will bring you a cup of tea up later.' Beatrice said nothing but like an obedient child she lay inert under the counterpane as her eyelids began to droop while the emotional exhaustion of the morning took its toll.

Sabine dressed untidily in yesterday's clothes followed her sister down the long landing into her bedroom. Thea motioned for her older sister to close the bedroom door quietly and then sit on the bed while she thought about how she was going to deliver the devastating news of their father as well as the bombshell her mother had dropped as the story had unfolded.

'You are going to have to brace yourself Sabby. There is no kind way to say it.' Tears were already beginning to glisten in her eyes as the shock of the news began to sink in.

'Say what?' Sabine asked nervously. Observing her mother's distress had disturbed her equilibrium. Beatrice was usually self-contained showing little emotion other than her affection for her children. Sabine had only seen her cry twice before in all of her twenty-two years.

'Daddy has died of a heart attack. There is no other way of softening the blow. It was announced in the paper this morning but there is something else which has been a huge secret. He is also the Earl of Westborough and has another family besides us. That is all I know. Mother has more to tell us.'

Thea watched her sibling's reaction to the news. It was heartbreaking to see the tears trace a course down her cheeks. Sobs racked her slight body as the news filtered into her shocked mind. Thea sat and watched her sister before taking her hand to caress it, to support her dear sister with the love that she felt for all her family but her thoughts drifted to her half-brother and -sisters wondering if their reaction had been the same. Had her father died at this Westborough Hall her mother had described? She had only concentrated on her father's death, not any other details concerning where it had happened. In fact she felt that the question was relevant to her feelings. She hoped that her father had died with the people he loved most around him and not by himself. This emotion choked her beyond reason for the people he loved most in the world had to be within the four walls of this house which had witnessed much love and laughter over the years. She thought about the times that would never be the same again, like

Christmas, but the harder she thought the more she realized that her father only spent short visits at home over the festive season. There were always reasons why he could not spend as much time as he wanted with them but he worked for the Government, some of his business so top secret that they could not be told what it was about. Now she knew the reasons which made her angry at the deception that had been played out in the dramas of everyday life. Her mother would have known but both of her parents had lied. She had no doubt that they loved both girls but to tell such blatant lies was hard to bear. Thea put her arm around her sister who continued to sob uncontrollably.

'Hush, Sabby. It will get better in time,' she said sagely, but she had little conviction on that matter. People whose grief was so raw rarely did. The luncheon gong reverberated through the house but nobody was hungry. After an hour Hetty cleared the table to be met by Mrs Platts' indignation that good food was going to be wasted. The news of their employer's demise had not filtered down to the kitchen quarters although they were aware that there was something terribly wrong.

'Must be bad news,' Hetty said taking a tray of dishes into the basement kitchen. 'I could hear the mistress crying upstairs.'

'Oh lordy, what a to do,' Mrs. Platt tutted as she placed their own lunch on the scrubbed pine table. 'There is great trouble up there mark my words.' Mrs Platt pointed a spoon upwards to emphasize the point that she was making.

'I wonder what it could be?' Hetty said as she liked a good gossip whenever there was an unfolding drama. Mrs Platt looked at the girl wagging her finger at her. 'What happens in these four walls my girl stays in these four walls. So you mind that you remember.' Hetty hung her head as she had been caught gossiping to the maid next door and had been in serious trouble with Beatrice, even to the extent of possibly losing her job. Raising her eyes to the older woman's face she said, 'I won't say nothing,' before scuttling out of the room to finish clearing the luncheon table, but it would still be nice to know what it was all about.

Later, still deluged by the great mountain of sorrow which lay heavily on their hearts, Sabine and Thea returned to their mother's bedroom where she lay awake waiting for their return. She was quiet now as she contemplated her daughters. Her arms flew wide to encompass them both in an embrace which seemed to say that they had to be brave for now it was the three of them against the world.

Chapter 3

James could not complain about Clarissa not fulfilling her uxorial duty for in the four years following their tempestuous marriage she had produced three children to fill the nursery at Westborough Hall. He had accomplished just what he had set out to do. He had kept Clarissa focused on her family and she had proved herself to be a good mother. It was a noisy, rambunctious nursery filled with the joys that only children could bring to such a large family home ruled over by Nanny Johnson, a large buxom woman who reigned over her territory with a rod of iron but had a kind heart and fiercely loved her charges with a passion. The oldest was Araminta (shortened to Minty), followed by Diana and lastly came Piers, James' heir, a boy of such sweet temperament that he charmed everybody who came within reach of him. He became the apple of his father's eye and when James was in residence at Westborough Hall the two spent much time together enjoying what most fathers and sons did. It was called quality time, for James spent much time away from home. Although Clarissa knew that she had lost the love of her husband over the years of her marriage with her domineering ways and complaints she still did not want to lose him. She needed him more than she was prepared to admit. Divorce was rare, particularly amongst the aristocracy, but it still happened and it was something she greatly feared. She had grown used to the affluence that the Devine money lavished on her and the lifestyle that she led. Her impoverished childhood by aristocratic standards was something that she did not want to repeat. She witnessed her struggling parents who regularly came to stay at the Hall to ease the burden on their finances. James was not concerned by the visitors that came to eat at his table rather than their own.

If it pleased his wife he was happy for it meant that he had a sense of freedom; and please himself he did. Not long after his marriage he had taken his seat in the House of Lords, which gave him the excuse to stay in London at the Westborough town house in Belgravia. Clarissa rarely joined him in London for the lifestyle did not suit her. Instead she enjoyed country pursuits and the company of her children and her parents. It was during this time that James met the lovely Beatrice Cavendish who was a socialite. They had met at a reception given by King Edward VII who was a lover of beautiful women. He had been accompanied by his mistress as he was on many occasions. Queen Alexandra only came to formal functions and rarely to such soirées. Beatrice had been accompanied by her uncle Lord Beaumont who was an acquaintance of James Devine. Their mutual attraction had begun from the very beginning and so an enduring love story ensued. Beatrice brought a sense of peace to James' life after the turbulence of Clarissa's domination. From the very beginning he had been truthful about his appalling marriage but it was the love for his children which had made his life worthwhile at Westborough Hall, a home he loved dearly except for the tempestuous presence of his wife. Beatrice made few demands on her beau, sensing that he would find it difficult to disentangle himself from the harridan of a wife whom he had described. Although her reputation was at stake having a liaison with a married man she led a very quiet life and kept just a handful of close friends who would understand the dilemma that she faced. It was a ménage à trois. When Beatrice became pregnant a few years into their relationship, plans had to be made to give the aura of respectability that was required during the Edwardian era.

'I have a plan,' James said one night as he arrived at Beatrice's home. 'I will set you up with a household of your own.'

'I have a home,' she laughed at him. 'Here.'

'This was your parents' home; you are known around here and as it is your sister lives here. What would people say?'

'I don't care what they say James. They only want to cause trouble. How can I care for people who do that?'

'It is my reputation too Bea,' he said, genuinely saddened. 'I'm a member of the Lords.'

'But James, the King has numerous mistresses so why should you be different?'

'But I am not the King,' he had laughed. 'I don't have mistresses everywhere nor do I want to. That is not my style. However, I want to protect you from Clarissa for there is no fury like my wife's scorn. Goodness knows what she would do if she found out.'

'All right as you wish,' Beatrice acquiesced, 'but I just want to be with you James. I am not asking to be your wife. I just love you.' James had enfolded her in a tight embrace showing the true love and affection he felt for her. He had blessed the day when Beatrice Cavendish had entered his life but his only regret lay in the fact that he had not met her before he had made the disastrous marriage to Clarissa for then they would have been together for all time. Her heritage was that of the aristocracy which would have made her an ideal wife in the eyes of the world and the fact that he truly loved her was the bonus in his life. It was since his meeting with Beatrice that he realized that he had never loved Clarissa and had only married her to move from his mother's clutches. It would cause a scandal to divorce his wife. Life was just too difficult to contemplate at times. The rules of the aristocracy separated them from other classes. Yet the lower classes had the freedom to marry for love much more than the affluent ever did.

Chapter 4

'Go on Mummy. There must be more to this story,' Sabine said. Her first wave of sorrow had finally abated as she stroked her mother's hand for comfort and encouragement.

'Did you live in this house from then on?' Thea asked with curiosity. Beatrice looked at the eager faces of her two daughters knowing that they were entitled to know all that had happened and should have been told the truth long ago, but the fewer the people who had been told the better it was for the little family. She was only too aware that she and James had lived a lie but it had not hurt anyone: then she corrected herself. It had hurt Clarissa when she discovered what had happened. Looking at the two beautiful faces in front of her she smiled wanly at them. The secret no longer mattered any more.

'I became pregnant,' she began. 'I gave birth to a little boy and we called him James after your father. However, he only lived for a few days because he had a heart defect and nothing could be done for him. He died in my arms in this very room.' Her face contorted in pain as she remembered the time as if it was yesterday. 'It was the saddest day of my life until today.' Beatrice lay back on her pillows exhausted by the recounting of the whole affair but Thea wanted to know more now that her mother had opened up to them. If she stopped that might be the end of the story.

'But you still stayed on in this house,' Thea urged her mother. Beatrice closed her eyes as if trying to remember all that had happened over the years. Her eyes opened wide as if remembering that her daughters were still there.

'Yes, Thea, I stayed here while your father lived between his two lives. This house is the town house belonging to the

Westborough estate. You two were born here like your brother.' Beatrice turned her face away from the daughters that she loved so much and let her memory take her back to happier times. This moment was just too much for us to bear for they were memories that she had shared with James. She thought about the last time that she had seen him. He had risen early as usual but that was the day that he was returning to Westborough Hall. He had taken her in his arms and kissed her passionately and had told her how much he loved her. It was almost as if he had had a premonition of death that morning, making his words something for Beatrice to remember and treasure for ever.

'Don't forget whatever happens that I have always loved you and our girls more than words can say. Tell them what I have said.' Those were the last words that he had uttered before he had hugged her for the last time and then he was gone, back to the other life and family. The girls' eyes blurred with the tears which were not far from the surface but Sabine was stoical in her attempts to continue pressing her mother for the rest of the story. But a great deal of anger was still there within her, fuelled by the deceptions that had taken place over the years. Her parents must have realized that the story would one day be told, just as it was now.

'Did you ever meet Clarissa?' Thea asked, now fascinated by the woman her father had married. Looking straight into the faces of her daughters, Beatrice gave a wry smile.

'Yes, I did just the once. I'm afraid that was enough.'

'What happened?'

'She came to the house here after our little James had died. The rumour mill had been working overtime and she had been told that her husband had a mistress. A friend of hers had seen us both out together in the city one night and had told her about it. It did not take her long to find out further details. She came to tell me to leave her husband alone as he was rightfully hers. She made it sound as if he was a possession.'

'But you didn't leave him alone because we are here,' Thea said with an explosion of laughter.

Beatrice gave a brittle smile, 'I told your father about the whole episode and he was furious. He went straight to Westborough Hall to have it out with her. I had never seen him so angry.'

'And what did Daddy do to sort it out?' Sabine asked. She had crept closer to her mother.

'He had told Clarissa that if she challenged the relationship he would divorce her and would cut her off without a penny. She had experienced poverty apparently and the threat silenced her. I never heard from her again. Your father lived between his two families. He had to keep up appearances for the sake of his other children whom he loved very much. He also had to see to the running of such a large estate. He had to keep his son's inheritance intact for the future. Your father would never have neglected such things.'

'When will the funeral be?' Thea wanted to know. Her face was grave and suddenly became choked with emotion at the thought. Everything was still so raw.

'I am waiting to hear from the solicitor. But you must remember that Daddy is no longer ours. Clarissa and her children have claimed him back as their own for legally he is theirs. We can have no hold on him anymore. I always knew that this would happen if Clarissa outlived him but it is something that you can't dwell on in everyday life. We will have to be strong as your father would have wished.' The three women knew how vulnerable they were in this uncertain world. What the future held could be anybody's guess now that they had lost the protection of James Devine. Beatrice hoped that Clarissa would not try and reap vengeance on them. She did not disclose this thought to her daughters. She began to cry once more as the three of them held each other until this new wave of sorrow had burnt itself out.

Chapter 5

Five days after the death of the Earl of Westborough, his widow Clarissa Devine sat proud and erect in the vast library at Westborough Hall. She was beautiful in a cold sort of way, her hair grey but twisted up into an elaborate coil at the back of her head. Her children had only ever known her wear her hair in such a style but it suited her, giving emphasis to her aristocratic features. She was dressed immaculately in black as the occasion demanded. Inside she still harboured grievances resulting from a long and unhappy marriage but, today, her unlined face was composed for she felt that the years of humiliation were at last over. Her children were good to her. They had been brought up that way and she felt that she could continue to rule over Westborough Hall with a rod of iron. Perhaps Piers would marry in the not-too-distant future and it was her job to discover a wife for him who was so sensitive and lacking in confidence that she would not be able to hold the reins of control over the house and would require assistance. Clarissa had decided that there was to be no retiring to the dower house as her mother-in-law had done in the past. She was not yet ready to release control over what had been rightfully hers for decades. Her place was to be here in the majestic surroundings of the big house for good. Sitting ramrod straight she glanced around her at the shelves of books, many of them ancient treasures from the past. There was gnarled dark oak panelling along one wall dating back centuries to the original building of the house. It was a room of exquisite beauty; at times its grandeur took her breath away. She had often sat in this room to read rather than in the drawing room, even on a stifling summer's day for its interior could be cool in summer, making a refreshing change from the heat outside, but in winter a log fire danced and spat in the huge fireplace lending comfort against the inclement weather outside. How she had grown to love this place over the years. It had become the home she had visualized in her youth when her penurious father could not afford to keep his family in the same style as much wealthier aristocrats. Across the large table sat Piers, the new Earl, still slightly unsure of the expectations that had been thrust upon him sooner than he had anticipated. His father should have lived for many more years. He was in a reverie wondering what the reading of the will would bring. Would it be straightforward? Who was to know? Beside him sat Minty and Diana; their faces were masked by the sorrow that was etched there. James Devine's daughters were also dressed in black as was the expectation of the occasion. Further down the table sat the Devines' solicitor, Ernest Fellowes, a partner in the firm Fellowes and Sinclair, solicitors to the wealthy. He was putting his papers ready for the reading of the will. He wore the suitable expression of one dealing with the bereaved. His manner was dignified and he spoke almost reverentially of the deceased whom he had served for many years and the firm for years before that. He coughed subtly to gather the attention of the family who had been absorbed by their own thoughts and emotions and then he began the task that he had come to undertake.

'All is in order Lady Devine,' he addressed himself to the widow whom he had never liked instead of to the young man who was inheriting his father's estate and fortune. He gave a wry smile knowing the contents of the will and was anticipating the furore which would surely erupt after he had delivered his client's instructions. Expectant eyes turned to him in readiness to begin. Their faces had turned suitably blank, inscrutable almost.

'There will of course be heavy death duties,' he began his preamble, 'but the estate and its wealth from all its resources is able to sustain such demands. In that way the Westborough estate is indeed extremely fortunate. But the Earl was always shrewd and had employed the best people to give him advice. It was his wish that this would be continued after his death.'

His eyes turned to look at the young Earl who did not speak but acknowledged the solicitor with a courteous nod of his head. He glanced at the widow believing that he had seen a hint of a smile, but it had gone before it had been allowed to develop. The mask was firmly back in place.

'There is to be a legacy for Lady Araminta and Lady Diana. Both legacies will be put in trust for the duration of your lives and you will be able to take the interest for your personal use. Your father did this to protect your interests.' He glanced up from his reading but neither of the sisters reacted to their father's decision. They were not surprised by their father's decision. It was well known that rich young women could be vulnerable to the predators who hunted for a fortune and he only had their interests at heart. Ernest Fellowes turned his gaze upon the Countess who sat dignified and serene, hoping that her husband had been generous with her to make up for his unfaithfulness. He began once more.

'I'm afraid, Lady Devine, that you will be left reliant on your son's generosity and charity for the rest of your life, however the dower house is at your disposal but will return to the estate on your demise.' Ernest took time to cough once more, this time with affectation, allowing him time to witness any reaction from the Countess. There was none. He felt that he had to admire the dignity that she maintained throughout this distasteful revenge of the Earl's. Fellowes had not thought that the relationship of his clients was so acrimonious although he had been aware of the contents of the will. None of this was easy for her. There was no flicker of emotion passing across the faces of the younger generation. Their emotions were tightly controlled and would only unravel when he had gone. The training to control their feelings had been taught them from the cradle. But there was something that he was to reveal which might cause a furore. He would be interested to see if there was to be a response.

'Now then, the rest of the estate will pass to you your lordship except,' he paused here and all eyes were focused on him now intrigued, 'except for the legacy left to Beatrice Cavendish which is to be paid annually for the rest of her life.

Finally, there will be a legacy for each of her two daughters, Sabine and Thea Cavendish who will also receive an income for life from the estate to be paid annually.' Ernest Fellowes replaced his papers on the gleaming surface of the library table before looking over his half-moon glasses which were lodged precariously over the bridge of his nose. Now he noted the reaction of all the members of the family. Their calm air of indifference had evaporated as they wondered who these women were. But nobody spoke at first expecting the solicitor to give an explanation, but he remained tight lipped on the matter expecting the dowager Countess to explain to her children in private after his departure. Already he had witnessed that Clarissa's face had darkened in anger; the mask had slipped as she assimilated every facet of her husband's treachery. But revenge appeared to be a more accurate word. Revenge on the life they had led together but mostly apart and there was nothing she could do about it, or was there? Could she contest the will, but again that would take money of which she had so little? James Devine's children were also rendered speechless, but for reasons that could not be more different from their mother. Eventually Minty, overcome by such curiosity, just could not contain herself.

'Who is Beatrice Cavendish?' Minty asked voicing what her siblings wanted to know, 'and her daughters.'

The three young people turned to their mother waiting for a response. Ernest Fellowes took his time to put his papers in order before placing them in his old, well used briefcase. Clarissa sat mutely, not wishing this humiliation to be made known to her children in front of the lawyer who no doubt would be amused by the whole proceedings. Her husband had vented his displeasure on her up to the very end. Diana, wanting to get to the bottom of this mystery, looked at the solicitor, one eyebrow raised in a quizzical fashion.

'Do you know Mr Fellowes?' she asked. He coughed again, not wishing to be drawn into a heated family debate. His silence spoke volumes.

'Will someone please tell us who these people are?' Piers, normally mild mannered, had stood up and banged his fist on the table jarring the fragile nerves of his kin.

'I think I need a glass of water,' said Clarissa, rising to leave. Normally she would have pulled the bell cord for assistance but all she wanted to do was to escape from the room, from such humiliation and the questions that her children demanded.

'Not yet Mother, not until we know. There is something going on here that I think that we need to be informed about.' Clarissa sat down again feeling totally defeated by her husband and now her son, who seemed to have inherited more of her husband's genes than she had realized. Recognizing defeat she said, 'Beatrice Cavendish was your father's mistress.' At this juncture Ernest Fellowes rose diplomatically from his chair, briefcase in hand in readiness to depart. 'I will take my leave of you all and will inform you of any outstanding matters. Otherwise I will see you at the funeral. Such a tragic time, I'm so sorry.' There was no comment from the family who were still looking aghast at Clarissa. Quietly, Ernest closed the library door behind him wishing that he could be a fly on the wall to witness the conversation. Voices raised in anger were audible as he collected his trilby from the hall table and his overcoat from the maid who stood in readiness to assist him. Her face remained impassive as good servants neither saw nor heard anything until they returned below stairs when the gossip began. The relief that the task was complete was visible on Ernest's countenance and he was more than satisfied that he had made his exit in time.

In the library Piers was in full flow, not mincing his words. 'Who is this woman Mama? It is obviously someone you know.'

Clarissa, head bowed, mumbled, 'She was your father's mistress and the two girls are his daughters. Yes he had two families and I had to suffer the humiliation of it all. I was probably the laughing stock amongst the aristocracy. It was one of the reasons that I stayed at Westborough Hall and rarely went to London but there were times that by doing so I was giving your father free rein to continue his subterfuge.' The tears of anguish streamed down her face and then she began to sob uncontrollably. Her voice had grown more highly pitched the longer she spoke. Her children gawped at her like simpletons as they assimilated this piece of intelligence. Their mother sat down again as if her legs would not take the weight of her body. Piers' attitude softened as he understood the blow that his father had delivered to his mother in financial terms and the ultimate humiliation of giving his mistress freedom to run her own life. But there were two sides to every story and, in this instance, his father would never be able to defend himself. Piers knelt at his mother's side and took her hands in his.

He felt her humiliation deeply for after all she was his mother. 'I'm sorry that it came to this Mama. Father has been cruel to you but don't fret; you will not want for anything. I will finance everything and secure an allowance on you. You don't need to worry.' The frigidity of his mother's demeanour thawed as tears ran down her face again and her hand rose to caress her son's cheek in gratitude. None of her children had witnessed her humility before and they were all touched by their brother's compassion. They put up a united front but it did not destroy the curiosity that they felt for these half siblings that they did not know.

'Tell us about this woman?' Minty asked. They just needed to know and Clarissa did not disappoint them.

'Beatrice was your father's mistress from just after the time that Piers was born. I gave your father an heir and he repaid me with humiliation and contempt. She was his mistress for all that time. She held his love and I had nothing,' the venom had returned to her face as she spat out the words as if they had left a nasty taste behind. The three siblings looked at each other in disbelief. They had always been aware of the enmity which had ruined their parents' marriage but all of them had loved their parents in equal measure. They had never witnessed the evidence of the spiteful woman that James had grown to hate for she loved each of her children unconditionally like any mother. Now they saw the rawness of their mother's hatred for their father. It unnerved them and they wondered what might happen next.

Chapter 6

The next day, just as it had been arranged, Ernest Fellowes arrived at the appointed time to attend his meeting with Beatrice and her daughters. He stood outside the front door of the town house in Belgravia admiring the elegant façade of the building before ringing the large, well-polished brass bell which had been carved into the shape of a lion's head. He smiled ruefully to himself feeling that this time he was not entering the lion's den. He laughed inwardly at his little joke but his features clouded once more, for he was not happy about what he had been instructed to do. After his return to London on the previous afternoon, a telephone call had been put through to him in his magnificent office which was beautifully furnished in wood panelling on one wall and book cases on the others containing great tomes of leather-bound law books which were only occasionally used. And there was highly polished antique furniture which had belonged to the previous partners of the law firm. Leather Chesterfield settees and comfortable chairs graced the outer perimeter of the spacious room where he could entertain his illustrious clients, the rich and famous of London society. But he had been sitting at his vast mahogany topped desk when the call had been put through.

'Ernest,' the now seductive voice of Lady Devine purred down the telephone. Obviously she had made a remarkable recovery after the shocks of the morning. 'I was wondering if you could deliver a message to Mrs Cavendish from the new Earl.' Momentarily he wondered why Piers had not telephoned him himself. Yet Clarissa delivered the request and, before he could say more, the telephone had been replaced in its cradle and the line had gone dead.

'I'm but a servant,' Ernest muttered to himself but smiled gleefully when he remembered how well paid he was for such services. He just hoped that he continued to serve this new era of the Devine family for sometimes such young men as Piers Devine wanted to forge their own destiny. In with the new and out with the old was a thought that occurred to him. He had not as yet got the measure of the young Earl.

His mind returned to the present as the front door of the town house was opened by Hetty whose uniform was slightly askew on her plump body. She looked as if she had been rushing as she was breathing heavily and her cheeks were slightly flushed by the exertion.

'Good afternoon sir,' she said in the flat intonation of her Yorkshire heritage. 'May I take your hat and coat? Madam and her daughters are waiting for you in the drawing room.' Ernest Fellowes divested himself of his outer garments which had shielded him against the inclemency of the severe cold weather that they had been experiencing. Witnessing Hetty knock on the door of the drawing room, he waited for the 'come in Hetty' before she opened the door wide for their visitor to pass through. Beatrice rose from her seat close by the roaring fire for the day had chilliness about it that she could not throw aside. Her hand extended in greeting to the solicitor and he felt warmth in this gesture that he had not received at Westborough Hall. It was no doubt where the old Earl's heart lay. Fellowes assessed the woman in front of him. She was indeed striking to look at but not conventionally beautiful like the dowager Countess. However Beatrice possessed a sunny disposition which put anyone who met her immediately at ease but he was aware of the sadness that lay in her intelligent blue eyes.

'Hetty, could you bring some tea please?' She smiled at the servant.

'Yes, Madam,' came the reply. Hetty and Cook had by now heard of the death of Mr Cavendish and were equally shocked as they had liked their employer who had always been good to them during the time of their employment. For once Hetty had not gossiped with the maid next door but had remained tight-lipped as a mark of respect to the family. She had liked Mr Cavendish because he did not possess a snobbish or condescending attitude like some employers she had heard about. The fact that he was not what he seemed to be had not reached the ears of the servants. Beatrice had tried very hard to shield her daughters from any gossip, but who knew for how long she could go on doing that? She did not know. Fellowes turned to greet Thea and Sabine who solemnly shook his hand and he observed the still raw grief etched on their faces. This situation never failed to touch him when he had to meet the families after bereavement and it was one part of his occupation that he detested. Years of working in law had not hardened him sufficiently against the unhappiness of others, however much he tried to distance himself from such emotional turmoil.

'I'm so sorry to see you in such circumstances,' he said to them all. He sat in the chair that had been indicated to him. It was positioned in front of the window which overlooked the road. He noted the passers-by who shielded themselves from the bitter cold but then he turned his attention to the purpose of his visit.

'Shall I begin?' he asked.

'Of course,' Beatrice said. She had no fears about James' generosity. He had always said that she and the girls would be well taken care of and she never doubted his promises. Hetty reappeared carrying a tray laden with tea and some delicacies which she had found in the kitchen.

'I'll pour tea Hetty. Thank you,' Beatrice said not wishing the girl to overhear what Ernest had to divulge. Hetty's gossiping was well known. Beatrice had only kept her on because it was so difficult these days to find new staff. On account of her grief she had not been aware how respectful her maid had been in recent days.

'Yes, madam.' Hetty dipped a curtsey and left the room rather disappointed that there was nothing to tell Cook but knew that it would go no further. Beatrice handed round the delicate Worcester china teacups while she listened to Ernest's monologue. There was nothing that surprised her for herself and her daughters. James had kept his word. After he had read their part of the will Ernest regarded the faces before him. They appeared happy at the decisions that James Devine had made, but now he had to deliver the instructions that he had received from Clarissa on the previous afternoon. How he disliked that woman and had often wondered why the Earl had ever married her in the first place. She was vicious and vindictive when her world was under threat, but at other times could be totally charming.

'I'm afraid that I have some bad news on two accounts.' Three pairs of eyes regarded him intently. They had received enough bad news in the past few days. 'What could be worse than the news of my poor James going like that?' Beatrice's voice was controlled as she had done most of her mourning in previous days, and the well of emotion that had hit her had nearly run dry.

'Yes well, I'm afraid that you all must brace yourselves for what I'm about to tell you. Lady Devine has specified through instructions from her son that your family must not attend the funeral. She said that he was her husband and she was not prepared to share him in death as she was forced to in life.' Beatrice rose from her chair and went to stand in front of the fire which blazed fiercely in the hearth as a chill ran through her. She had her back to the other occupants of the room momentarily before turning to look at them; her face was ravaged with pain and sadness.

'Very well Ernest,' she spoke softly and her voice was barely audible. 'I am fully aware that James was only mine when he was here but my children should be able to see their father laid to rest.'

'I'm afraid that is not possible. Her ladyship made it quite plain that nobody from your family was to attend. His lordship will be laid to rest next Friday at Westborough Hall or rather at the Church of Saint Peter. The funeral service is at one o' clock. I am so sorry to heap more sorrow upon you at a time like this. If I could have prevented it I would have done.'

Beatrice looked at the kindly face of the solicitor and smiled wanly at him.

'I know,' she said and the tears trickled down her cheeks as they had done so regularly since James' untimely death. Sabine went to her mother to give what comfort she could but her own heart was breaking, too.

'It looks as if our whole world is crashing down around us,' Sabine said as she looked at the solicitor, 'and none of it is of our making.' Earnest made a face of great sympathy but said nothing. It was not his job to side with one part of the family or the other wherever his private inclinations lay. Thea calculated the date of the funeral which would make it just five days before Christmas. What a sad time they would have. Her father's presence had always been like a beacon in the dark. A voice broke into her reverie.

'I'm afraid there is more bad news,' Ernest began once more. He felt that he had delivered enough of a blow already but he was only doing his job. 'This house belongs to the Westborough Hall estate and as such must be returned. The Earl did not make any provision for a home for your family in his will. It was clearly an oversight on his part so I'm afraid at your earliest convenience you have to vacate these premises. But not before the festive season ends. I am sure his lordship will be lenient on that account.'

Ernest Fellowes hated to be the bearer of bad tidings but the instruction that he had received from Clarissa had been made very clear that the Earl's second family had to depart as soon as possible after Christmas. The property had to be used by the young Earl when he took up his seat in the Lords in the New Year. Fellowes was fairly sure that the words had been Clarissa's own. As yet Piers Devine had not got the full measure of the momentous task that lay ahead of him and he did not bear the hatred to his father's second family that Clarissa possessed. Beatrice's daughters sat mutely unable to fully comprehend the events that were changing so swiftly or the deep animosity which existed between the two women who had occupied rival places in their father's life. The fact that they could be homeless within weeks was abhorrent. Why was Clarissa Devine being so uncharitable because they had all lost someone they loved?

'I have no knowledge about any of these instructions Mrs Cavendish other than to pass them on. All I can say is that I am very sorry about it. I just wish the Earl had made provision. It was his one oversight.' Ernest's words were genuinely felt but it was not within his power to negotiate on the part of Beatrice and her family. Suddenly he looked up from his papers.

'You could write to the Earl explaining your predicament and he may allow you more time to find somewhere else to live, for your daughters are his half-sisters. He is a very amenable young man and much liked by everybody he meets.'

'Thank you Ernest. I might just do that,' Beatrice smiled, grateful for the concern that the solicitor felt. Fellowes took his leave of them to return to his office in the city. He felt that he had accomplished his task for the moment except for his attendance at the funeral of his client. Then James Devine's file would be closed and a new business venture would begin with young Piers providing that he wanted to continue to use the law firm like his forbears. Fellowes' departure had released a mixture of emotions in the family he had left behind. But it was mostly feelings of anger at the way they had been treated. They had become social pariahs overnight without the protection of James Devine. This was the trouble with being the mistress and not the wife. At least Clarissa could claim to be the victor in the moral high ground but Beatrice knew in her heart that James' love had been hers alone. From that piece of knowledge she drew comfort. The Devines could take possession of James' body and lock him away from the rest of his family, but he remained securely in her heart and that of her children. Of that there was little doubt. After Ernest Fellowes' departure Thea had become angry and wilful, raging against her father's other family. She stood up and looked at her mother and Sabine. Mutiny was there in her eyes for all to see.

'How dare they keep us away from Daddy's funeral?' she fumed, 'I shall be going and they will not stop me. Are they going to lock me up if I go? They will stop a grieving daughter, I don't think so. Sabine, do you wish to go?'

Sabine looked nervous. 'Of course I want to go but won't they guess who we are? Two girls together; I even look like Daddy. Thea, you know that you have always looked like Mummy.'

'Well that settles it. I shall go on my own. I will go by train for the day. I think that should be all right and I will report every detail to you both on my return. Nothing will prevent me from saying farewell to my father.' It had all become too much for her and then she promptly burst into tears, showing how much strain the little family was under.

Chapter 7

James Devine, even in death, was dominating everybody's thoughts. That night after the visit of Ernest Fellowes Beatrice sat in the drawing room after dinner and recounted the rest of her story. It was the only way that the family could find solace by talking about happier times.

'What happened when the Great War began, Mummy?' Sabine questioned. It had been strange to glean that they had had an older brother who, if everything had been different, might have been heir to the Westborough fortune.

'Your father and I lived like husband and wife for all those years. He took my name of Cavendish as you two have done and we kept a façade, a pretence of respectability. Nobody seemed to guess or if they did they respected our privacy and it never became a scandal in the public domain. Your father knew that a scandal would not do the Devine name any good.' Suddenly Beatrice looked at her daughters, 'I don't want that to happen ever, a scandal I mean.' She twisted the gold band that she wore on her wedding finger. 'I don't ever want to be known as a mistress or you two to be called.' The sentence was left unsaid but her daughters knew what she meant. 'When you two marry it should clear the air of your illegitimacy. There is still a stigma attached to such things. But James and I should have been more aware of such protocol. Then of course I would not have had my lovely girls. But we made the right decision.'

'Of course you did. Times will change and it has not affected us so far,' Sabine said, wondering now what the future held for the three of them.'

'What about your family Mummy?' Thea asked. 'We don't seem to know much about them.'

'There isn't much to tell. Our parents died when I was fourteen and my sister Ruth was seventeen. We went to live with my aunt Celine but she died when I was nineteen. By that time I had met your father and the rest was history, as the saying goes.'

'And Ruth; what happened to her?'

'She died. She had been ill.' Beatrice went quiet as the memories were just conjured up by the mere mention of her sister's name. 'I still miss her every day. We were very close.'

'What caused her to die?' Sabine asked aware of another wave of sadness engulfing her mother. Beatrice remained silent for a few moments without knowing how to answer. In fact it had been quite some time since she had thought about Ruth. Her life had been completely taken over by her own family. Eventually she said, 'I find it difficult to talk about Ruth at length. Let me just say that she had been ill for a while and her premature death caused me much heartache. I loved her so much.' Sabine knew that it was no use pursuing any further on the subject for experience told her that when her mother decided that was the end of an issue, she could not be drawn any further.

'And what happened when the Great War began?' Thea asked.

'Your father had a commission in the Army. If I remember correctly he was a colonel. It was a most terrifying time because we went months without hearing from him. Most families did and we never knew whether our men were alive or dead. But when he came home on leave he spent his time between his two families. It was what we became used to and when the War was over it did not matter that he was not here all the time because we were used to the way of life. Any way I had you two to look after and to love.' Beatrice smiled at the two faces before her.

'Two little bastards,' Thea said grimly and then in a rush of affection she took her mother's hand and held it to her cheek before kissing it.

'Don't mind me,' she said. 'I wouldn't have it any other way.'

The three women drew close in an embrace which encompassed them all, displaying the love they shared. Even Clarissa Devine's hatred could not quell the emotions that dwelt in their hearts.

Chapter 8

The Friday morning of James Devine's funeral was cold and frosty but the sky was a translucent blue, adding poignancy to the occasion. His body had been lying in state overnight in the candlelit Norman church of Saint Peter in the village of Durston. This had been a tradition dating back several generations because the Westboroughs were well thought of in the surrounding area. In the intervening days since James Devine's death, estate workers and members of the local community had filed past his coffin which had been placed before the altar in the parish church. Caps were held in hands and heads were bowed as a mark of respect for the man that he had been. He had always been approachable and only wanted the best for the people who worked for him. This had been taught him by his father who had believed that if you looked after your own people there would always be respect and loyalty in return. He had always hoped that Piers would continue in the same tradition when it became his turn to inherit the earldom. Now the coffin was being borne out of the church and placed in the horse-drawn hearse; the horses were restless, their heads dipped and their black plumes danced in their eagerness to depart. The old Earl was returning to his ancestral home for the last time in readiness for the mourners to walk the short distance to the church behind the coffin. Clarissa and her daughters were clad in black with veils covering their faces. They stood erect and dignified as they looked at the coffin shrouded in lilies. Piers stood dry-eyed and proud as he reflected on the father he thought he knew but had never known at all. James Devine had kept his secrets well but so had his mother. They were conspirators but for different reasons. As they waited for the cortege to depart

Piers' thoughts turned to the mother who had always been there for her children, but her behaviour of the previous few days had shown her in a new light. She had qualities of character that he detested but perhaps after his father's funeral she might revert to her true self. This he prayed would be true. But his father had never been honest with his legitimate family either and this perfidy had also angered Piers. The hearse began to move at a respectful pace and the family followed, each member harbouring memories of the past and wondering what the future would hold. As they neared the ancient church, estate workers and members of the Westborough household lined the lane that led into the graveyard. As the hearse passed the men dressed in their working clothes, doffed their hats and bent their heads as a mark of respect.

The church lights blazed brightly and mourners had seated themselves in readiness for the final celebration that the Earl would attend. At the back of the church a slight, lone figure knelt; head bent in grief waiting for the service to begin. Her hat was pulled low, concealing her face from public scrutiny. Thea had left London early in the morning just as she had said that she would. It had been a difficult and protracted journey; also it was a journey of discovery into her father's other life, one of great sadness that she would see him interred without being able to grieve openly like his legitimate family. On the train she had been left to her own gloomy thoughts and memories of happier times. There had been one stage of the journey where an elderly woman had tried to make conversation when she saw how sad the young woman was; she was the only other person in the carriage. Thea had rebuffed the old woman who took the hint not to bother her again. The six pall-bearers carried the coffin up the church steps and down the central aisle; their pace was measured almost like a mark of respect for the position that he held in the community and the wider world. As the slow procession passed her, Thea looked at the coffin carrying her father's remains. Tears filled her eyes as she said silently, 'Goodbye Daddy. I love you.'

She bent her head again but overwhelming sensations of curiosity made her glance up to see for the first time these relations that she had never known. Clarissa Devine, dowager Countess of Westborough followed the coffin on the arm of her son Piers. She looked dignified as the occasion decreed a true daughter of the upper classes. Her high-heeled shoes dragged and clattered on the stone flags of the church, almost as if they said, 'We have seen many occasions like this over the centuries.' Piers, eyes red-rimmed, looked straight ahead wishing that he had had more time before he had inherited the title from his prematurely deceased father. The sadness had been overwhelming. His sisters, Diana and Araminta, walked solemnly behind, arm in arm, giving each other the support that they both required at this time. They appeared composed but Thea wondered for how long knowing that her own heart was breaking. These were her half siblings. She wondered if she would ever meet them face to face to be able to discuss the love they shared for the one parent that they held in common.

The service began. The priest's voice intoned the rituals of the service and the choir and the congregation sang out as one, but it all passed Thea by. Her thoughts were elsewhere. Before she had realized it the service was over and the pall-bearers lifted the coffin onto their shoulders while the congregation stood to the organ playing, *All Things Bright and Beautiful* which had been her father's favourite hymn since childhood. And her father was making his final journey to the resting place he would occupy for all time. Again the family passed by disappearing into the fading daylight of a December day. The coffin was borne solemnly to the mausoleum where James Devine was to be interred with his forebears. The family followed in readiness to listen to the final blessing which was to be held in private. Mourners from other aristocratic families streamed from the church either to go home or to visit the Hall where refreshments had been prepared by the kitchen staff. Thea did not know what to do but she was not ready to go home without seeing her father's last resting place. She wanted to describe every last detail to her mother and sister. How their hearts must be breaking at not being able to be here and utter their last goodbyes. The thought was insufferable. She wondered if her funny, caring, sophisticated father had ever given a thought about what would happen to his illegitimate family after his demise. He had covered the financial aspects of their future, but what about the trail of emotional destruction and chaos that were bound to follow? Few people rarely wished to face their own mortality.

The family reappeared from the little service by the door to the mausoleum. They appeared sombre in the gathering twilight. They walked down the path towards the hall to the party that her father could not attend. How sad he would have been at that thought. Thea felt that it was safe now to venture from her hiding place at the side of the old Norman building where she had witnessed the activity. She made her way along the front of the church and turned the corner of the building into the area where the mausoleum was found at the side of the church itself. The iron door was still open as James Devine's coffin was placed in the recesses of its interior. Peering into the gloom, she saw very little except for glimpses of the beam of a powerful torch and she heard low murmuring voices. Footsteps resonated on the stone flooring and then two men made an appearance. Thea stepped back into the shadows but she could still witness what was happening. One man she recognized as Piers Devine and the other was unknown to her but he held a large key in his hand and the door of the mausoleum closed and the key turned in the lock, imprisoning her father for eternity. The two men shook hands and began to depart in different directions, but Piers suddenly stopped in his tracks. He half turned to take one last look at the place where his father now lay; it was almost as if he could not quite believe what had happened over recent days. During that brief glance he had become aware of a slight movement as Thea had recoiled deeper into the shadows but it had been enough for him to fully turn once more to see for himself what was happening. He caught sight of Thea in the gloom of a winter's day.

'Hello,' he said recognizing a female form. 'Can I help you? Were you one of the mourners? I don't recognize you. Should I know you?' His voice was fuelled with grief as he spoke but his words were meant kindly. Thea did not know what to say. It had not been her policy to be caught like a thief in the night. She had edged closer to him to try to explain her presence but she did not know how she would do it, for she expected him to be angry as he had forbidden their attendance at the church.

'I just wanted to come,' she stuttered, her confidence and defiance of recent days had evaporated as she contemplated this new half-brother in her life.

'I'm Piers Devine and you?' Piers offered his hand. His face was kind as he witnessed her inner turmoil but not quite understanding why she was there or why his father's death seemed to have so much effect on this young woman. Thea put out her hand and shook the proffered one. 'Thea Cavendish,' she whispered, wondering if her revelation might cause some furore as she was not meant to be there. Piers' face took on a puzzled expression. He had heard the name only recently but he could not quite place it. However, suddenly the dawn of realization appeared in his eyes and he smiled.

'You're my half-sister. Have the rest of your family attended the service? I am sorry that we did not invite you but it was very remiss of us. I know that my mother would not have approved but...' His voice broke off as he watched Thea's expression change. 'I'm sorry,' he reiterated.

'You said that you did not want us to be here.' Thea's voice quivered with emotion, sounding bleak at the memory. 'Ernest Fellowes said that you had banned us from the service.'

'I did no such thing.' Piers' voice bristled with indignation at such an accusation.

'Your mother sent a message to Mr Fellowes on your behalf. My mother was not allowed to see the person she loved most in the world laid to rest. That was a terrible thing to do to her.' Thea's voice had become vitriolic in tone as she remembered the heartache in her mother's eyes as she had gone to say 'goodbye' before she left for the railway station that morning. Why did these rich people feel that they could do what they liked with ordinary mortals such as herself? Piers' facial expression changed from bewilderment to anger. 'My mother you said. Now I understand.' Thea had no comprehension at all. 'My mother does not like yours I'm afraid. As far as she is concerned my father should have danced to her tune. They were always at loggerheads. I did not send that message. But it was purely my mother's malice or a type of revenge on your mother for taking my father away from her in the past. I am glad that you defied her.' He bent and kissed her cheek. 'Come along with me.' This gesture Thea found disarming and did not know what to do.

'I can't as I have to catch my train back to London,' she said warily looking up into the face which reminded her so much of her father.

'Not tonight you won't. It is too far in this kind of weather. You can telephone your mother so that she doesn't worry.' Piers took her gloved hand and placed it firmly under his arm turning to walk the short distance to Westborough Hall. Thea resisted. She had only just met this young man even if he was her brother, her half-brother she corrected herself.

'Where are you taking me?' Thea asked trying to take back control of this strange situation.

'To the Hall, of course, as my guest; it is my home now. My mother won't interfere again, that I promise you. It is where your ancestors have lived for hundreds of years and it is time that you were acquainted with it.' They walked on as the dusk began to turn into night.

Chapter 9

The Elizabethan Hall came into view and they could see the brightly lit windows which illuminated the ancient building. Thea was transfixed by the beauty of her father's ancestral home. She knew that many of her own forbears legitimate or otherwise must have set foot inside these portals to have experienced the same set of emotions that she did now. They stood for a few minutes viewing the front façade of the black and white majestic building. Piers studied Thea's face closely in the gloaming as she breathed in every facet of the property. It was easy for Piers to take so much for granted for he had lived here all his life and knew nothing different, but he was trying to see it through the eyes of his half-sister who was only just beginning to come to terms with the secret life of their father. Her face, not conventionally beautiful, but full of life and character captivated him as the emotions that swept through her mind danced on her features.

'It's beautiful,' he said not expecting her to disagree. His voice contained pride now that he was the guardian of this sumptuous place. His father had instilled it into him from the earliest of times that the family never owned the house but were the caretakers, keeping it for future generations.

'Love the house and the land where the people dwell and the rest will take care of itself,' he had said.

'Welcome to Westborough Hall,' was all Piers could say as he led Thea forward for her to experience the delights that lay inside. Piers placed his hand under his sister's elbow to draw her forward through the magnificent entrance into the wood-panelled hall where people drifted in and out, some taking their leave while others spoke sotto voce about the old Earl and his passing.

'Good evening your lordship.' A footman had suddenly appeared to divest the young Earl and the young lady of their outer garments.

'Thank you Perkins. Do you know where the dowager Countess is?' Piers' voice was suddenly sharp.

'In the large drawing room, my lord.'

'Please ask her to meet me in the library, Perkins.'

'Yes my lord.'

While this conversation had been taking place Thea had stood wide-eyed drinking in the ambiance of the splendour that surrounded her. She saw the grand staircase as it made its ascent to the upper floors of the house. She imagined her father here, growing up as a boy and then his life as an adult culminating in his inheritance of the house and all it must have meant to him. Her father and his forebears were part of the history of the place. They had earned the wealth which allowed the estate to grow and prosper, even during the times when other great houses had not been as fortunate. Thea knew that she and Sabine had had a privileged life. They had never been short of anything but here there was a different story being told. There was status and grand inheritances and splendour. Did she really know her father? Were there other secrets they had to discover? Time would tell, she thought, as her attention returned to the brother she did not know. She found Piers looking at her quite fascinated by the discovery of another sibling and there was still Sabine to get to know. He found Thea to be an enigma, but of course she was bound to be as he still had to get to know her. She was young, beautiful and intelligent. Suddenly, he was angry about the deceit of his parents having kept him and his sisters in ignorance of the true facts of their half-siblings' existence and the crumbling ruin of a marriage that had lasted a lifetime, based on lies.

'Come,' he said kindly. 'Let's go to the library. I will find you a brandy to warm you up. The cold must have gone to your bones like it has mine. It is not just the chill of the day but it's also the emotional roller coaster which has played havoc with our nerve endings. It is not every day that one buries their father.'

Thea followed Piers across the flagged floor of the great hallway towards a closed door. In the distance Thea heard voices, some subdued and others louder and there was also laughter. On entering the library, Thea observed the same oak panelling as in the hallway. Old and valuable volumes of books covered the shelves behind glass doors. On the highly polished library table stood a silver tray gleaming in the artificial light. A crystal glass decanter and several brandy blooms had been placed upon it. Piers pulled the stopper from the decanter and poured two generous measures of the amber liquid and handed a glass to Thea. She took a sip and the fierceness of its affect was instant. At that moment the library door opened and closed and before them stood Clarissa; a smile hovered around her lips but did not meet her eyes. It was unusual for her to be summoned to her son's presence but she was gradually beginning to understand the old ways had gone and she was no longer in charge. The very thought was like a stab in the dark.

'You wanted to see me Piers,' she purred, and then her attention focused on another presence in the room; it was someone she did not know. Her face creased into a frown as she tried to think who it could be. She was unaware of a woman in her son's life. She was not ready to be usurped by a stranger in his affections.

'Are you going to introduce me Piers?' she asked as her eyes drank in every nuance of the young woman from her demeanour to her clothing and hairstyle. It was Clarissa's wont to be over critical but it was difficult to find fault. This friend of her son's looked charming and demure.

'Mother, I would like you to meet Thea Cavendish, my half-sister.' Clarissa was mute but the expression on her face spoke volumes. She stood and looked at the young woman in horror as if the Devil himself had appeared before her. Piers looked at Thea, who was now feeling uncomfortable under the close scrutiny of her father's wife. She had never intended to come face to face with the woman her father had not loved in a long time.

Piers turned to Thea, his words warm. 'Thea could you give me a moment with my mother alone, please? If you go into the grand hall you will find a fire blazing. Please make yourself comfortable. Take your brandy and I will call you when I am ready. Thea said nothing but was only too pleased to flee the presence of the formidable Countess. The library door closed quietly behind her as mother and son regarded each other hostilely.

'Sit down Mother,' Piers said. It was more of a command than an invitation.

'I won't sit down,' she hissed venomously at him through gritted teeth. 'How you can bring that woman's daughter into my home I will never know.'

'I said sit down Mother and may I remind you that it is my home now.' It had become all too much for Clarissa. She sank onto the nearest chair and leaned on the library table for support. She felt her age after recent events and her legs had told her that they would not hold her upright any more.

'I have to know Mother. I need the truth. Is it correct that you telephoned Ernest Fellowes to tell Father's other family not to come to the funeral and you gave instructions in my name?' Piers waited for an answer. He wanted the truth from his mother's own lips. He did not doubt that Thea had spoken the truth but he had to gain the measure of his mother who he thought he had known and loved. But after recent days he wondered if he had known either of his parents at all. There were too many secrets and lies. That was not the way he wished to conduct his own life now or in the future. Clarissa had lowered her eyes. She could not bring herself to answer the question. She had heard the timbre of anger grating in her son's voice which she had never heard before. She remembered him as the sweet-natured child who used to run to her for a hug, a mother's love. He had been her boy even if he was his father's heir. She knew that he loved his father too; he had wanted to please him but a mother's love was special, unconditional. Now that love had disintegrated as she heard the anger, hurt and the fact that he knew that he had at last grown into the inheritance which was rightfully his. Overnight she had become a 'has-been', a nobody and soon there would be a new countess to usurp her place, her position which she believed should belong to her alone. Her anger was full of hatred for the husband who had died too soon, who had cast her aside in death as he had in life for that strumpet who had borne him two children out of wedlock but would forever hold the key to his heart and his love would be with her for all time, whereas she could weep and rail at the world which had turned against her, left her feeling bereft and alone. The tears coursed down her ageing cheeks as the thoughts took hold. Piers remained unemotional as he watched the turmoil mind change the contours of her face and in her eyes. He had never had less sympathy for her and bore some understanding of what his father had experienced. He wanted the truth and have it he would.

'I want the truth Mother,' his ice-like words sliced through her, making her shudder. Clarissa had the feeling that woman had won and her daughters, too.

'Yes,' her voice was low and muffled but the normally mild-mannered Piers banged the table with the flat of his hand making the crystal decanter and the brandy blooms tinkle in their tray.

'The truth. I want the truth.'

'Yes,' her voice had risen several decibels. 'What of it?' She rose from her seat to face him. Her anger had suddenly made her strong once more.

'And you delivered this ultimatum in my name?'

'Yes,' she hissed at him, the contours of her face had twisted in anger and rage. 'You will never understand the humiliation I have suffered at the hands of that woman and her illegitimate children. How can you, my son, bear to have that girl in the house? Where does your true loyalty lie Piers, or are you your father's son who condones deceit and subterfuge?' Piers had had enough. He had never seen such venom in his mother or ever thought that she was capable of it. He felt some sympathy for his father who might have been driven into the arms of another woman. Now he would never know, for his father had taken such secrets to his grave. But he had made a decision that he was not going to be ruled by his mother. He was his own person, now and forever. His demeanour was now calm. 'You will never do that again Mother. I am the master here now. My word will be law. From tomorrow you will pack your belongings and move into the dower house. It will be made ready for your comfort. I will continue to pay your allowance but if you ever do such a thing again I will withdraw it. You will only come to the Hall when you are invited. Have I made myself clear?' The old Countess' face had turned sheet white but there was still a fire burning inside her. Her warrior nature would fight on. It was not going to be this son of hers who was going to dominate like his father. Not for the first time she thought that the Devine genes had much to answer for.

'How dare you?' she spat at him. Piers faced her across the library table. He now had every sympathy for his father and what he had done over the years.

'Don't defy me Mother. Tomorrow I will see that your maid packs your things and they will be taken to the dower house. My word will be law around here, I promise you.'

Clarissa said not another word, but holding her head high as she had done on many other humiliating occasions she walked from the room as if she was moving into oblivion.

Chapter 10

Clarissa had left the library chastened by what had happened. She held her dignity to her as she had been trained to do in her youth and straightened her lips into a tight line when mourners spoke to her. She was not prepared to show any emotion on the subject. This was banishment like a courtier sent away into exile. If Piers had suggested the death penalty she could not have felt worse inside. The only thing she had left was her pride. Her husband and son had robbed her of everything else. As she re-entered the drawing room she made excuses to her guests that she had the most severe of headaches and felt that it was imperative that she retire to her room. Sympathetic noises were clucked by her friends about the sadness of the occasion and of course she must go and lie down. It was no wonder that she felt as she did straight after burying her husband. This must be the worst day of her life, they exclaimed, having no knowledge of how bad it was for her. It felt as if the end of the world had arrived.

The Countess left the room feeling that with the death of the Earl the old humiliation was over but now she knew that it was only just beginning. Her banishment she saw as the end of everything. Would she ever be able to hold her head up high in society ever again if it became public knowledge of what Piers had done? She would become a general laughing stock. Climbing the stairs she listened to the hubbub of noise emanating from the drawing room; glasses clinked as they were refreshed by the staff and, as she turned to go to her bedroom for the last time, she cast her eyes into the hallway below where she spied her only son talking animatedly to the daughter of the whore who had supplanted her in her husband's affections. Now they had inveigled their way into her home who knew what would happen next? Tears stung at the back of her eyes as she reached the door to her bedchamber, opened it and then locked it against the world which had treated her so badly. Some of the guests took the Countess's departure as a signal to leave. They presumed that it would not be good manners to linger, but Piers had been conspicuous by his absence which had been regarded as rather odd behaviour considering it was his own father who had been buried that day. However, his appearance with a young woman at his side was enough to quell the gossip that had begun, but it also encouraged speculation as to whom the young woman might be. Some mourners had seen her at the back of the church as if she was of no consequence to the family, but now she had made her appearance by the young Earl's side. It was all rather curious. Minty and Diana broke free from a group of middle-aged matrons who had detained them for long enough.

'There you are,' Minty said to Piers, 'we wondered where you had got to.'

'Have you seen Mother?' Diana asked.

'Yes a while ago.' Piers did not expand on the conversation that they had shared. He was not about to tell the tale of his mother's sudden departure here in a public place where guests and servants could overhear. However, he took them to a corner of the room where they could not be overheard. A footman carrying a tray of drinks began to approach them, but Piers waved him away with impatience.

'Poor thing; she went to bed with a very bad headache,' Minty continued. 'It is not surprising after a day like this.' Minty's eyes filled with tears at the thought of her mother's anguish. Diana put her arms around her protectively. Piers suddenly remembered his manners. 'I would like to introduce you to Thea Cavendish.' Both girls looked at their brother's companion for the first time. The name of the young woman seemed familiar but, with the heartache of the day, they had not registered the connection to their own family. Piers could not help but smile as he realized what had happened. He lowered his voice. 'Thea is our half-sister, Daddy's other family.' Minty and Diana looked at each other. Light had dawned in both of them and now that they contemplated this most extraordinary event they did not know what to think. But what they realized was Piers' acceptance of the whole situation. If he had accepted the fact then so should they regardless of their mother's feelings. Hatred and animosity could last a lifetime and it was a destructive element as they had witnessed with their mother in recent days. She had harboured ill feelings for decades and where had it got her? More embitterment was not desirable. Piers had placed a protective hand on Thea's shoulder to give her courage in this oddest of scenarios.

'It is lovely to meet you,' Diana smiled genuinely. Her face had lit up with pleasure. She was left in the dark about her mother's actions concerning the funeral. Minty took her cue from her sister. She bent forward to kiss Thea's cheek.

'It is lovely to have another sister or two,' she corrected herself.

'Thea is staying the night. It is not right for her to return to London at such an hour.'

'Oh, but I don't want you to put yourselves about on my account. I can–'

Piers' raised his hand to prevent any more protest. 'It will not be of consequence. We are more than happy to have you here. Minty do you think that you could show Thea to her room and find her appropriate clothing for the night?'

'Of course I will. You look about the same size as me. Come on, let's sort you out.'

'When the rest of our guests have gone we can have dinner in the small dining room. There will only be four of us,' said Piers, 'and then we can become better acquainted.'

'What about Mother?' Diana asked.

'Mother won't be joining us. If she wants she can have a tray in her room.' Piers' voice sounded strange, almost bitter, as he delivered this ultimatum. His sisters looked at him sharply but said nothing, knowing that they would find out what had happened between their mother and brother eventually.

'I think that I will need to circulate amongst our remaining friends otherwise they will find me rude and discourteous,' and with those words ringing in Thea's ears he left her to her fate with her half-sisters.

Chapter 11

The following morning Thea was woken abruptly by heavy footsteps striding out on the landing outside her bedroom. She felt disorientated by the unfamiliarity of her whereabouts but, as her head cleared, she began to remember. Scurrying footsteps could be heard passing along the landing this time.

'Tibby hurry will you?' Piers' slightly impatient voice could be heard calling to the maid.

'Yes Lord Piers,' came the reply, followed by a very audible sigh. 'I'm sorry I mean my lord.' Tibby was finding it difficult to keep pace with all the changes that had been taking place in recent weeks. It was all too much. It went quiet again as the footsteps died away. Thea curled herself into a ball in the huge bed hoping to return to the luxury of sleep. Her mind drifted in and out of consciousness but eventually she was fully awake wondering what time it was. The hands on the bedside clock pointed to seven thirty and she distinctly remembered Piers telling her that breakfast would be at nine in the small dining room where they had eaten on the previous evening. Again she snuggled down and allowed her mind to drift back to the events of last night. Dinner had been a joyous time amongst her new siblings, even considering the sad events of her father's funeral. The four of them had memories to tell of the father that they had shared. They began to see him as a full, rounded person, not just the individual persona who had only shown one facet of his character to each family. There was laughter and tears as they continued. The one item that came strongly from these memories was the fact that he had loved all his children in equal measure. Suddenly Minty said, 'Where do you live in London?' For the first time Thea looked grief stricken. 'We live in the town house belonging to

Westborough Hall but not for much longer. After Christmas we have to move out. Mr Fellowes informed us when he came to read father's will.' Her face had turned to look at Piers to see what his reaction might be. His face was inscrutable.

'I didn't know we had a London home,' Diana had said, also regarding her brother.

'Neither did I. Father never mentioned it,' Piers had suddenly found his tongue but his suspicions had begun to deepen.

'Do you know who had issued this instruction to Fellowes?' Diana had asked.

Thea was wide-eyed with fear believing that she might be in trouble for revealing the truth but she knew that she could not lie. It was not her way.

'I do believe that it was your mother,' she whispered.

'Ah Mother again.' Piers' face had taken on a grim expression. He had been correct after the discovery of the previous day. He felt that his mother's banishment was truly warranted and he was going to let her know that he had discovered the truth.

'You do know that Mother is moving to the dower house tomorrow,' he told his sisters. It was time that they were aware of the situation.

'Why?' Minty was forever curious. 'It does seem a little cruel to make her move out of the Hall so quickly. Surely it would be better to let her get used to the idea slowly.'

'It is time that Westborough Hall was mine and soon I will be thinking of finding a bride. We must have an heir here too.' He did not want to spoil the evening by explaining his mother's misdemeanours. That was a story for another day when they had the Hall to themselves. There was no need to inflict the arguments on a new member of the family. Thea stretched in her bed and then her thoughts turned to her mother. She had telephoned her just before dinner. Beatrice had been worried by Thea's prolonged absence and relief could be heard flooding her voice when she knew that her daughter was safe.

'You are where?' she said into the telephone. The line was bad again.

'I'm at Westborough Hall. I hope to be home tomorrow or the next day but I will be back before Christmas.' Her mother was amazed at what had happened. Thea did not want to say too much as the telephone was in the corner of the great entrance hall and she knew that many of the servants were around and could overhear her conversation. Thea was only too aware of the machinery of the rumour mill which worked over time in the depths of the basement kitchen. A box was dropped on the landing. The footsteps had begun again too. Tibby could be heard uttering gutter language much to the despair of the housekeeper, Mrs Pardoe.

'Don't you use language like that in these walls my girl,' Mrs Pardoe could be heard scolding Tibby. 'The mistress would be aghast if she heard. It could mean instant dismissal.'

'Sorry Mrs Pardoe. I didn't mean to use them words.' Tibby's tone was contrite. She did not want to lose her job but she had been pushed from pillar to post this morning with all this feverish activity on account of the old Countess moving out. Life was hard enough as it was without all this bother going on. Then there was Christmas to prepare for but she had heard that there were to be no guests this year on account of the old Earl's passing. It was a mark of respect. How could they all party with his lordship so soon to his grave? She had heard Cook sigh with relief that it was going to be an easier time this year. And Mrs Pardoe did not have as many rooms to oversee as other years the house had been teeming with visitors coming and going.

'Get on with it girl.' Mrs Pardoe was not prepared to put up with any slacking from her staff as she liked to think of them. Tibby sighed loudly, but without comment she continued with her lot. But later on she would grumble to the new maid Lottie who had become her kindred spirit in recent weeks. They often found somewhere quiet where they could gossip about the happenings in the big house or they would grumble at the amount of work they had to do. This was going to be something huge to feast and speculate on in the next few days. The old Countess had her comeuppance was the general consensus of opinion downstairs among the servants, but Tibby knew a little more for she had heard snatches of conversation which were only for Lottie's ears.

Thea rolled over now fully awake. She had listened to the entire fracas on the landing and knew that sleep would not come again. She turned to look at the clock and the hands confirmed that fact, for they told her that it was nearly time for breakfast. She did not want to spoil the friendships that had been formed only a few hours ago by being late. She already loved this house and felt near her father here in the more spiritual sense. This had been his true home for all of his life and she was aware that she had known so little about him. In London he had only touched their lives with his presence, but here he had roots going back hundreds of years. She wanted to know more about him for in a way it was her heritage too. She knew that she would never live here on a permanent basis but it meant much to her to be accepted by his other family and she hoped that this would be extended to Sabine, even possibly her mother, but maybe that was a step too far.

Clarissa sat at the head of the table in her usual place at breakfast. She said nothing about leaving the Hall and her body language was as normal. She was brusque with the staff and smiled as her children seated themselves at the table.

'Piers dear,' she feigned humour and lightness in her tone. 'What are your plans for the day?' Piers had been reading the newspaper as his father did when he did not want to become involved in conversation, but he folded his paper neatly to finish later. He looked coldly at his mother who now knew that the argument of the previous evening was not forgotten. She shivered slightly at this frostiness. She had been hoping that her son would relent. The activity on the landing had not dispelled any hope on the matter.

'You know what I am doing. The purpose of the day is to see you comfortably settled into the dower house. I might have relented for a little while longer but it came to my attention last night that the Cavendishes have been asked to vacate the town house. Again Mother that was not your decision to make so the move into the dower house still goes ahead.'

'Am I never to be forgiven for any indiscretions?' Clarissa asked humbly, which had never been her style. 'Am I to be banished forever?'

Diana and Minty regarded each other but said nothing, waiting for Piers to answer. Last night they had whispered to each other that they had never seen their brother so determined or masterful before. The inheritance of the estate and title had made him grow up very quickly. Perhaps it was all the responsibility that accompanied it which had made this happen. Even the mention of taking a wife had surprised them, but there had to be an heir.

'You will have to earn your forgiveness Mother,' Piers continued in the same vein with the edge of authority in his voice, 'and as for being banished you will be invited for all the big events as usual, but the dower house is now your domain for you to rule over as you wish. The Hall is mine. Diana and Minty will remain at the Hall until they wish to leave, as in marriage.' Just at that inopportune moment Thea opened the door into the small dining room. The silence in the room was deafening and she looked anxiously at the sea of faces before her. Minty and Diana flashed her warm smiles but Clarissa could not bring herself to look in Thea's direction. She deemed her the cause of her downfall since Thea's untimely appearance the day before. Clarissa never felt that she was in the wrong even though the family disagreed with her. Piers glanced up from eating his breakfast and indicated the spare place that had been set for her.

'Do come and sit down Thea.' His voice was warm and welcoming. 'Please help yourself to any of the hotplates.' His hands wafted in the general direction of the dresser where the food was laid out. She went to see what was available and helped herself to a small portion of bacon and eggs. Her appetite was lacklustre but Clarissa's presence had made it almost non-existent. She was unsure of the older woman from what her mother had divulged in recent days, but she knew that she had revealed details to Piers that the solicitor had passed on from Clarissa which would not help the poor relationship between the two branches of the family. But she could not fault the warm welcome from her other relations.

'I think I should go home today,' she directed the statement to Piers feeling that she did not want to spend another moment in the Countess' company. She was feeling vulnerable in such close proximity to the dowager Countess and felt that she could become a victim of her razor-sharp tongue.

'Are you sure?' Piers asked. 'You are welcome to stay longer. In fact we would all like you to stay. We want to get to know you better.' Thea shook her head, 'I must get back. It is almost Christmas and there are things to do to help my Mother. But I am very grateful for your warm welcome here.'

'Then you must come again soon after Christmas with the rest of your family.' Clarissa found it difficult to conceal her anger at the mere suggestion that Beatrice Cavendish should set foot inside the walls of Westborough Hall. It would be a step too far but pride made her listen rather than air her opinions. She was no longer mistress here. Soon someone else would fill those empty shoes.

'That would be lovely,' Minty added kindly. Diana smiled her approval. Clarissa stared straight ahead. All this politeness was becoming too much for her agonized soul. Piers folded his copy of *The Times* with a flourish.

'Then I will escort you back to London if you cannot stay and then will return on the late train.'

'Really you don't have to Piers. I am very grateful for your concerns but I have travelled alone before.' Thea had noticed Clarissa's demeanour which had been ignored by the others. She did not wish to cause more trouble in the household.

'Nonsense,' Piers said adamantly, 'If you can be ready shortly we can catch the ten thirty. Denham will take us to the station and then he will be able to pick me up this evening.' Turning to Minty and Diana he said, 'And can you lovely ladies help Mother in sorting the dower house? It has been aired and cleaned and made welcoming for her arrival. Come on then Thea, eat up. We have a journey to make.' He rose from the table looking neither to left nor right, otherwise he would have been aware of the fire that was burning on his mother's face. She looked as if she was going to have an apoplexy. It was only Thea who had noticed the Countess's colour but she quickly hurried after Piers, fearful of any comment that the sour-faced woman might make when Piers had moved out of earshot. Thea was not a vengeful person by nature but for once she felt that the ageing matron had received her comeuppance for the wrongs she had inflicted on others. As she left the room rushing after her brother she dismissed the very thought, swiftly feeling that it was beneath her to be so uncharitable. Yet she knew that she would endeavour never to be alone in Clarissa's company any time in the future.

Chapter 12

Beatrice had been puzzled by the fact that Thea had stayed at Westborough Hall. The information that Beatrice could not hear properly due to the poor connection had been only scant and to the point to prevent her from worrying. She had spent the evening on her own as Sabine had gone to stay with a schoolfriend overnight and the solitude had given her an opportunity to think deeply about the Devines. Feeling that Thea had made an impression on James Devine's other family and there had not been any animosity had amazed her. Perhaps there was less rancour than she thought or the Countess had mellowed over time, but she had to wait until her daughter's return to learn the full facts. Then her thoughts returned to her husband, as she thought of him. It had been a permanent liaison not just an affair. She did not like to think of him as a lover because they had raised two wonderful daughters. Her eyes filled with tears knowing that his remains were lying in the cold mausoleum where she could not pay her respects to him ever again. Now they were facing Christmas without his dynamic presence and life would never be the same again. She knew that she was being maudlin but, with nobody else in the house, she did not need to rein in her thoughts; they had the freedom to roam at will. Beatrice knew that she had to make a life for herself particularly knowing that the girls would leave home and then she knew that she would be bereft. A new year was approaching and with it a new beginning she had promised herself but, in the meantime, it was her duty to make Christmas as joyful as she could. But her heart was heavy as it struggled to cope with all that had been thrown at them as a family.

The front door to the town house opened allowing a blast of cold air to tunnel through the hallway. It closed loudly heralding Sabine's return. She did not bother about divesting herself of her outer garments but rushed into the drawing room where she knew her mother would be waiting. The two women hugged; neither needed to say anything. Sabine felt guilt ridden about leaving her mother on the day of her father's funeral but she could not settle to do anything knowing that they would talk about her father all day and that would depress both of them beyond measure. She had wished that she had had Thea's courage to attend the funeral but it had been too late by the time she decided that. Beatrice knew her daughter well and had pointedly sent Sabine to visit her friend. She wanted the day to herself to think about James and all he had meant to her over the years. She knew that he was to be hers for all time. Had he not said it just before his death but his body lay stiff and cold in another place, the property of his legitimate family.

'Are you all right Mother?' Sabine asked concerned at her mother's pale complexion.

'Yes of course.' Beatrice smiled wanly.

'How did Thea manage yesterday?' She was surprised at the absence of her sibling.

'I don't know yet because she has not returned from Westborough Hall. She telephoned to say that she was staying the night.'

Sabine looked surprised. 'It must have gone well then.'

'Yes, I think that it must have.'

*

Piers and Thea had caught the train at Worcester. Denham, the chauffeur, had driven at a hair-raising pace along the narrow country lanes making Thea feel that they would have an accident, but Piers had only laughed and had reassured her that they had the best driver in the county at the wheel. It was going to be quicker to catch the train from a main station instead of stopping at the small stations along the way. At Worcester they had arrived as the London train steamed into the station hissing and spluttering as its great machinery grated and clanked to a halt. Surprisingly they had found an empty compartment in first class and were surprised that the train was not busy, considering that the festive season was nearly upon them. Piers was thankful that they were alone for he desperately wished to get to know his new sister and by so doing he would come to understand his father better. The last twenty-four hours had given him much to contemplate and gain a greater insight into the man he thought he knew. He understood his mother better and abhorred her meddling ways. He believed that his father had taken the easy way out by acquiring a mistress and living a secret, harmonious life rather than having to battle with the Countess on a daily basis, but each woman knew about the other. However, as his children had reached adulthood James Devine had not been honest enough to tell both families the truth. It was now in death that he had left his children to battle the emotional legacy that he could not face explaining in life.

The Countess, though, had disappointed Piers for he now understood her animosity towards Beatrice; which was self-explanatory but it should not be at the expense of the relationship that she shared with her children. It was his right to be treated with respect now that he was the new Earl and she should have aired her views on all the matters that had embittered her for most of her marriage. If he had not taken such prompt action it might have happened repeatedly in the future and a new Countess could be treated like a doormat. And it was his intention to marry in the not too distant future for the continuation of his line. Having roused himself from such a reverie he glanced across at Thea and found her looking through the window at the passing countryside, but she seemed deep in thought too. There had been much happening in their young lives in such a short space of time. Thea seemed to have been aware of Piers watching her and she turned to him, her face etched in sadness as she had been thinking about her father too. She smiled at him, but it was a smile of grief.

'I was thinking about him too,' Piers said reading her thoughts.

'I just can't believe that he has gone. I keep thinking that he will appear at any moment but of course, if he did, we would not be here together either. It is only his death which has brought us all together.'

'I was thinking something similar too. I just wish that he had had the courage to have told us all about the existence of his two families.' Piers smiled at her, feeling a sudden affection for this young woman.

'I never thought of Father lacking courage. I always felt that he was strong, invincible almost and with him we could face the world as a family. Together we were strong, but now I wonder if I knew him at all. He was away so much but we now know the reason why.' Piers nodded sagely, also thinking of the times when he had wanted his father but had been told that he was in London at the House of Lords. Life had kept his father busy and made him into a liar too.

'Your mother hates my mother, doesn't she?' Thea said. Piers regarded Thea and saw no evidence of recrimination. 'Yes I'm afraid she does, but she did not like my father much either. But the will was the last resort when Father left her no inheritance at all and she felt that your mother had everything. All that prompted her to take revenge on your family, but it does not give her the right to take the law into her own hands. I had to do what I did to make her realize that she could never do that again. I will take care of her but from now on she must know that she has her place like we all do. I haven't abandoned her, although she thinks I have. She will realize that in time, but in the meanwhile she can rule the dower house with a rod of iron and nobody will mind.' Thea looked at Piers for a few minutes without saying anything, and then she said, 'You are very strong, Piers.'

He smiled his lop-sided smile. 'Not really. But if needs must...' His voice trailed off. He looked at her affectionately, 'I feel that I have known you forever Thea, not just a few hours.'

'I feel like that too. It is rather good having an older brother and sisters, although I have Sabine. I think wherever our father is he will be looking down on us giving us his blessing of approval. He probably wanted this all along but did not quite know how to go about reuniting us.' Piers nodded but could not quite voice what he thought. His father had dropped in his estimation, but he did not want to say this to Thea whom he found idealistic and too kind-hearted for words. He knew that he was that bit older than her with more life experiences, which made him more cynical about the world in general and the people who populated it. But that was life. What else could be said? The train was drawing into Paddington. Here the station was much busier than it had been in Worcester and there was hustle and bustle as people moved along the platforms hefting suitcases and bags. There were women who hailed railway porters to carry excess baggage and others carried parcels obviously having shopped for the Christmas season. Other people stood ready to board the train while some passengers disembarked as doors opened and others slammed. Thea turned to Piers and said, 'Thank you for seeing me back, but I will be fine from here. I know London like the back of my hand. I've lived here all my life.'

'Nonsense,' Piers said, 'I'm seeing you home. We will get a taxi and it won't take long. Anyway, I want to meet your mother, as I have something to say to her and I also want to meet my other new sister.' Thea looked alarmed at his statement. He laughed. 'Don't look that way. I only want to tell your mother that she can stay in the town house. I would never dream of evicting you all.' Thea visibly relaxed. She was lost for words but she reached up and kissed her brother spontaneously on the cheek. Piers could not express how he felt at that precise moment, but it was a sensation that was anything but brotherly. Guilt poured through his veins as he took a step backwards having shocked himself into keeping a physical distance between them. Thea had not noticed that anything was amiss. She was just excited about introducing Piers to the rest of his family. She knew now what a good person he was.

Chapter 13

After Piers and Thea had departed for London Minty and Diana had taken the responsibility for directing the Countess's move into the dower house.

'Please don't let her persuade you otherwise,' Piers had instructed his sisters. 'When I return, I want to know that she is comfortably settled. I know that you aren't happy about the move but she does have to learn her lesson, obviously the hard way. She can dine with us regularly but as a guest from now on. It is always traditional that the dowager Countess moves into her own premises in readiness for the new Earl to bring home his wife and family. If you miss her that much you can live in the dower house but I would like you to stay in the Hall. That will always be your home.'

'Couldn't it have waited until after Christmas?' said the soft-hearted Minty.

'No, I'm afraid not. It is a hard lesson our mother has to learn, sooner rather than later,' Piers said soberly. He had made a decision and was not prepared to renege on it. His lack of compassion had even surprised himself, but recent events had changed his view on life, most particularly the business of his parents' marriage when they had lied to their children by omission. The two sisters had organized their mother's most important possessions which were to be transported in the old car that was kept for just such purposes. Tom, the ageing gardener, was to drive the loaded vehicle to the dower house along the country lanes and up the short gravel driveway. It was only a mile and a half by road and the drive would not take long. There was also a short cut through the magnificent gardens of the big house, past the Italian gardens and the walled kitchen garden, all of which could only be made on foot. Some of the maids and the two footmen had taken the short route carrying armfuls of the Countess's most valuable items. They had begun early in the morning when Tibby had dropped some of the valuables on the landing, waking Thea. Now she groaned as she scurried on her sixth visit to the house. She was slightly out of breath and her arms ached from holding awkward parcels. She dared not say anything because she had already received several scoldings from the housekeeper. Mrs Pardoe was supervising the transformation of the dower house under strict instructions from Piers. It was already looking more comfortable. The whole building had been aired with coal fires lit in every fireplace and the old, cold building had taken on a vibrancy as the rooms were sprinkled with the Countess's possessions. Clarissa was to bring her maid, Libby and two others with her to make her life comfortable. The under cook Mrs Thoms was to take over the full role of cook and, after the festive season, more staff were to be appointed to fill the gaps that had been left behind in Westborough Hall. The basement kitchen came to life as Mrs Thoms prepared the room which had not been used since the previous Dowager, James Devine's mother, had passed on. Mrs Thoms tutted to herself as she assessed the old fashioned kitchen. She hoped that some aspects of it could be updated before too long otherwise she would be looking for a new position. She was used to the luxury of Westborough Hall's basement kitchen, which was a miracle in modern convenience and had spoilt her, for the old-fashioned technology of the dower house.

The Countess stood in the hallway of the George III building and smiled. Amongst the flurry of activity she gave instructions as to where everything should be taken. She suddenly felt happy knowing that this was to be her home, her domain and even Piers could not hold sway here. She was not answerable to anybody else. Her husband was no longer around to make her life a misery and good riddance to him, she thought; he was lying in that stone cold mausoleum at the village church with his dead relations. When her turn came she felt that she did not want to lie with him but would find somewhere peaceful where she could spend eternity. The mere thought made her laugh out loud. Her mind was diverted from such maudlin thoughts with the arrival of her daughters. They had concluded their activities at the Hall and now wished to see their mother comfortably settled as Piers had directed. Although they had visited the dower house on many occasions it always amazed them how small the property appeared compared with the big house. They explored the downstairs rooms checking that everything was in situ and then ordered a pot of tea from Mrs Thoms in the basement kitchen with some scones to accompany it. After their departure they failed to hear the cook take her frustration out on the scullery maid.

'Scones indeed!' she shouted to the walls. 'Am I supposed to be some miracle worker? Look at the state of the place.' Her hands rose in despair heavenwards as if she was challenging the Almighty. Diana and Minty had been quite oblivious of all the fuss and the ordeal that the staff had to organize from chaos into an organized home for a member of the peerage. All they wanted was for their mother to play hostess as she had done over the years in the big house. It would make her feel more at home. After all they were only following their brother's instructions. Their instincts had been correct for Clarissa poured the tea and her mood had lightened as she felt for the first time that she was entertaining on her own terms. She was determined to hold her head up high once more in society and was already beginning to plan her first dinner party for old friends, once the staffing situation had been settled.

Chapter 14

The taxi carried Thea and Piers through the busy streets of central London. The shops that they passed were bright and colourful and the whole place was alive with shoppers who were making their last purchases for friends and loved ones for the festive season just three days away.

'We're here!' Thea cried joyously. She wanted Piers to meet her family and love them as much as she did. It was also special to her that he loved her mother who was so unlike his own. But she then rationalized her thoughts. Beatrice was partly responsible for inveigling their father away from the Devine family. It was all so strange, this brand new complicated world that their father had willed to all of his children. Piers' thoughts were full of curiosity to meet the woman who had supplanted his own mother in his father's affections. The driver pulled up the taxi alongside the kerb and drew to a halt. Thea pushed her face forward to speak to the driver about the cost of the fare but Piers was far quicker and had stepped out of the vehicle and produced a wad of notes from his wallet which he handed through the open window.

'Keep the change,' he instructed the driver who saluted before driving off. Piers regarded the town house which he had never seen before. It was a glamorous-looking building and not for the first time his thoughts returned to his father who had lived here with his other family. Thea was regarding her half-brother closely, almost as if she could read his thoughts, but she said nothing. Instead she knocked on the door waiting for Hetty to open it for them.

'Miss Thea, you're back,' Hetty said in her thick Yorkshire accent. 'You look proper perished.'

'I am Hetty. Can you tell me where my mother and sister are?'

'They are just finishing luncheon. I can set two more places for you and your, er, friend.' Hetty was looking at Piers very unsure as to whom he could be. Miss Thea had not mentioned his name but he must be staying for luncheon. The news of the true identity of their employer had not as such reached their ears, which might have thrown more light on this unexpected guest. Thea opened the door into the dining room where she found her mother and Sabine. Their heads turned in unison as the door opened interrupting their tête-à-tête.

'Thea, you're back at last.' Beatrice's voice was filled with happiness as her daughter entered the room. Then she realized that she was not alone. Here was a striking young man who looked vaguely familiar, but she could not quite place him.

'Mother and Sabine, can I introduce you to Piers?'

For a moment Beatrice was none the wiser, then realization dawned. No wonder she knew the face. It could have been a young James standing there before her. It was her dead lover looking at her through his son. Her heart flipped. Sabine remained none the wiser. Just at that moment Hetty entered the dining room to lay the two extra places at the table.

'Excuse me madam,' she said taking her time to lay the places hoping to hear some snippets of news, but there was nothing forthcoming that she could gossip about below stairs. Hetty disappeared, which gave Beatrice the cue to greet Piers.

'I'm so happy to meet you Piers.' Her voice was warm and inviting as she extended her hand to shake his. Piers never took his eyes off her face. He had noted her good looks, not conventionally beautiful like his mother, but he saw what his father must have seen in her. It was the warmth in her smile, right there in her eyes in contrast to the coldness and hauteur of his mother. His father must have truly loved this woman who had a trace of sadness about her from the loss of his father and was holding herself together for the sake of her children. This must have been what true love was about, not the bitterness and torment of souls that was endemic in his parents' union. But Beatrice had also played the game which had kept her own children ignorant of the circumstances concerning their heritage and their birth. Piers held out his hand and shook that of his father's mistress. He was mesmerized by her and saw what had enchanted his father for all those years.

'I am so pleased to meet you too. I have heard so much about you from Thea. I just wanted to come. I hope you don't mind,' he said sincerely and Beatrice saw evidence of her dead James in his looks and demeanour. The tears glistened around her eyes but she was not going to succumb to shedding them now or ever. Enough grief had been experienced since his death and she knew that they all had to move forward with their lives however difficult it may be. They all had to be strong. Beatrice did not answer him for he had now turned to his other sister. Sabine had understood what was happening. Like Thea it had taken her time to absorb the fact that she had a brother, a very handsome one at that.

'Hello Piers,' she said blushing slightly under his close scrutiny. He bent and kissed her cheek. 'It's good to meet you at last.' As luncheon was served for Piers and Thea the conversation flowed despite the fact that Piers had only just made the acquaintance of Beatrice and Sabine. Finally Piers turned the conversation to the true purpose of his visit.

'I'm sorry that you never came to the funeral. It must have been unbearable for you. I just want you to know that this was my mother's doing in my name. I knew nothing about it, but I am so grateful that Thea had so much courage to come despite everything.' All three pairs of eyes were riveted on his face as he continued. 'This house belongs to the Westborough estate and should revert back on the death of the Earl so that the new Earl can make decisions for its use.' He paused here looking at the anxious faces of Sabine and her mother. 'But it is my decision that you continue to use it for as long as you want. You are part of our family and I wish my father had shown the courage to introduce us and keep us close despite the most difficult of circumstances.' Tears filled Bearice's eyes as the knowledge that they did not have to leave their home registered with her. It was a huge burden lifted from her shoulders and she was amazed at his generosity of spirit. 'But you will be taking up your seat in the House of Lords, so you will require a property in the city?'

'Yes I shall,' he agreed, 'but I will ask Ernest Fellowes to find me a small place to rent for that purpose. I have to sort out Westborough Hall and the estate so I do not expect to be in London more than I have to be for the foreseeable future, but I would like to call on you again when I am in town, if that is all right?'

'Of course it is Piers and thank you so much for your generosity.' They lingered around the table talking, finding a common ground of conversation.

'How is your mother faring?' Beatrice asked. Her voice held no animosity towards the woman who had found ways to degrade them in recent days. Piers looked closely at the older woman but, seeing no guile in her features, he said, 'She has not found the situation easy even though she and my father were separated in all but name.' His eyes drifted towards Thea who had witnessed the debacle at Westborough Hall but she gave no indication of having seen or heard anything. Piers wondered whether his new sibling would tell the secrets after his departure. He felt that as much as he had enjoyed meeting this extension of his family they remained an unknown quantity. As the winter dusk was descending on London, Piers Devine left the town house to catch his train to return to his family seat feeling happier than he had done since the funeral. He had promised that he would return to see them in the New Year of 1937 when he made his first visit to London after the festive season. He had sincerely meant what he had said and had every intention of being a frequent visitor to the town house. He had enjoyed the easy relationship that the three women shared and hoped that their closeness would spill over into his own family as time went on. Both families would be facing a very different Christmas due to the absence of James Devine. They were all due a little happiness after recent events. Not for the first time Piers, normally mild mannered, cursed his father for what he had done to the family. There was even a vestige of sympathy for his mother but he had no intention of changing his attitude to her for a while yet. Lessons had to be learned.

Part 2

1938

Chapter 15

More than a year had passed since James Devine's death and, to the people who had loved him, his passing had affected them in different ways. Piers had probably been the least affected of all of them. His time had been spent learning to run the estate which was in the capable hands of his manager John Burns, a hardy Scot who had helped his father for many years. It was well run and maintained an annual profit. This had not changed in the year that Piers had been at the helm but he wished to update the farm machinery in order to bring it into the modern era and he also had his own ideas about how things should be run. He had discussed these facts at length with John who could not fault the young Earl's enthusiasm or love of the land; this was shared by both of them. However, John Burns had advised caution. One step at a time he had said so that they could view how everything was working out. Piers was a young man in a hurry but he was prepared to listen to the older man and agreed that he was right on this account.

There were other life changes too. Piers had taken his seat in the House of Lords as his father had done before him. It fascinated him to listen to the political debates and how the elder statesmen amongst the peerage conducted themselves in the chamber. He looked around him in this historic place and noted the young men who had recently inherited their titles like he had and knew that they had much to learn. His father was constantly in his thoughts but not in a maudlin way, though he asked himself what his parent would have done or decided in certain circumstances. He was to make his maiden speech in just a few weeks and the subject that he had chosen was close to his heart. The rumblings towards war in Europe had made him thoughtful and concerned and he had decided to talk about his grave worries about the rise of Adolf Hitler and his ever more threatening war machine. Piers had very strong views and wished to make his thoughts clear to those who held doubts about the German leader. Once he had done that he truly believed that there was little else he could do for the decisions for his country's future lay in the hands of the Government. Piers had also wanted to secure his dynasty. He had felt that it was the right time to seek a wife and although he would have preferred to marry for love, he would be quite happy to form a union with someone who could be a friend but not necessarily the great passion of his life for that belonged elsewhere and she was unattainable. So he had attended the London social world where he met young women who were not the marriage material that he was looking for. He did not want the coy damsels who wanted the title but not the responsibility that went with being the life partner of a titled man who ran an estate and looked after the interests of the estate workers as well as producing the next custodian of Westborough Hall. As Piers became more and more disillusioned about his marriage prospects he attended a dinner party at the home of Sir Giles Boardman who had been an acquaintance of his father. Not feeling excited by another round of introductions to more people he felt he would attend the party on account of the fact that it was an evening where he had little to occupy himself and the next day he was returning to Westborough Hall for a few weeks to help John Burns with various matters concerning tenant farmers and the oversight of the arrival of some of the new farm machinery.

During the course of the evening Piers had held forth with Sir Giles on the demerits of Hitler's policies in Germany. Both held opposing opinions of the matter but their debate had been amicable. They had been joined by other members of the aristocracy who held sway one way or another and, as they entered the dining room, Piers suddenly became aware of a pretty fair-haired young woman who had been seated near him at the table. When the gathering was complete he introduced himself only to learn that he was seated next to Mary Boardman, the only child of Sir Giles himself. During the course of the evening they had engaged each other's attention almost to the exclusion of the people who had been seated to the other side of them. Their discourse was about getting to know each other and their personal interests. Piers had found the young woman to have a mind of her own and a remarkable intelligence. During the course of the evening they had learned much about each other. Piers found her charming and self-assured without being arrogant as many of the women he had met in recent times had been. He had compared them to his sisters who, considering their titles and upbringing in an aristocratic home, remained unassuming and pleasant. At twenty-six Mary Boardman had been out of circulation in London Society. She had nursed her mother until her death just weeks previously. Now she had been freed from the constraints that had been put on her as an only child and was free once more to pick up the threads of her own life. This she was eager to do but she did not appear flighty and the responsibility of her ailing parent had matured her beyond women of her own age. At times Piers became aware of Sir Giles's covert glances across the table and wondered, not for the first time, if the ageing baronet was assessing their future as a potential couple. Piers, though, was thinking along the same lines but a courting process would have to ensue before any decisions could be made. He wanted to marry sooner rather than later, but he did not wish to make the same mistakes as his parents.

During the following months he became the escort of the young woman to dinner and luncheon parties as well as to the theatre and concerts where they shared much the same interests in music and theatre. Neither of the young people had declared their feelings towards the other but Mary was hopeful that marriage might be a prospect after a while. She had felt that at nearly twenty-seven she was becoming an elderly matron. After spending so much time in nursing her mother this might be her last opportunity to make a life of her own. But it was after a courtship of several months that Piers eventually approached Sir Giles. He felt that this was a marriage of convenience in some ways. However, he and

Mary could say they had a friendship which could possibly lead to love in the future. She was a lovely woman but his heart lay elsewhere. He had an appointment with the older man when he knew that Mary was away from town visiting her aunt, her mother's only sister. As the two men sat in Sir Giles' study in the beautiful town house where they lived in London, they regarded each other momentarily.

'I think you know what I am going to say, sir.' Piers looked at the older man.

'I think I do, but I will not presume but will let you tell me.'

Piers looked into the shrewd face and smiled wryly. 'Very well. I have now been courting your daughter for the last few months and I do believe this to be the right moment to ask for her hand in marriage.' Sir Giles rose stiffly from his chair and walked to the window to look out; but as he did he saw nothing, for his thoughts were working overtime on this request. It was one that he knew was inevitably coming but it did not make it any easier to answer.

'Before I agree to this question I have a few things I want to say and then I will never repeat them again. Mary is very naïve. She has been sheltered by myself and my late wife rightly or wrongly. She was devoted to her mother, having no siblings of her own, and it was Mary's choice to care for her through her final illness although we could have brought in nurses to do the job; but my daughter would never hear of it. Now she is free to lead her own life and make her own choices. You are the first man that she has really known and consequently fallen in love with. As any parent I want to see my daughter happy and taken well care of. You see Piers, what I am about to say may insult your ears I'm afraid.'

Piers looked startled. 'Go on sir.'

'Everything I see about you I like, but I want to know if you love her and will cherish her. I won't be around forever. I am in my seventieth year and have no family left for Mary to turn to in her hour of need. She has her aunt, but she is ageing too so, Piers, you would be her family. And please forgive me for saying this but I witnessed the disintegration of your parents' marriage and I would never want history to repeat itself. I have met Beatrice and her daughters and regard them highly but I would not want Mary to have to face such trauma.' For a moment Piers looked shaken, then angry as he contemplated the older man's words.

'Is this a case of the son inheriting the father's sins?' he retorted. 'I think that you are out of order there Sir Giles for I would never do that to Mary. I love her.' But he knew that he did not love her as he should. If he was honest he was very fond of her but love meant passion and deep feelings which were not at his disposal. But he was happy for her to be the mother of his children. He was not unkind and it was not in him to be cruel, but to really love? He could never agree to that. Sir Giles smiled at the young man's impassioned plea mistaking it for the real thing. He held out his hand to his future son-in-law. 'We will not speak of that subject again, but I will take you at your word. Welcome to my family.' Piers took the proffered hand and shook it. He knew that love could grow out of friendship, but in this instance he thanked the older man and hoped that when he next saw Mary she would accept his proposal. Then they could move forward with their lives.

It was several weeks later on a mild autumn day when Piers had been staying in London on one of his visits to the Lords that he had met Mary and taken her to lunch. They had talked about their love of the theatre and the plays they would like to see soon in the West End. Her face was animated as she spoke and on this occasion she looked particularly lovely wearing a jade green dress which emphasized her curvaceous body. He watched her face as she spoke feeling that, at some point, love would grow between them given time and her father had been correct to make sure that she was cherished after his days. Over dessert he had taken her hand across the table and brought it to his lips to kiss. She had stopped talking and looked at him, wondering what was to come because Piers was not demonstrative by nature.

'I love you Mary,' he said.

Not knowing how to answer she looked down at their entwined hands and her eyes returned to his face. He was smiling at her and she blushed, knowing that he was waiting for some response. Awkwardly she said:

'I love you too Piers.'

They smiled at each, the embarrassment having faded away.

'Will you marry me?' he had asked and waited to see what happened. Mary regarded him and smiled happily, her eyes twinkling with merriment.

'Of course I will marry you Piers and thank you.' Suddenly Piers wondered if Mary realized how he felt and guilt spread through him like a tidal wave.

'I know that you don't love me very much but it can grow,' she suddenly said with great sagacity, 'and we can be friends, which is sometimes better.'

'I, I....' Mary held up her hand. She was grateful that he had proposed. She knew that she loved him but he had never given any indication before this moment about his true feelings. She did not want any dishonesty between them. 'I do love you Piers in my own way and I am flattered that you have asked me. I will be a good wife and bear the next heir to Westborough Hall, but don't deceive me with great emotional talk of love. We are each from old historical families who do not expect passion but just to unite our dynasties and our wealth. One day I will bring a fortune into our family but not yet, I hope.' Piers felt that he had to return honesty with honesty for this was to be the foundation of their relationship from then on.

'Am I so shallow? I have a great affection for you Mary and as you say, our relationship will be built on friendship and care. I do want you in my life and I have already promised your father that I will treat you well and look after you. He requested those assurances and I have given them to him.'

'So be it. We will marry soon I hope,' she said looking questioningly at him. She was not totally sure what true love was or even passion for that matter. Her months of nursing her mother had drained her and love for a parent was not the same as the love of a man. She cared about Piers and wanted to marry him partly because she knew that there might not be many offers left. She did not want or need his money for she was her father's only heir, although the baronetcy would go elsewhere.

'Of course, I hoped April would be a suitable month and then perhaps you will be providing us with an heir soon.' He now laughed happily that they had an understanding and he promised himself that he would not let her down. She deserved the best that he could give, particularly if she gave him a son.

Chapter 16

The months following the engagement had not quite gone to plan. There had been hiccups which had caused much in the way of rows and at one point Mary had felt that it might be easier to cancel the wedding plans. She had wanted to plan the wedding herself which Piers was happy for her to do and Minty and Diana had offered to give assistance too when it was required. It was to be held at Westborough Hall. That had been decided as soon as the marriage proposal had been accepted. Neither prospective bride nor groom wished to marry in London near the Boardman home. The city was always busy and neither of the couple wished to have a Society wedding which London would have demanded. Mary was quite happy to use the venue of the Hall over which she would reign supreme, once the ring had been placed on her finger. The Boardmans did not have an ancestral home. This had been sold during her great grandfather's day to pay off his considerable gambling debts, but the fortune which she would one day inherit had been remade by her grandfather Sir Guy. He had learned from the errors of his father's ways and invested the little money he did have in industry. This investment had done well and from the little acorns grew huge oaks. All this was reinvested and when her father had inherited he continued in the same vein. Sir Giles had now retired and had sold all the assets, making him rich in monetary terms. This had prompted his conversation with Piers about his daughter's future. He did not want any fortune hunters to seek his daughter's hand in marriage after his death. Fundamentally he had been delighted about the union of Mary with the Devines for he knew that they were among the richest of the aristocracy. While some fortunes were declining the Westboroughs' was in the ascendancy.

The first problem with the wedding plans had been caused by Clarissa. She had partly been forgiven by Piers for she had kept herself to herself in the dower house, entertaining her own circle of friends and only returning to the Hall when invited for special occasions. She was fully aware of her son's thawing in past matters and this gave her opportunity to find the chink in his armour and to slide through unobtrusively. As Piers was so heavily involved in all these aspects of his life he had not noticed. On the numerous occasions that Mary came to stay at the Hall Clarissa made every attempt to befriend her, but it was for her own ends. She had made the assumption that Mary was a timid, pathetic creature who needed guidance in the future running of the Hall and the organization of the wedding. Mary on the other hand had not been warned of Clarissa's dominant personality and she had fallen for the golden hand of friendship which had been proffered. Her own mother had been a lovely woman and naively she had assumed that her future mother-in-law would be the same. Gradually as the weeks progressed and the date of the wedding grew nearer, Clarissa had sown seeds of doubt in Mary's mind about the organization of the wedding and insidiously was beginning to take over. But as time wore on Mary began to see the dowager Countess as she really was. There were times when Mary would not tell Clarissa what some of the arrangements were and then the Countess would ask her daughters about decisions. They would give the appropriate information for they had not grasped the fact that their mother was trying to interfere and take over. Clarissa would try subtlety, persuading Mary to change the plans for something else. However, Clarissa had not quite discovered the full measure of Piers' future wife for Mary was beginning to see the older woman for what she was, domineering and manipulative.

One morning during her stay Mary found Piers alone at breakfast. That was a rare event for usually his sisters were present. It was only six weeks until the wedding day. Mary sat at the table and drank a cup of tea which had been poured for her by the maid who waited at table. When she had disappeared she looked across at Piers who was reading *The Times* as he did most mornings. He had acknowledged her presence with a "Good morning" and a beaming smile but, while Mary had been instructing the maid, Piers had returned to the article which had gripped him about the war-mongering in Europe. As his speech was only weeks away, just after the wedding, he was busily acquiring as much information as he could to fuel his case. It was now or never Mary felt. She could not go on feeling as she did.

'Piers, I think that I am going to have to call off the wedding,' she said matter of factly as if it was an everyday occurrence. Her voice was level without any hint of hysteria. For a moment Piers appeared to have not heard or noticed, but then slowly he lowered his paper and looked at her intently.

'Did I hear you correctly?' he asked incredulously. 'You want to call off the wedding at this late stage when the invitations are nearly ready to be sent? Why for heaven's sake?'

Mary looked him straight in the eye, her gaze never faltered. 'Yes,' she said, but gave no reason for her statement.

'Why? Have I done something wrong?' he asked again.

'No. It's just I don't want to marry your mother as well,' she said without a flicker of emotion. Piers burst out laughing at the statement and then he became serious. 'What in damnation has she been doing now? Has she been interfering in the plans?'

'Yes,' said Mary not wishing to beat about the bush. 'Why did you not tell me that she was like that?'

'Because she has been living at the dower house and I thought that gave us a distance from her here; obviously not. I will deal with it today, I promise.'

'If you don't I will call off the wedding. My own mother never interfered so I cannot live with someone who does.' Mary had delivered her ultimatum knowing that she was quite serious about the whole affair. Piers had to bite his tongue for although he had never met Mary's mother, he felt that the woman had never had a daughter who was marrying an Earl during her lifetime and Mary could be viewing her saintly mother through rose-tinted glasses. Piers did not have any conscience about thinking such malicious thoughts, either.

'She won't be living here and I shall deal with it straight after breakfast. I have just promised you that.' There was no argument on that score but Mary knew that he would speak to his mother for, if nothing else, Piers was a man of his word. She smiled at him flirtatiously and seeing a new side of her he returned the smile, then bent forward to kiss her cheek. Their relationship was growing warmer. Both had taken cognizance of this fact.

The other factor in the lead-up to the wedding had been the list of guests. It was not going to be a huge list as the church of St Peter was only small, so it had to be carefully and diplomatically chosen. Both of them were in accord on the decision. Mary had such a small family which made it no great issue for her and they chose friends who were the closest to their heart. But Piers was adamant that his father's other family was to be present. Mary had no agenda with this. She had met the Cavendishes in London on one of the few occasions that Piers had stayed at Sir Giles' home. They had dined at the town house specifically for his family to meet his prospective bride. Mary was fully aware of the circumstances surrounding this 'other family' who had only been discovered so recently. She knew how close Piers had become to them and she felt much the same herself for they radiated warmth that was not felt as such at Westborough Hall, something that Mary wished to remedy in the fullness of time. Over weeks she had become close to the two sisters who were slightly younger than her, but they had grown up after the death of their father. Beatrice had told Piers that she felt that she should decline the invitation on account of Clarissa's feelings, but he had remained adamant that she was to attend. He no longer cared what his mother felt for, when he had challenged her about the incident, she had once more tried to bluff her way out of the situation. She had become a mistress of subterfuge over time but now Piers could see through her. He was no longer blinkered by the love he had once felt for her and now could understand why his father had acted as he had done, although he still would not condone his father's behaviour. The invitations were sent out and heading the list was the little family that he loved. Clarissa was kept at a distance. Personal invitations from the big house were not issued and Clarissa became a pariah within the family. Even her daughters shunned her presence and gossip began to ripple through the downstairs regions of the house about the tiff which had occurred between the Earl and his mother. But eventually the news that Beatrice had been invited to the wedding had filtered through to the dower house when, Minty on a visit to see her mother with an olive branch to try and restore peace and harmony, had carelessly let the information slip out. Minty, although she did not realize it, was the eyes and ears of what was happening at the Hall. Minty's easy-going chatter and lack of guile were her let down within the family on such occasions. As a result of this faux pas Clarissa summoned her son to the dower house for a discussion on just this subject.

'I don't want that woman at the wedding Piers. This is just too much. Your unkindness at such a thought is beyond my comprehension,' she had stormed.

Piers had listened quietly until the tirade finished. 'But she has been invited, Mother, whether you like it or not. That is our decision. I am beginning to see why my father did what he did.'

Clarissa's face tightened in anger. 'And you my only son are like your father. You have developed his cruel streak. If you continue along this path I shall not attend your wedding and then you will have Society tittle-tattling at your door.' Piers looked unfazed by his mother's words. 'It is up to you to decide what you want to do, but Beatrice is invited.' And with those words ringing in her ears he turned his back on her and left the room and the dower house to wend his way through the beautiful gardens of Westborough Park to cogitate on his mother's decision. It was a situation that he hated but she had to think about what she was doing to the family and particularly its newest member. It never occurred to Piers to think about his mother's feelings, for there was a stalemate on both sides. The war had begun.

Chapter 17

On the morning of the wedding Mary, dressed in her white, lacy dress and veil knew that it was too early to go to the church. She looked radiant, almost beautiful. Her fair hair had been piled onto the top of her head in intricate twists and curls and from that her veil hung around her shoulders. It was held in place by the Devine tiara which had last been worn by Clarissa a long time before. She sat by the window in her bedroom in the east wing of the old hall looking onto the still wintry garden, but the day was glorious even by spring's standard. She was thinking of her mother wishing that she could have been here to see how happy she was. Then her thoughts turned to Piers and she smiled. She had grown to love him in recent months and hoped that it was possible for him to return the emotion now that they were to be finally united as husband and wife. Everyone wanted to be loved, she thought. She was going to make him proud of her, his new countess and then finally to be mistress of Westborough Hall was an amazing privilege. The building had worked its magic on her months before and she had fallen in love with its beauty and history. To fill it with children and their laughter was her greatest ambition. She so much wanted to be part of a large family. Being an only child had had its merits and drawbacks. The responsibility she had felt for her mother had weighed heavily upon her over the months leading to her death and now she looked at her father and saw someone who was getting old and weary missing the wife he had adored and lastly losing his daughter to a new husband. She had wondered if in time she could ask Piers if her father could come and live with them, perhaps in this wing of the house where they had stayed during the last few days. He would be no trouble and he could have his own private quarters where he would not bother them, for that was not his style. A soft knocking came at the door to interrupt her reverie. She smiled believing it to be her father, come for a last few words before he handed her to her husband. These were to be the last minutes that she was his. A tear tickled the corner of her eye but it did not fall. There were to be no tears today of all days, only happiness.

'Come in,' she called fixing a smile onto her face. He must have no doubts about her happiness today.

The door opened but it was not her father but Polly, her maid, who was to stay with her in her new role as Countess.

'You look beautiful miss,' Polly said taking in the vision of loveliness and truly meaning what she said. 'His lordship will believe that he is the luckiest man placed on this earth. I have been asked to tell you madam that it is time to go to the church.'

'Thank you Polly. I am ready,' she said walking to the cheval mirror to make a few final adjustments. Polly followed her to arrange her veil and to tease an errant curl back into place. Mary just wished she could spend a few more minutes in this room to compose herself. It was her prerogative to be late, but tardiness was not her style.

'Has Lord Devine left yet Polly?' she asked. Her superstitions were legendary. She did not want to meet Piers before she saw him at the altar. It was bad luck. She had also gone through the ludicrous charade of something borrowed, something blue, beseeching friends as well as Thea and Sabine to lend her items. She knew that it was foolish but it had mattered to her.

'Yes, Lord Devine has gone with his best man.' The maid smiled at her mistress knowing what was going through her mind. 'And your father is waiting downstairs for you miss. He is looking very handsome.'

'Yes, I expect he is.' Mary smiled as she pictured her father in her mind's eye. He was a handsome man even though he was now ageing.

Downstairs the house looked empty except for staff who hurried hither and thither making the large baronial entrance hall ready for the wedding breakfast. This was the largest place to seat the guests. It had been used in the time of Queen Elizabeth to entertain Her Majesty. At least that was how the story went. She had been on one of her numerous progresses living at the expense of her subjects. Mary could almost believe that knowing how wonderful it was to stay in Westborough Hall. Polly had gathered the long train in her hands as Mary walked down the stairs where her father stood waiting for her at the bottom. He had smiled encouragement at her but felt bereft inside, knowing that he was losing her. This was a moment in time which he wished he could have shared with his wife but he pushed the thought aside. As Mary walked beside her father, her arm tucked beneath his, he looked down on her from his great height and whispered, 'You look beautiful and I am so proud of you.'

'Thank you,' was all she could say. She was too emotional about everything hoping that her relationship with Piers would be as good as he had promised. Sir Giles walked her towards her fairy-tale carriage, for that was what it was. It had been taken out of one of the barns on the estate and cleaned to perfection for just this occasion. The pair of chestnut horses had been groomed to within an inch of their lives, their satiny coats shining in the spring sunshine, waiting patiently to take this young woman to the man who would be her husband and she would return as the new Countess. On the short journey to the church of St Peter the estate workers had turned out in force with their families to see the new bride. They waved and shouted their good wishes. Mary waved in return ridiculously feeling like the new King and Queen she had seen so recently at Saint Paul's Cathedral in London. The carriage pulled up outside the church and Sir Giles helped his daughter down as she coped with the lengthy train of her dress and her only bridesmaid, Thea Cavendish, moved from the church porch to pick up the train in readiness for the long walk down the aisle to meet her future husband. A woman had been standing on the steps of the old Norman church and, at the sight of the bride and her father, she dashed inside and waved frantically at the organist whose nimble fingers ran over the keys of the organ to begin the wedding march as the couple began their journey to the altar where Piers Devine awaited, his bride wondering if he had done the right thing. He had turned to look at his approaching bride on the arm of her father but all he saw was his half-sister looking radiantly beautiful in her pink dress holding the train of the sumptuous wedding dress. Feeling bereft, Piers turned his attention on his bride and smiled warmly at her. This was the woman he had asked to spend his life with and that was what he was going to do. Other thoughts must be erased from his mind as they started their new life together.

As they stated their vows clearly at the high altar steps Beatrice became aware of the absence of Clarissa. She had not thought to look at all the family members for she had wanted to see Mary in her dress and then Thea. It had been a lovely gesture on Mary's part to ask her daughter to be a bridesmaid and it brought the two families closer together. However, the absence of Clarissa at her own son's wedding was odd at the very least and Beatrice felt that she knew the reason why. She wished that she had not come because the old feud would never go away, but Piers had wanted her there which had made it difficult to refuse. She also wondered what James would have thought at the bizarre goings-on but that did not matter anymore. If the news of Clarissa's absence reached the newspapers it could make headline news, particularly so close after James' death. She thought about her dead lover, feeling so near him here. It was the first time she had visited Westborough Hall and it was just as he had described it to her. On their arrival at the church she and Sabine had found the mausoleum where he was buried and it had upset them all over again as if his death had happened only yesterday. She had lingered at the door of the mausoleum and offered up a prayer for his soul. She was not religious but it all seemed appropriate at this moment, when his two families had come together as one.

Chapter 18

The time since James Devine's death had been difficult for Beatrice. There was little purpose to her existence and now she realized just how much she had depended on her children's father to be the sun, moon and stars of her reason for being. She leant on her daughters for company, who were far more resilient than herself. She had always considered herself as a strong person but now she saw herself in a different light and wondered what the future would bring. A huge depression hung over her, a mantle that she could not throw off easily. Sabine and Thea whispered in corners of the house away from their mother's ears; their concerns were evident. They tried to make sure that one or other of them stayed with her to jolly her along, to find a new purpose for living. However, this could not continue indefinitely for their own lives were beginning to gather momentum.

Six months after her father's death Sabine had met Peter Jordan, the heir to a baronetcy. His father was a financier in the City of London and they owned an estate in the Home Counties. It was not large on the lines of Westborough Hall but it was a beautiful Georgian mansion built in extensive grounds. Most of the land had been leased to other landowners who farmed on a grand scale. This provided a steady income for the Jordans who were not rich by conventional standards but could hold their heads up in county society like the best of the aristocracy. Peter had been smitten with Sabine from the moment they had been introduced by Piers. He was a friend of her brother from their days at Eton and over the intervening years they had continued to keep in touch. Peter's friendship with Sabine had blossomed into love. Sabine, who was as smitten as her beau, was worried about her pedigree. It was all right being the daughter of an Earl but it was her illegitimate status which caused her grave concerns. Things like that still mattered in certain stratas of society and the stigma of such a status weighed heavily upon her shoulders. However, one day she found Piers at the town house having come to visit as he did regularly. He felt at home among this part of his family and whenever he was in the capital he visited them. On this occasion he was sitting in the drawing room waiting for the first member of the household to return home. It was early evening and he had helped himself to a brandy from the decanter on the occasional table by the sofa.

'Piers!' Sabine cried out, moving swiftly to him to give him a warm hug. He had jumped to his feet to reciprocate the greeting. He found Sabine charming but there was a moment of disappointment that Thea had not been the first person home.

'How are you Sabine?' he asked.

'I'm very well, thank you. And Mary?' she added.

'She is well too. May I ask how the big romance is going with my friend, Peter?' He grinned knowing how well Peter spoke of Sabine. Sabine flopped down on the sofa and made a face which brought Piers to believe that things were not turning out favourably.

'Piers, may I ask your opinion?'

'Of course,' he said, suddenly frowning as he observed the distress on his sister's face.

'I have a feeling that Peter might propose soon which is wonderful but it's my illegitimacy which is worrying me. I haven't told him yet and you know how people talk about such things. There I have said it. Only a few months ago I did not know so it did not figure in my life.' Piers looked seriously at her for a moment and then said, 'I hope you don't mind Sabine but Peter has already spoken to me about this. He wanted to know how we were brother and sister, for at school he knew that I just had two sisters. I gave him the full story.' Sabine looked shocked. 'What did he say, or would it be better if I did not know?'

Piers smiled the warm smile that she had begun to know so well. 'He said it didn't matter to him and once you were married nobody would think anything of it.' Sabine sat up excitedly and said; 'He said married.' She jumped up from the sofa and began twirling around in excitement and just at that moment the drawing room door opened and she bumped into Thea, who stood laughing at the spectacle that her sister was making of herself. Piers' laughing eyes left Sabine and stared intently at Thea. She was dressed in blue from head to toe which reflected the blueness of her eyes; they sparkled with happiness and laughter. Her cheeks were red from the chilly wind which was blowing a gale and this picture took Piers' breath away. He had to avert his eyes so that nobody could tell what he was thinking. It was wrong to be thinking these thoughts for a sister that he had not long met and the fact that he had so recently married.

'What are you doing Sabby?' Thea laughed at her sister. She looked young and vivacious as if she had no care in the world. She appeared as if she had moved on from her father's death and she had. Life was for the living, she had determined, but sometimes she felt a stab of pain for her mother who was still bereft. Then she became aware of Piers who once more was sitting, watching her.

'Hello,' she said. Her face became open and warm as she regarded him and then, flinging her arms wide, she went to hug him. Piers hugged her back and kissed her, experiencing the same emotion as he always did when there was physical contact. He pecked her cheek, then pulled away to look at her.

'Have you been having fun?' he asked wondering if she had acquired a male escort in the few weeks since he had last seen her. Her effervescence had never been as high as this in the few months since their first meeting.

'Yes,' she said but did not embroider further on her day's activities. Piers did not press her further as he knew that it was none of his business, but he so wished to know what happened in her life. However, he knew that to be unfair as he did not own her and there was to be no relationship between them.

His quietness had gone unnoticed as Sabine was telling her sister about Piers' news that Peter could propose any day.

'Oh Sabby I'm so thrilled for you,' Thea purred at her sister's uplifting news and then she focused on her brother, 'and Piers what news do you have for us?' Piers smiled sheepishly knowing that he did have wonderful news which he had only learned about a few days before. 'Go on Piers,' Thea enthused. 'I bet I know what it is. Is it to do with Mary?'

'Yes, it is to do with Mary. She is now pregnant and we are so proud.' Piers felt a huge guilt at his earlier thoughts but he could not help how he felt deep down. He had been so thrilled when she had brought the news to him in his study. They had both cried with the sheer enormity of the fact that they might have produced the heir to Westborough Hall and if it was not this time, it would surely be the next.

'I think that deserves a celebration,' Sabine said.

'What does?' Beatrice asked as she entered the drawing room. She had been resting as she did most afternoons if she had nothing to fill her time.

'Mary is expecting a baby,' Sabine said excitedly. Beatrice looked at Piers with a warm smile and held out her arms to hug him, 'I'm so thrilled for you both. Have you told your mother yet?'

Piers face darkened slightly. 'Not yet. We have only just found out ourselves so I thought we might keep it secret a little while longer.'

'Of course,' Beatrice said, but deep down she thought that it was strange to think that her family knew before his own mother. The animosity between them must be worse than she thought.

'I think that we should open a bottle of champagne.' Sabine fizzed as if she had already drunk a bottle.

'What a wonderful idea,' Beatrice said, wondering why she had not thought about it herself.

'It is only half past five,' Piers sounded disapproving but there was a conspiratorial smile on her face.

'The hour doesn't matter,' Thea chipped in. 'This is a wonderful occasion. Sabby and I are going to be his aunt.'

Beatrice said nothing but wondered where this placed her in this great scheme of things. She would never be related to the new baby but perhaps she could be an honorary grandmother. After all, this was James' first grandchild.

Clarissa had survived her time at the dower house far better than she could have imagined. In some ways Piers had been correct when he had stated that it was her domain. She had started socializing on quite a grand scale, sending the bills to her son to pay making her feel like royalty. He had also given her quite a generous allowance for which she was very grateful. Her time on her own at the beginning of her banishment had made her think deeply and she felt perhaps wisdom came with age and she should behave better, but all that had gone when Mary had come upon the scene and then old jealousies had reared their head. There was a new Countess at the Hall and all the old habits of taking over had occurred once more; making mischief had been a habit that she had practiced all her life and now she was mistress of her craft. Her new daughter-in-law had not been the timid person that she had imagined and in some way she had met someone who was willing to stand up to her instead of quaking in her shoes. However, the deepest hurt had come when she discovered the invitation sent to her husband's mistress and her daughters. The ultimatum that she had delivered to Piers, she knew, she had to carry out and not lose face. The day of the wedding had caused her more anguish than even she could have imagined. What was the use of principles if she did not abide by them but her heart had broken beyond measure? On the day of the wedding she had locked herself in her bedchamber and howled her eyes out. Her staff had heard the anguish and wondered if they should send for the Earl, for they feared for her sanity. Having requested not to be disturbed they knew that it was more than their lives were worth to interfere with their mistress' orders, but in the basement kitchen the atmosphere was clouded with worry at the turmoil which seemed to have eaten its way into the family like a cancer since the old Earl's death.

'Someone needs to tell his lordship what is happening here. He should come more often to see for himself what is happening.' Cook was standing at the kitchen table, arms akimbo, spouting forth her opinions. 'It's like it was under the old Earl, trouble and strife. Why can there not be peace in the place?' The staff gossiped in corners not wanting to make their opinions general knowledge but, when they saw staff from the Hall, they were informed about what was happening at the dower house.

'It is a disgrace that the Dowager is treated this way,' Mrs Pardoe said in the kitchen. She knew that she should not be so vociferous in her opinions but she had always found Clarissa kind and thoughtful, but not everybody agreed with her. The wedding, so everyone said, had been a lovely occasion. It had been on a small scale just as the young couple had wanted with the people who had meant much to them. The wedding breakfast had been a large dinner party on a grand scale and when it was all over Piers and Mary had not left on honeymoon as was the tradition, but she had requested that she wanted to wake up as the new mistress of Westborough Hall and start the most exciting adventure of her life so far. They could go away at any time they wanted. Piers had been amused by this request and had gladly fallen in with the plan. He felt that his relationship with his new wife must turn a corner and he wished to spoil her, for he now guessed that she really loved him. He was trying hard to make their future together a happy one and hoped that in time he would love her too as he should. He was very fond of her, but it was not his intention to hurt her or make her feel second best to a relationship that was going nowhere.

Mary was aware very early on that she was pregnant, but had waited a few days to absorb the fact herself and to enjoy the secret before it reached the public domain. Her news was received just as she knew it would be as a very special event to continue the Devine line into the future. Piers had done his duty to make his wife feel special. They had time in London to attend the theatre and dine intimately so that they could savour the moment. Mary had never felt happier or closer to her husband. Piers felt gratitude that he was to become a father for the first time and made a mental note that his wife required cherishing. It was after his visit to Beatrice and his sisters that Piers had a stab of guilt about his mother. He had witnessed Beatrice's face concerning the fact that they were the first to know about the baby. Although he knew Beatrice had been treated badly by his mother over the years, Clarissa had been his father's legal partner and had provided the heir to the estate. She had done her duty like Mary was doing now. On his return to Westborough Hall he had decided to offer an olive branch to his mother. The rumour mill had worked between the dower house and the Hall and the news of his mother's state of mind over her isolation from the wedding, even if it was of her own making, had reached his ears. Finally on his return from London he had stopped at the dower house uninvited, but he went through the formality of being a guest in his mother's home. She welcomed him stiffly; all the hurt of the previous year was foremost in her mind and etched on her face.

'Would you like tea?' she asked in a strained fashion and Piers, knowing that he had to break the giant iceberg between them, had agreed. As they began to talk the thaw set in and mother and son had begun to build bridges that would put them in a better place for the future.

'Mary, would like you to take tea with us one afternoon next week?' he lied, knowing that Mary found his mother difficult but if he was there it would help. 'And by the way Mother we are to have a child, hopefully an heir.' Clarissa's response baffled him as tears ran down her cheeks before she said, 'I'm so happy for you.' And with that comment he went over to kiss her cheek, knowing that at least they had brought a little happiness into her world. Perhaps there was hope that their relationship would turn a corner at last. The thought felt impossibly good after all the turmoil in their lives and Piers was not somebody who wished to harbour grievances indefinitely.

Chapter 19

Piers knew that it was time to establish himself in the House of Lords by delivering his maiden speech. He had achieved much since his father had died. The Westborough estate was run like a well-oiled machine and now that he was married with a possible heir on the way, he felt he could turn to the political arena which, to his immense surprise, had captured his interest. He had opinions which he wanted to share publically even if he was shouted down in the process; he felt confident enough to do just that. He had listened to many speeches based upon the uncertainty of war, a possible war which would lie at Britain's door and cause more heartache only twenty years after the Great War had ended. For mostly he was fervently patriotic and did not want to see the country he loved torn apart by the dictatorships of Germany and Italy which were emerging in Europe and the rise of Japan in the Far East. While Piers had been involved in his own personal life, the political world on the home front was changing. Only weeks before his wedding Lord Halifax had become Foreign Secretary, replacing Anthony Eden. It had enraged Piers that Lord Halifax had reluctantly agreed with the Prime Minister, Neville Chamberlain's policy of appeasement which was to give some ground to the dictators Hitler and Mussolini.

In the House of Lords Piers had stood up to intervene in a foreign policy debate addressing his thoughts to Lord Halifax. He expressed his grave concerns of giving way to Adolf Hitler who, he felt, if given an inch would take a yard. History showed how through the years dictators had done just that. Politicians should learn lessons from the mistakes of the past to provide a better future. He thought that he was being idealistic but nevertheless he believed that he was right and was prepared to be dogmatic about such things. Piers had no qualms about speaking out amongst the most illustrious of politicians. It was his self-belief on this very subject that he wanted to air. It was his way of issuing a warning which, whether right or wrong, was up to the government to listen or dismiss as was their will but he had done what he thought was right. He had also read the warning speeches of Winston Churchill, who spoke his rhetoric with authority and self-belief from the back benches of the House of Commons; for had Churchill not said that you could not feed dictators for their appetites were insatiable? He believed the man to be a genius in how he articulated the English language in that timbre of voice which was distinctive and specifically his own. Love him or hate him, Piers believed that at some point in the not too distant future Churchill would one day return to the front benches where he felt that he truly belonged. The reaction to Piers' speech was mixed as he knew that it would be, but it had been well received generally by people who did not have the courage to stand in the House and say what was on their minds though, in reality, they agreed with him. Having returned to Westborough Hall two days later he was greeted at breakfast by Mary smiling at him as he entered the dining room. She had served herself a large plate of bacon and eggs and toast which she ate hungrily. Piers looked at her appetite in amazement and then laughed. Normally she picked at food, unlike his sisters who had always eaten heartily.

'I'm eating for two,' she laughed with him. 'And by the way, in *The Times* page six is an article that I think you should take a peek at.' Her smile had become enigmatic. Piers regarded the newspaper, which was always folded neatly by his plate. It was in an untidy fold having been read by his wife. He poured himself a cup of tea and then shook out the paper into the tidy creases that he normally liked before turning to the appointed page. His eyes scoured the page wondering what he was looking for, and then he saw the subheading near the bottom of the second column:

New Earl Makes Debut Speech.

He read the short article which described how he had made a public declaration in front of Lord Halifax concerning the onslaught of dictators and their greed for advancement. He continued his perusal noting how his words had generally been well received by his peers. Mary regarded him proudly. Her cheeks were glowing as she looked at him with love.

'You're famous,' she said, smiling shyly at him. 'I'm proud of you.' He laughed at her thinking how pretty she looked this morning. There was a bloom about her, obviously her pregnancy agreed with her. 'Hardly famous Mary, but I'm glad that my speech was generally well received.' He bent to kiss her. She really was rather sweet, he thought, and was making herself into a good wife and Countess. Since their marriage they had hosted several dinner parties and he had been very proud of the way she had coped at such a level. Her mother had taught her well to be a hostess on quite a grand scale.

'Oh, by the way, I called in at the dower house on my way home yesterday to see Mother. She was asking about you and our infant and I decided to ask her for afternoon tea today.' He waited for the inevitable reaction.

Mary pulled a face. 'I know that she is behaving better Piers, but I wish you had asked me first.' She made a little moue with her mouth which wiped away the happiness from earlier.

'I'm sorry, I should have asked, but I will be here to keep her in order. Now that she is more thoughtful I think that we should be too. Oh, by the way is your father coming at the weekend?' He knew well how to deflect unhappy thoughts by referring to more pleasant matters. Her father visited regularly so she really had little to complain about concerning his mother, who hid herself away at the dower house for most of the time.

Mary's face brightened again at the thought of her father. 'Yes, he is. He is arriving on Friday. I had thought that we could invite your mother to dinner and Diana is bringing her new young man to stay. So we should have a lovely weekend.'

She realized that this should placate Piers for her earlier gaff and now he had fully recovered his sense of humour, for he knew that her father had a certain respect for his mother. He often wondered why that should be but, if it lightened the mood of the evening, he was all for it. He also wanted to meet Diana's new friend. As the head of the family he felt that it was his duty to inspect any prospective husband his sisters might bring home. He felt that he was being a little stuffy on such matters, but his new position as Earl had given him a different perspective on life and much more responsibility, to boot.

*

Sabine had been in a world of her own in recent days after her brother's revelation that Peter was in love. She had spent more and more time in his company and was becoming desperate for him to propose, but it had been very quiet on that front. They had wined and dined and attended theatrical productions in the West End and still nothing had been forthcoming. She was nearly beside herself with anxiety and tension while Peter remained oblivious of her inner angst. Then she had been invited to Peter's home to stay for the weekend where there were several guests staying including Piers and Mary. Sabine had been so relieved to see such familiar faces and, on the Saturday afternoon, she had taken her brother aside and the tears had flowed, relieving the distress that had taken its toll over time. She had managed to suggest a walk in the garden where their private conversation could not be overheard.

'Are you sure that you were right about Peter? The suspense has become too much for me to bear. We are in each other's company so much but he says nothing about marriage.' Her beautiful face looked saddened through her genuine anxiety. 'What am I going to do Piers?' He looked at her with compassion, knowing how he felt about the woman he truly loved and who would always remain unavailable to him but Sabine's story would probably turn out differently; in fact he knew that it would but he could hardly confess what had been secretly shared with him. Peter had met Piers for lunch one day to see how the land lay in seeking Sabine's hand in marriage. He had thought that he was doing the correct thing in asking Piers' permission. Although Peter was going about it in the right way Piers had said that he should seek permission from Beatrice first. Neither of them had met, which might cause friction, and Piers had offered to take Peter to meet Sabine's mother one day when his half-sister was away and Piers had arranged for his two half-sisters to spend some time with Mary at Westborough Hall. Mary always had enjoyed their young company.

The exact moment for Peter to meet Beatrice had been well engineered. Piers had arranged to have afternoon tea at the town house and had informed Sabine's mother that he would not be alone. Beatrice was always pleased to see Piers for he had been good to her family and their times together were always harmonious. However, she was curious that he was bringing a friend to tea as well. It was not that she was displeased, for she enjoyed young company and it prevented her from thinking too deeply about her own circumstances; but she knew that she was often lonely, particularly in the evenings. Her circumstances were beginning to change as friends began to invite her as the single woman to their dinner parties. She had often been placed next to a widower or a single man, but she was wary at meeting someone for the first time as she was not ready to find a new person who was a prospective husband or companion; yet part of her wanted just that. She wished to be escorted to the theatre or wined and dined at the best restaurants, as she had done with James in the early days of their relationship. She was still a comparatively young woman; the early forties was not so old for the modern woman and now she wanted to open the door to a new life, but by clinging to the memories of James Devine she could not quite shake him off. Perhaps she did not want to do it either. Her emotions were still in turmoil.

Sometimes she felt guilty at the thought of letting go of the memory of James, but the old adage said that life had to go on and, by gradually letting go, she would be moving forward for herself and her daughters who were so worried about her emotional well-being. This train of thought came and went on a regular basis but now her reverie was interrupted by the arrival of Piers and his friend. The drawing room door opened and Hetty put her head round to introduce Beatrice's visitors.

'Shall I prepare your tea, madam?' the maid asked.

'Yes, Hetty, that would be lovely. Thank you.' Hetty made a hurried departure, but there was just enough time to take a glimpse of the visitor whom she had not met before. Piers gave her a smile and closed the door after her believing that she could be eavesdropping at the door.

'Beatrice, I would like you to meet Peter, an old friend of mine and now he is a friend of Sabine.' Beatrice looked puzzled for Sabine had not mentioned this young man to her before, but good manners had always been her style and she stretched her hand to welcome him. 'It is good to meet you Peter,' she said, and then proffered her cheek for Piers to kiss.

The occasion was pleasant as she found the two young men to be amusing company and she had laughed more than she had done in a long time. Her hand went out to pull the bell rope to order more tea when Piers looked at her and said, 'I'm sorry Beatrice but I have to be going now. I have arranged to meet my father-in-law for dinner later and I have a few things to do before then, but Peter can stay a while longer I am sure.' Beatrice felt flustered at being left alone with a stranger and Piers, sensing this, said, 'Peter wants to ask you something important.' Piers rose from his chair and bent and kissed her cheek once more but whispered in her ear, 'Don't be alarmed, you are quite safe in his company.' Having shaken hands with his friend Piers had made a quick exit. Hetty hovered and helped Piers with his coat and handed him his hat. She closed the door behind him. He just hoped that the interview with mother and the prospective new husband would go well.

Chapter 20

Before Peter had an opportunity to begin his diatribe about Sabine and how wonderful she was, Beatrice had regarded him quizzically with an intuition as to what might be coming. She knew that this would have been James' territory had he still been alive, but now the female world was changing. With the lasting social affects from the Great War women had played a more proactive part with their men away at the Front; and women drove ambulances in France to help save lives, often putting their own in jeopardy. This was a wake-up call for her to take her life in her own hands and be decisive. She prevented Peter from speaking by asking him questions to which she required answers.

'Tell me about yourself, Peter. I have an inkling what all this might be about.' He had the grace to blush but it was not the best of introductions to a possible new mother-in-law. Although Peter Jordan was a similar age to Piers he appeared much younger in years. The recent experiences that Piers had endured had made him mature quickly and he had thrown himself wholeheartedly into all that the new challenges had placed in his path. However, Peter was still strongly attached to the demands of an autocratic parent who expected his son to jump a mile high when the lion roared. But he had made decisions of his own in an attempt to cut the umbilical cord. Although his father had met Sabine and had approved of her merits as a personable human being, he still was unaware of the emotional entanglement between the young couple. Peter wanted to present an engagement as a fait accompli rather than allow his father to pick away at what might lie below the surface. If the engagement was announced Peter's father would have to accept the situation because he would not wish to cause a fracas in the public domain as he had always considered his family's life as a private affair. Public quarrelling about such events had never been his style.

'I um...' Peter faltered feeling gauche all of a sudden when he had wished to feel debonair and make a good impression. Then he took his courage in both hands. 'I am in love with Sabine, Mrs Cavendish, and I would like to ask for her hand in marriage.' Now that it had been stated Beatrice was at a loss for words. She wondered what James would have said. What would the young man's prospects be? It was difficult not to laugh at this thought for Piers had already introduced Peter as the heir to his father's baronetcy. He would be a good match for Sabine and the fact that it was obviously a love match touched a spot in Beatrice's heart when she remembered the love that she and James Devine had shared, for what had seemed a lifetime.

'Do you really love her and will cherish her?' She had to ask the question and hear the answer from his lips.

'Yes I love her, very much and I can make her happy.' Beatrice averted her eyes from his face which was suffused with the love he had declared. 'You know her family history?' she asked tentatively. The parentage of her children had to be declared, although she wished otherwise.

'Yes, Piers told me about sharing a father with Sabine.'

'And that will not cause a problem in the future?' Beatrice asked.

'No. There might be some gossip initially but given time it will disappear and people tend to forget such things. After all, she is the daughter of an earl' He looked at Beatrice and found her deep in thought. She had heard all that he had to say but the words 'and the daughter of his mistress' circled in her brain.

'And you wish to marry my daughter?' she said.

'Yes, I am asking for her hand,' he repeated the fact. She had no reason to deny their happiness nor would she want to, but she was dreading being left alone as her children departed the nest; but such thoughts were selfish, she knew. Regarding him she smiled at him, 'Make her happy is all I ask. There has been enough sadness in recent times with the passing of her father. You have my blessing.' With those words she rose to her feet and offered her hand, which he did not take but kissed her cheek as he had seen Piers do.

'Thank you Mrs Cavendish.'

'Beatrice,' she murmured to him as she saw him collect his possessions in readiness to depart. His urgency lay in the fact that he wished to ask the question that his prospective bride was waiting to hear.

'Tell her you both have my blessing,' Beatrice said as she saw him to the front door. Peter turned to her. 'Thank you for that,' he said as he leant forward to kiss her cheek once more, relieved that his duty had been done.

Chapter 21

The summer months of 1938 brought highs and lows for the relatives of James Devine. Thea felt stifled in London by the heat and the atmosphere in the city. The place seemed airless and dusty. Conversations were limited to the crisis looming in Europe. Different age groups had different fears. The older generation could remember the lives sacrificed by the young in the trenches and on the battlefields. Many families had been almost wiped out when their sons had paid the ultimate sacrifice. Grief was an emotion which transcended all classes of society. It had been a unifying factor which brought the country together. Now though there was another generation of young men who would enlist to keep their country safe from the threat of Hitler and Mussolini, if it came to that. Others felt that nothing untoward would happen and some of these people were members of His Majesty's government. Opinion was divided but London was restless with the possible threat of war, for Hitler was an unknown quantity and he was not trusted although he built a façade of friendship.

All this had added to Thea's mood. Yet there were other factors which had contributed to her emotions, but the underlying one was the fact that she was lonely. Her world was changing and crumbling. It had begun with the news of her father's death. Out of that had come some positive things such as meeting with her half siblings and the closeness that had developed very quickly between them. This she cherished more than she could say but, in recent weeks, she had not heard from Piers or Mary. She knew that she was being selfish but Sabine's obvious happiness had made her slightly jealous of her older sibling.

After Peter's conversation with Beatrice he had headed out to the country to the family estate where Sabine had been staying. His proposal had left Sabine breathless with happiness. Her life now revolved round her fiancé and she had neglected her own family. About this time Peter's father had suffered a mild heart attack and the fact that he had been ordered to rest gave Peter greater freedom to run the estate. In fact it had given him increased confidence while his father was incapacitated. Despite his father's illness a notice had been placed in *The Times* of the engagement and without losing face his father had not been able to protest. Thus, as his father's health had improved, the planning of the nuptials had begun to take place. Piers had intervened in the proceedings by saying that the wedding planned for the autumn should take place at the family home of Westborough Hall. This was now beginning to proceed with everyone's blessing except for Clarissa who had offered no protest, knowing what the outcome would be if she took that route. Now that she was once more in the family fold she was not about to sacrifice her lot for pride, but it did not make it easy for her to know that the other family had scored again. However, a lesson had been learned the hard way and she was never going to lose face again. Beatrice, seeing her daughters picking up the threads of their own lives, had accepted an invitation from a distant cousin to visit for a few weeks. She had left Thea in charge of the town house and made her way to Bournemouth on this extended stay. She knew that this was not a long term answer to her problems but it was the beginning of a new adventure and there had been talk of possibly taking time to meet more relatives who lived in the West Country. Her feelings of ennui and sometimes descending fits of gloom and despondency had lifted as soon as this letter had dropped through the letter box. She had not considered herself selfish for she had devoted her life to a man who could not marry her, and to her daughters whom she loved very much but had reached adulthood now. Her girls were beginning to make lives for themselves just as they should.

The summer recess of Parliament was to allow Piers an extended period of time at Westborough Hall. He viewed this with mixed emotions, for it meant that he would be spending more time in the company of his wife, who was beginning to place greater demands on him, and Westborough Hall required his attention. It was going to be pleasant to be away from the doom and gloom of the talk of war however concerned one might feel about the situation. He knew that the Cabinet would be monitoring the action in Europe, but he did not rank highly enough to be involved in any decision making. However, the balmy period of his marriage to Mary seemed to be over for now. The happy days of the news of a possible heir had evaporated as Mary grew larger and the days grew hotter. She did not know what to do with herself, if truth be known. She felt lonely and abandoned by Piers as he had had to spend more time in the House of Lords. It had not been his fault or been done deliberately, it was a case of needs must. Piers had understood about her loneliness but it was her constant moaning which had made him feel as he did. Other women had to endure pregnancy in the heat, he would remind her, and not all women were as privileged to lead such a life of luxury. If she did not want to do anything she did not have to, for others were paid to do it for her. He did not love Mary sufficiently to be patient when everything was not going the way it should. His reaction was always to escape, which compounded the problem. He knew it was being selfish but he also had other things on his mind. He had made sure that Mary was well cared for but apparently that was not quite enough. He also realized that she needed a mother figure to help her through the crisis and, as her own was deceased, he had to find a replacement. Clarissa was no good in that department for she would make the situation worse by believing that you should just get on with it and would start on a diatribe of 'In my day we...'. As it was Mary saw as little of her mother-in-law as she could, for both women were stubborn in their own way and would not find a common denominator that would make for any progress in their relationship.

Before he left London Piers had thought long and hard about ways of solving the dilemma and had hit upon the idea of inviting Thea to keep Mary company for the few months until the time of the birth. He had intended to keep Thea at a distance for a while but, knowing the close friendship which existed between the two women, he found that it was the only solution to the problem. The reasons which lay at the core of keeping Thea at arm's length were personal to himself. He knew that he was infatuated by her but if he was honest, he loved her deeply and he had hoped, by keeping away from Thea, that a love for Mary would grow deeper. His love for Thea was forbidden, he knew, but since their last meeting he had become obsessed by her. He could not keep her out of his mind. Perhaps if she were constantly in his presence she might begin to irritate him, and these nagging thoughts and doubts might end his inner turmoil. So on the day before his return to Westborough Hall he took a taxi from Westminster to the town house in Belgravia. Hetty as usual opened the door to him and led him into the drawing room where Thea was writing her neglected correspondence, which she always found irksome. She had found the day particularly long and was gratified to find that she had a visitor to divert her attention from her letter writing, which she willingly put to one side.

'Piers, how lovely to see you,' she cooed. Her face was alight with pleasure at his visit.

'Would you like some tea?' she asked as she turned to look at the clock on the mantelpiece.

'No thank you Thea,' he said, looking at her radiant face alight with a kaleidoscope of emotions. As usual his heart had flipped as he took in the tumble of curls and her pretty face; and the childlike figure which never seemed to change. He tried to think of her age. She still must be only twenty-two, so young and unspoilt.

'Is this a social call, Piers?' she asked, wondering what this visit was about after so many weeks of silence.

'Yes it is and I also want to ask you a favour.' Momentarily her eyes clouded. 'Yes of course. There's nothing wrong I hope?' Her eyes had observed the change in his demeanour. She had wondered if there was something wrong with the baby, for his face was quite serious.

'Well yes and no. It's Mary.'

'The baby is all right?' She cut across his sentence, concern etching her features.

'Yes, yes,' he wafted the question away impatiently. 'It's just that Mary is not coping with her pregnancy very well. She is lethargic with the heat and she yearns for company. As she has no mother she wants company to divert her and Mother just gets under her skin after only a few minutes.' He pulled a half-smile knowing that Thea was perfectly aware of his mother's behaviour as she had witnessed it first hand and then he continued, 'I was wondering if you could come and stay with her for a while. You are good friends after all. I know it is a bit of an imposition but...' His voice drifted off as he watched Thea's reaction, hoping that she would come.

'Of course I will come, in a few days when I have informed Mother that the house will be empty. She is staying in Bournemouth with an elderly cousin. Tell Mary that I shall look forward to it.' In fact the suggestion had been an answer to a prayer. 'And how are your sisters?'

Piers' face clouded again. 'Have you not heard? Diana and Minty are both to be married this autumn. We have been neglectful of you lately Thea, but we will be inviting you. As you know the invitations will not be going out for a few weeks yet. Three family weddings, all within such a short space of time, can you believe it? It will be quite a festive time and then Christmas will be just around the corner.' Thea smiled. 'Yes it will be fun, and there is me heading for the shelf with no beau in sight.' She giggled but, deep down, it was how she felt. Also she had been aware how neglected she had felt, but it was not her way to moan and criticize. She was not called Mary.

'I am much afraid that I have neglected my wife lately. The House of Lords has held my attention recently with so much talk of war on the horizon.'

'I know Piers. That is all you hear in the streets or read in the newspapers. It is so depressing. Do you think there will be war?'

Piers looked saddened, 'Yes I do believe that it will come to that soon. This fellow Hitler has the world dancing to his tune. He wants to add to Germany's territories in Europe fully aware that civilized countries like our own don't agree with what he is trying to do.'

Thea looked worried, having felt much the same herself although she did not proclaim to have a great knowledge of the political arena in Europe. Yet regarding Piers' facial expression she felt suddenly afraid.

'And if it comes to that?'

'I think we must hope that our politicians can keep a peaceful process in mind. But they have to be firm with him. War should be the last option. It is not long since we were at war with the Hun before.

'I really must go, though. Mary will be wondering where I have got to. I shall be catching a later train as it is. Thank you, Thea, for your kindness. Let us know when you will be arriving.'

They rose from their seats and looked at each other for what seemed quite a while. Then Piers put out his arms to give her an affectionate hug and kiss but, as she walked into his embrace, his mouth hungrily searched for her own and they stood locked together until Thea reluctantly pulled away, puzzled by what had happened between them. She was naïve in matters of the heart, having only experienced mild flirtations across a room or had danced with the brother of a friend who might have drunk too much and a hand wandered off course, but was easily put back where it was meant to be. She was not used to chaste brotherly kisses. Even her father had kissed her on the forehead when she had gone to kiss him goodnight. She was left feeling confused by the little nugget of desire which had stirred inside her. But most of all, that kiss she knew was not right. But there would not be a next time for she had decided that she would not be alone with her brother again. Piers was anxious to go now, for he realized that he had gone too far. He had never intended for it to happen but his desire for her left his emotions in turmoil. He took his leave knowing that he had a fight on his hands and would have to tread carefully to keep his emotions in order. His own inner angst was the enemy at the door.

Chapter 22

Mary had accepted Piers' news of Thea's pending arrival with excitement and gratitude. She had begun to feel that her husband had not cared about her enough with his constant absences from home and the fact that, when he was at the Hall, the estate claimed much of his time. The tension between them over the following days had begun to ease and the easy affection and harmony that had existed in the early days of their marriage had begun to return much to the relief of both parties. Thea had written to her mother concerning her visit to Westborough Hall. She knew that she would have to leave a list of instructions for the staff and it was a suitable time for the house to be cleaned from top to bottom. Hardly a spring clean in early August, she mused, but she knew her mother would take the opportunity for such action to be taken. There would be moans and groans from Hetty and the young girl Maria who came to help on a daily basis. Neither of them enjoyed hard work of any kind. Thea had started wondering if they would be able to keep staff if a war started. There was more money to be made outside domestic service and, no doubt, there would be more pressure placed upon women in general to do their bit. Depression descended on her once more as she thought so deeply, as she often did. A thought struck her too about Piers who might have to go to war. She knew that she could not even contemplate that. She had spent too much time alone in recent days and, if she had had her mother or Sabine to talk to, they would have brushed such thoughts away as nonsense. She could hear her mother saying, 'Why worry unnecessarily when nothing might happen?' Of course her mother was correct but Thea was a worrier by nature. She had also worried incessantly about the kiss and knew that she could not confide in anyone about that, not even Sabine who was her closest confidante. The inevitable reply came from Beatrice, who expressed her pleasure that Thea had something useful to fill her time. As she had predicted Beatrice wished for the house to be cleaned from top to bottom but she had no date as yet for her return to London. She was enjoying her extended visit to the south coast and her relations were due to set off for the West Country at the end of August. She felt that it was unlikely for her to return to normal life much before Sabine's wedding, now dated for October. Thea sighed deeply. She was missing her mother but at the same time she was pleased that she was making a life for herself. She could not begrudge her that, for such thoughts would be selfish and unkind particularly now that her own time was to be taken up with caring for Mary. Thea issued her mother's instructions to the staff, who she could see were not thrilled by the orders that they had to undertake. Hetty twisted her mouth into a wry smile knowing that she would take her time to follow such directives. Even Cook had no control over her in matters of the general house. Here Hetty held sway and she had every intention of thrusting much of the work onto the willing Maria's shoulders.

Packed and ready for her journey, Thea looked around the house nostalgically knowing that only a matter of months before, if Clarissa had had her way, the house would have been returned to the Westborough estate and her family would have been homeless. She was fond of this house as this was where she had grown up with happy memories, but the thought of the elderly Dowager made her shudder for she knew that she would be in close proximity to her when she finally took up residence at the Hall. These thoughts dissipated when she observed a car pull up outside the house. Piers had said when they had last spoken on the telephone that the very least he could do, would be to send the car for her. He had jested that if she was like Mary or his sisters she would be weighed down with luggage which could not be carried onto the train even with a porter's assistance. She had smiled at this statement for the amount of luggage which was stacked in their entrance hall bore testament to that. She continued to look through the drawing room window. The morning had clouded over and a slight drizzle came down, cooling the heat that had been unbearable over the previous few days. Then she observed Piers' Bentley draw up outside. It was Piers' chauffeur who had come to collect her and her volume of luggage to transport her to Westborough Hall. She was beginning to feel excited by the prospect of returning to the Hall. She was forever eager to find out more about her father and his youth and also previous generations of her family who had lived there. It was a constant voyage of discovery every time she visited. What would her father have thought of the circumstances that had unfolded since his unexpected death? She wished she knew. Hetty appeared at the door of the drawing room.

'The chauffeur has arrived, miss. Shall I help you with your bags?'

'That's kind of you Hetty. Just the small ones mind.' She smiled at the maid but deep down she wondered if she was happy to see the family disappear for a while. She knew that such thoughts were unkind but the whole family had the measure of the young woman. The front door stood wide open and the chauffeur carried the heavier bags with ease to the car and spent a few moments arranging the items to fit into the limited space. This was an art form in which he was well practiced. Thea sat in the back seat enjoying the comfort of the leather-seated vehicle. It was a luxury that she was not used to. Her family had never owned a car for her father had declared that they were unnecessary in London, with taxis and the tube so easily at hand. The car pulled away allowing Thea to settle into her daydreams and observations of London as it went about its business.

The journey through the suburbs was long and protracted. The roads were full of traffic probably heading to the coast for some respite from the relentless activity of the capital, but eventually they were moving into the countryside with its greenery and undulating hills and valleys. Her mind also left the weariness of London behind. Here the pace of life had slowed and they seemed beyond the talk of war. Was it possible to believe that those thoughts did not exist here? She smiled to herself at such absurdity and then her eyelids grew heavy and her head flopped to one side as the rhythm of the engine lulled her into sleep, as it would a fractious child.

Chapter 23

Piers had smiled at the new Mary who sat across the table from him at breakfast. Her mood was effervescent and flirtatious as she watched him put his newspaper to one side and give her his full attention. The fact that the storm that had existed between them had broken and they had entered calmer waters had been a relief to both of them. It had also made Piers think that Mary had not been imagining her traumas but she had been genuinely lonely in such a big house as Westborough Hall, with little to fill her time or mind for that matter. She was an intelligent young woman who required to be fulfilled intellectually in order to stay happy. She was no fly by night who only thought about clothes or partying. Her whole being demanded more than that to keep her happy and, if he were honest, that was one of the reasons why he had married her. He had wanted someone whom he could communicate with as his equal and he knew that he had failed her on that score with his constant absences from home. Loneliness was not something that he knew much about for his life had always been full. He thought about his father wondering if so much bad feeling had partially been some of the discord between his parents. Now he would never know as he would only hear his mother's version of the truth. However, Mary required friends of an equal status who would call on her during his time away from home, but she had had very little time to do just that. To make true and loyal friends took time and probably the best ones were those who one had known for a lifetime. Poor Mary had had to become used to the ways of life at the Hall which was run like a well-oiled machine. He had his mother to thank for that for she had run a tight ship and so it continued, even though there was a new

Countess at the helm. And then there was a new baby on the way only weeks into the marriage, and these thoughts had absorbed them initially; but eventually as they had become used to the news the excitement had been absorbed into everyday life, leaving Mary wanting new stimulation to feed her brain and imagination. So the excitement of Thea's visit had reignited the fire in his wife, making her find ways of how to entertain their long term guest.

After breakfast Piers had disappeared onto the estate. He was casually dressed for working alongside his men out in the fields. Like his father he enjoyed being in the open air and experiencing the hard toil of the farm workers. He was not above such things; this aspect of his life, which was in complete contrast to his life at Westminster, had brought him much pleasure. This was his summer vacation and he loved the freedom that such times offered, but he felt a great responsibility to keep abreast of the news out in the wider world, avidly reading the newspapers to keep up to date on the events in Europe and the government's stance on such matters. Herr Hitler and Benito Mussolini had much to answer for. However Mary, although excited by Thea's imminent arrival, felt that she could not settle to do anything specific. She felt restless and suddenly energized by what they would do with their time together. She had planned to take tea in the gardens as Westborough Hall was so beautiful in the summer months. There were only a few more weeks of summer left and every opportunity had to be taken to enjoy the outdoors. They could take walks and explore the estate, for neither of them knew it well; also the nursery floor had to be planned out and everything checked in readiness for the baby as well as hiring a new nanny. They could travel to Worcester or Birmingham to choose a layette for the child. All this she would have done with her mother had she been alive. They would have had such fun for they had been more like sisters than parent and child. Feeling a little wistful Mary tried to dismiss these feelings, but it left a sensation of emptiness that had plagued her since her mother's demise. Planning their prospective activities sustained her during the hours between breakfast and luncheon. Mary climbed the stairs to the top floor where Piers and his sisters had lived in nursery days under the strict regime of Nanny and her staff. She smiled, feeling contented for the first time in months. She also wanted to be a mother who did much for her child instead of handing the infant over to Nanny all the time. They had to bond from the very beginning. Her daydream saw her filling the nursery with little replicas of Piers. She thought that she would produce a string of boys and the line would be secure for the future. She smiled to herself knowing now that her love for her husband had flourished over time despite little domestic tiffs. Even the best of marriages were susceptible to such disputes but, given time, she was certain that their love would flourish as her parents' marriage had done.

Having climbed the stairs and walked along the landing she opened the door to the nursery suite to look around. She was amazed at how it sparkled with cleanliness and she could smell the carbolic soap which had been used to achieve such perfection. Some of the staff had worked there recently rubbing and scrubbing to make the place shine for the new arrival. She had heard the army of footsteps moving up and down the old creaky staircases and bangs when something was carelessly dropped. Mrs Pardoe had supervised such activity. Under her close scrutiny no speck of dirt would be left; she was a stickler on such matters. She wondered if Piers had given specific orders for the job to be done, or had it been Clarissa who returned to the Hall more frequently these days? A feeling of guilt overcame her as she should have been the one to give such instructions, but her own circumstances had overtaken her whole being and she knew that she had been selfish. This time she promised herself that she was going to be a better wife than she had been over the past months. Piers would see a remarkable improvement in her demeanour and the running of the Hall; after all, she was mistress of the great house. As she moved around the nursery suite she opened cupboard doors where toys, left over from previous childhoods, were revealed. She wondered which of the teddy bears had belonged to her husband; but they had all been well loved, she noticed, for their threadbare appearances were a testament to that. The rocking horse which stood by the window had been well loved too and had seen better days. She stroked the tangled mane and placed her fingers in the cracks in the old leather saddle. She had time to take the horse to be reupholstered before the birth of this child and everything to be renewed, but that would take away all the love that had been lavished on it over the years. It was part of the history of this family that she had married into and her children had to be aware of this great heritage that was theirs. Her hand touched the precious place where the next heir to Westborough Hall lay. She was convinced that the baby was a boy for when she gave him a son her husband would love her truly. For some time now Mary had been convinced that there was someone else in his life but she had no real evidence of it, just a strange feeling inside her. When he kissed her or made love to her his thoughts seemed to be somewhere else. She did not want history repeating itself as she had heard about James Devine and Clarissa. It was time to make Piers happy and by doing that she must rise above all her own personal problems and put them well and truly behind her. As she looked up and out of the nursery window she drank in the spectacular views across the great expanse of garden to the front of the Hall. It all took her breath away. In only a few months she had grown to love this place; its tranquillity, after a life lived in the hustle and bustle of London, was soothing to the soul.

Suddenly moving steadily along the winding drive she saw the Bentley approaching and she knew that Thea had arrived. Mary flew down the two flights of stairs in her haste and excitement at the arrival of their guest. She had not given any thought to her unborn child in case she tripped or fell but Piers, who stood at the bottom of the grand staircase in readiness to great Thea, looked at the high colour in his wife's cheeks and the brightness of her eyes and smiled knowing that this was all down to Thea's visit.

'Mary, be steady. You don't want to fall and harm the baby or harm yourself,' he admonished her, but not unkindly.

'Sorry. I forgot. Thea's arriving and it made me feel excited. I've seen the Bentley.' Her face was flushed with happiness as she spoke. Piers could not help but smile for she seemed like an excited child might, knowing that Christmas was approaching soon. 'I knew Thea would be here at any moment so I decided to change from my work clothes into something smarter. And then I saw the Bentley approaching as well. It is good that we are both here to greet our guest.' Piers slightly turned away from Mary, trying to mask his pleasure at Thea's arrival. Mary looked at her husband and saw how spruce his appearance was and how impossibly handsome he looked. Despite her reservations that he did not love her, she felt quite buoyed by the fact he belonged to nobody else but herself. She also knew that all the Devine children had that je ne sais quoi about them, including the Cavendish branch of the family. Beside them all she felt incredibly plain and dowdy and cumbersome with her increasing girth. It was always the custom to change before sitting at the table and it would soon be time for luncheon. That was part of their good breeding and traditions died hard amongst the ranks of the aristocracy.

'You look nice,' she said smiling and leant her cheek forward to be kissed. Piers obliged out of politeness but, deep down, he was more interested in seeing Thea.

'Well it is nearly luncheon and we do have a guest,' he explained away his appearance.

'Indeed we do,' she said and opened the front door just in time to see Thea alighting from the back of the Bentley. Mary walked towards her and flung her arms wide to hug her friend. The delight at seeing each other was obvious from the expressions on their faces. Piers stood back and looked at every facet that was Thea. Her beauty was taking his breath away and he suddenly felt a great sorrow that she could not be any more to him than just his sister. He knew that he had to tread carefully for his own sake as well as hers. Mary was not to know about his feelings towards Thea and in the fullness of time he hoped that he could put all this behind him and forget.

But he believed that it would take an awfully long time as he had loved her for all the time he had known her.

'Come and say hello to your sister Piers. I don't know why you are skulking back there.' Mary's happiness was palpable.

Piers stepped forward and gave Thea a chaste brotherly kiss on the cheek. 'You look lovely,' Piers whispered into Thea's ear as he greeted her. She looked at him smiling uncertainly and wondered for the umpteenth time whether she had imagined the kiss of only days previously. There was an anticipation and a thrill about being in his company but her feelings were confused. She wondered where all this was leading them but she was aware that this kind of love was forbidden. Mary linked her arm through her friend's, noticing nothing amiss as they turned towards the house. Piers walked towards the chauffeur.

'Denham, can you put the luggage in the hall for my sister please?'

'Of course my lord,' he replied touching his peaked cap as a mark of respect before emptying the boot of its contents, which he hefted towards the house wondering for the second time that day why women could never travel lightly. It was beyond his comprehension. Thea had asked if she might go to her room before luncheon. The journey from London had left her feeling that a change of clothes might make her feel better as it had been so hot in the car. She also wanted to touch up her lipstick and generally feel more presentable. After a few moments, feeling better, she found Mary and Piers in the small dining room which was only used by the family when they were not entertaining. It was a pleasant, homely room facing the lovely gardens at the back of the house and allowed the warm sunshine to filter through the open French windows. Her hosts were already seated and the footman hovered in readiness to wait at table. A white wine was poured into her glass as she settled herself onto her chair.

Piers raised his glass. 'To family,' he said, smiling at his wife and sister.

They raised their glasses to the toast as the footman served them the most delicious-smelling beef and Yorkshire pudding outside of the county after which it was named.

Chapter 24

The weeks of August were the happiest that Mary had known since she had first arrived at Westborough Hall. She had enjoyed playing hostess to their guest and on a few occasions her father had visited from London. Minty and Diana had also come with their prospective husbands. Now that the Hall had a new Countess they resided with their mother at the dower house and, once they were married, they would move away all together. Minty was going to be the first to be married at the end of September followed by Diana in early November. Sabine had set the date for her wedding the following spring. At first she had planned an autumn wedding but with all the chaos of her half siblings' nuptials she had decided to wait. There was no way that she wished for her star to be eclipsed by her relatives. There was just too much happening including a birth along the way. Mary's life was suddenly full with all the planning that the forthcoming events entailed and she felt happier with the buzz of activity than she had done in all the months of her marriage. She found Piers attentive and Thea just a delight to be with. So as the weeks progressed Mary had carried out her plans that she had made during that morning in the nursery. The two friends had explored the estate finding new joys and ways to entertain themselves. There was the summer house overlooking the small lake. Here they took picnics when Piers was away, for occasionally he had to return to London for various reasons, some of it estate business or to see his lawyer. He still had several weeks before the House was due to sit again. There was a little boat house near the edge of the lake containing two rowing boats. Here Thea was in her element, for her father had taught her to row as a child. She and Mary rowed across the lake and it brought them to a little jetty near the dower house. On one occasion in a fit of madness Mary declared that they should visit her mother-in-law but Thea declined, for she had not set eyes on Clarissa during the time that she had been staying at the Hall. She still felt intimidated by the elderly woman but she knew that at some point over the following months she would have to meet her. Cowardice was not usually her style but prevarication on such matters helped to keep the meeting at bay. By chance Piers had found out about the escapades of the two women. The three of them had been alone one evening in the small dining room when Piers had looked at his wife and sister with quite an angry expression on his face.

'It has come to my notice,' he began looking intently at them, the image of his father Thea thought, 'that the two of you have been seen rowing across the lake unattended.' Mary and Thea regarded each other waiting for the other to interject.

'I have to say that I am appalled that you have been so reckless, particularly you Mary. You could be putting our child or yourself at risk if anything happened. You will not do it again is that clear?' His voice had risen in his anger.

'No Piers I won't do it again. It was thoughtless of me. Please don't be angry with Thea. It was not her fault.' Mary looked down at her hands, tears brimming in her eyes. She had not heard her husband so angry before and could not bear raised voices, particularly ones aimed mostly at her own inadequacies. Her own parents had never raised their voices at her. Piers' face softened as he saw her distress realizing how austere his face must have been and the fierceness of his voice. Suddenly he smiled, believing that he had made his point.

'Well, enough of that then. But I am pleased that the pair of you have been enjoying yourselves. What do you plan for tomorrow?'

'I thought that we might enjoy a quiet day in the sunshine if it still holds.' Thea has been searching the library for something special to read. She wondered if there might be some local history which might give her information on the Hall and the Devines. 'We could then take a picnic into the orchard which will be cooler for us.' Mary knew that she was rambling but she wanted to divert her husband's attention away from her previous misdemeanour.

'I do believe that there is some old dusty relic of a book that would give you the information that you require. We could have a look after dinner if you like.' Piers had turned his attention now to Thea.

'That would be wonderful,' she said. 'The Hall feels so much like home these days that I feel I must know more about everything here.'

'And so it should. Part of you belongs here like any of us.' Piers' manner had mellowed now with the amount of wine he had consumed and he was once more affable and feeling great affection for these women. The footman cleared the table of the remnants of the meal while the threesome left the dining room for the library. The evening was still balmy and the windows were flung wide, allowing the scent of the roses which grew just below to waft gently upwards, mixing with the smell of freshly cut grass and honeysuckle.

'I'm sorry but I think that I must go and lie down. I have a headache coming on. Please excuse me.' Mary suddenly stood up, putting a hand to her forehead and then made for the library door. Thea rose to go with her, quite worried about her friend's sudden departure. She wondered whether Piers' harsh words of earlier had caused the headache. 'I expect that I shall be asleep in minutes Thea dear, so don't come with me.' Mary left the room closing the door silently behind her. Piers momentarily looked concerned. He wanted no problems with the health of his wife or unborn infant. He needed this child to be his heir. As every aristocrat or person of wealth knew, an heir was as important as breathing; but he made no comment on the matter.

'I suspect that she has overdone it in the sun today,' Thea said, looking at Piers wondering how he would react after his outburst at dinner, but he said nothing. He helped himself to a cigar from the box on the mantelpiece, cut the end of it and then lit it, taking his time to enjoy the first inhalation. His attention then focused on the brandy decanter. Thea felt unnerved by his silence for this was the first time they had been alone since their meeting at the town house. He turned to smile at her. 'Brandy?' he asked, raising a brandy bloom in her direction. Generally she did not drink spirits but, somehow, she felt so unnerved by his close presence that she nodded, hoping that the amber liquid would quieten her mood. Piers passed her a generous measure which she sipped, but the fire hit her throat as it moved downwards making her cough.

'Steady Thea. Take your time with it.' Piers' voice was stern as he watched her over-enthusiasm with her intake of the brandy. His perception at the rapid speed that she had sipped it made him wonder if she suspected his feelings for her or even if she reciprocated them as well. He wondered whether he should speak to her to clear the air between them and to assure her that he had no intention of doing anything wrong.

'Do you think that I should check on Mary?' she said, placing her glass on a silver coaster.

'I think Mary will be fine. I will look in on her later before bed. Thea, I think that I need to speak to you on a very serious subject. I have a feeling that you might know what I might say. Please sit down. I will return shortly.' Thea sat on the chair nearest to her, her legs felt weak with nerves and mental exhaustion as well as the anticipation of what he was about to say. She had never felt so flustered in her life. Piers left the room but returned quickly.

'I have instructed the staff that I must not be disturbed.' His voice was choked with deep emotion. He sat on a chair facing Thea not quite knowing how to begin. She sat with her head bowed plaiting her hands in her lap. Then she reached out for her brandy glass hoping that she would obtain some courage from its contents. Piers could tell at a glance that she suspected what was in his heart which made him fearful at the outcome of this meeting.

'Please look at me Thea.' His large hand covered hers as she raised her eyes to his face, but said nothing. He continued, 'Ever since I set eyes on you on the day of our Father's funeral I have had great affection for you, but I'm afraid that it is more than brotherly love. I also know that it is wrong but one cannot always control the matters of the heart. I have no intention of doing wrong or forcing you to do what you don't want to do, but I want you to live here at the Hall so that you can be near us. The love I bear you is so strong that I don't want you to be away from me. I know that this is wrong for Mary and for the child she bears but I have great respect for her as my wife and you must be assured that I would never wilfully hurt her.' Thea now knew that what she had suspected for several months was true. 'You want me here, but what if I want children one day and a man to openly love me? Can you deny me that?' Her voice sounded brittle with the emotion that she did not know how to cope with.

'No I cannot deny you what every woman has a right to have. It is not fair, but I am asking you how you feel and what you want to do?' Thea took her handkerchief from her pocket and dabbed her eyes which swam with tears. Piers brought her hand to his lips and kissed it with true affection.

'Would we be better not seeing each other again so that all of this might go away and we give the people we love a fair chance of happiness?' Piers regarded her intently and then, pulling her to her feet, he took her in his arms and held her tenderly. 'We do not intend to hurt people Thea. All I want to know is if you love me, too.'

'Yes Piers I love you too, only I have been trying to quell such emotions for so long now. I feel so guilty and I know that it is wrong to feel this way. We do not have a future together. You have too many responsibilities and society would shun us for how we feel. And think about the hurt and shame that we would inevitably bring down on ourselves and our loved ones, who don't deserve any of this. We would be being selfish.'

'Yes, but we will not do anything wrong. It is not wrong to love someone so much that it takes one's breath away. Mary is my wife and I never intend to hurt her, but we know there is surely a war coming in Europe and if we cannot take some happiness in life, what is there for us? If war comes I will have to go and fight like so many of us. And if it does come to that I want to know that you are safely living here and not in London, which will probably be a target for Herr Hitler and his Luftwaffe. I fear Mary will not cope if anything happens to me and I want someone to look after my son until he comes of age to inherit all this. Only you Thea, with your strength of character, could hold all this together for the future.' Suddenly he pulled her into his arms and kissed her passionately, taking her breath away. But just as quickly he pulled away from her and looked into her eyes as tears poured in torrents down her face. Gently he wiped the tears from her cheeks, and kissed her again.

'Please don't say such things,' she hiccupped through the flow of tears.

'We have to be realistic Thea. If we are prepared it makes it so much easier to cope when the day of war is upon us, for I do feel so strongly that it will happen. Hitler is intent on pulling the wool over our eyes even though he says there will not be war. His intention is to acquire other territories to give him power. Mark my words.' She snuggled closer to him for some reassurance, but only moments after they heard footsteps outside the library door. Pulling away from each other they felt like the guilty lovers that they were becoming. Both knew that it was going to be difficult to resist each other and, by living under the same roof, temptation was continually by their side. Would they have the courage to live apart? Neither of them knew the answer to that question, but if they did not the alternative could ruin their lives by causing scandal should the news ever reach their family and the wider world.

'I'm going to bed,' Thea said, and left him to his own thoughts while she went to wrestle with her own and ponder on her future. It was a dilemma that said logically common sense should prevail, but the heart said something else. It was a difficult task to find the right answer and with nobody to confide in only Thea could make the ultimate decision.

Chapter 25

The lovely weather seemed to linger through the long days of late summer. Thea and Mary continued their lazy outings to the shade of the orchard or the summer house continuing to take their picnics and books from the Hall's library which they read to each other, enjoying the joint appreciation of the literature which they discussed endlessly. They lived the lives of the characters of this fantasy world and educated themselves far beyond their days in the schoolroom on such matters. They even walked further afield through the cornfields, which were now golden stubble after the harvest and before the fields were then burnt and ploughed in readiness for winter sowing. They were halcyon days of fun and humour; days without responsibility as the Hall was run like a well-oiled machine, much of the credit down to Clarissa's skills as the former chatelaine of the house. Mary had seen no need to alter what had worked well over the years. She had no great affection for her mother-in-law but she had to give her credit for her housewifery skills. But deep in her heart Mary knew that these days of enforced idleness could not continue forever and, at some point, she had to pick up the reins of the role of Countess and accept that was her position in life. She kept telling herself that this would not be until after the baby made an appearance, allowing herself a breathing space or interlude to enjoy a life of luxury and pleasure. The arrival of the baby would put an end to such dalliances. There were no visitors of consequence to the Hall and neither woman felt inclined to invite company. They were happy with their own world, spending time reading in the coolness of the orchard as the sun blazed on. Thea was beginning to learn about the history of her father's family and the generations of Devines who had inhabited the house that she loved. It was her wish that she had known this place during her childhood, managing to spend time with all her siblings under this ancient roof. This thought constantly filled her psyche and she could not quite forgive her father, and the deceit that he and her mother had kept from herself and Sabine. She often felt that she and her sister had been second-class citizens in the family. Obviously that was what a bastard child was, not to be officially recognized by the rest of the family. But she knew that was not the full truth for her half siblings had taken both of them to their heart. However, there was the other issue of her illicit love affair. It was another secret which could never be divulged to anyone. How she hated all this subterfuge knowing that only heartache could come from it. Did this secrecy make her any better than her parents? Then there was the deceit that played upon her mind; Mary was so sure of Thea's love and friendship but, deep down, there was so much treachery from herself and Piers. All of this made Thea feel that she had to be true to her sister-in-law in other ways to amend for the transgressions that were of her own and Piers' making. Thea had not seen Sabine for weeks and was beginning to miss her older sister too much. But Sabine's life revolved around her beau and the new life that would overtake them in a few months. And there was her mother who was still embroiled with these relations in the West Country and was not in a hurry to return to an empty house in London or a meaningless life. Thea knew that she could not blame Beatrice, whose life had been empty for a long time now. It must be difficult to be cast adrift after loving someone like her father for so long. And then there was her own life here at Westborough Hall. It was not as it should be but there was nothing that she could do. There would be no marriage between them, ever. In fact the whole situation remained futile. She had two choices. The first was to stay at Westborough Hall or she could find someone to marry her and hope that a love might grow. She could have a family and a home of her own. The choice was hers and hers alone but she could find no solution to the problems. She felt trapped, for

Mary had become like a clinging vine wanting her to stay on for the birth, and thereafter no doubt. Sometimes Thea had felt resentful that she was wanted or needed so much, for it made too many demands on her and her time. She had always been the courageous one but now she was in a dilemma caught in the net that others had cast overboard to ensnare her. As time progressed Thea found that her attention was distracted by what was happening at Westborough Hall and in the political arena. As it was Piers was spending more and more time in London at his rented apartment. He was not avoiding the two women in his life but he wanted to be near the action if Europe exploded into war. He wanted to know everything that was happening. Although Parliament was not sitting the Cabinet was coming and going continually from Downing Street. At times he returned to Westborough Hall to see his wife and Thea, but nothing remiss had taken place between the two lovebirds. It became almost as if the conversation had not taken place between them. And so the days passed without a decision being made on her future. Prevarication appeared to be the name of the game and so life continued. However, on the political front Germany was busy acquiring new borders. Only in March around the time of Piers and Mary's marriage Germany had annexed Austria. There had been much protest from the Austrians as they had requested help from the British but none was forthcoming except in the form of Chamberlain, uttering his country's discontent to Berlin; but otherwise they were left to their own devices. Hitler was looking unstoppable as he had turned his attention to the Sudetenland where many Germans resided outside of the mother country. The Cabinet had agreed that there was little they could do in this crisis to help the Czechoslovakians. And so Europe had wrestled with its conscience as it watched the Nazi flag spread across borders during the course of the summer months. As the month of August drew to its conclusion Neville Chamberlain had called his Cabinet to secure their agreement that Britain was in no position to go to war. And so Britain waited with bated breath to see what would happen next.

The capital was buzzing with the prospect of war and Piers had returned home full of fears about what the future might hold. Deep in the Worcestershire countryside life continued almost untouched in such a rural setting. In their snatched moments together there had been no private discussions between Piers and Thea concerning their illicit love affair. There was just too much going on but, occasionally, their eyes would meet across a table at luncheon or dinner and they smiled their secret smile that those in love shared. Occasionally they could touch hands and a tingle would run through their bodies; but Piers had kept his word and only the two of them knew how difficult the situation really was. Both wondered how long they could go on with the ever present volcano inside them erupting into full passion. In some ways it was easier when they were apart and they had to get on with life without living under this enormous strain of pretence and wondering if anyone had noticed any nuance of indiscretion between them. At every mealtime the family discussed the ever deteriorating state of affairs in Europe and few personal remarks were mentioned between himself and the women in his life. Mary in a high degree of angst could not control her fear that Piers might have to go to war and she would be left with a baby and having to run the estate. She had imparted these fears to Thea, who had tried to calm her and tell her that it might not have to come to that; but in her heart something told her that it perhaps would and she was not sure she could cope without the man she loved, who could even die in battle. But there were times when common sense prevailed and she knew that life would continue chance what may.

The annual Nuremberg rally was held in the middle of September and, as Hitler was due to speak, Britain held its breath and waited while people stood in Downing Street hoping to know more about what was happening. As time moved on, Hitler disclosed that the Germans in the Sudetenland were being badly treated as a minority in Czechoslovakia. The Reich could not tolerate such happenings so foreign countries had to be convinced that these were not empty words.

Chamberlain with the backing of his Cabinet had offered to go to Germany to discuss the state of affairs and what help Britain could bring to the solution. Hitler had agreed and on the 15th of the month Chamberlain flew to Munich, then travelled on by train to Hitler's country retreat at Berchtesgaden. The feeling of unease continued throughout September, leaving the country in a state of limbo, but news bulletins continued to be listened to with increased regularity. Thea had received a letter from her mother informing her that she was enjoying the peace of the countryside and that she was considering putting her stay in Devon on a more permanent footing. She had found a cottage to rent overlooking the sea and was taking it for six months. She hoped that in the not too distant future both of her daughters would come and visit her. She also hoped that Thea might like to come and live with her if she could tear herself away from these new relatives who seemed to claim so much of her time. It was not like her mother to take umbrage at such circumstances, but it meant that she was still missing her father. Thea put the letter down and looked thoughtful. She was sitting at the breakfast table not eating her toast while Mary chatted on. Suddenly stopping mid-sentence, he noticed Thea's face.

'What's the matter?' she asked, worried about the contents of the letter. Thea looked up and then smiled, 'My mother wants me to go and live with her in Devon, at least for a short time to see if I like it. She says that she doesn't want to return to London with all the uncertainty of this talk of war. It would be nice to go for a visit just for a short time as I haven't seen her for several weeks. She also said that there is someone she wants me to meet. I think that it might be a man. It looks as if she could be matchmaking.' Thea's face had taken on a closed expression as she uttered the last few words, but Mary had not noticed as she considered the fact that she could lose Thea. The thought made her feel uncertain. Thea's presence had given Mary a newfound confidence during her pregnancy.

133

Mary made a little moue of discontent with her mouth. She wanted her friend to stay with her. She knew that it was a selfish thought, but the time that her friend had been living at Westborough Hall had been the happiest she had been since her marriage to Piers. Although she had grown to love Piers Thea's presence at the Hall had helped ease her feelings of loneliness during her husband's constant absence.

'And what do you intend to do then?' she asked as a small frown creased her forehead like a cloud passing over the sun. Thea noticed Mary's expression and knew how much her company meant to her. But Thea was also a free spirit and did not like to be held back by others. She also owed her mother a visit. Thea's thoughts ran riot as Mary sat anxiously waiting for an answer to her question. The reply did not come as Thea rose from the table to say that she had letters to write before luncheon. There was no talk of them taking an outing that day as autumn began to close in. The skies were grey as the leaves began to change, their colour matching the sombreness of Mary's mood.

Chapter 26

The outlook in Europe looked more and more uncertain. Piers on one of his rare visits home had discussed the ever more likelihood of war in the not too distant future. His face was solemn as the conversation turned to what seemed inevitable.

'I have learned that they are making gas masks in the factories around Blackburn, to be moved to distribution centres around the country if it should come to that.' His face was grave as he looked at the family who sat around the dining table in the large dining room, for this was a special occasion.

'It sounds like the Great War all over again,' Clarissa said as memories of those dark days returned to haunt her thoughts, as they did those of that generation who had watched the young men go valiantly into the service of their country only to return mere shadows of their former selves; that was, if they returned at all. Many families had lost several sons and the agony of their loss was unbelievable and would haunt them until the day they died.

'Don't people learn from the past?' Minty said, looking anxiously at Alexander, who was to become her husband the next day. If war was imminent she did not want to lose him now that she had just found him. It was not Alexander who answered her question, but her brother:

'Dictators like Hitler do not learn. They are suffused with their own greed and self-importance and it looks as if the German people are encouraging this man, Hitler, by their adoration of him. He holds them spellbound. Have you not seen some of the newsreels showing their hero worship of him?'

The conversation around the table had gone quiet as they ate the superb meal set before them. There was just too much to fill their thoughts of a serious nature. They were on the eve of Minty's wedding, but it was the political arena which dominated their conversation when a light-hearted banter should have been the order of the day. Once again Neville Chamberain had only just returned from another meeting with Adolf Hitler. All the agreements of the previous meeting had been dusted aside with Hitler demanding immediate occupation of the Sudetenland as well as making German territorial claims in Poland and Hungary. The country knew that Chamberlain had objected strongly but, on his departure to meet the Führer, he had been booed as he had boarded the aeroplane. Some people thought that Chamberlain had been too weak in his handling of the German leader; others held their own council waiting to see what the outcome would be. Earlier that evening the family had gathered around the wireless to listen to the Prime Minister as he addressed the nation about a quarrel in a faraway country and about a people of whom they knew nothing. The circumstances were grim. Chamberlain had asked Hitler to invite him once more to discuss the situation through a summit involving other nations. Hitler had agreed. At this point the company present at the dinner began to look uncomfortable and depressed about the whole affair. It began to look as if the real reason why they were there had been completely forgotten.

'Let's change the subject,' Mary said looking at Piers. She knew that her husband was obsessed by the politics of the moment and she did not want this precious family time to be spoilt by the talk of war. As she had surveyed the faces before her she knew that it was time to lighten the mood. It was Minty's special day and the family was gathered for a time of harmony and love before the wedding. Even Clarissa was full of bonhomie towards Thea and Sabine, who were deemed members of the family now. All the members present had their suspicions about her new approach to life and wondered uncharitably if a leopard could really change its spots so quickly.

The autumn day was pleasant and the sun shone, but the strength of its warmth had cooled after the days of August when Mary and Thea had taken full advantage of the long days to seek some freedom before the onset of winter. The wedding was to be a small affair, not in the style of Piers and Mary's which had been reasonably lavish. Now into her early thirties Minty, always pragmatic, had deemed it not fitting for a woman of her years to be married in white; this was much against her mother's advice but she had managed to have her way, after all it was to be her occasion. Instead she had chosen an ivory silk two-piece suit which she had found in a London boutique, kindly paid for from her brother's generous stipend which he had bestowed upon her weeks previously. Piers being diplomatic had not commented on the subject of his sister's wishes. He was happy to fulfil whatever they were with his blessing. It had never been known why the Devine sisters had left the idea of marriage so late. It had been discussed at length in the Society papers as well as in the local village communities. They were beautiful women who could have married into the crème de la crème of English society with their pedigree of wealth and titles. It was usually the norm to be married young but, like all of James Devine's children, they only did what they wanted to do when it was right for them. And so Minty had met Alexander Spencer at a Society wedding and their acquaintanceship had been of short duration when they decided to marry. It had not been a difficult decision to make for both of them had fallen madly in love. Alexander had no title to offer his new bride, nor did he come from a titled family. Minty's decision had broken the mould as far as this was concerned. However, Alexander's family was wealthy. His father had made his money himself for he had been a medical practitioner to the rich and famous and his son had followed in his shoes. Alex was some ten years older than his bride, having been married before, but his wife had died unexpectedly from a rare blood condition and left him bereft and childless after several years of marriage. The union with Minty was an answer to his prayers.

The next day Clarissa's eyes filled with tears when she saw her daughter walk down the aisle on the arm of her new husband. There had been no question that Clarissa would not attend the wedding of her daughter. Piers had noted this tender gesture on the part of his mother and smiled broadly at the happy couple who after the wedding breakfast were leaving on their honeymoon to the south of France. It had been a difficult decision to make with the storm clouds of war gathering so quickly but, as Minty said, if they did not go during a time of peace then they might not be going at all if Europe did not pull itself together to subdue the Hun. On the day of Minty's and Alexander's wedding Mary had forbidden Piers from listening to the wireless. There would be no talk of war, only happy times. Piers had acquiesced knowing that as soon as the nuptials had finished and the couple was safely dispatched on route for honeymoon, he would listen to the news hoping that the tidings were good although, like many others, he had his doubts. That very morning of the wedding Chamberlain had flown once more to Germany to meet the Führer, Mussolini and the French Prime Minister Deladier and, after much debate, the Munich agreement had been signed. After he had flown home Chamberlain was greeted by cheering crowds in the streets as he drove to Buckingham Palace to meet the King. Not all people were as jubilant about the course of events granting 'Peace in our time'. There was a descent of gloom upon the minds of Winston Churchill and his adherents. Piers had returned to London only hours after his sister's wedding to sit in the House of Lords and hear what his peers had to say about the pact that had been signed. Again opinion was divided and in the House of Commons Winston Churchill had spoken as forcefully as usual; as he predicted, 'England has been offered a choice between war and shame. She has chosen shame and will get war.' As Piers read this quote in the newspapers he was inclined to agree with Mr Churchill, as he usually did.

Part 3

1939

Chapter 27

Thea wanted to be alone. It was a beautiful June day; the sky was a translucent blue making everything seem to glitter as the sun's rays touched every surface of this external world. It was claustrophobic in the house as it seemed stuffy and airless even with windows flung wide open. As usual she had spent the morning pandering to Mary's demands, which had become insatiable over the previous months since the birth of the baby. Even Piers when he was at home had fallen victim to his wife's temper and tantrums which erupted when events did not go her way. There was no doubt that Mary had changed from the calm woman that she had been into the shrew that she had now become. The doctor when summoned had said that she was suffering from a form of melancholia and in time she would return to her normal self when life had settled down. But he could not put a time limit on such things. It could be weeks, months or even a year or two. Thea's heart sank at the mere thought, but she felt sorry for Piers' wife because it was some kind of illness of the mind that she could not shrug off like a cold or influenza, but it certainly made it difficult for the people who loved her. Piers and Thea kept Mary at a distance for some of the time to keep their own sanity, but they were aware of their selfishness and tried to make amends when they could. They whispered in corners not wishing to be overheard and also took comfort in the love they shared. Sometimes they spent as much time as they could snatch together aware of each other's physical attributes, but the one act which would give them most comfort was denied to them. Instead they would touch and hug but it was still not enough. They had remained strong in the promise they had made each other just months before, but it was becoming more and more difficult to be abstemious. Piers' frequent regulated absences helped the situation, but it was a love that was not going away now or possibly ever. Piers was in London, as he frequently was now that it seemed almost certain that war would come. It appeared to be when, not if. Europe was in turmoil waiting to see what Herr Hitler would do next. London was a hotbed of unease feeling vulnerable against the might of the Hun. The capital would surely become a victim to the Luftwaffe if war came. The country was making preparations for the war that was deemed inevitable. Sandbags had been filled and were already being used, particularly in the capital. Air-raid precaution wardens had been appointed across the country and air-raid shelters had even been erected in many gardens as well as in the capital, where drills were frequently practiced so that people would know what to do if raids came. There was to be no panic if people had been informed, or at least that was the theory and there was no accounting for human nature. Pathé newsreels in the picture houses showed the arrival of German Jews and their families into Britain while others chose the United States of America, seeking a safe haven away from persecution. This attack on the Jews had been happening for some time in Germany where their homes and businesses had been smashed and now they were forced to wear the Star of David as a badge on their sleeves to distinguish them from the rest of society. It was all too much to comprehend for a nation that was regarded for its tolerance. Many of these stories were brought home by Piers who was so close to the centre of the political world. It had left him feeling helpless, unable to contribute much to the plight of others, but deep down he prayed that if war did come the control of the government might lie in the hands of a man like Winston Churchill.

In the sleepy backwater around Westborough Hall much of what was going on in the outside world passed them by, for it appeared unreal. The locals were more concerned about their daily life within a rural community. For many it was only the wireless that kept them fully informed and it was an inconvenience to travel into the towns just to view the newsreels about an approaching conflict that was far away and nothing much to do with the politics of their own country. Even Thea, now that she was not living in the capital, felt slightly detached from the life she had lived there. Her thoughts turned to her mother, hoping that she would not return to London to live in the near future; and then she wondered what would happen to the town house. Piers had not mentioned the fact that it was left empty apart from a maid and a cook to keep it in order. It was these daily spats with Mary that Thea could not cope with and regularly she left the house to find peace in this beautiful part of England. Today she walked through the gardens of the old Hall which were a riot of colour of summer flowers, particularly the roses which gave a heady scent into the fragrant summer air. She took the path towards the lake where the air would be a little cooler from the water giving some relief to the unrelenting strength of the sun's rays. As usual she had a book in her hand to read which often calmed her mind, a mind regularly in turmoil these days after one of her frequent quarrels with Mary. Only that morning they had fallen out about something trivial.

'Mary,' Thea said not for the first time, 'I can't cope with your mood swings. I think that I will have to go and live with my mother in Devon. It is quiet and calm there and really beautiful. The summer months would be glorious and far away from the talk of war.'

Mary, suddenly contrite, pleaded, 'Don't go Thea. I need you here.' She would smile and suddenly would be consumed by guilt until the next conflict reared its head, and so their lives continued. Thea walked around the edge of the lake where a copse of trees bordered the southern side and gave a cooling shade. She had brought a tartan rug with her which she spread over the tufty grass under the trees and away from view of the main path, thus affording her privacy from prying eyes and also from Mary should she come searching for her. This had become a frequent haunt over recent days and afforded an escape for her mental well-being. She sat looking around her at the breathtaking views. In the not too far distance the blue undulating form of the Malvern Hills could just be made out in the summer heat haze that hung over the skyline. She had thought of climbing the hills on a good day to view the spectacular sight of numerous counties from the summit, but time had not made that possible with all the family events that had taken place in recent months, giving the impression that they were a happy family, although Clarissa could still not accept Beatrice after all that time. The two women rarely met but when they did they exchanged not a word. It was as if the other woman did not exist. After Minty's wedding, Diana had married Daniel Martin-Jenkins, a barrister. Like her sister she had not married an aristocrat for they were few and far between or already spoken for. After the Great War it was almost as if a generation of young men had been killed and many of these brave soldiers had been from the aristocracy, for they had led their men over the top from the trenches and many had suffered the same fate as their men. Diana was pragmatic about not marrying a man of equal status, although her mother had not been happy about her two daughters marrying outside the aristocracy; but Diana knew that it was a changing world and the halcyon days of long ago before the Great War would never be recaptured. If you did not move on and accept that it was a new world, then you would be lost. Now Diana only wanted what other women wanted, which was a home life that she could call her own. She had had her day of the debutante and the life of indulgence to find a vacuous husband who only wanted to dangle a pretty woman on his arm and to discard her when he wanted a mistress. This had made her think of her father who had done just that and had never had the courage to tell either of his two families. The fact that everything had worked out well was a blessing to the strength of character of all his children and their generous acceptance of their father's weaknesses. The blessing of her marriage to Daniel was the fact that her new husband would be unlikely to go to war, for he was well into his forties. But he had served his country honourably in the Great War having spent four years in the Royal Navy. His maturity and perspective on life had made her respect him as well as love him. He had made his name in the legal world and, over time, had risen to become a Queen's Councillor in London and regularly defended his clients at the Old Bailey. He had made his wealth through his profession and two inheritances from his parents, his mother having been a woman of means in her own right as his new wife was, too. His wealth had afforded him a house in London and eventually a country property not far from Westborough Hall. It had been at a dinner held by Piers and Mary where he had met Diana and, much like Minty, a mutual attraction had grown quickly between the couple. They were mature enough in mind and age to know that love might not happen again like the one they shared and had decided on a swift courtship which had occurred in haste, causing much speculation in the local community and in the London gossip columns whether there was a special reason for such a hurry to the altar. The innuendo had not escaped Diana's ears or her mother's and it was with a smug satisfaction that Diana could answer her mother's allegations that she had nothing to worry about. Time was always the judge on such matters and this thought had amused Diana's quirky sense of humour. Again the nuptials had been held at the village church which stood on land belonging to the Devines and now, in the tradition which had been set by her sister, Diana and Daniel were married in a simple ceremony and returned to London to start their life together. There had been little mention of a honeymoon but both of them were content to start their life as they meant to go on. Holidays could happen later and it was no time to travel abroad, with the upheaval that was happening in Europe.

It was at this point that Thea had been able to see Sabine, who was so excited about her own wedding that she had little else to talk about and it became the start of the two sisters beginning to drift apart. There was sadness in Thea's heart that this should be the case but, perhaps when her own life began to change and she shared a husband and children of her own, they might draw closer together. But deep down she knew that she was chained to the man she loved and there would be no family for her. To this she had become resigned.

She was destined to become an old maid, only loving the children of her friends and family. Her own children would be a figment of her imagination.

Chapter 28

As Christmas moved into the New Year of 1939 the outlook in Europe was still alarming, but life moved on regardless on the home front. Piers had opted to stay at Westborough Hall for the festive season. He felt that his home and most particularly his family required his presence amongst them. It had not been a festive season full of house parties and noisy guests but Minty, now pregnant, and Diana with their spouses had brought some life into the walls of the old house; but Mary had remained in her room for most of the time except to make an appearance at meal times. She was finding the last stages of her second pregnancy a trial. Thea had stayed with her much of the time, reading to her or listening to classical concerts on the wireless. Both of them were savouring their friendship after Thea's absence in Devon to visit her mother. To Thea the time in Devon had given her a chance to think about her circumstances and her true feelings for Piers. She and Beatrice had spent a treasured three weeks together enjoying each other's company after so many months apart and, on days when her mother was engaged in a whirlwind of a social frenzy, Thea would walk on the beach, the bracing November air tingling her cheeks and adding colour, giving her a healthy glow. Here she could give free rein to her thoughts, working out what she wanted from life. The answer was always the same. She wanted the man who was forbidden to her but she would have to sacrifice what other women of her generation had, that of a happy home life and children. She would watch Mary produce a string of children for the nursery at Westborough Hall with the man she loved, and in time she would be regarded as the maiden aunt who had failed to find a husband of her own and she would grow old gracefully helping the wife of the man she loved. The unfairness of it was wearing her down. Part of her felt that she would sacrifice her love for Piers for a lesser love in order to make a life of her own. She had never been a woman who would live out her life in the service of others. Like her siblings she was a Devine by birth if not by name. It had become her plan to leave Westborough Hall after the birth of Mary's baby and return to live with her mother, hoping that at some point she could find some inner peace, and perhaps she might meet someone; but most of all she wished to have a purpose in her life and not be at the entire beck and call of others. Was that a lot to ask of life? She knew that Piers wanted her to stay at Westborough Hall, but he had a life in politics and was expecting to produce a family, while she made the sacrifices. But when she returned to Worcestershire real life had taken over and she once more became ensnared by Piers' attentiveness and their total desire that was unobtainable.

During this time Mary went into labour early. She was not finding the first stages of childbirth easy as the pain was traumatic. Her wails rebounded through Westborough Hall, making everybody feel useless to help her. Piers had invited his mother to come for she was the only woman within the family who had experienced childbirth, and he had envisioned her holding his wife's hand and giving comfort now that the birth of the Devine heir was imminent. Clarissa came but her response was not quite what her son wished to hear. He should have known what his mother would be like. They stood in the magnificent hallway listening to Mary's cries of anguish.

'Where is her pride?' Clarissa asked, always aware of keeping face in a crisis and looking askance at her son. 'I brought three children into the world without the true love of a husband and never made as much as a whimper. It is the duty of a wife of a member of the aristocracy and the royal family to be stoical in such circumstances. She is not the first woman to have a child and certainly will not be the last.'

'Oh Mama, don't be so hard on her,' Piers retorted, having reverted to using his childhood name for his mother. 'I shall go and hold her hand and give her confidence.' He started to turn to mount the staircase. Clarissa laid a hand on his arm to prevent him. He turned back to her as she said, 'No you won't. There is a doctor and a nurse up there as well as what's her name, Dorothea. Your place is down here away from all that. Go and have a stiff drink.' Piers regarded his mother and, despite the differences between them in recent times, he felt a measure of pride in her attitude and her strength of character which gave him more backbone to deal with this novel occasion for him. The fact that his heir was to be born filled him with great pride but he was also nervous that something could harm the child with Mary in such a state. However, he knew that his mother's attitude towards childbirth was out of date in this modern era, but she did have a point that the aristocratic lines had to produce an heir if they were to continue into the future and that it was still a wife's duty to do just that. He heard his mother's voice again interrupting his reverie, 'It's not as if you love her. You married her out of convenience like previous generations.' Piers stood open-mouthed regarding this woman who had given birth to him wondering how she was so intuitive and hoping that she had no other knowledge regarding his personal life. Having said her piece, Clarissa moved towards the library. Opening the door she walked towards the library table and poured two generous measures of brandy, offering one to her son who looked in desperate need of its calming affects. Just at that moment a knock on the library door sounded and then it opened. The face of Daisy the parlour maid appeared round the door.

'Yes Daisy what is it?' Clarissa said as if she was still the resident Countess.

'I'm so sorry to bother you my lord,' she directed her reply at Piers and ignored Clarissa, 'but Doctor Brown would like a word with you.' Piers' face suddenly looked anxious as he expected the worst. 'Send him in Daisy,' he said, for there was little point prolonging the agony.

Daisy opened the door wider allowing Doctor Brown to enter. He was a short rotund man of Irish descent despite his name. His balding head made him appear older than he was but he had served the local community well all his long working life. Daisy closed the library door and lingered for a moment hoping to catch some of the conversation, but a noise behind her made her move swiftly away to continue her chores.

Inside the library Piers waited with bated breath for what was to be said.

'How is my wife?' he asked.

'Well,' began the doctor trying to be tactful, 'her ladyship is not helping the situation by her anxiety but at the same time the baby is in distress, for labour is taking longer than it should. The baby has not turned in the womb in readiness for its arrival into the world.' Piers looked puzzled about this statement. He had never thought about such matters and the whole situation was completely alien to him. Noting this confusion Doctor Brown continued, 'Babies should come into the world head first, but this one is feet first my lord. I have failed to turn it in the womb so we must use other methods to ease the mother and baby's plight.'

'You have got to do what you have to do,' Clarissa said pragmatically without giving her son chance to answer. If it resulted in the death of the new Countess, so be it. A new wife could be found. There would always be a woman amenable to the delights of the Devine fortune. The current wife was proving to be too much of a trial, the old woman thought acidly.

'We will have to operate to relieve the problem. I would rather do it at the cottage hospital if I am honest, but I don't feel that I can move her ladyship at this stage. I will have to perform the operation here.'

'You must do all that is necessary for both mother and child,' Piers said, not wanting to lose this child at any cost.

'I will inform your lordship as soon as the child is born.' He inclined his head and left the room without another word. Neither mother nor son spoke as they sipped the brandy which had become more than medicinal in recent minutes. Piers rose from his seat to pour another generous measure into his own glass only to find his mother holding out her brandy bloom to be refreshed, too. Clarissa could not tell what her son was thinking although it was not difficult to guess. He wanted the safe delivery of his heir and before too long another to join it in the nursery to ensure the future of their house, but he was also concerned about Mary's health. If she had a difficult time would it mean that she would have to wait some time before considering another child, or would she even refuse to have another one? What would he do then? Divorce Mary? Life was too difficult to contemplate such thoughts. While his thoughts were adrift he thought of Thea, if she had been his wife and in the same situation as Mary. He could never have put her through any more suffering and divorce would never have entered his head. This was surely all the proof that he needed to convince himself that he did not love Mary and never would as long as Thea was foremost in his thoughts. Clarissa's own thoughts were far more practical, but she knew that she could not voice them to her son. His was of a more romantic nature. It would seem that the old ways were beginning to disappear. Suddenly, in a rare moment of affection much to her son's surprise, she patted his hand.

'It will turn out all right, you will see,' she said almost jovially before rising to refill their glasses for a third time. Piers did notice the unsteadiness of her step and the slightly slurred speech, despite his worries.

Chapter 29

Lady Jane Devine was born a healthy, bouncing infant but her difficult arrival into the world had left her mother weak and drained and in need of much care from the doctor and the two nurses whom Piers had employed to assist her recovery. A nanny had been appointed before the child was born and in recent days had transformed the nursery suite into a sterile unit in readiness for the new occupant. Mary had hardly seen the child who had caused so much trouble to her well-being, for she had been whisked away and tended to allowing the new mother to rest after the ordeal. After the news of the birth, which was delivered by Doctor Brown, to Piers and his mother in the library as they sipped their third brandy; he had felt a great pang of anticlimax that he still did not have an heir. He sat silently by his mother who watched him anxiously across the library table. In her new phase of being a pleasanter person to the world she looked at Piers, waiting for him to comment, but the disappointment was etched on his face. There was no need for words to describe how he felt. He had had a feeling that the child was a boy, but there had been nothing to base those thoughts on.

'I know that this is a huge let-down for you but there will be an heir next time,' Clarissa said, knowing full well that there was no such guarantee. She continued, 'Look at me. I produced an heir on the third attempt so there is plenty of hope and time to accomplish it.' By the way you must not let Mary know that she has failed you.' Piers regarded his mother and he smiled wryly. 'Of course I won't do that. I'm not that unkind.' He drained his brandy glass and rose to leave the room. 'I had better go and see my wife and my new daughter,' he said, knowing the right thing to do and to show his appreciation of what she had suffered for the future of his family. But what he really wanted to do was to find a quiet corner where he could have free rein to let this overriding emotion of disappointment have chance to dissipate. He would get over it; he just had to. After the door shut quietly behind him Clarissa sat rigidly in her chair musing over the events of the day. It would have been easy for her to reach out to refill her brandy bloom, but normally she was not a great drinker and the last thing that she was going to do was make a spectacle of herself where the servants would gossip. She could almost hear the whispers down in the basement kitchen where there was little respect for their employers except from the servants who had status and authority. As it was there would be gossip that the new Countess had failed in her attempt to give the Earl an heir. Piers had made his way up the main staircase and had arrived at his wife's bedroom door. He knocked quietly and it was opened by one of the nurses. Putting a finger to her lips she beckoned him inside and pointed to the bed where Mary slept the sleep of the dead. Piers stood by her bedside and saw for himself how she had suffered during the past few hours. Her face was drained of all colour and the efforts she had made to bring the child into the world were etched on her features. He felt that he should touch her, lift her hand to his lips to show the gratitude he felt at her suffering; but the nurse shook her head, guessing what had been passing through his mind.

'She will be stronger tomorrow. Let her sleep.' Piers nodded his agreement and, after taking a last lingering look at his wife, he opened and closed the bedroom door. His next mission was to see his first child up in the nursery. It was a long time since he had visited this haunt which he had shared with Diana and Minty. He had fond memories of the mischief that the three of them had got up to, plaguing Nanny Thompson to death so much so that she had seriously considered handing in her notice until his mother had come to the nursery to sternly tell them off. A smile crossed his face as the memories tumbled back. Would the new arrival have such happy memories, in years to come?

The outer door that led into the nursery suite was firmly closed but Piers could hear the strange mewling of a young baby. This was alien to his ears but, unfazed, he opened the door which led into a rabbit warren of rooms which were still familiar after all these years. He followed the sounds of the baby to what had always been the night nursery. Nanny looked up uncertainly and then frowned at the interruption. She was holding the baby whom she was about to place into her Moses' basket.

'Isn't it a bit late your lordship for visiting the nursery? I am trying to establish a routine from the beginning,' she said churlishly. Piers knew very well that nannies could be territorial and possessive about their charges, almost believing that the children were their own. He remembered his mother regaling stories along such lines and he knew that the formidable Clarissa had not allowed that to happen. She had been a regular visitor to the nursery. For all her faults, she had always loved her children.

'I have come to take a look at my daughter,' he said firmly. 'May I hold her?' It was a rhetorical question. His hands were ready to receive this child and begin a bonding process from the start. Nanny hesitated for a moment but, capitulating, handed the infant into the strong arms of her father. Piers moved the white shawl back from the small face and regarded her closely. The small but perfectly formed child filled him with awe and thus began a love affair which would never die, chance what happened. His eyes filled with tears as he contemplated her future, hoping fervently that soon there would be an heir to keep her company. But this moment in time was going to be the most special of his life, holding his first child and feeling the overwhelming rush of love to protect her from the world, particularly from a world that was hurtling towards disaster. The doctor had advised that Mary must have time before they contemplated another child to allow her body and spirit to heal after such a traumatic ordeal, but Piers was anxious to begin the whole process once more. There was this nagging feeling that war would begin and he would be caught up in it like so many others. If he went away soon there would be no heir to the earldom and then what would the future hold for them all? He pushed away the thoughts, but they would always be near the surface of his mind.

Chapter 30

The talk of war still rumbled on making the country feel that it could happen at any time. As it was Herr Hitler had invaded the remainder of Czechoslovakia, claiming that it was a protectorate of the Third Reich. By performing such an action he had torn up the Munich agreement which gave credence to Churchill's viewpoint that the man had an 'insatiable appetite', but somehow life went on. Mary had made progress physically after the birth of her daughter, but the mental scars had left her with an abject fear of giving birth to another child. Piers had been gentle with her, trying to give her confidence that they could wait to have another child, but this was the time that her melancholia had descended on her like a great hanging cloud and her fits of unreasonableness and outbursts of temper, brought on by fear and anxiety, had made her difficult to live with. Thea had sat with Mary explaining everything patiently to her.

'The doctor says that it might never happen again. Not all births are the same,' she tried to explain. But Mary was having none of it, her ordeal was still too raw. 'What if I should have another girl?' she said. 'Piers would not be satisfied and the title and estate would go to another branch of the family.' Tears had filled her eyes as she looked hopelessly at Thea, who said nothing but in her heart knew that Mary was telling the truth. Every titled or rich person wanted an heir, that was only natural, but Thea had no more answers. Deep down she felt that Piers should know how his wife felt, but it was not her duty to tell him. One of the midwives had stayed on at the Hall for a time to help with Mary's recovery but, after a while, the poor woman had decided that the whole situation was more than she could cope with. Piers had returned to London for short spells, thus distancing himself from the problems on the home front, which left Thea coping alone to maintain the status quo. Through all these problems little Jane began to thrive under the auspicious eye of Nanny Barnes, but the child's mother kept her daughter at arm's length for she was a constant reminder of the trauma that she had experienced. It was also Thea who treated the child more like her own daughter that she would have loved to have had with Piers. Clarissa had made herself indispensable at the Hall. She loved her first grandchild more than she would have thought and her appreciation of Thea's presence in the bosom of this difficult family situation knew no bounds. It was Thea's fundamental goodness which had won the matriarch over and the two had formed a truce and a friendship which had seemed impossible to envisage in the early days of their acquaintanceship. Regularly Thea would wheel the ancient perambulator through the garden to the dower house where she shared a cup of tea with the old Countess and then returned the child to the nursery, to Nanny's joy. On one of her ever increasing visits to the Hall Clarissa witnessed Mary rampaging when Thea had taken the child to visit Piers' mother. The infant wailed as the pitch of Mary's temper reached full volume. Unable to stand the situation any more Clarissa opened the door of the small sitting room where this theatrical scene was played out and witnessed for herself the tantrum that her daughter-in-law was performing.

'Leave us,' she said sharply to Thea, who was trying to placate the wailing infant. Thea fled to the nursery where she handed the baby to Nanny, who clucked disapprovingly. 'It's not natural to reject your own flesh and blood,' she said, but Thea, who had been brought up to be diplomatic in front of staff, left the room and sought solace in her own bedroom wondering why she was in such a situation. If she was not here Mary would have to do something for herself. Clarissa never revealed the conversation that had transpired in the small sitting room that day, while Mary remained tight-lipped about the whole affair but from her observations Thea had found a different Mary; occasionally she tried to bond with her daughter and made an effort when Clarissa was invited to tea. But the tears and tantrums continued at other times.

In March Sabine's wedding was close and the family was growing excited. As with her half siblings, the ceremony was to take place in the local church of Saint Peter at Westborough Hall. Although it was going to be mostly a family affair Sabine had no intention of getting married in a suit but had chosen a white dress and veil which had been made especially for her by her mother's dress maker in London. She had required several fittings and on those days she chose to stay at the town house. It had been a shock to stay there on her own. Much of the furniture was shrouded in dust sheets which gave the house a sad neglected feeling and it showed how much such a place needed people to make it a home. It gave Sabine the opportunity to do some deep thinking; thoughts that she had never contemplated before. For the first time she realized why her mother had taken to living in Devon. This large house was too big for her on her own and, although she lived in the heart of a large city with the hubbub of life all around, it did not prevent the feeling of loneliness which had plagued her mother since her father's death. Then there was Thea who was living the life of a drudge at the beck and call of their newly acquired family. Sabine could not understand the attraction of living in the back of beyond, albeit in luxury. Her own life was full and exciting. Before the Christmas festivities Peter's father had died leaving his son the baronetcy, thus giving Sabine a title once she was married. All this, she felt, would go some way towards the compensation of the lack of a legitimate status, which had left her feeling so insecure. She had never discussed this at great length with Thea or her mother, but she did hope that her sister would find a husband soon; but it did seem rather unlikely in the depths of the country away from the busy social life that could be found only in the heart of the capital. Sabine arrived at Westborough Hall three days before the nuptials, chauffeur driven and laden down with three incredibly large suitcases which contained her wardrobe for her honeymoon. During her stay in London she had used her time profitably to shop for all these outfits, often wishing that her mother and sister were with her to enjoy the fun that such occasions could bring. Her arrival at the Hall had caused much excitement for Thea and Beatrice who had arrived just that morning. For the three women to be together again after such a long time was manna from heaven as they laughed and talked endlessly of their separate lives. On one rare occasion on their own Sabine had taken Thea aside to speak to her about her concerns for her mother and for her sister's life at the Hall.

'Thea, you can't stay here indefinitely you know. Look at you! You are withering away with so much boredom in your life. What does Piers say about it all? Surely that wife of his can do more for herself. How old did you say the child was? And look at your hair. What a mess!' Sabine's criticisms seemed to be endless. Thea had to admit she did feel inadequate beside her sister who was dressed in the latest London fashions with a fox stole draped around her shoulders to keep the March chill at bay. They were walking in the gardens of the Hall and, although the day was bright, the winter drabness had not left the plants as they stood decked in the brownish hues which lacked any cheer. Thea found it difficult to answer her sister, but she knew that she was correct. Her clothes were dowdy but women in the country did not dress up as much as their counterparts in the town unless it was for a special event. What was the point in getting new clothes covered in mud when you rode along the pot-holed lanes on a bicycle, or put on elegant footwear when wellington boots were the better option? Looking at Sabine's footwear made Thea smile as she knew that she was right. Sabine would never be seen wearing wellington boots.

'I have a new outfit for your wedding Sabby. I had it made in Worcester only a few weeks ago, and tomorrow I shall have my hair done so that you won't have to be ashamed of me,' she said, smiling at her sister.

'Good, that sounds better. I have noticed that you have grown you hair long. It doesn't suit you, you know.'

Thea allowed this particular comment to pass without some kind of retort. It was Piers who had persuaded her to grow her hair long. He liked the silky feel of it as it ran through his fingers and it made her look even younger than her years. Thea was not really sure because she had liked her short, curly mop, but here in the country it was not as easy to find a decent hairdresser as she had done in London. It meant a trek of several miles into the city to accomplish the fashionable style that she had worn. However, her life here at the Hall dictated a more practical approach and for that she could put it up, as she had decided to do for Sabine's wedding, under her fashionable hat. Thea did not take offence at Sabine's words for they were not meant spitefully. It had always been their way to be honest with each other over the years. Sabine had become confident and stylish in herself since her engagement to Peter. It was not that her husband had lavished money on her, for the Cavendishes had always had money and their father made the decision that should be the case after his death. All his daughters had their financial independence if anything went wrong in their lives. The thought that her sister was to become titled in only a matter of days had made Thea believe that Sabine was practicing her role before the event. Sabine had seen much of her half-sisters since they had left their country roots to live in London for most of the year, and what came naturally as a member of the aristocracy had had its mark on Sabine as she waited to be Peter's wife. It was not her intention to look down on Thea, but an outsider who did not know either sister well would have reached that conclusion.

'Anyway Thea, I am not out to be critical but I am concerned about you buried out here in the sticks not having a life, no husband on the horizon and so on. When Peter and I return from honeymoon you must come and stay and we will introduce you to some of our single friends. I don't know what Piers is thinking about burying you out here.'

'I like it here,' Thea defended herself lamely and flushed scarlet at the mention of Piers' name, but Sabine had not noticed as she continued her diatribe concerning the woes of her sister's way of life.

Chapter 31

Westborough Hall was beginning to fill to capacity as the day of the wedding approached. The staff spent their time moaning below stairs about the amount of work such an event entailed. They whispered together huddled in corners afraid that if they spoke too loudly the senior staff would overhear them and it could all become a discipline issue or even result in dismissal if it should reach the ears of the Earl and dowager Countess. They were not afraid of Mary, who had never used her authority within the Hall, and now they ignored her and took their orders from Clarissa. This was the third family wedding in just a few months and everybody was exhausted. Guests were arriving at all times of the day and the maids and footmen were dashing around everywhere. The new arrivals had to be shown to their rooms, their luggage unpacked and food had to be served at all times during the day and then, in the evening, the large dining room was used where a formal dinner was served. This was only the start of it all for there was the wedding breakfast to prepare. His lordship was not prepared to stint on anything. Below stairs the staff knew all there was to know about Piers and his relationship to the new bride. Some of the servants who had been with the family for years had often wondered how the old Earl had managed to keep his second family so quiet. They had often witnessed his unpleasantness with the dowager Countess and, when the news broke after James Devine's death, they were not surprised that the Earl had taken his affections elsewhere. However, they were full of admiration when the young Earl and his sisters had taken so well to their half-siblings. As for Miss Thea, they had taken her to their heart. She had no airs and graces and the way she had taken the new baby under her wing made them all teary eyed. The servants might moan but there was true affection for the family these days since the Dowager had gone reluctantly to live in the dower house, although she had appeared more and more in the big house since the birth of the infant Lady Jane. Piers was aware of the strain placed on his staff and he had approached his mother, who was ridiculously overstaffed for one person in the dower house. To ease the situation in the Hall if only for a few days he intended using some of her servants. Clarissa, not well pleased that her husband's illegitimate daughter seemed to be receiving more attention on the marriage stage than his two legitimate ones, felt upset; but her better judgement told her to bite her tongue on the matter since she was desperately trying to foster a better approach to life and in particular to her own family, to whom she was obligated for her standard of living. She had to admit that Piers had maintained his promise to her to keep her financially afloat and had increased her allowance once the iceberg had thawed between them. It was now her policy to keep all the family on her side for it was to her benefit in the end. If anything Clarissa was nobody's fool. Yet she still had an agenda towards her husband's second family. She had made friends with Thea and what had been a sour, resentful encounter in the beginning had turned into a genuine friendship over time. Even Thea, feisty by nature, had passed through the phase of being afraid of Piers' mother and had helped to break the ice between mother and son after all the difficulties that they had faced; for that Clarissa was grateful. However, her grievances were still directed towards Beatrice whom she blamed for stealing her husband, but forgot to acknowledge the fact that neither she nor James Devine could stand the sight of each other, which had been the case for most of her marriage.

A wedding invitation had been sent to the old Countess who had felt churlish not wishing to attend the nuptials, believing that if she did so she would be giving credence to her husband's liaison with Beatrice Cavendish. She still could not bring herself to speak to the woman who had held her husband's love for so long, right up until the end of his days.

James Devine had always had an eye for a pretty woman in his youth, but his loyalty to his mistress had not wavered over the years. It had been a liaison made in heaven, never to be broken. If she was honest with herself she would have liked a relationship like that where she had been loved for herself, but she knew that she could only blame herself for her intolerance of the man she had married so long ago.

'Let bygones be bygones with Beatrice,' Piers had said to his mother as the wedding drew closer, knowing her feelings on the matter. 'Try and rise above such things, showing your mettle and forgiveness, otherwise you will be giving the locals and the Society press a reason to gossip. If you are there, there will be nothing for them to gloat about. You don't want the public to think that you are still bitter and twisted after all this time. Remember this is not just about us but Sabine and Peter. They have a right to their place in society like the rest of us. Once it is over that will be that. You will never have to see her again.' Piers knew that he was right for it had happened before and the press would probe and probe until something juicy was discovered. Skeletons in the cupboard, it was called. Clarissa knew that her son was correct, but it was her pride which was finding it hard to surrender to the situation. Pride came before a fall, Clarissa told herself.

'I will think about it,' she said, which was all she would promise, but deep down she knew that she had no choice but to attend the wedding. Piers felt that it would be a final battle to the end, but it was Thea who let slip a nugget of information one night over dinner when she and her brother were together in the small dining room, Mary having taken to her bed with one of her frequent headaches.

'I went to see your mother today with Jane. She really does love the child, not like the image she often displays to the world.'

Piers looked at her and smiled. He was pleased that the truce had finally been signed between his mother and sister. But what had delighted him most of all was the fact that his mother saw her grandchild regularly which, if it was left to Mary, would not happen at all.

'How was she?' he asked, as he had spent most of the week in London at the House.

'Quite subdued really, but she told me that her dressmaker had come to measure her for a new outfit.' Thea beamed at Piers who suddenly understood the significance of her words. He covered her hand with his own and brought it to his lips to kiss. A tingle of anticipation wormed its way down her spine at his touch and his closeness still had that affect upon her. 'This is all you're doing you know,' he said. 'She is fond of you as she is of so few others, and if she snubbed Sabine and your mother she would be doing the same to you.' Thea blushed at the compliment and then their heads bent forward as they kissed passionately.

'I wish I could take you upstairs,' he said, looking at her longingly.

'I know. I want to too, but Piers, how long can we go on like this? I love you but I want children, and it will never happen.' Piers looked at her strangely for a moment. 'I cannot alter the situation, Thea, as much as I would like to. We have a lifetime of this situation ahead of us unless...' His words trailed off but Thea knew what he meant. She shook her head, 'We can't.' Her voice came in short breaths as the emotion of the moment overcame her. 'It would be wrong,' she continued.

'Well, I see that we have two options open to us. We can continue as we are or you must find a husband worthy of you. I will never hold you here against your will, you know.' Piers stretched his hand over hers and once more brought it to his lips to kiss, but as he looked deep into her sad eyes his own filled with tears and great gulping sobs emanated from his body. She had never seen him like this before.

'I'm sorry,' he said, 'I just cannot imagine a life without you.'

'I cannot either Piers, but we must just see what happens. I will always love you. Nothing will prevent me from doing that, ever.' His face still showed the trauma of his emotions. Still holding her hand he suddenly said, 'I don't love Mary. I care for her, but that is different from the true feeling of love, and the fact that she is behaving so strangely makes it the more difficult for us both. I went to see the doctor the other day and he said that we could start a relationship again, but she won't let me near her. I do have to have an heir. I have been thinking of divorce but it would be a public scandal at this moment in time and there is too much going on politically with the talk of war.'

'Could you ask the doctor to talk to her about the situation?' Thea said, feeling sorry for him.

'I could do, but I will wait until after Sabine's wedding before I take such action.' Again they kissed, wishing that they could change their world. It seemed as if the odds were totally stacked against them; both of them consumed with guilt because of the intensity of their feelings.

Chapter 32

On the day that Sabine and Peter were due to marry on 31st March much had been happening on the political front in London. The Anglo-Polish military alliance had been formed between Britain and France to guarantee Polish independence in case of attack from Germany. However, Neville Chamberlain still hoped to strike a deal with Hitler. The Prime Minister and his Cabinet optimistically believed that war could be avoided. Sabine looked at her most beautiful that March day. Her white lacy wedding dress suited her slim figure and her face, the window on the soul they say, was radiant with happiness. On the arm of her brother she walked down the aisle of the old church as the sun shone brilliantly through the stained-glass windows heralding spring's arrival. Every pair of eyes turned to view the bride as she passed by and her radiance filled them with joy. The news about what was happening in Europe cast a shadow over people's lives but a day such as this allowed people to forget even just for a short time. The church was not full but the guests who were there were special to the couple who were about to say their vows before the altar. The previous evening a special dinner was held in the large entrance hall at Westborough Hall as it would have been done hundreds of years before. It was a family affair for the Devines and, on this occasion, two women came face to face for the first time in over two decades. Piers had had his way and the two families were here together for the first time. The two women who had loved or hated the same man faced each other across a table while the family held their breath to see what would transpire. Clarissa could hardly raise her eyes to the woman who had stolen her husband, but Beatrice saw little point in the rancour that lay between them. Their war had died with James Devine and life had to move on. Life was too short for such hatred.

'It is good to see you Clarissa. Let us hope that the day will be set fair for tomorrow.' Beatrice was looking straight at the older woman who knew that, if she ignored her husband's mistress, she would be held in contempt by everybody seated around the table. She had to conquer her pride once and for all. Lifting her head high she looked every inch the aristocrat that she was and suddenly that gave her confidence to confront the other woman. Looking directly at Beatrice she noted that time had been kind to her counterpart. Her face was unlined and she had retained her beauty. It was no wonder that James had been smitten to the very end. She saw Sabine mirrored in her face but there was less of Thea's likeness there, but what did that matter? All eyes watched as she opened her mouth and uttered, 'Let's hope so.'

Almost in unison the family relaxed. No other exchange was necessary between the two women. Piers beamed at them, inwardly proud that neither had made a scene. At the wedding they sat only a few seats apart but there was no need to say anything more. Nothing else was required of them. Beatrice shed a tear at the sight of her daughter and new husband, wishing that the girl's father could be present to witness this of all days. There was happiness but most of all the harmony of the whole family was a testament to the young people to overcome the problems that the older generation had created.

The young couple had decided not to honeymoon in Europe. The consensus of opinion was that it would be unwise to travel with all the problems that the Continent was experiencing. Instead they had decided to visit Cornwall now that the weather was improving and had made a promise to visit Beatrice in Devon on their return journey. Sabine had looked at her sister with new eyes. 'You look lovely Thea,' she said, approving of her sister's choice of a wedding outfit after admonishing her only days previously. 'I won't forget to let you know when you can come and stay with us.' Her eyes had drifted to look at her new husband. Peter would welcome her with open arms once they had settled into their new life.

Piers had been standing behind Thea listening to the conversation. As Sabine turned to kiss her mother before seating herself in Peter's new sports car, Piers leaned closer to Thea.

'It is true you look lovely today.' He leaned a little closer so that nobody else could hear, 'I wish it had been us here today getting married.' Thea blushed as she felt Piers' hand brush her own. Her head turned to see if anyone had noticed and she found herself staring into Mary's blue eyes, which appeared brighter than normal. Had she seen anything or overheard Piers' careless remark? The thought filled her with trepidation. Moving away from her brother Thea sought the company of her mother. She and Piers could not afford to be careless, now. She did not know what had put the idea to take such risks into his head in such a public place. Suddenly there was much chatter and laughter as the confetti was thrown over the car as they pulled away, laughing and waving at their loved ones while the cans tied to the back of the car jumped and bumped over the ground, clattering, telling the world of their happiness.

Chapter 33

The rumblings of war still continued in Europe with Germany withdrawing from agreements which had been set up only a few years previously and, as tension mounted, Hitler had turned to an aggressive diplomacy. Talks between the Germans and Poland had broken down over Danzig and the Polish Corridor, and the Soviet Union was interested in an alliance with Germany against Poland. At this time too the Germans had learned that France and Britain had failed to secure an alliance with the Soviet Union against Germany. In May Hitler and his generals began to plan the invasion of Poland. Against this growing backdrop of unrest, Sabine and Peter had returned from their honeymoon, refreshed by their holiday and more dewy eyed than ever. They had stayed in Devon with Beatrice and met the horde of relatives that they had never seen before. The May weather was balmy, as summer approached; they were halcyon days but, as they listened to the news from Europe, fear of what was to come filled their hearts as it did the people who had never wanted war in the first place.

'Live for the moment,' Beatrice said sagely as she remembered the insecurities of the Great War. There were months when she had not heard from James and had learned to be stoical and convince herself that everything would turn out all right. For her it had been fine, but there were millions who never returned to their homeland. Why was this all happening again? Avarice and the wish for power on the part of some of the dictators was something she could not comprehend. However, Sabine had not forgotten the promise that she had made to Thea about the visit to their home in London.

The letter written in Sabine's careless handwriting had come when Thea was feeling at a low ebb. It was at this time that she had begun to escape from Mary and the confines of the Hall. Mary had been difficult and cantankerous again of late, but there was also something secret and furtive about her which Thea could not quite put her finger on. Nothing had been mentioned about Piers' indiscretion at the wedding, which made Thea believe that Mary had not noticed anything after all, but she felt that she should mention her feelings to Piers. She found the opportunity one morning when Piers was in the library looking through the open windows. He appeared to be deep in thought as he stood staring into the distance, but not really seeing anything. Thea shut the heavy door of the library noisily to warn him that there was someone there. He turned to look and then his face creased into a tender smile. He had not seen much of Thea recently and she seemed to have been hiding from him, making it difficult to seek her out for a secret tryst without them being seen.

'Hello,' he said, 'I have missed you.'

'Yes,' she said, not attempting to go near him although his hand had stretched out to take hers. But she resisted him, nervous in case Mary entered the room, or one of the servants. She was not prepared to be caught out again.

'What's the matter?' he asked, frowning at the seriousness of her expression.

'Not a great deal, although I keep wondering about Mary. She appears to be very secretive at the moment.'

'Ah, Mary. Of course you won't know but I have tried to find a moment to tell you alone.'

'What is it?'

'Well, good news I think. Mary is expecting another child. We hope it will be an heir this time.' Thea's face turned to one of astonishment. 'I thought she did not want another child or to be intimate.' If she was a little honest with herself she felt jealous that Piers was forbidden to her in that way.

'So did I, but she came to my room a few weeks ago, just after Sabine's wedding and the rest is history, so they say.' He smiled sheepishly.

'She knows, Piers, about us.'

'She can't do,' he said, suddenly feeling uncomfortable. But the thought of her wanting another child so soon after all of the problems had amazed Piers too, but he had not given it a great deal of thought owing to the nature of his hectic life between London and Westborough Hall.

'I have had a letter from Sabine,' she said changing the subject. 'She wants me to go and stay with them in London. She asked me at the wedding.' Piers frowned. 'London,' he reiterated. 'I really don't think you should go. It is so unsettled there with all this talk of war.'

It was Thea's turn to look unhappy. 'Are you forbidding me to go and see my sister? Am I a prisoner here?' Her indignation had risen to the fore. She was a free spirit to do what she wanted to do. She had given much to Piers and his family over the last months.

'You have misunderstood me Thea. I have no right to keep you here, but I worry about your safety. I already have three sisters who live in the capital when they are not at their country estates. I worry about them, too.' He smiled again the smile that she loved and the contours of her face relaxed as the intensity of her love for him flowed through her like a tidal wave.

'I shall be careful and then I will return. At the moment I cannot take much more of Mary's tantrums. I try to escape whenever I can.' Piers was aware of this. 'Go to London then, but take care of yourself and perhaps we can meet away from prying eyes and take time to enjoy ourselves. There is no harm in a man taking his sister out.' He leaned forward and kissed her as she leaned forward, eager once more to enjoy their closeness.

Chapter 34

Clarissa was in a state of agitation now that Thea had gone to London to see Sabine. She knew that the girl was entitled to see her family wherever and whenever she wished, but the Hall seemed empty without her sunny presence. She missed the regular visits to the dower house and most of all seeing her granddaughter, who seemed to have changed at every visit. Clarissa was worried about the Hall and her granddaughter's well-being. Mary had changed since her marriage to Piers. The depression that had engulfed her so badly after the birth of Jane had only lifted slightly and Clarissa was frightened that, if she were alone with the baby, something awful might happen. Thea had kept an eye on the situation and Nanny was one of the best, but Piers had tried to persuade Mary to be a hands-on mother as well. A child needed its mother and Mary's neglect of the child seemed unnatural to him. He loved his daughter and when time permitted he spent as much time bonding with her as he could. Mary had witnessed some strange sort of episode at Sabine's wedding. Her clouded mind had picked up some strange code of behaviour on the part of her husband, but she had not worked out the true nature of it. She knew that he and Thea had formed a close bond since their first introduction and the only emotion she felt in her numb state of mind was jealousy. The closeness that had started to appear in the early days of their marriage had long gone and she knew that she was partly to do with that, with her fears of the birth. By trying to turn it all around she had wantonly thrown herself at her husband and hoped that the result of the pregnancy, which deep down she did not want, would return Piers' love back to her. If she gave him the heir that he desperately craved she would feel secure in his eternal gratitude. She also missed Thea's soothing presence but did not realize how badly she had treated her over the ensuing months. The close bond that they had shared had long gone and the damage was not likely to be repaired. One afternoon at the end of June Clarissa had walked from the dower house in the warm sunshine, through the magnificent gardens of the Hall and entered the house through the French windows of the large drawing room. All she could hear were the cries of a baby. She came upon Mary who sat gazing into space while her daughter had been laid on the carpet, screaming loudly in a fit of temper. Her legs and fists were moving at a furious pace, as she lay ignored by her mother and the world at large.

'Mary, pick that child up at once!' Clarissa shouted.

Mary promptly burst into a fit of tears and shouted, 'I don't know what to do with her! She won't stop crying. It's not my fault.' Clarissa, slowly and with great difficulty owing to her advancing age and arthritis, knelt on the carpet and picked up the angry and neglected child. Rising slowly she carried her granddaughter to the safety of the sofa and gave her comfort, and the storm began to pass. The gulping sobs abated as her grandmother rocked her and hummed a lullaby which she had sung to her own children years before. Leaving Jane on the sofa propped against the cushions, she walked to the bell pull and rang for assistance. Daisy the parlour maid opened the door to the sitting room and expressed surprise at seeing the ageing Dowager.

'Daisy? Fetch Nanny. Tell her to come quickly.'

'Yes ma'am.' She dipped a curtsy, for she was in awe of the older woman and fled the room. Only minutes later Nanny knocked on the door and entered the room. She, too, was surprised at the scene before her.

'Nanny, take the baby to the nursery please and I will be up shortly.'

Her face a mask, Nanny scooped up the baby in an expert fashion, talking to her as she did so. At last happy and content, the baby gurgled as she was spoken to and the door closed behind them quietly. Mary looked as if nothing remiss had happened.

Clarissa looked at her daughter-in-law for a few minutes wondering how she could connect with the young woman. She knew that she could shout at her and, deep down, felt like doing so but that really was not the answer. The situation of Mary's health, or to be honest her mental health, was an issue that she felt was not going away. Something had to be done about it and soon. Piers was not due home for several days and Thea was enjoying a well-earned holiday and it would not be fair to bring her back to keep an eye on the situation. Thea was not an employee but a member of the Devine family. Clarissa found it strange to admit that to herself, but she knew that she had changed over the last few years and with this had come a measure of calm after the turbulence of her married life. She could even think about her husband more objectively these days, though her unhappiness with him would never go away.

'Mary, my dear,' she said, touching the young woman's hand. 'Are you listening?' Mary, calmer now that the screaming child had been removed from the room, looked at the older woman and nodded.

'This situation cannot go on, you know. You need help. You are anxious all the time and you have never been close to your child, and now you are expecting another. This is what I shall do until Piers' return. I shall move back into the Hall to keep you company and take some of the responsibility away from you. You need a rest to overcome the problems.'

'Yes,' was all her daughter-in-law said.

'I think that you should go and rest now until dinner and then we can dine together in the small dining room later.' Mary never answered but mechanically left the room and ventured up the wide staircase to her own room. Clarissa was busy forming plans of her own. She did not think that Piers would like her taking over, but it was in a different capacity this time. He should know better than neglect the problems on the home front and, if war came, what would happen then if he had to join the forces, as it was more than likely that he would as an officer? She rose stiffly from the sofa and made her way across the room into the magnificently panelled hallway. She stood for a few moments looking around her, breathing in the atmosphere of the great room as if she was seeing it for the first time as she had done when she came with James Devine as a young bride, in happier times. A fire blazed in the hearth as it did on most days as the dark interior was often cold, even if it was hot outside. When she was ready she climbed the familiar staircase slowly and stiffly, cursing her ageing bones not for the first time. Then she made her way to the nursery suite. The door was open as Nanny expected her arrival. Inside Nanny sat nursing the infant, showing her pictures from a book which had been used in Piers' childhood.

'What a lovely sight,' Clarissa said taking a seat in the day nursery, forbidding Nanny to rise whilst she held her charge.

'I would like to say, Nanny, that there is a wonderful atmosphere in here and Jane is well looked after.' Nanny Barnes beamed at the compliment.

'But,' continued Clarissa, 'I must ask you never to leave Jane alone with her mother again. When I entered the sitting room the child was in such a state, and the Countess did not know what to do with her.'

'She won't care for the lovely little thing. I had hoped I could help the situation.'

Clarissa waved her hand to silence the other woman. 'This is no criticism my dear. I just want the child to be safe and well looked after. The Earl might make other arrangements but until then...' Her words drifted off for the nanny had understood the full implications of what the dowager Countess was saying.

Chapter 35

Thea had travelled up to London with Piers. The two-hour train journey had given them a special time together to talk about what they wanted from life. It was an uninterrupted time as they sat in the first class compartment which they had almost to themselves. Nobody would comment about their being together for at least they were brother and sister. They explored every facet of their lives as well as the subject that was nearest to their hearts. But nothing could change for them. There was no solution that would free them to be together unless they renounced their responsibilities and could live as husband and wife in a small community away from the world. But Piers had been strictly brought up to accept his responsibilities to Westborough Hall and the estate. They could have a pipe dream, but that would be all it was. Thea learned about Piers' feelings concerning Mary. She had always known that he did not love her as he should but, since the birth of Jane, she had been a source of anxiety and he feared for her sanity. The news of the second child had only worsened the situation instead of bringing joy. Thea listened broken-heartedly at his sadness and wished that they could rectify the situation. He took her hand and squeezed it... and then it travelled to a forbidden place, momentarily causing a spasm of pleasure, but it was gone almost as soon as it had come.

'At least we can steal some time together while you are staying at Sabine's,' Piers said, looking at her intensely, his eyes burning with the love that he felt for her. 'If you travel into town we can meet for luncheon or dinner, perhaps take in a show in the West End, almost like a normal couple.' He then smiled, the smile that he reserved for her alone, but there was still a sadness between them that it could not be anything else.

Thea moved a little closer to him, her head almost lying on his shoulder, and they sat quietly in their different worlds cursing the card that fate had handed them. At Paddington Station amongst the melee of bodies Piers gave Thea a chaste kiss before they parted company. Piers had appointments to keep in the city, but Thea was not going straight to Sabine's home. She had decided that she wanted to go shopping and to see the haunts that had been hers in her childhood and adolescence. She felt happy and content wandering along by herself, enjoying the freedom that she had seemed to have lost in her long sojourn in the country. London's streets were abuzz with life, almost as if its citizens had not a care in the world; but Thea looked for a deeper meaning which seemed to shout to the rooftops that if life was not lived to the full now, in the not so distant future it could all be very different. This thought made her sad for she loved the city of her birth. However, there were signs that war could be imminent as sandbags were piled in brick-like precision under shop windows or near doorways, in readiness for the threat hanging like the sword of Damocles above their heads. But the British bulldog spirit and stoicism were ever present and the sense of humour led to laughter and an enforced gaiety. It was lovely to be back but it would not be for long, for if the threat of war came the capital would not be safe. She knew though that for most of London's citizens they did not have the option to leave but had to carry on life as normally as possible. Thea shopped as she had never done before, knowing that she would be socializing during her stay with Sabine and her sister would give close scrutiny to the clothes that she wore as she had done only weeks previously at the wedding. At Westborough Hall Clarissa had made herself comfortable in her old room. It felt strange to be reinstated in the house that had been her home for decades for she had settled into the dower house and enjoyed her independence as she had never done before. Her motives for returning to the Hall had been the right ones, she believed, but she did not want her son to feel that she was interfering. From the humiliation of her exile and her son's wrath she had learned a lesson never to be repeated. She had tried to telephone Piers at the House but he had been involved in meeting after meeting and she had left a trail of messages for him to ring the Hall as soon as he could. Eventually the telephone in the hall rang. Clarissa was not so swift of foot these days to answer, but Thomas the butler entered the library where she had taken up residence with a medicinal glass of sherry now that it had reached the acceptable time of day to take a measure of alcohol. He told her that the Earl was at the other end of the telephone, requesting to speak to her.

'I will take it on the extension in his lordship's study Thomas,' she said. It was important to her to speak privately to her son. It took her a minute or two to walk the short distance to Piers' study. She lifted the receiver to her ear. 'Piers are you there?'

'Yes Mama,' he said dutifully using his childhood name for her. She was pleased about that because at least he was in the right frame of mind to listen to her. It suddenly occurred to her that she had not heard the click of the receiver at the other end of the telephone being replaced into its cradle. She knew that if she continued her private conversation its contents would be made common knowledge. She would have to speak to Piers about such indiscretions.

'Thomas,' she said frostily, 'could you replace the telephone receiver at once?'

'Yes, my lady,' he said, a sheepish note entering his tone of voice at having been caught out. He knew that there would be repercussions later. Clarissa heard the click as the hall telephone was replaced into its cradle and now felt ready to impart the news of the day to her son and expressed her anxiety. Piers listened to his mother's rendition of the events of earlier on in the day. He was tired from the numerous meetings that he had attended and felt that more anxiety was exactly what he did not need. His expression was grim as Mary's misdemeanour was revealed. Did he need to hear this now when he was about to dine with important members of his party, including Winston Churchill? How he wished Thea was present at the Hall. She would have known instinctively what to do. Then, his conscience admonished that thought. He could not use Thea in that way. The telephone was silent as he allowed himself time to digest all the information that his mother had told him.

'Thank you Mama. It is a great consolation to me that you made the right decision and if you can stay there until I return either tomorrow or the day after, I would be most grateful. I cannot impose upon Thea to return to the Hall for a while as she has already done so much for us over time. I think that I need to see Doctor Brown to discover what he recommends.'

'I can stay as long as is necessary. Thea deserves to have her break in London. She has been splendid,' Clarissa eulogized, much relieved by the fact that she had not been accused of interference. Despite his anxiety about the situation at home Piers had to smile to himself about his mother's obvious attachment to Thea. Never in this world would he have thought that events would have turned out that way. He was also grateful that his mother was at hand to take control of the situation. After his father's death he never thought that he would ever think that again.

'I'll ring before my return, Mama. Thank you for being so good about the situation and coping so well. I am very pleased you are there to take charge.'

'I have always been one who copes,' Clarissa said, her voice a little strained, even waspish in its tone.

'I know Mama. You always have coped,' Piers said in a placatory tone and rang off. Clarissa sat in the study thinking about the conversation. She slowly sipped her sherry and then smiled. She was certainly back in favour and of use to the family she loved more than anything. She had always loved her children but her life with James had left her disgruntled and bad tempered, but she had mellowed as old age enfolded her to its bosom. At least that was one advantage of this time of life, and she decided that she would not want to be young again and experience the angst that came with it.

Chapter 36

Thea had taken a taxi after she had finished her shopping expedition in the West End. She was loaded down with her suitcase and the parcels and bags containing her purchases. But now she was tired and just wanted to arrive at Sabine's home to be spoilt and looked after for a short time. She knew that her sister would fuss over her like a mother hen just as their mother had done. It would probably not be long before Sabine had a child of her own, Thea thought with a smile, and Peter would want an heir for the baronetcy. That was the constant demand of the aristocracy. Her thoughts turned to Piers who had been upset when Jane had been a girl. Perhaps Mary would produce a male child this time, providing she managed to keep healthy in mind and body? Thea hoped that everything went well with the new baby, for it might make Mary feel better, otherwise she was not sure what would happen between Piers and Mary. She shuddered at the thought of divorce, but Piers was adamant that he must have an heir. He was not going to allow the title to go to some ageing distant cousin if he could help it. The taxi drawing up outside Sabine and Peter's very elegant town house brought her back to the present. It was Sabine who opened the door, a rare event indeed, but she wished to be the one to welcome Thea personally. There was to be no standing on ceremony now that she had a title unless it was for a special occasion. Thea looked at the very elegant person waiting to greet her. Sabine was classically dressed and her hair was coiffed in the latest style, looking the epitome of class and money. All this made Thea feel dowdy as she looked down at her own clothes, which were creased from travelling and her day in town. The taxi driver opened the door for her to climb out, then proceeded to the boot of the vehicle where all her possessions were bestowed. Polly, Sabine's maid, appeared proceeding to carry some of the parcels indoors followed by Parks, the general factotum, who picked up Thea's suitcase as if it weighed nothing, and carried it upstairs. Sabine took Thea in her arms and kissed her cheek affectionately, feeling genuinely pleased to see her sister.

'I'm glad that you could make it. It is wonderful to see you.' Both sisters knew that their time together was special now that Sabine was married to Peter. Thea was led into the drawing room which was filled with natural light; it was elegantly furnished with antique furniture which was left over from Peter's father's days, but Sabine was already beginning to put her mark on the house by subtly changing just small items knowing that, as time went by, she would have her own way as mistress of the house. But she had decided that she was not to embark on married life by upsetting her husband straight away.

'This is a lovely room Sabine,' Thea began as she heard the door open and Polly circumnavigated the furniture to place a cumbersome tray on an occasional table loaded with teatime essentials, including a large chocolate cake which just happened to be Thea's favourite.

'Thank you Polly,' Sabine said as Polly bobbed a curtsy as if her new young mistress was royalty and left the room, taking one last glance over her shoulder at the newcomer. She knew that they were sisters but this newcomer looked dowdy and careworn, while her mistress was the height of fashion. Funny that two people, both of whom were good-looking, could appear so different. Thea removed her hat, fanning her face with it as the heat of the afternoon had been unbearable for someone who had spent her time rushing around. Her cheeks were red from the exertions of shopping and hurrying about in order not to be late. The windows were open wide to allow a movement of air to fan them and street noises could be heard filtering in, but it was still stifling with the heat.

'You look tired Thea,' Sabine began as she had studied her sister, noticing large dark smudges under her eyes and a weariness in her general demeanour. 'I want you to have a little rest while you are here.' Sabine had taken note of her sister's dowdiness, leaving her worried by the exhaustion that was reflected in her face. Sabine had made the decision that Thea required to be looked after and have a little fun. She was young and if she was not careful she would enter middle age before her time. They would shop for more flattering clothes and she would take Thea to have a makeover. She needed a more flattering hairstyle to return her to the beauty she had always been. It was so unkind of Piers to put on her as he had done. She knew that her brother had not done it on purpose but he had to be made to see that her sister was not an unpaid housekeeper. Minty and Diana had not been put upon but they were full sisters to his lordship. It was difficult not to be bitter and twisted when she observed such things happening. She and Thea were only bastards after all. Even after all this time Sabine had never quite come to terms with what her parents had done and the base level they had reduced them to by their irresponsible actions. It was almost like gutter behaviour, she thought snobbishly. Sabine poured the tea and offered cake, but Thea shook her head and promptly burst into tears. Feeling baffled by such behaviour, which was most unlike her usually ebullient sister, Sabine replaced what she had been holding back on the tray and knelt down by Thea, taking her hand in her own and stroking it as if she was her child.

'All this is Piers' fault isn't it?' she said, looking into Thea's eyes. 'Just look at you. You are tired out.' Thea's eyes clouded with misery and anxiety as she wondered what was coming next. There was just no way that she could confide her dark secret. The world would be against her if it knew what lay in her heart.

'He's let you look after that useless wife of his until you have worn yourself out. I shall have strict words with him when I see him. I think a sleep would do you good and then I will wake you for dinner.' Thea was too tired to argue and followed Sabine upstairs to her bedroom without argument. It was a beautiful room, tastefully furnished in chintzes and light colours, but Thea had not noticed. However since her arrival her clothes had been neatly unpacked and hung in her wardrobe by Polly. Her night attire lay neatly folded by her pillow, but Thea lay down on the bed while Sabine closed the curtains against the vivid sunlight. Turning round to say something to her sister she saw that she had fallen into a deep exhausted sleep, looking dead to the world. Sabine stood for a few moments looking at Thea. She had not seen her normally feisty, vibrant sister look this way before and she knew that while she was under her roof Thea was going to experience all that had been forbidden to her for so long. There would be parties, the theatre and they would accept invitations to meet unattached young men of a certain class who would no doubt fall in love with Thea Cavendish once she had had her make over. There would definitely be some changes. Sabine was on a mission.

Unbeknown to Thea, Piers had been invited to dine with Sabine and her sister that evening. He had failed to inform Thea feeling that he wanted to surprise her. It was to be an evening of the three siblings together as Peter was away in the country dealing with problems of the estate. At the weekend there were plans to go out to the theatre in the West End. Sabine had had fun planning it all and it was all aimed at entertaining her sister and trying to keep her social life on track, instead of burying herself away in the country without house guests to light up their lives. Sabine just shuddered when she thought of Mary and her self-indulgence and Piers' ghastly mother. There was nobody else whom she could socialize with. Piers was due to arrive at eight. An hour earlier Sabine left her chore of letter writing to think about changing for the evening ahead and to check on Thea. Creeping into her sister's bedroom she discovered that Thea had not moved but lay soundly asleep as if she had been drugged. Sabine again left the room with the thought that it was sleep that Thea required more than anything and she would entertain her brother alone, giving him a piece of her mind.

Promptly at eight Piers arrived, dressed in his evening suit carrying a vast bouquet of flowers for his hostess. It would have been even better if he had been having dinner with Thea on their own, but there was still an opportunity for that before her return to Westborough Hall. Polly opened the front door and allowed the Earl to enter. His face was flushed but she did not know why, for the evening was just beginning to cool. She showed him into the drawing room where Sabine, elegantly dressed as always, sat alone sipping a sherry. Rising from her chair she moved forward to greet Piers, who thrust the huge bouquet at her.

'For my lovely hostess,' he gushed, becoming aware that Thea was not present.

'Why, thank you,' Sabine smiled but was not going to lose sight of her objective for the evening. 'Polly, could you arrange them for me? And while we are dining could you bring them in here and place them over there?'

'Dinner is ready ma'am,' Polly intoned, opening the drawing room door wider for her mistress to pass through. It was unusual for Sabine and Piers to be alone together. He followed her into the dining room where a large table was only laid at one end. It was an elegant room and could sit twelve people quite comfortably, but it seemed incongruous to see it laid for so few. It would have been wonderful to see candelabra down the table with a full complement of guests. It was on occasions like this that Piers appreciated the small dining room at Westborough Hall where more intimate dining could take place. It was unlike him to be critical. Sabine directed him to the head of the table where he took his seat rather uncomfortably, noticing that the table setting was only for two people. 'Is Thea not dining with us?' he asked regretfully, really knowing the answer all ready.

'No Piers she is not, and that is something I wanted to talk to you about.'

Piers looked at Sabine quizzically, wondering what she was going to say.

'Poor Thea is exhausted,' began Sabine. 'She is asleep and has been for a few hours. I did not want to wake her. I shall look in on her later. Have you taken a good look at her lately and noticed anything amiss?' Sabine had put down her knife and fork to look directly at her brother. Piers was taken aback by such a question. Of course he had looked at Thea. It gave him the greatest pleasure to do so, but he was not going to admit such a thing to Sabine.

'What do you mean looked at her?' he asked cagily.

'Really looked at her. Have you noticed how dowdy she has become? She wears clothes that don't suit her. Her hair makes her look older than her years and she has dark shadows under her eyes that suggest she has not been sleeping or has been doing too much. Has she not been running Westborough Hall for you while your wife just moons about feeling sorry for herself? And to cap it all you are hardly there because you are more interested in the war in Europe that has not even started yet. If you loved her you would not let any of these things be happening.' Her tirade over she picked up her knife and fork again and resumed eating. It was unlike Sabine to be so forthright but she could not let all her feelings go without being said. 'As it is,' she continued, 'she should be living the life of a young person, not a recluse. She is a wonderful person, loving and giving and if you thought enough about her you would make sure that this did not happen.'

'But I do love her,' Piers protested and then wondered if he had said too much.

'Well all I can say is that you have a funny way of showing it,' Sabine said, the double entendre of Piers' declaration passing her by. The evening was not turning out the way Piers' had hoped. He had to sit through Sabine's anger and now he had lost his appetite. He placed his cutlery on the side of his plate, pushing it away as if it offended him.

'Look Sabine, I am sorry. I have taken her for granted I admit, and when she returns to the Hall I shall make sure that this does not happen again.'

'I shall try and make sure that she does not return to the Hall. I am hoping that we can introduce her to someone so that her life can change. Nothing has quite been the same since Daddy died. She has no permanent home of her own since Mummy went to Devon and she cannot live in London on her own. I'm sure Peter won't mind her living here for the time being.' Piers was taken aback by Sabine's reading of the situation. Thea had to return to Westborough Hall or he would hardly see her.

'But she has a home at Westborough Hall for as long as she wants. We love having her there.'

'But don't you see, Piers, that the same thing will happen again being worn down by Mary's demands, being at her beck and call. She is entitled to a life of her own and not to be at the beck and call of your family. I know she cares for you all, even that witch of a mother of yours. But you must see sense.'

'Has Thea complained about any of this?' Piers asked, wondering if she had taken Sabine into her confidence.

'No,' admitted Sabine, now feeling that she must have gone a little too far.

'I am leaving for the Hall first thing in the morning to deal with a few matters. Give my love to Thea and tell her that I hope she will be better soon.' He rose from the table with as much dignity as he could muster. 'Thank you for dinner. I will see myself out.' With those words ringing in her ears Sabine looked dumbfounded at his abrupt departure, but there was no feeling of guilt on her conscience. Her concern was for Thea alone and Piers had to be aware of the situation. However, when she next saw her brother, she expected there would be a very strained atmosphere between them.

Chapter 37

Piers left London early the next morning anxious to be back at the Hall so that he could see the problems for himself and to find viable solutions. The previous night he had been so shocked by the verbal attack on him by Sabine that he had felt that he had to leave, for her stinging words held a measure of truth which he did not want to hear. But having had a wakeful night he had had plenty of time to reflect on all that she had said. He saw nothing of the countryside as the train sped along but had sat in a quiet area of the first class compartment, continuing to ponder on all that his half-sister had thrown at him. He had taken advantage of Thea's good will and self-sacrifice while she stayed at Westborough Hall for all these long months, fulfilling the role that should have been Mary's. His wife had turned out to be disappointing after what had been a promising start to their union. The fact that he had never loved her was something that he had tried to hide, hoping at some point during their marriage a love would grow or at least a mutual respect that would keep them together, as well as the love they would share for their children. His love for Thea was a torture to them both. He now saw that Thea had given up everything to be near him while he still had a life outside the home. There were his interests in the political storm that was unfolding in Europe and the running of the Westborough estate kept him occupied during his time at home. But he had neglected his wife and the woman he truly loved. Thea had no life along those lines and there was only so much self-sacrifice that a person could give without feeling used and hurt. Thea was entitled to a husband and children if that was what she wanted. He hated the thought that she might move away and the fact that she could have a normal relationship with another man, and not with himself, was totally abhorrent to him; but it was unfair and selfish of him to stand in her way. They could never have a normal relationship. He wondered what had got into him over all this time, believing that he could hold her close to him while he continued his own life? Sabine had been more correct than she realized without knowing the whole story. He finally decided that he had to let Thea go. He had to be fair to her but what was he left with? The answer that came back to haunt him was a marriage like his parents' unless he could resurrect his relationship with Mary. There were the other issues that Sabine had mentioned about Thea's dowdiness and exhaustion. He could see it now. The weight of all that she had to shoulder on his behalf had worn her down and was making her ill in the process. It was all down to his selfishness and Mary's, who demanded more of anybody he knew but gave little or nothing in return; this included her own child. First of all Piers had decided that he must put his house in order on the home front before he made further decisions.

His chauffeur met him at the railway station in Worcester and drove him on to Westborough Hall where his mother was waiting. He gazed out at the lush countryside, viewing it through new eyes. How he loved this part of the world and the history of his family who had lived here for generations. These thoughts brought him back to the present and the need for an heir. He half laughed to himself, for the suggestion for the need for an heir made him think of the Great Harry who had required an heir to rule England. The great lengths he had gone to were mirrored in Piers' own thoughts if Mary did not produce an heir this time. In the small drawing room Clarissa, so pleased to see her son's return, recounted the details of the day that she had found her only grandchild neglected on the floor in the drawing room. Tears ran down her face making Piers warm to the woman he had treated so cruelly only a year or two before. He had to remind himself that at that time she did deserve such treatment, but their relationship had turned a corner in recent months.

'Mother could you move back here on a more permanent basis until I have sorted out what I have to do? It should not be for too long. Also thank you for looking after the situation here for the time being.' Clarissa was happy that Piers had acknowledged her assistance in the situation and pleased to be asked to stay on for the time being, but it was strange that she now thought of the dower house as home, no longer this huge rambling house where she had lived for decades. It was too big for the few people who inhabited it. It required a large family to fill it, not a reclusive countess and a baby.

'Of course,' she said magnanimously, 'but, when will Thea return?' Piers regarded her for a moment. It was happening again. Thea was the one they relied on most of all. 'That I don't know,' he said evasively. 'She is not well at the moment. I will let you know. Sabine is like a mother hen looking after her.'

'Ah. Sabine,' Clarissa said enigmatically without uttering anything further.

'Besides, she should have time to herself sometimes as much as we love having her here,' Piers continued by way of explanation.

'Yes, we love having her here. I miss her when she is away. I have become so fond of her since she came but not Sabine. I can't take to that girl. She reminds me of your father.' Piers could only just keep his face straight. He had to admit that Sabine had given him a shock with her long tirade the previous evening, but at the same time she had been correct in her train of thought. Her protection of her sister had been her main focus and was only natural, and who could blame her for that? In this, Piers had to admit, his half-sister had been correct after all. Piers left his mother in the drawing room reading the daily newspapers. It was something that had consumed her for weeks now trying to keep abreast of the daily happenings in Europe and the British response to it. She dreaded another war. Her memory was too vivid of the Great War and the atrocities that had occurred to 'our boys' as she often referred to them. The Great War had been the war to end all wars and here was another brewing and simmering, with nobody taking notice of the past.

'That man Hitler needs somebody to assassinate him,' she thought out loud, not for the first time. Piers was now about to cause strife in his own home. There would be no negotiation or diplomacy used to deal with a situation that was partly his fault through neglect and not wanting to know what went on. He climbed the stairs like a man on a mission, striding purposely towards his wife's bedroom. There was no subtlety to his approach as he opened the door and walked straight in. It was nearly luncheon but here was Mary, lying wanly in her bed making no attempt to dress and ready herself for the day. She half rose on her elbow, expressing surprise and pleasure at his appearance.

'Piers! What a lovely surprise,' she murmured.

'Why are you still in bed, Mary?' he asked coldly.

'Oh Piers, I don't feel well with this child. I am better lying here to make sure nothing happens to it,' she cooed sweetly. Mary had not observed her husband's look of contempt as he regarded her. He sat on the edge of the bed remembering the young woman he had married. She had changed beyond recognition in the year and a half since then. His hand felt her cool forehead, which gave no hint of illness. Pulling the sheets back he noticed that now she had a slight bump where their second child grew strongly inside her. Her melancholia seemed to have dissipated as she was sweet in her disposition towards him.

'I think that I will call Doctor Brown to come and see you. It is not good to be languishing in bed all day. You know Mary you have a job here to do in running the hall. My mother did it for decades and she had three children to look after. What about our daughter Jane? She needs a mother's love.'

'Jane has Nanny to look after her. She does not need two of us all the time.'

'What about your childhood? You had a nanny but you had a mother's love as well. Remember how deep your feelings were for your mother.'

Mary looked down at her hands and wrung them together in anguish for she could not answer that.

'Piers I fear that I don't have it in me to be a good mother. I love Jane, but…'

'I am on my way to telephone the doctor to visit today.' Piers ignored her excuses with the contempt that was beginning to rise in him.

'No Piers. Please don't. I shall be fine. There really is no need to waste his time. Thea will be back soon.' Piers had stood at the open door of the room and he turned back to look at his wife.

'Thea is not our servant Mary. She has been good to look after things while you have been ill.'

'I thought you enjoyed having her here,' she sneered as if she knew everything that lay in his mind. The expression on his face never wavered. He and Thea had not done anything of which to be ashamed.

'Thea is not well herself and might not be returning any time soon. She is staying with Sabine in London. Apparently she has worn herself out with all that she has had to cope with. She has been doing your job, Mary. She has been running the Hall for you and playing mother to our child.' With those words still ringing in her ears Piers left the room, closing the door with a resounding bang behind him, while Mary turned her face into her pillow to howl her eyes out.

Chapter 38

Thea had slept for two days on and off. Sabine had crept in to see how she was and let her sleep on. On other occasions she had woken Thea to make sure that she had eaten delicate morsels which had been ordered from the kitchen prepared under Sabine's watchful eye. Today Thea was wide awake when Sabine, on silent feet, opened and closed the bedroom door to take a look at her patient. Thea smiled to watch her sister go through this procedure.

'Hello Sabby,' she said. Sabine turned to see a much brighter Thea. Colour had returned to her cheeks, giving her a healthy glow.

'Well just look at you,' Sabine said with delight, viewing Thea through new eyes. 'You look wonderful, almost radiant. Sleep has done you the world of good.'

'I feel great,' Thea enthused. 'Did Piers come last night?'

'Not last night but two nights ago,' Sabine laughed. 'You have lost all track of time.' Thea made a small moue with her mouth, feeling thwarted that she had missed him. 'Was he all right?'

'I don't think so,' Sabine answered honestly. 'I gave him a piece of my mind. I told him how much he had taken you for granted, which had made you ill.'

'You didn't?' Thea said, quite aghast at her sister's temerity. 'What did he say?'

'Absolutely nothing, at first. He just took it on the chin which was admirable of him because I told him the truth. Then halfway through the meal he made some excuse about having to leave. I was left to eat dinner on my own.' Thea did not know what to think, but she giggled at the thought of the normally quiet Sabine asserting herself. Marriage to Peter had given her a confidence that she had never had before.

'I think our half-brother will be wary of me in the future but it won't hurt him. Anyway I have plans for us in a day or two, but I want you to take it easy until then.'

'But I am fine now,' Thea protested feebly trying to get up. Sabine raised her hand with authority, 'do you wish me to treat you to some of the medicine that I gave Piers?'

'No I don't,' Thea said laughing, making them erupt into a fit of the giggles. It was so much like old times when they had been children. Sabine sat on the edge of the bed and they hugged, knowing how much they loved each other. Nothing could tear them apart. Three days later Thea could not wait to leave the confines of Sabine and Peter's home. It was good to be back in London but she did miss Westborough Hall and the countryside. The fact that you could walk straight into the gardens and into the fields gave a sense of freedom which was never possible to experience in the metropolis. However, for the moment she was happy here wishing to meet some of the people that Sabine had spoken about. Her new circle of friends, some of whom had been Peter's before their marriage, had taken to their friend's new wife. All stigma of illegitimacy had been taken away by her marriage and her new status. Thea had insisted that Sabine and Peter follow their plans which had been made long before her arrival. She had been happy to have a tray in her room for supper followed by a good book, which she had found in her sister's small library; this also doubled as Peter's study. For part of the day she had dressed to come downstairs to enjoy some company and the warmth of some of the last days of summer. She felt wistful about that as summer had always been her favourite season. There was also music on the wireless to be enjoyed which was sometimes interrupted by news of the events from Europe. The Polish and British Defence Pact had been signed. Britain had committed itself to the defence of Poland to preserve Polish independence. The British were hoping that this would lead to a position of opening up discussions with Hitler.

Just as she had promised Sabine took Thea into Town. They had taken a taxi to Oxford Street where they shopped, buying evening dresses and clothes for the autumn now that it was nearly the end of August. They crossed London to the West End where Sabine had booked both of them in for the full beauty treatment. They came out feeling rejuvenated with up-to-date hairstyles. Thea had returned to her short curly bob which she had always loved and suddenly felt more herself, not looking how somebody else wanted her to look. It was a flirtation with freedom, something she had not known for quite some time. Sabine had been correct in the way she had read the situation of Thea needing to enjoy her youth. To crown all the fun of the day, the evening ahead was dedicated to launching Thea into London Society. Thea was a mixture of nerves and excitement, not knowing what to think. She also missed Piers wishing that he was with her to take her in his arms to whirl her round the dance floor. As she descended the stairs Sabine and Peter were waiting for her. Sabine gasped when she saw her sister for the transformation was unbelievable. Thea looked sensational, an utter contrast to her arrival of only days before. Even Peter could not but be moved by the beauty he beheld. Her blue, silk evening dress which flowed around her ankles suited her slim frame and the colour complemented her fair hair and blue eyes, with a light summer stole completing the ensemble. But most of all it was the happiness reflected in her face that captured the moment. She had not looked like that for a long time. The three of them were dining at the Ritz with three other couples. After that they would dance the night away to the big band sound which was so popular these days. It was a fabulous night, a night to remember. They had dined superbly and then the tables were cleared while the music played. Couples of all ages rose to dance. Thea sat and watched transfixed by all the glamour. She felt confident, elegant, even beautiful. Peter took hold of her, whirling her around the floor while Sabine laughed at the pure pleasure on Thea's face. In turn the other men at their table did the same. The fact that she did not have a partner did not seem to matter. They were just there to enjoy themselves.

London seemed to have an air of excitement about it as if nobody had a care in the world. *Live for the moment* seemed to be the message thrown at them, so they did; for tomorrow's story might be very different if Mr Hitler had his way.

A handsome young man came striding across the dance floor towards Thea. Bending down he whispered in her ear, making her giggle. He held out his hand to help her to her feet before he whisked her off onto the dance floor where they remained for the rest of the evening. Sabine and Peter looked at each other before smiling, hoping that this was the beginning of a new life for Thea. As the band began to wind up for the night Thea handed her Prince Charming an address and a telephone number before leaving in the early hours of the morning, feeling less like Cinderella than she had done in a long time.

At Westborough Hall Piers had been active in sorting the problems on the home front. After his discussion with Mary he had telephoned Doctor Brown asking if he could visit the Hall as soon as possible that day. Although it was a matter of urgency, there was no illness as such to diagnose but he wanted his advice on a matter that required the Doctor's specialist help, but it was not possible to discuss it over the telephone. Doctor Brown sighed with annoyance at the intrusion. This was a rare day off in a long time. A doctor hardly had such luxury in a rural community, being at the beck and call of all and without a partner to help ease the burden upon him. But he decided to go and do his duty before spending the rest of the day doing what he had promised himself that he would do. The weather was so pleasant that he had decided to go fishing before visiting his widowed sister who lived nearby and would cook his catch as only she could. He drove up the long driveway as he had done many times over the years and pulled up outside the Hall and, not for the first time, marvelled at the grandeur of the building on this wonderful summer's day, the sun's rays working its magic on the mellow stonework.

Piers had been awaiting his arrival. He joined the older man as he descended from the vehicle and closed the door.

They shook hands and together the two men, who were comfortable in each other's company since the doctor had known the young Earl since childhood, walked around the building into the gardens at the rear. Piers had not wanted to be overheard by any of the staff, nor did he expect to inform his mother of the doctor's presence until it was necessary. The two men sat on a wooden seat overlooking the lake which shimmered in the late summer heat. The Malvern Hills were partially shaded by the heat haze in the distance; it was a day that made you glad to be alive, as only an English summer's day could.

'It is Mary, Doctor,' Pier's began to explain. 'She won't get up in the morning and does nothing with Jane except ignore her despite all that I have said. It is a situation that cannot go on. In fact I want your advice because I believe it is becoming a medical problem. She is lethargic, without purpose to her existence even though she has a child and another on the way. There is no excitement that another baby will fill the nursery with fun and laughter. It can't be natural surely?' Doctor Brown felt sorry for the young man who appeared to be at the end of his tether. They were a privileged family, the Devines, with the money that other families could only dream about; but the dilemmas of real life touched them just like people who had less of life's worldly goods.

'I think that what you describe is more of a malady of the mind, a kind of melancholia, which does not heal as quickly as the body, but I have little expertise in such matters. She has already suffered after the birth of your daughter, but she seems to fear the same thing happening to this new baby. What solution I have you could try, but if that fails you might have to seek more specialized help for the Countess.'

'We will try anything to make the situation more bearable for my wife and for all of us.' Piers' voice was tinged with the sadness that he felt.

'Well I would suggest that she has a companion who will keep her company. That might prevent her mind from dwelling on sad thoughts and worries. I know you are away a lot in London with all this talk of war.'

'We have tried that with my sister staying here and, yes, I am often expected at the House,' Piers felt a twinge of guilt that he could not give his wife his undivided attention. Doctor Brown held his hand up to silence Piers, 'I mean a trained nurse who will be firm with your wife to make her get up and dress herself, look after the baby under supervision at certain times of the day. However, this nurse will not wear a uniform or be acknowledged as a nurse, just a companion. This is not a new train of thought but one that has been practiced before and proved that it can work. It will give her ladyship confidence to find a daily routine and fit once more into society by your side as a wife should do, given your personal status. She requires a focus and interests without dwelling on her own problems all the time.' Piers leaned back against the wooden seat contemplating the Doctor's advice. 'You really think that could work?' he asked.

'I do, but her ladyship must also want to be better. She must try hard to improve her health.' Piers nodded, still deep in thought, and then he said, 'Do you know such a person?'

The doctor laughed, 'Oh yes. I shall set it in motion for you, but you must tell your wife that she will be coming next week and also your mother must know, too. The Countess should not be told the person is a nurse, but perhaps you could suggest that the young woman is to help with her duties here at the Hall. Make it sound as if it is the most natural thing in the world. Her ladyship obviously can take advantage of your sister, but a trained outsider is less malleable.'

Piers shook the doctor's hand out of gratitude for all the sensible advice that he had received. His heart had lightened considerably after their discussion. Doctor Brown, having done his good deed on his free day, resurrected his plans to go on his well-earned fishing expedition with an excellent meal at the end of it, which deserved a glass or two of good claret to wash it all down.

Chapter 39

Thea was enjoying London Society. Her mother had never been part of this scene and had not encouraged her daughters to be either. Their father had left those heady days of his youth far behind and no longer wished to be seen in London with Clarissa on his arm so it became a late lesson for Thea to learn on the back of Sabine's liaison with Peter. La dolce vita was an aphrodisiac in which the wealthy youth of London Society liked to indulge. Both girls found it a heady experience and somehow could not quite get enough of it. There had been no contact from the young man who had danced the night away with Thea on the night of their visit to the Ritz.

'He said his name was John,' Thea had said to Sabine, who was indignant that her sister had not heard from this young man. Thea was not bothered for there were plenty more fish in the sea, as she said. She was enjoying herself for the first time in a long time, with no immediate wish to be tied down or to take on the responsibilities such as she had known at Westborough Hall. She often thought of Piers with nostalgia but now accepted the fact that he was beyond her reach. She had not seen him since the day that they had travelled to London together, or heard from him. Sabine had made sure of that. But along the way she had gleaned the fact that Minty had given her husband a son. This would have made Piers jealous she was sure but she knew that he only wanted the best for his family and, deep inside, he would feel pleased at their joy. There would always be a part of her that would never be over Piers no matter how hard she tried. She still wanted to see him but only as her brother. It was all so difficult not to be able to confide in someone. As close as she had become to Sabine again she knew that her sister would become outraged at what had happened between the two of them. The French would call it a coup de foudre but it would outrage Society if it ever became public knowledge. It was still a taboo subject, one not to be raised now or ever even though both of them had been responsible adults. Incest it was called, which was the ugliest of words. Summer was beginning to wane. There had been a touch of autumn in the air for a few days; the sun was becoming lower in the sky without the same warmth as it had only days before. Along with these depressing thoughts the country had heard the news on the wireless that Germany, in the early hours of September first, had marched into Poland making the British people feel that war would now be inevitable. There seemed little hope to cling on to; even the most positive of citizens were now believing in the 'when' not 'if' scenario. Two days later Sabine and Thea, like many other people in Britain, sat close to their wireless sets waiting for Neville Chamberlain to tell them their fate. Precisely at eleven fifteen on that Sunday morning he announced that "a state of war" existed between Britain and Germany. Although the country had been half expecting those words it was still a shock and, for the previous generation, something they had never wished to contemplate ever again.

'I would like you both to go and live in the country out of harm's way,' Peter had said seriously that night over dinner.

Thea groaned inwardly, for it was going to be like living at Westborough Hall all over again and the time she had spent in London had been more exciting than anything she had known in years; but she knew Peter spoke sense, particularly now that Sabine had declared herself to be expecting their first child. Peter was not taking any chances for, like Piers, he wanted a son.

'We will go when it starts to become nasty,' Sabine had declared. She did not want to wither away in a parochial backwater either.

'It might be too late by then,' Peter said sagely, but for once he did not press the subject too hard; but there would become a time when his word would be law.

In the next few days as Thea and Sabine shopped in the West End it was hard for them not to notice the subtle changes that were happening around them. The plate glass fronts of the shops were covered in long criss-cross strips of sticky tape to prevent any flying glass if a bomb should be dropped. Even bus windows had been strapped in the same sort of way. More sandbags had been introduced to protect public buildings while gas masks were carried by the population at large. There were more soldiers on the streets in readiness for being shipped abroad. But what Thea noticed most of all was the stoic attitude of the people. Their sense of humour never wavered; the cockneys would rib each other and laugh. Yet it all masked the deep anxiety that each and everyone felt that this could be their last day; they were going to enjoy it, chance what. Piers had stayed at Westborough Hall far longer than he had intended, but he knew that he had to take control of events there before he returned to Westminster. His mother had now returned to her former home with a view to overseeing the running of the house. His gratitude to her had been immense and the love that they had shared during his boyhood had resurfaced. Each had learned a huge lesson, most particularly Clarissa who was aware of the boundaries that she could and could not cross. Once more the house operated like a well-oiled machine, the servants fully aware of what they could and could not do. Doctor Brown had kept to his word and found a charming young woman called Betty Drew to perform her role as a companion to Mary. She had qualified as a nurse a few years before but, having had to nurse her mother through a long and protracted illness, had decided that she did not want to return to her former profession. As a consequence she had taken work of short duration as a companion to older women. When Doctor Brown had been given her name, which came with good references, he had invited her to the Hall with the permission of the Earl to take part in an interview, which also outlined the problems that she would have to deal with.

'My wife is really not herself these days,' Piers had been profusely apologetic to the charismatic young woman who had not yet met Mary and would probably be a similar age. 'I don't want her to feel like a prisoner in her own home, but she must be allowed to regain her confidence in the world which includes her status as a countess, and then there is the fact that she is carrying our second child. This unnerves her after the problems that she encountered during the birth of our daughter Jane. I am afraid that they have not bonded well, which is not good news.' Betty had listened very carefully to this tale of woe. After her previous experiences, what she had heard did not present her with any feelings of trepidation. She was fully aware that she would have to be firm but kind to the woman who was to be assigned to her care. They were to become friends instead of the nurse-patient situation. Betty stuck out her hand to shake that of her new employer. 'You can count on me, my lord. I will not find it a daunting task to help the Countess after some of my previous encounters. I can only hope that she improves before too long. It must be very worrying for you all.'

'Indeed it has been,' he said, but his features looked a little less tense after the reassurances that Betty Drew had given him. She seemed a capable and sensible young woman in more ways than one. Piers shook her hand firmly and with gratitude. As he showed the Doctor and the young woman out he walked with them to the physician's car.

'Thank you,' he said to Doctor Brown, who smiled as he opened the car door for the young woman and, as she climbed in, he doffed his trilby as a mark of respect before driving away. Time would tell if Betty Drew could work miracles on her new patient. From an upstairs window Clarissa had observed the departure of the doctor and nurse, hoping that everything would work out for the better.

Chapter 40

Piers had left Westborough Hall for London soon after his interview with Betty Drew. He had felt happier at having made the arrangements and that he could leave his affairs in safer hands. He had taken his mother into his confidence concerning the situation which, she had agreed, had been good advice on the part of the Doctor. Her interest in the whole affair was to monitor the situation and to keep her son informed. Piers, knowing that his mother was now quite elderly, did not want to place too much responsibility on her shoulders and hoped that Mary as her mental and physical health improved would once more take up the reins of what was her responsibility as Countess, but he had a lingering doubt that she would be up to the task. However, he hoped that he was wrong.

The day after his return to London he had, quite by chance, bumped into an old friend of his father's, Lord John Gort, who was a man of distinction and held in high regard by his peers and the Government as a whole. He was a military man through and through having been mentioned in dispatches in the Great War on numerous occasions and had been decorated with the Military Cross and the Victoria Cross. Once again he had been given a leading position in the armed forces. Piers had known and respected the man for most of his life but they had never been close. However, as a small boy he had listened to his father tell stories of the great man's heroism in the Great War. But this chance encounter in the corridors of Westminster all these years later had given Piers an opportunity to briefly discuss and seek advice about his own part in this second conflict. He had had it on his mind even before war was declared that he would join up. He felt that it was only right to be part of the war effort and, as a member of the aristocracy, he had to lead by example.

Lord Gort had looked upon Piers favourably as a man who was not one to make excuses about not joining the conflict. He would be a leader of men as had always been the tradition of the aristocracy. His advice had been simple. As nothing untoward had yet happened it was a good idea to join the local Worcestershire Territorial Army to receive his military training and to become a commissioned officer. It was sound advice from such a distinguished man, which Piers took to heart and was prepared to act upon. Piers was also anxious to see Thea but not at Sabine's house in Belgravia. He was not usually a coward but he felt that his half-sister would prevent him from meeting Thea if she became aware of the encounter; so it was advisable to take Thea out to dinner. If he found an exclusive restaurant which was private so that they could talk on a more intimate scale, he would be able to tell her of his plans to join up and the steps that he had taken at Westborough Hall to improve the intolerable situation. She had a right to know for they still loved each other and he wanted to tell her that he would not take advantage of her generosity of spirit again. That had caused him a few sleepless nights after his meeting with Sabine. He had rung the house late in the morning, taking a chance that Sabine would be lunching with one of her numerous friends. It was difficult to know what time of day was best but he had made his decision and was not going to deviate from it. Luck was on his side as Thea answered the telephone. She had just returned from a walk to post some letters to her mother and friends. As she passed through the hallway, the telephone had rung.

'I'll get it,' she called as Polly appeared from the depths of the basement kitchen. Polly retreated as quickly as she had come.

'Hello, Belgravia 239,' Thea said into the telephone. For a moment there was silence and then a voice said, 'Thea, is that you?'

'Piers,' she said, delighted to hear his voice, 'how are you?' She had gone weak at the knees at the sound of his voice. She had tried to reassure herself that she was over him but she knew that if she was honest that was not true. But they did have to make an effort to live their own lives, knowing that nothing could possibly come of their relationship.

'Thea I want to see you,' he said. 'Can I take you to dinner tonight?' Thea was silent, weighing up the pros and cons of the situation. Sabine would be angry if she knew for she would think that Piers was inveigling her to return to Westborough Hall. Sabine could be quite vociferous on the subject once she started.

'When?' she asked, trying to think straight.

'Tonight. I have found a restaurant not too far from where you are. It is not the Ritz but it will give us a chance to talk in private. Will you tell Sabine?' Thea laughed as she heard these words. 'Of course I shall tell Sabine. I don't have to ask permission to go out to see my brother.' But she was not as confident as she sounded. Piers flinched at the word 'brother' for he would have wished it could have been lover or wife. 'I will pick you up at seven thirty.'

'All right I will see you then.' Thea replaced the telephone in its cradle wondering how the evening would go. It was now several weeks since their last encounter. Sabine had returned home from her luncheon party only to say that she and Peter had been invited to go to the theatre and then to dine later, with friends.

'I hope that you don't mind, Thea. It is only one night. Tomorrow we shall return to the Ritz as we did before. I am making the most of my freedom before this young person prevents me from enjoying myself. I shall be too ungainly to dance the night away very soon,' she trilled, rubbing her stomach and laughing. She had been unsure at first about wanting a baby so soon after her wedding but Peter's enthusiasm had been infectious winning his wife over. He had also spoilt her which had made her feel so wanted after the dreadful months after their father died. The illegitimacy factor had cut her to the quick.

'Sabine,' Thea began, wanting to tell her sister about her own evening ahead, but Sabine's mind was on other things as she rushed from the room to begin her own preparations for the evening. Sabine and Peter had driven off to their evening's entertainment before Piers' arrival. Thea was feeling sick with apprehension. It had taken her quite some time to choose an outfit and to tease her short curls into the way the hairdresser had shown her. Viewing her reflection in the mirror she smiled, feeling pleased with what she saw. Polly knocked and put her head around Thea's bedroom door.

'Is there anything I can do for you, Miss Thea?' she asked, observing the mess that Thea had left strewn around her room as she had tried on a variety of outfits until she had decided on the one she was wearing.

'I don't think so Polly, thank you.' It had not occurred to her to ask the maid to clear up the detritus that she had made.

'Oh Miss Thea, you look beautiful tonight!' the girl exclaimed, picking up some dresses to arrange on the coat hangers.

'Thank you Polly.'

'You go along miss and I will tidy up.'

'Are you sure Polly?' Thea asked surveying the mess that she had made of the room.

'Of course miss. You go and take your time and wait for your young man.' Thea looked at the maid quizzically. 'It's not my young man Polly, only my brother.' Thea had waited by the window of the drawing room for at least half an hour before the chauffeur driven car drew up outside Sabine's town house. It was taking her a while to still her nerves as her mind whirled, wondering what Piers wished to see her about. Opening the front door she then pulled it behind her with a resounding bang. Piers leaned forward to take a good look at the woman he loved. He gasped as he viewed a different Thea, a woman who was sophisticated, beautiful and elegantly dressed for such an occasion and she felt empowered, giving her a new found confidence that he had not seen before. The chauffeur held the door open for her to sit in the back of the car next to Piers. They looked at each other, the love they shared shining from their eyes, and it told the story which they would have liked to sing out to the world. Piers slid his hand along the seat to grasp hers and his lips moved silently, telling her how beautiful she was and how much he loved her. The car slid gently forward to the restaurant which was just a short distance away. The restaurant Piers had chosen was a small French bistro with a secluded interior. It was not the Ritz in style and grandeur but it would give them the time to be themselves and to talk privately about personal issues. Inside the bistro they were shown to a corner table which was just as he had planned. They took their seats opposite each other and were handed a menu to scrutinize, but Piers only had eyes for Thea. She blushed and looked down at her menu, but he continued to stare at her. His hand slid across the table to take hers as her eyes wandered around the restaurant to see if anybody had noticed. Not all the tables had been taken, but all the people who were there were intent on their own lives.

'Are you aware how beautiful you are tonight, Thea? You have blossomed since leaving Westborough Hall. I am so sorry that I neglected you there and that Mary was so difficult over the last few months. Your stay with Sabine has done you good.' Thea did not know what to say. The days after leaving Westborough Hall had been difficult for her; in fact she had not realized how ill she had felt until she had arrived to stay with Sabine.

'Yes I was quite ill for a few days. Sabine was very good to me, more like a mother than a sister.'

'Can you forgive me?' he asked, taking her small hand in his.

'Of course,' she smiled, 'I don't think there is anything to forgive. Tell me how is Mary?'

'Much the same at the moment but I have employed a young woman called Betty Drew who will hopefully help the situation. She will help Mary sort out her personal problems and give her confidence to return to a more normal life. The real reason I want to see you is to tell you that I shall be joining up as soon as I have had my army training. I have to do my bit for my country.'

Mary's problems were suddenly forgotten. Thea's eyes filled with tears as he said this and large droplets fell down her cheeks. Piers used his fingers to brush them away. 'Hey, there is no need to cry. I will come back, you will see.' He kissed her hand but the flow did not stop for a few minutes. The waiter brought their first course, tactfully placing the dishes in front of the couple pretending not to notice the heartache that was being suffered. This was not the first time he had witnessed such sorrow. It was happening all the time now that war had been declared. There was also the other extreme too when the young men and women in uniform partied as hard as they could but never thought about tomorrow. Live in the moment seemed to be the philosophy of the day, for there might not be another.

'What will you do?' Piers asked her, still holding her hand, feeling so sorry that he could not soften the blow of such news.

'Oh, I don't know Piers. I feel like a loose cannon or a ship without an anchor. Sabine wants me to stay with her. Peter wants her to go to the country for safety with the baby coming, but she loves London so much. This has always been our home town. And then there is Mummy in Devon. She has done well for herself making a life down there. I could go and live with her, but I might join some part of the war effort to do my bit.'

'You are welcome to return to Westborough Hall, but on a different footing. Mother misses you. She keeps asking about you.'

'You know Piers, your mother is not so bad. I am quite fond of her really. She was quite a tartar when I got to know her but she has mellowed over time.' They both laughed as they thought of Clarissa, who had turned out to be the most stoical of them all.

Chapter 41

Piers had left Thea at Sabine's house. He would have liked to have stayed longer to make sure she was all right because he did not like to see her upset at his news, but she had promised that she would be all right and would return to Westborough Hall sometime in the future, just for a visit so that they could be together before he went away. She had told him how she missed the place completely but both of them knew that she could not return on the same footing as before. There was too much at stake for them both. Now that Piers was considering joining up she had to come to terms with the news like any woman in the land who was to wave her man off to war, but the good news was that it would not be for some time yet as he had to complete his training. People were beginning to joke that there was no war at all. Some were calling it the Phony War, but who knew when everything would start in earnest? That was the question on the lips of people throughout the land. Piers had had much on his mind since leaving Thea the previous night. There was nothing worse than seeing her upset but he was resolved to do his duty for his country.

He made his way to Paddington Station to travel back to Westborough Hall. There were people everywhere. However, it was like a normal day on any large station in the country but the one difference was that there were many men and women in uniform, some arriving and others leaving for secret destinations. There were women crying copious tears taking their leave of loved ones; holding hands, kissing, hugging as if they might not see them again. It was a world turned upside down by a sense of greed and power of one man in another country. This was not the personal argument of the man in the street, but he would have to deal with the consequences which would separate him from family and friends for months or possibly years or make the ultimate sacrifice for King and Country. Piers felt that it could be worse for the people left behind, dealing with uncertainty and the unknown. Across the platform small schoolchildren were standing in crocodile-like formation with their belongings carried in anything that had been available. There were pillowcases and brown paper parcels stuffed to capacity; some of the contents spilled all over the place as children dropped their possessions. They all carried their gas masks slung across their bodies but what Piers could not get over was the look of bewilderment etched upon their faces. The War, which had not really happened in reality yet, was affecting every age group or strata of society. He thought about his own daughter who would not have to endure such conditions being separated from family and housed with strangers; also he wondered about his unborn son or daughter. What would happen to his little family during the duration of the War? How long would it last? This contemplation was just too much to bear. The train to Worcester was full. The evacuated children sat three to a seat subdued by the bewildering circumstances of their departure. The autumn weather was bright and cool but everybody seemed not to notice. They looked unseeing through the carriage windows as the countryside passed swiftly by. Piers was the same. He had wanted to take the train to give himself time to think and had sent his chauffeur ahead to meet the train in Worcester. His chauffeur liked to talk to his employer but Piers was not in the mood to discuss inanities. His mind was full of Thea and the events of their meeting the night before. He knew that she was beautiful, but she had looked radiant and full of love for him. Their time apart had not distanced them but drawn them ever closer. Their love was alive and strong and would be so forever. He thought of reckless schemes that might enable them to be together, for all time; but that was just what they were, stupid and futile. He sat in his first class compartment and placed his head in his hands full of despair for a situation that could not be resolved, now or ever.

On returning to Westborough Hall he had much to do. He would not be returning to the House of Lords for some time if ever, his mind was in a downward spiral of depression wondering what the future would bring. First he had to set everything in order for his departure, whenever that might be. Work was an answer to keep him busy, to prevent him thinking too deeply on the matters that were uppermost in his mind. One consolation was that all families would be dreading separation from their loved ones. The chauffeur, Denham, dropped Piers in front of the old house before driving away to garage the car. That would probably be one of the last times that the vehicle would be used on a lengthy journey. There was talk of petrol rationing and people using public transport or their bicycles. Everything that could be useful was to go towards the War effort. He stood in front of the house looking at its magnificent façade, drinking in every nuance as if he needed to remember it for all time. He sighed heavily as thoughts somersaulted through his brain. On entering the house he saw his mother descending the stairs slowly and stiffly. This made him aware of how much she had aged in recent months, but it was on her shoulders that he was going to place much responsibility during his time in the forces. What else could he do? His sisters had their own lives and visited the Hall rarely, but with reluctance he felt there was still Thea.

'Piers,' his mother said in delight. 'It is good to see you home.' She had reached the bottom of the stairs and walked to him to kiss his cheek fondly, just as they would have done in the past. Recent recriminations appeared forgotten.

'Hello Mama,' he said, feeling pleasure at seeing her. A lesson had been learned on both sides and a mutual respect had developed over time. Piers had needed his mother more and Clarissa had realized how much she wanted to be needed too. It brought about a feeling of belonging that most people required to keep them grounded. They walked into the large sitting room to speak privately. Piers closed the door while Clarissa walked stiffly, leaning heavily on her walking stick as she made her way to the window seat where warm autumn sunshine spilled into the room, making it feel like the last of summer; but a fire roared in the fire place telling a different tale. Piers seated himself on the sofa to await his mother's report on events at the Hall.

'Well,' she began. 'It would appear that things are looking up. That Betty is trying her best to work miracles with Mary. She has made sure that she is up every morning and dressed ready to come down to breakfast. That is indeed an achievement. After breakfast she spends time with Jane under the supervision of Nanny, but Betty is always with her. She has not rejected Jane but I would not say that she is a natural mother. Also Doctor Brown has visited again to make sure that everything is as it should be and has said the pregnancy is advancing as it should do. But–' Clarissa paused for affect. Piers had been smiling at the good news that he was hearing, but suddenly his face clouded at the change of tone in his mother's voice.

'We had a telephone call yesterday with bad news. It would appear that Mary's father has had a stroke and the prognosis is not good. We have not told Mary as yet. She is not fit or strong enough in mind or body to go to him. I have consulted Doctor Brown on the matter. He came very promptly soon after the news yesterday. He is a good man.'

'Yes he is,' Piers agreed, somewhat taken back by the news his mother had imparted. 'Where is her father now? Is he well looked after?'

'He is receiving private care but he is not expected to live very long.'

Piers was thoughtful for a moment. This was another unforeseen complication to Mary's return to full health. 'Should I take her to see him? If I am with her surely she would not come to any harm. Betty could come as well.' Clarissa looked thoughtful for a moment then shook her head. 'I don't think so, for I believe that it would wreck all the progress that has been made so far. It would set her back considerably. I think that it might only be days before he dies. That was what the matron of the home seemed to think.'

'I will need to tell her mother for she is her father's only heir. There will be all the legal issues to sort out and it will make her a very wealthy woman. It will be difficult to keep it all from her. She is an intelligent woman and will work out that there is something wrong.' Clarissa mulled over these facts. She had not thought about those complications to the situation. 'I would go and see her and make a decision afterwards. She has been very close to her father over the years so you could be right on that issue, but I don't think that it will help her mental state.'

'I think you are right Mama but there is no other way around it. She must be told. She has a right to be told.' Piers gave his mother an affectionate kiss on the cheek, making her blush with pleasure at his warmth. There was most definitely no turning the clock back to those days when they had been at loggerheads. Piers left his mother to her cup of tea in front of the drawing room fire fully aware of what was passing through her mind. He climbed the stairs to Mary's sitting room and opened the door. The scene before him made his heart somersault. Mary was sitting on the floor playing with Jane. This was a genuine bonding moment between mother and child, one that he had never thought would happen. Jane was playing with a pile of bricks while her mother helped her build them. Betty sat in the chair watching over them, as had been requested. She too was enjoying the scene before her. Both women looked up and Mary's eyes shone with pleasure as she saw her husband standing there. He closed the door quietly behind him, not wishing to startle Jane. Lowering himself onto the floor by the side of mother and child he entered the game as his daughter looked at him and laughed with happiness. Despite what had happened she was a happy baby, which filled Piers' heart with love. They played on for a few minutes and then he indicated to Betty to take Jane back to Nanny in the nursery.

'Mary I need to speak to you,' Piers' said. 'I'm afraid that it is bad news and I want you to brace yourself and be strong.' Mary's face which had been open and happy suddenly clouded. She rose from the floor and turned to sit in one of the armchairs. It was this movement which made Piers notice the bump of her pregnancy. He pulled an armchair close to where she was sitting and reached for her hand, which he kissed tenderly, for she was his wife and needed him more than ever. It was this thought that made him think back to the promise he had made to her father before their marriage. He was sure that he had not been a good husband. His thoughts had been with Thea or the work that he had to do at the House. A measure of guilt and a feeling of selfishness rushed through him, making him shudder at his own audacity at having played God with the emotions of his wife, the mother of his child; after all it had not been Mary's fault that he had loved Thea. Both of them had used Mary in a way, but most of all himself.

'What is it?' she asked with fear in her eyes. She had often thought that Piers would divorce her after all the problems. Perhaps that was what he had come to say. Perhaps he thought this new child was another girl and he could have a boy with someone else. Her hand carefully touched the place where the baby grew.

'Mary, you have to be strong,' he said as gently as he could, still holding her hand. The tears brimmed in her eyes as she waited for the blow to fall, but what came was not what she had been expecting.

'It is your father Mary. He is very ill and not expected to live very long. At the moment he is in hospital but I wondered if you are up to seeing him. I will go with you.' The tears fell in channels down her cheeks and the resounding sobs racked her slight frame. 'I want to see him,' she continued to sob, 'but I feel that I cannot leave the house. I have lost all confidence in going out even with you beside me, Piers. What am I to do?' Piers now realized the problem that had begun with the dramatic birth of Jane had developed into a more serious situation than they had first thought, and not for the first time he believed her problems were beyond Doctor Brown's own medical capabilities.

'I will be with you every step of the way,' Piers encouraged her.

'I cannot do it Piers, not even with you beside me.'

He sat with her for a while feeling her body shake with the grief that had engulfed her. He held her hand, stroking it softly and his emotions overtook him too, experiencing the guilt and sorrow of his conscience telling him how badly he had treated this woman in his misguided pursuit of Thea, the forbidden apple. He knew that once the child was born he had to seek specialist help for her in Harley Street in London. There would be someone there who could alleviate the troubled mind of his wife. But before then he had to fulfil his promise to Mary's father that he would try to love and protect the woman he had married. However, there was a war and with every good intention that he might have, fate would play a major role in the lives of every man, woman and child in the country.

Chapter 42

Thea had not told Sabine about the evening she had spent with Piers. There would have been an investigation of some magnitude if she had. But she had grasped at the invitation that her sister and Peter proffered to dance the night away at the Ritz. It was a way of obliterating the knowledge of Piers going to war in the near future. It was a frivolous diversion which she would take as often as she could. These thoughts had remained prominent in her mind ever since her last meeting with Piers. She knew that he had fleetingly visited London on behalf of Mary, but the full facts had escaped her. He was more concerned about meeting her again without fully disclosing his reasons why, but Thea had been evasive saying that she was not sure what she would be doing on that date. It was not that she did not want to see him but the great pit of pain that she had endured on their previous separation had been just too much to bear. She had still promised to visit Westborough Hall soon, but it was going to be difficult to endure. She wondered how other women found such separations; she was one of many thousands in such a predicament, yet she must live her life instead of pining for the only man she could truly love. There surely would be another man out there who could claim her heart and give her the family that she so longed for. When Sabine retreated to the country under Peter's orders, Thea decided that she would remain in Town at the Devine house. The Phoney War still continued; some said it would be the calm before the storm but nobody knew for certain. The new dance at the Ritz had blown away many of the cobwebs that had clouded her mind recently. Receiving many invitations from Sabine and Peter's friends in her own right had lifted Thea's spirits. She could be found regularly dancing the night away and sleeping until the early afternoon before repeating the process the following evening. Life was one long party but it prevented her from dwelling on the problems which haunted her. When she did have an opportunity to think, it made her new lifestyle seem frivolous, while other young women were helping with the War effort any way that they could. Sabine often telephoned her bemoaning the fact that she was in the country, bored senseless. She envied her sister and the freedom that she had. Deep down it was Thea who envied Sabine to have the security of a husband and the imminent birth of a child. Thea felt her own life had little purpose. Frivolity was not truly in her nature but she was enjoying it while she could. There might be a time when she had to leave London. Her mother was strongly hinting at the prospect of her daughter joining her in Devon, particularly if the War took a turn for the worse. London would no longer be safe.

Then, one night at the end of October, Thea met Jack Carson, a handsome young man dressed in the uniform of a captain in the army. He was one of many young men and women dressed in uniform that night. While Thea chatted to her group of new friends, Jack had been drinking a pint of beer watching her, totally mesmerized by her beauty and her vivaciousness. When the band played a Glen Miller number he witnessed the members of her party rise to dance, leaving Thea tapping her foot in time to the music. She had obviously come unchaperoned. Looking around at all the couples dancing, she suddenly became aware of someone watching her. Their eyes met and locked momentarily, but she turned her glance to another part of the dance floor where she saw somebody she knew. Automatically she raised her hand to wave, a smile lighting her eyes. Jack had witnessed this and felt truly smitten by the young woman. Suddenly her eyes were drawn back to the young man, who still continued to stare. Shifting uneasily in her seat under such intense scrutiny her eyes drifted once more in his direction. It was as if she was now hypnotized by his presence. But he was not there anymore; before she knew it he was standing in front of her asking if she would like to dance. Rising from her seat as the band played on, she found herself in his arms where she stayed for the rest of the evening. At one point they wandered from the heat of the dance floor and found themselves in the cooler lobby.

'I'm Jack Carson,' he introduced himself with a smile which brightened his already handsome features.

'Thea Cavendish,' she replied, wondering what would happen next.

'It is lovely to meet you, Thea Cavendish.'

Thea did not know what to say. She was not well practiced in the art of flirtation but she need not have worried, for Jack Carson had kissed the Blarney Stone at some point in his life. He had enough to say for both of them. Suddenly they discovered that the band had stopped playing now as the evening was growing late. The musicians were beginning to pack away their instruments and a buzz of conversation could be heard as groups of people began to gather their belongings to make their way home. Jack and Thea returned to her table.

'Thea, there you are,' Cassandra Constantine said to her friend, her voice full of ennui at the trouble she had gone to find her. '-We have been looking for you. Are you ready to leave?' She had not troubled herself to look in Jack's direction, as if he was not worth contemplation.

'Can I take you home?' Jack suddenly asked, feeling that he would not see her again if he did not ask now and then she might be lost to him forever. Cassandra picked up her stole and handbag while Jack stood waiting for Thea's answer. It took quite a while to come.

'Yes, all right,' she said, wondering what would happen. Cassandra flashed her warning look, then kissed Thea's cheek.

'I will telephone you soon,' she said and then, sotto voce, she murmured into her friend's ear, 'be careful,' before disappearing towards the rest of her group.

*

The news had not been the best at Westborough Hall. A telephone call had been put through in the early hours of the morning explaining that Sir Giles, Mary's father, had passed away in his sleep even before Piers could go and see the old man on behalf of his wife. Mary had taken the news badly as had been expected. Her refusal to leave her bed came as no surprise to the people who surrounded her. On this occasion Piers had given orders that she was to be allowed to grieve in her own way, but not for too long. He was not prepared to undo all the good work that had taken weeks to achieve. He also asked Betty to take Jane to see her so that she knew that she had something to live for. Piers knew that he was being rather overdramatic with such thoughts, but Mary could not afford to take a retrograde step into the melancholia that still engulfed her at times. Piers had been the chief mourner at the funeral of his father-in-law. A few people who had known the baronet for years had attended but it was a very low-key affair. Mary's mysterious absence was cause for speculation but Piers did not feel that other people should be concerned by the private business of the family. As the mourners congregated outside the small church of St Asaph, Piers acknowledged them and thanked them for attending the service, but there it ended. There was to be no wake for the baronet who had been laid to rest next to his wife. When Mary was feeling stronger physically and mentally he would bring her to see the grave and, if time permitted, there would be a small memorial service to celebrate her father's life. There was also the question of Mary's inheritance. The will was simple in the fact that everything had been left to Mary. She was indeed a wealthy young woman, as Piers knew from her father's revelations some years previously. The solicitors could deal with the paperwork without Mary having to be bothered by the affair. After the funeral Piers returned to Westborough Hall to enlist in the Territorial Army and had been given the rank of major on account of his standing in society. There was also the issue of securing the lands which were under his ownership. There were more and more men who were joining up, leaving their tenant farms without adequate resources of manpower. The older generation had to take on more responsibility along with the younger boys, who were not eligible to go to war on account of their age. It was going to be difficult to run the farms as it was, but they could only do their best.

There were other issues that concerned Piers regarding the Hall and his inheritance. He had to make his will in case of his never returning from the War. It was a dismal thought for quite a young man but it still had to be done. He had summoned Earnest Fellowes to the Hall to discuss and draft the will. In case Mary did not present him with the expected heir, he had to make provision for the future of the earldom, the title and everything that went with it. Inheritance had its own rules of working. Other than this he had to name a legal guardian for his children. Mary would always be their mother but, under present circumstances, he had to find a suitable adult who could support her in any decisions that had to be made. It had to be his mother with all her experiences, but if anything happened to this elderly parent he decided to name Thea as their joint legal guardian and to separate the London town house from the Westborough estate. This would give his family a roof over their heads and a large inheritance as his father had given his Cavendish family. When this was complete it made him happy to know that all eventualities had been covered. There was also Mary's inheritance to will. He did not want it willed to himself for if his wife predeceased him and then he died, the money could go into the Westborough estate and line the pockets of others. It would have to be left to the children in trust until they came of age.

Part 4

Chapter 43

The day that Thea had feared the most had arrived. Piers had done his military training and had been posted to the first Light Armoured Reconnaissance Brigade as a major. He was due to be in the second wave of the British Expeditionary Forces to land on French soil. The first wave had gone out in October and had been deployed along the French and Belgian borders; but the Phoney War continued, leaving both soldiers and the civilians at home wondering whether anything in military terms would occur.

Now in February 1940 there were constant shiploads of soldiers leaving from ports along the south coast of England with Piers being amongst them. Prior to his leaving Piers had been given a week's leave and had naturally returned to Westborough Hall to say his farewells to his family. Thea had been invited for part of that time as Piers had issues which he wished to discuss with her, as well as the fact that he was desperate to see her again. As she had promised on that evening when they had dined together in London she returned to the Hall for the first time in nearly six months. The atmosphere was very different from Thea's time there. She had not known what to expect but was mildly surprised to find that Mary had blossomed during her time away under the guidance of Betty, her constant companion. There had been a bonding with Jane, now well over a year old and walking on sturdy legs. She was a pleasant, pretty child with her father's good looks and steadfast nature. Mary had accepted the fact that the birth of her second child was only weeks away but that had not stilled the anxiety she felt for the physicality of bringing the new infant into the world. Her relationship with Piers was also on a firmer footing and they were easy in each other's company. However, there had still been hurdles to overcome. Mary had been grateful for Piers' dealing with the legalities of her father's death, which he had explained to her and his mother so both would be fully aware of the problems which could ensue. The passing of her father had been most traumatic and the fact that she had not seen him at the end of his life had left a sadness that she found difficult to shake off. Finally, now that Piers' departure was imminent, she had begun to feel bereft once more at the thought that she could lose him too. Clarissa, who was still living at the Hall now on a permanent basis, had taken control of her daughter-in-law giving her the backbone that she needed to cope with the situation. What Clarissa did not confide to anybody were her private feelings of dread if Piers did not return. Those dark thoughts were relegated to a place so deep inside her that they were not allowed to surface ever. Her determination to run the Hall so efficiently in readiness for her son's return was the only purpose she would allow herself. This was the situation that Thea returned to in early February on a cold day with snow lying on the tops of the Malvern Hills, the view as breathtaking as ever. It was Piers who had opened the door to Thea as she stepped out of the car that had met her at Worcester. He ran down the steps to greet her and this was when she had noticed his weight loss. It suited his frame and gave him an athletic air. It was all the training he had done over the previous months and a less luxurious diet brought on by a different lifestyle. He was wearing a light pullover over an open neck shirt and his hair was shorter cut in a military style. He swept her off her feet without a care about who was watching and hugged her closely, planting a kiss on her cheek.

'Piers!' she exclaimed laughing at such an affectionate greeting, 'you don't know who is watching,' she whispered as the chauffeur smiled at them as he took her suitcase from the boot of the car.

'Can I not greet my sister whom I have not seen for a long time?' he said, laughing with happiness at her presence. 'Come on in. It is far too cold to be loitering out here.'

Thea followed him into the hallway of the old building and, as usual, she luxuriated in the history of the place. She realized that she had missed it after all these months of self-imposed exile. 'Go and make yourself presentable. Luncheon is to be served shortly.'

Thea disappeared to the room that she had occupied during her previous stay. It was like returning home for the first time in months. After feelings of trepidation she felt relaxed and happy. She glanced in the mirror at her appearance. Her eyes were bright with the expectation of the visit and her face glowed with health. She was no longer dowdy as she had been then. Running a comb through her short curls she wondered if she should tell Piers her news, but instantly decided against it. It was not fair to upset him when he was going away. The future on his return would be soon enough to divulge the momentous decision she had made. Enjoying the moment had become her motto; it was the only way to cope with the uncertainty of war. She entered the large dining room to find everyone seated. Her place had been laid between Piers and his mother. Enthusiastic greetings of welcome warmed her heart, making her feel part of this large family. Even Clarissa squeezed her hand in greeting smiling warmly at her. She really was a very different woman these days. Thea looked across the table at Mary who appeared reserved, but their last meeting had been plagued by problems. She said nothing, but looked down at her hands. Thea made a mental note to seek her out when the opportunity presented itself so that they could both make their peace with each other.

As luncheon finished, Piers indicated that he wanted time alone with her. They wrapped up warm and ventured into the garden making their way down to the lake, away from prying eyes.

'You look well Thea, and beautiful. There is a sparkle about you which is new. How is life treating you?' She did not answer him. This must be the time to tell him, she thought, but again she could not bring herself to do so. At the folly which overlooked the lake they took shelter from the raw wind which blew treacherously. Inside the building with the door closed they unwound their scarves momentarily before he took her hungrily in his arms and kissed her.

'How am I going to cope without you, without being able to see your beautiful face and to talk to you?' He nuzzled her neck. She allowed it for this would be the last time in a long while, maybe forever. She dismissed that thought almost as soon as it surfaced.

'I need to talk to you, Thea. I have made you a legal guardian of the children along with my mother. I hope you don't mind. Mary is still not fully capable of taking on that role,' he said, 'and I feel you are the only one I can trust with that. I know you will take care of the children as if they were your own.'

'Piers, don't worry so much. Everything will be all right. I do see that you have to make such plans, but rest assured that we will do our best for everybody concerned.' Again she did not tell him what was in her heart; it would only complicate matters before he left these shores. Before the end of the day Thea had knocked on Mary's sitting room door. There was a reckoning which needed to happen before she returned to London, and most particularly in the light of what Piers had told her about the legal side of matters that he had established so recently. Mary shouted out for her to enter, thinking that it was one of the maids. On seeing Thea she recoiled; Thea had noticed it, too.

'May I come in?' she asked jovially and continued to walk into the room, but knew that she was not going to take 'no' for an answer. Mary had been having a rest as she did most days now that her stomach was so huge. But she had picked up a book and had been reading; it was the one occupation which prevented her from thinking depressive thoughts when she was on her own. Now that the baby was only a few weeks away, she had begun thinking about the problems that she had had with Jane's birth; but she had not voiced her fears for she knew that they would be relayed to Piers and the doctor, so she chose to keep her own council.

'How are you Mary?' Thea asked, perching on the end of an armchair without an invitation. She was regarding the other woman with concern for their parting had been quite acrimonious. Mary did not give her eye contact initially, but then raised her face to look at Thea.

'I'm not too bad,' she said stiffly. 'I am not far off my date now.' She placed a comforting hand over her bump and smiled. 'Have you seen Jane?'

'Yes. She is lovely, a little imp though.' Thea had seen her when Nanny had brought her down to the drawing room earlier in the afternoon. She was walking now and had enjoyed the exploration of the room, reaching for expensive china which made the adults' nerves jangle as Nanny chased after her. Mary smiled again at her daughter's antics. Piers had been correct that Mary was bonding with Jane at long last. Thea moved closer to Mary and placed a comforting hand on hers. 'I want us to be friends Mary, like we were. Do you remember when we would sneak off to the lake with our books and have picnics? Those were good times.' Mary's eyes misted over as she recalled the fun their friendship had brought them. 'I want those days back again, Mary, once you have had this little one. I will come and visit as often as I can once Piers has gone off to war. You should not be on your own too much because it is not good for you.'

'It would be good for you to come and see me,' Mary said, accepting the olive branch that had been offered. On the other hand Thea knew that she was laying down the foundations for Piers' plans. She could not just walk back into their lives and take over. The process would have to be subtle so that Mary trusted her and did not think that she was being spied on. Piers had not thought out that part of his plan too clearly. But Thea doubted that her friendship with Mary could ever be what it had been before; she would try for Piers' sake but, now, she had to reserve time for herself because her future was changing. Thea's day of departure from Westborough Hall had come. Feeling emotional she wanted to go quickly so that the agony of separation and the 'goodbyes' were not prolonged. She was due to catch a late afternoon train to London but now wished she had made a reservation on an earlier one. After lunch Clarissa asked to speak to her privately in the library. They walked in together, Thea wondering what was to transpire.

'My dear,' Clarissa began, guiding Thea to a seat at the well-polished table. 'I have to admit to a feeling of trepidation at having so much responsibility after Piers goes to war. I am getting old and feeble for such a job. It is not just the running of the Hall but overseeing the land and the tenant farms with so many men volunteering to join up. Usually I am stoical but my body is feeble these days. Old age comes with lots of worries and I cannot confide in Piers as he has enough worries of his own.' Thea regarded this woman who, in the early days of their acquaintance, had seemed a demon with her demands and interference; but over time she had grown to know her better and, if she was honest too, to love her. She had been her father's wife but Thea had grown to believe that her father had not been the saint they had all thought. He had certainly had grave faults and had led this woman a dance. It had always been thought that the old Countess was in the wrong and causing trouble. The truth, Thea believed, was that they were not compatible, had never had anything in common except their children whom they had both loved. She knew her father had loved her and Sabine. Clarissa's children spoke affectionately of James Devine. He had also loved Beatrice, but not this very proud woman of the upper classes with her stiff upper lip, not until the barriers came tumbling down. Thea took Clarissa's hand with genuine affection.

'You don't have to worry, you know. I will come regularly and we can telephone each other often. You will not be alone in this.' The old woman's eyes brimmed with tears as she whispered, 'Thank you my dear. I just knew that I could depend on you.' Thea's tender heart turned somersaults, but she dismissed the fact that Clarissa doubted her personal qualities to run the estate. She was no different from any other mother in the country of any class; she wanted her son to come home safely. Thea's eyes watered too and, in a moment of affection, she took Carissa's hand and squeezed it, then kissed her cheek.

'I have to go now but I will see you soon.' The two women had formed a close bond which crossed the generation divide and they knew that they could trust each other implicitly. Thea slipped out of the library to find Piers before her departure. He was in the garden dressed for the elements as clouds threatened snow.

'I shall drive you to Worcester. It will give us more time together.'

'No Piers,' she replied, 'let us say our goodbyes here before I go.' She pulled her coat more tightly round her, her scarf was wound round her neck as they walked into the gardens to find a secluded place away from prying eyes. His arms went round her as he pulled her closer and her head lay in the space between head and shoulder, drawing courage from his presence which would soon be gone. How would they bear such a parting? He released her, turning her to face him.

'Do you think we could just this once?' Shaking her head she said, 'No Piers, we have vowed that we won't. It would not be right.' He smiled at her weakly, 'It was just a mental aberration. I have tried to find ways round it in my mind but I cannot find a solution. Will you write to me telling me what you are doing and what is happening here?' Tears filled her eyes knowing that the time of their parting had nearly arrived, 'Yes of course I will. You must write to me and promise to keep yourself safe.'

'I'll try my best.' He pulled her to him and they clung together as if they could never let go. Suddenly Thea pulled away.

'I have to go now, but I won't look back or I won't be able to go.' They both cried as they clung together for the last time. 'Try not to stay long in London. I think that it might become a target,' he said. She nodded.

'Goodbye, my love,' she whispered. Turning her back on him she walked away with great gulping sobs shaking her body. What she had not witnessed were the tears streaming down Piers' face as he wondered if he would ever see her again. The next day Piers left with his regiment for France.

Chapter 44

Thea had returned to London, to her father's town house. She lived there on her own, well not quite on her own. The servants had left knowing that they could earn better money in the factories which were keeping the Phoney War going. Most of the rooms in the house were covered in dust sheets except for her bedroom and the drawing room. She ate in the kitchen but sometimes she went out to dinner with her new friends, or to be honest they were Sabine's friends. Deep down she was not frivolous by nature and she knew that she was becoming bored with them and the never ending parties. There was more to life than frivolity. Her heart was broken by her brother's departure but she knew that she had a life to live; one that she did not wish to divulge to Piers to upset him or alarm him before he went to fight, but feelings of guilt engulfed her. A week after his departure she sat at her dressing table placing her wedding ring on her finger. It was just a plain gold band which fitted her snugly. There had been no time for an engagement ring or an announcement in *The Times*. She had not told anyone about what she had done, not even her mother or Sabine. There would have been questions to answer and interference from her sister who had married well. It had all happened so quickly, but that was what war was doing to couples these days. There were no prolonged engagements, just instant decisions, living for this moment in time. Perhaps that would be the only time they would have together. Would there be subsequent weddings? Nobody had an answer to give. She heard a key turn in the lock and a voice calling her name.

'I'm up here,' she answered. Only minutes elapsed and the bedroom door opened. Jack Carson poked his head round, smiling broadly at her. He had returned home on leave.

'How's my girl?' he asked, imitating a Cockney voice. Although her heart was full of sadness she laughed at him as he held his arms wide. Rising from the chair she went into his embrace, taking comfort from the love that he bore her. She could not quite reciprocate those feelings, but nevertheless she had grown fond of him and he treated her well. Not all marriages were made in heaven. She had wanted Piers, who she could not have and so she had settled with someone who was a substitute, and that person was Jack. There was no knowing how long their marriage would last but she would endeavour to make it work if she could. Jack was a good man and deserved the best, which she intended to give him. They hardly knew anything about each other. However the attraction was mutual for he was good-looking and treated her well. It had all begun on the night that they had met at the Ritz. He had hailed a taxi to take her home and he had stayed the night, something that Thea had promised herself that she would not do. They had been carried away on a tide of emotion which continued for the entire two days of Jack's leave before he had to return to his unit. If they were not making love they spent the time talking, finding out about each other's family. Thea was honest about her family situation, only omitting the part about her relationship with Piers. Jack had told her his story. He was an only child and his elderly parents had died ten years before. He was on his own, rootless rather like a loose cannon. In civilian life he was a banker in the City, living in the capital in a small house in North London. It never felt like home for there was never anyone to anchor him to it. When war had been declared he had offered his services for his country. It was his time in the forces that had given him his first feelings of belonging; the camaraderie of his fellow officers had grounded him more than anything since the death of his parents. Meeting Thea had given his life another dimension; something that he had wanted for quite some time but had never found the right woman before. Now whenever he was on leave he had something to look forward to, coming to stay with her and so their relationship had flourished. He had been in love with her from the first time that he had set eyes on her. He had worked out that she did not return his love as readily but, given time, he was convinced that it would happen. It was still early days in their relationship. On the other hand Thea was fond of Jack, who gave her commitment which Piers could never do. Piers had a wife and children which she could never have with him and to remain an old maid was not on her agenda. She wanted children and the life others took for granted. In the four months since they had known each other, there had been two months of marriage which had held them together like glue. After the first six weeks of their relationship Thea had known that she was pregnant. She was happy; the child was wanted but not without a ring on her finger. She had witnessed her mother's anguish after her father's death. It was not a pretty picture to be the mother of two daughters and not have a wedding band on your finger, and there was to be no illegitimate stigma for her child. Thea had not held back at telling Jack how she felt. Although she had not known him long she did not doubt that he would marry her. Her instincts had proved correct. His reaction had been one of sheer delight as he pulled her close and kissed her realizing that, when he did go to war, he would be like his peers with a wife and baby to come home to. His eyes shone with happiness when he rested his hand on the place where the child lay. It was too soon to feel anything, but that did not detract from the excitement that he felt.

'I think it is wedding bells for us my girl,' he had said firmly, 'I will get a special licence. It will be no problem as it is done all the time now.' Thea could not help smiling at his infectious attitude. Her child would be legitimate. That was all she wanted right now. Jack had been correct in his judgement. He had rushed off that day to buy a ring and had returned with the licence and the news that they were to be married at Caxton Registry Office the following day. And so it had happened with two witnesses, whom they had not known, signing on their behalf. Their wedding breakfast had been the two of them dining at the Ritz celebrating their happiness. A whole new world was opening before their eyes.

But here was Jack home on another leave wondering how his wife and his son and heir were coping with his absence. He made the assumption that the child was a boy but deep down he did not mind. He felt anchored now that he had Thea to come home to as well as the child. He did not want anything to go wrong to spoil for what he had waited a lifetime. It was on this occasion that Thea had told him about Piers' idea of making her a legal guardian for his children and the affairs at Westborough Hall.

Jack's face clouded. 'That's a big commitment which he has placed on your shoulders, especially now with our son.' He did not want anything to jeopardize the health and well-being of his family. He was serious and unhappy about the burden her brother had placed upon his wife's shoulders.

'There is no need to worry, Jack,' she said as she stroked his face, looking into his eyes. His heart melted.

'If I am there you must come too if you are on leave. I will give you all the details you will need before you go.' For once he was placated, kissing her passionately. He loved her so much.

Piers had left a tearful wife and mother behind when he left to return to his regiment. He had felt beleaguered too, not wanting to leave the people he loved; but the stiff upper lip so often used by the aristocracy had come into good use as he departed. He knew that tomorrow was the day of their departure for France. During the night Mary went into premature labour, probably brought on by the stress of Piers' departure. She woke feeling a pain in her back. Lying there wondering what it was, she made no attempt to seek help and it was only as the intensity of the pain increased that she began to realize what it was. Her fear had surfaced, making her agitated wondering if she could give birth to the child naturally without another operation. This time she hoped that it was a boy for she had no intention of having any more children with Piers, despite the fact that he wanted an heir for Westborough Hall. She cried out, but nobody heard her pleas for help. Climbing out of her bed she dragged her cumbersome, aching body to the door of her room and shouted before slithering to the floor where she had been standing. Clarissa, a poor sleeper these days, heard a commotion. It was only faint but her overactive imagination thought that someone had broken into the Hall. Picking up the nearest object to her in the form of a bedside torch, she held it as a weapon to lash out at any intruder. She would not allow some upstart to steal any valuables from the Hall. She was past caring for her own safety. The landing outside her room was dimly lit like it always was but, as she stepped from her room, she became aware of something or somebody lying partly on the landing floor writhing in pain. It was impossible for her to kneel down these days with her arthritis making her stiff, so she too cried out for assistance. Betty, in a nearby bedroom, was suddenly aroused from a deep slumber. At first she was disorientated, but another cry from the landing alerted her senses and she rose from her warm bed, flinging on a dressing gown as she opened her door. Witnessing the scene before her she bent down to take a look at Mary. 'Stay with her,' she instructed Clarissa, 'I'll go and telephone Doctor Brown.'

Nanny, hearing the rumpus, clattered down the nursery stairs. She also knelt down by Mary, speaking to her in a reassuring voice. Slowly she managed to bring her to her feet and walked her slowly back to bed. Betty returned to the scene, breathless but offering the news that Doctor Brown was on his way. However, the waiting seemed interminable.

'It looks as if the baby is well on its way.' Betty looked at Clarissa, noting the strain on her aristocratic face, and said, 'why don't you go back to bed? You look tired. Nanny and I will stay with the Countess and see what the Doctor says. Don't forget that really I am a nurse so she will be in good hands.' Clarissa, not normally someone to take orders, looked at the kindly faces of the two women and nodded her thanks. 'Let me know what happens as soon as it happens.' Then she stiffly returned to her own room, but lay awake not being able to sleep with all the problems that Piers had left firmly in her hands as he went to fight for King and country. She offered up prayers to the Almighty that the child would be born well and a boy, an heir for the earldom, and then Mary could be left in peace for she would have done her duty. Her fears over childbirth would be a thing of the past, allowing the family to move forward. True to his word Doctor Brown came quickly, huffing and puffing up the steep stairs, his stout little body making him breathless after all this exercise and the hurry from his own home. The door to Mary's room lay open and he observed that arrangements had already been made for the birth by the two efficient young women. He hoped that it would not be a repetition of the previous birth when young Lady Jane was born, but now the Earl was abroad which made him feel uneasy if anything went wrong. He rebuked himself for his maudlin thoughts but, looking at the grey face of the young woman lying on the bed, did not fill him with hope. As an experienced doctor he would use all the skills God had given him and pray that it all went well. He removed his outer jacket and then rolled up the sleeves of his shirt before attending to the matter in hand.

Chapter 45

Thea had not been awake long. She and Jack had had a long, luxurious lie-in until nearly nine o'clock. After all they were both exhausted from her surrendering her body to his with the maximum of pleasure during the night. What struck her most of all was the fact that what they did was legal, as they were husband and wife. That was a luxury which had been denied her for several years. Although there had never been a coupling between her and Piers, they had always had to be on their guard about being seen together. Any body language would give them away and if he kissed her in public it had always been a chaste, brotherly kiss. She was missing Piers dreadfully and often during her most intimate moments had made herself believe that it was Piers making love to her. Then guilt would overtake her when she thought about Jack, who did not need such unfair treatment. He would never be Piers; he was himself and quite rightly so. She could have a complete lifetime with Jack and bear more of his children. Would she still feel this way? Guilt made her play her part of the doting wife, which made Jack more amorous than ever.

'You could have been on the stage,' she told herself, giggling at the way life had made her act over the past few years. She had never thought that she could be so good at deception, having been an open book in her childhood. She then thought about the hand of deception that her parents had played and there was her answer. She had been critical of their actions when she had discussed the subject with Sabine. Now she felt a total hypocrite masking her conscience by treating Jack as if he was the only man in the world. He deserved her love and attention, for he would be returning to his regiment in twenty-four hours and then she would have a break again until the next time he came home. Who knew when he would be sent away like Piers? But could she spend a lifetime with him? Only time would be the answer to that. However, if her marriage did not work out, she knew that she could always lead a different life funded by the nest egg that her father had left her. Funnily she had not told Jack about that. That was her secret and would become the inheritance of this much wanted child. As Thea pulled back the bedclothes to go down to the basement kitchen to make them a leisurely breakfast the telephone could be heard ringing in the hallway. Putting on her warm dressing gown she tried to rise when Jack's hand reached out to pull her back to him.

'Don't,' she said to him rather sharply. 'I must get that.' He released her rather taken back by her tone of voice. Thea had never liked the sound of the telephone ever since it had brought the news of her father's death, confirming her suspicions after the newspaper article. Running down the stairs quickly she snatched up the telephone from its cradle and had to stand still for a moment to regain her breath.

'Hello?' she said after a moment. At the other end of the receiver she heard the sound of a very cultured voice speaking, but it was not one she recognized. Suddenly, she heard weeping. Something deep inside her instinctively told her that it was Clarissa Devine.

'Clarissa is that you?' she asked.

'Yes,' came the reply. Her voice had regained its self-control now. 'I have to tell you that Mary has had the baby. A girl. Mary is not at all well.' Thea stood speechless at the news. There was still no heir for Westborough Hall. How would Piers react to such news so far away from home? But regaining her composure, she said, 'How is the baby?'

'The baby is thriving. She was large but Mary could not give birth naturally so had to have an operation again. Doctor Brown feels that it would be unwise for her to have any more children. Piers will be so disappointed at such news.'

Feeling horribly dismayed at this prognosis the Countess had imparted Thea did not know what to say. Then she suddenly thought and said, 'Do you want me to come?'

'Would you?' Clarissa's voice was full of relief.

'Of course I will come,' Thea said decisively, 'as soon as I can.' There was little else she could do but go to the family who needed her the most, for were they not her own family too?

'Thank you. I hoped you would say that.' Clarissa's voice was lifeless, as if all emotion had been drained from her. She put the telephone down leaving Thea holding the receiver, wondering what she could do for the best. She did not return upstairs to give Jack the unhappy news. Making her way down to the basement kitchen she knew that she had to give herself time to think. Abstractedly she pulled crockery from cupboards, clattering as she went. There was little to eat now with rationing in full swing, but she made toast with marmalade scraped thinly across its dry surface. The butter had run out days ago. Thea decided that she would catch the latest train in the day to Worcester so that she could spend more time with Jack. She hoped that he would not feel too snubbed that she was leaving him so soon, but she had already told him that she had agreed to help the old Countess with any problems after her promise to Piers; as it was Jack would have to leave by late afternoon to return to his unit and could leave for the front at any time soon. There was no certainty in anything anymore. Thea took the toast and coffee upstairs to tell her tale of woe. He rolled over onto his back grinning happily, but her face told the unhappy story that she was about to unleash on him. Why was life so difficult? Jack had not been too pleased about the circumstances of Thea's departure, feeling that the Devines put upon her more than they should. Piers had two full-blood sisters who should do their share as far as he was concerned, but he did not want to leave Thea after a row knowing that it could be a long time before he saw her again. He thought about Mary Devine's circumstances and the birth of her child. The thought made him shudder as he touched the snug place where his own child lay. There was no way that he wanted Thea to be on her own when her time came to give birth. Perhaps the best place for her would be at

Westborough Hall surrounded by family who would look after her. He made no comment about her early departure.

'Do you think that it would be a good idea for you to go and live at the Hall for the duration of the War? I don't like the fact that you are here in London on your own,' he said, 'it is not the best place to bring up a child in case there are air raids.' His face looked grave as he thought about such things. He wanted to go to war feeling that his little family was safe. Thea looked into his honest open face, loving him a little for the care he wanted for her now that he could be going away quite soon. She laughed in order to lighten the heaviness of his thoughts. 'You are a worrier Jack,' she said, kissing his lips. 'You are probably right as always. You could come and see me there on your next leave. They won't mind.'

'Have you told them about us and the baby?' he asked, doubting that she had.

'No but I shall as soon as I know Mary is all right. It would not be right to throw it all at them straight away. It would be like throwing our happiness at them while their world is upside down with poor Mary's health.' Jack looked at Thea and smiled, 'Do you know, Mrs Carson, that you have a big heart? I suspect that is one of the reasons why I married you, that and the fact that I love you.' His eyes had misted sentimentally as he took her in his arms and made love to her all over again. And that was where they stayed until it was time to go their separate ways.

Chapter 46

Jack and Thea had travelled into central London together to catch their different trains. It had been a journey of reflection for them both. Jack had morbidly wondered if he would see his wife again and if he would ever see his unborn child. He had been overwhelmed by Thea's affection for him; in fact, since their marriage he had often wondered if she had only married him to legitimize the child that she carried, but this leave had calmed the troubled waters and he felt differently about their relationship. She could not have been more loving and giving of herself. If he was not sent away soon maybe another leave would permanently cement their relationship that had been on such a short foundation. Thea on the other hand had enjoyed her short time with Jack, but her mind was beginning to move on to events that were taking place at Westborough Hall. She wanted to satisfy herself that Clarissa had reported the situation accurately before she wrote to Piers to tell him the facts. But there was also the fact that she did not want to bother Piers too much to worry him about affairs at home which, if she were honest, he could do little about. She tried to empathise with his situation but found that she could not for she was not able to visualize what it would be like on the front line. As yet people were still calling it the Phoney War and that was how she hoped it would stay. It was time to say their goodbyes. Jack had travelled on the tube to Paddington Station to see her onto her train. He still had a couple of hours before he needed to catch his own. As it was now the custom the station heaved with uniformed personnel coming and going. There were couples who held hands and tears were shed as the journey into the unknown began for them all. Thea's train arrived early. Jack carried his wife's suitcase into the carriage and hefted it up onto one of the racks above their heads. He stayed with her for as long as possible but eventually the whistle blew, announcing the train's imminent departure as doors banged shut. Jack hugged her to him before saying, 'Write to me. I want to know everything you are doing and this young man.' His hand gently touched the small curve of Thea's normally flat stomach. It lingered there, reluctant to move, wanting to know this child more than anything but a small nugget of doubt filled his heart as his lips sought those of his wife for the very last time. Thea laughed as she pulled free of his embrace, 'Of course I will write. You will know every thought that passes through my mind.' She stroked his cheek for one last time and kissed him, and then he was gone as the whistle blew again, reminding other lovers of the imminent departure. The train began to inch forward and to gather speed but Jack kept up with it, sprinting ever faster while Thea leant out of the carriage window waving and laughing at him. As the speed of the train gathered momentum he was lost to view in a cloud of steam and the suburbs of the city flew by at an amazing pace. Thea sat in her seat gazing out at the dusk which was ever darkening, until she could see her own reflection in the glass of the window. The thought of returning to Westborough Hall did not bother her, but what she would find worried her beyond measure. The stoic old Countess was struggling to hold all the threads of life at the Hall together. Even Piers did not quite understand that his mother, who had always been so strong over the years, now just wanted a peaceful old age which she would not be able to have for the foreseeable future. At Foregate Street Station in Worcester the Devine Bentley was waiting for Thea as she descended the steps onto the pavement below, carrying her suitcase which seemed to be becoming increasingly heavier with every step that she took. There was now another chauffeur to replace Denham who had volunteered to go to war. Perkins, the new chauffeur, must have been seventy at least she thought, regarding him intently. He recognized Thea from her time staying at the Hall where he had been a gardener but, as time wore on, he had found the physical side of that too demanding; but driving the Bentley was never a chore but a pleasure to be behind the wheel of such a vehicle. He did not drive at speed as the old Countess did not hold with that, and as for distance, that was restricted by petrol rationing. It had all fallen very nicely into place for him. Quite often men of his age could feel a burden on society but he still felt needed or useful. The Devines had always been known for the care of the people who worked for them. Perkins touched his peaked cap in respect before taking Thea's suitcase from her, to place it in the boot of the car.

'Cold evening miss,' he said, opening the passenger door at the back of the car.

'Yes,' she replied, 'but I do believe that spring is on the way.'

Thea settled herself into the luxury of the back of the car and settled down for the ride to the Hall. She would be there in time for dinner. Clarissa had promised to wait for her. There was much to discuss. Perkins was not a talkative person. After their initial conversation he had returned to his usual taciturn self, but it was a situation which was favourable to both. Thea was still deep in thought knowing that once she had returned to the Hall there were many decisions to discuss and put into practice. Half an hour later they arrived but, instead of seeing the welcoming blaze of lights that normally greeted a visitor, the place appeared to be in darkness.

'Of course, the blackout,' she thought to herself. That must have been a herculean task for the staff to complete, particularly now that many of the staff had left to do War work either in the forces or on the home front. It was Clarissa who opened the front door to the Hall, something that she would never have dreamed of doing over previous decades; but it brought home to Thea how much the world was changing, not just for women or the humbler classes, but for the aristocracy as well. Perkins carried the suitcase into the hallway, but there was nobody to heft it upstairs to her room. These were certainly new times.

'Thank you Perkins,' Clarissa said, dismissing the chauffeur. Her hauteur was still intact and probably always would be. It was too ingrained to disappear completely. Thea smiled at the old woman, who responded by kissing her cheek. How times had changed. On Thea's first visit to the Hall she had been in total awe of this woman, probably fear was the correct word to use.

'I gather dinner is ready, but I shall detain it for a few minutes while you go and refresh yourself after your journey.'

'Thank you. I won't be long.' Thea lifted her case and carried it up the stairs to her usual bedroom. Just a few minutes later she entered the small dining room where the table was set for the two of them; Clarissa was already seated, awaiting the young woman who she badly needed to help with the colossal task which lay ahead of them. Dinner was not served but set out on the hot plates which had been used for breakfast over a number of years. This was another innovation which surprised Thea, but it was one that Clarissa again had grown used to over time.

'Shall I serve you Clarissa?' Thea asked, as she now used her hostess's Christian name.

'Yes please my dear,' she replied with some manner of warmth for the young woman who had risen in her estimation over time. They ate in a comfortable silence for some time before Thea asked about Mary and the baby.

'The doctor believes Mary should recover from the birth more easily this time unless complications set in. As for the baby, she is thriving. We have not named her as such yet. Mary has not bonded with her, but I expect that she will in due course. Betty has been a great help in that area.'

'Has Piers been told of the baby's arrival?' Thea asked.

'We have sent a telegram to his regiment, but whether he has received it I do not know. It is so chaotic out there, I believe. Though, I have no doubt that he will be disappointed that it is another girl. All aristocrats want an heir. It is different for the Royals these days. Look at King George, for example. He has two daughters, which makes Elizabeth the heir to the throne.'

'Clarissa, I have so much to tell you about what I have been thinking about the Hall and the estate in general. I believe that we should make some changes until the War is over and Piers is home again. But firstly I must tell you about my situation. I am married to Jack Carson. It happened very suddenly because of the War. It is happening all the time now. However, there is one other thing.' Thea paused looking at the reaction of the older woman, but there was no look of surprise or condemnation on Clarissa's part.

'You are pregnant,' the Countess said without rancour.

'Yes,' Thea breathed heavily. 'I know it is a complication under the circumstances but–'

'What is one more in the nursery while we have staff to look after it?' the dowager Countess said sagely, 'but we will have our work cut out to run the estate with most of the able-bodied men going to war.' The two women left the small dining room to return to the small sitting room. The Countess wanted her nightcap of a large brandy which helped her to sleep but, before she disappeared, Thea wanted to tell her what had passed through her mind about making the hall and estate more manageable. She dispensed the brandy herself and placed it on the occasional table next to Clarissa. Clearing her throat to begin, she said, 'There aren't enough staff to run such a big house as this. A lot of the women servants have left to go into the War effort, so I wondered if we closed most of the rooms and placed the furniture under dust sheets; it would be more practical. We could live in the places which are mostly used now. That way there would be less work to do. Even the dower house could be closed for the time being until the War is over. Any servants there could be brought back to the Hall. Then there is the estate. The country is expected to grow more food and we could have Land Girls to help like they did in the last war. It is all the talk as the way forward at the moment. Even the young boys who help on the land will go off to war if it lasts much longer. It was all done during the Great War. Women can do anything they want these days.' Thea stopped as she looked for a response from the old woman. She had drunk half of her brandy and Thea thought that she had gone to sleep, but her eyes opened and she looked at the young woman who sat in earnest in front of her. 'I could not agree more,' she said. 'We will start putting the whole thing into operation this week.' With that she consumed the rest of her brandy and rose to her feet, just a trifle unsteadily, and after bidding Thea goodnight she left the room in pursuit of her bed. Thea could not help but smile at the scenario she had just witnessed vowing that she would begin the day after tomorrow the task that she had highlighted. However, the next day she would go and see Mary and the new baby to find out what the situation was so that she could write to Piers to put his mind at rest. She had also promised to write to Jack informing him of what was happening and to tell him that she loved him. She knew that he was a good man and she owed him that to give him comfort before he was sent to a foreign field. She wondered why life could be so difficult, particularly when it was none of the country's fault to be at war with Germany.

It was time for bed too, she thought, rising to her feet tired from travelling and the exertions of the day. Her hand touched the place where her child lay and she smiled. She was looking forward to its birth. She knew that she would have to recover quickly after the birth in order to gain control of all that was happening at the Hall. It had become her responsibility to keep it in good order for Piers's return. The thought that he might never return she kept secretly locked away in a place that she never visited in her mind. She was one of millions of women who had to think positively about their menfolk. All they wanted was to keep them safe.

'God keep you both and protect you,' she said softly to herself, thinking of the two men who fought for attention in her thoughts. Yet deep down it was Piers who held her heart, and always would.

Chapter 47

Thea had tossed and turned for most of the night. There was just too much on her mind which had been in turmoil deciding what was best to do on many levels. She glanced at the clock on her bedside and was pleased to see that it was time to get up, but she was still tired from lack of sleep. It would be so easy to roll over and snatch another hour. However, she rose deciding what she would do straight after breakfast. It was obvious that she had to see Mary and the new baby. She touched her own stomach where her child lay, wondering what it would be like to hold her own baby in her arms for the first time. Her thoughts turned once more to Mary. Again she had had a bad experience at the birth, but Thea hoped that everything would be different from now on and when Piers did return, either on leave or at the end of the War, he would find a wife who had fully recovered from her mental and physical traumas; but whether there was another baby, an heir, that was a different matter. Time was always said to be the greatest healer of all.

Thea found the nursery a hive of activity as the daily routine began. Young Jane was proving to be a boisterous child. She was now walking and kept her nursemaid fully employed by her antics as she opened cupboards, pulling out the contents and strewing everything around the floor. Nanny sat nursing the new baby, of which only a fluffy dark cloud of hair could be seen above the edge of the shawl. The child had just been fed and was contentedly drifting back to sleep. Thea noticed a frown crease Nanny's forehead at her appearance. It was well known amongst the nursery staff that Nanny did not like the routine in her domain to be disrupted at any time and this unheralded appearance of Thea was not acceptable. Thea was made of sterner stuff not allowing the Nanny's demeanour to faze her mood. Before too long her own baby would join the Devine children and nothing would prevent her from visiting then.

'May I hold her? 'Thea asked as her head bent over the sleeping infant, wondering who she looked like. Nanny made a moue of disapproval with her mouth before allowing this young woman to take the baby from her arms. Thea gently rocked the child, humming a lullaby that she loved. Thinking for a moment the title of the music came to her. It was by Brahms and her own Nanny had sung it to her as a young child. The child snuffled, stretching its limbs before falling back into a deep sleep. Thea bent to kiss the soft down of the baby's cheek. She was beautiful with a look of her father, even at such a tender age.

'Can I put her down now, miss?' the nursery maid, asked ready to take the precious bundle back to the night nursery. She was afraid of Nanny's tongue if she did not keep to the strictly regimented routine.

'Of course,' Thea smiled, reluctantly handing over the infant. Having retreated from the nursery floor, Thea's next port of call was to see Mary, who was still recovering from the birth. Tiptoeing silently along the bedroom floor she arrived at Mary's door. Putting her ear to listen for any sounds she then turned the knob before quietly entering the room. As she made her advances across the carpet she was met by Betsy, who put her finger to her lips before indicating Mary's sleeping form. Thea sat by the bed looking at her friend's wan face, showing the torment had taken the toll of Mary's frail body. The bedroom door had closed behind Betsy but Mary stirred and woke from her much needed slumber. Looking up she saw Thea sitting beside her; both smiled at their reunion, now as friends once more after their difficult relationship of months before.

'Thea, how lovely to see you; is this a flying visit?' Thea bent to kiss Mary's cheek. 'No Mary I have come to stay for a while.' She did not want to tell her that she would be at the Hall until Piers's return.

Mary's hand touched Thea's rounded stomach. 'Is that Piers's baby?' she asked with a measure of insight making Thea turn her head away to hide the redness of her cheeks. 'No Mary, Piers is my brother not my lover,' she said, wondering what her sister-in-law would say next.

'I know Piers loves you,' Mary continued, 'more than a brother should.'

'Hush Mary, you do not know what you are saying. I am married to Jack Carson. It is his baby.'

'But I have seen the way Piers looks at you. He never looked at me that way in all the time we have been married and I have borne him two children.'

'This is all a fantasy,' Thea said, looking at the woman lying in the bed. She wondered if she had said anything to other people.

'I have not told anyone about this Thea, for they would think that I was mad. I am not mad but I see things that other people do not.' Thea made no comment but drew her chair closer to the bed; taking Mary's hand she hoped that the conversation would end, and so it did as Mary closed her eyes and returned to the land of sleep. Thea looked at the pale face before her wondering how she would recover from the birth of the child. The signs were not good, but she prayed that Piers's wife would recover. However, these thoughts concerning herself and Piers had unnerved her, making her wonder who else had noticed the feelings that passed between them. They had tried every way they could to keep their desire for each other a secret. Leaving Mary to sleep, Thea tiptoed from the room to start her next project of the day which was to find out what was happening out on the estate and within the house. She would then report her findings to Clarissa and, together, they would make decisions for the immediate future of the Hall.

Chapter 48

The Phoney War ended abruptly on 10th May 1940 and the people who believed that everything would fizzle out were made to change their minds. The Allies had believed that time was on their side and had hoped to postpone going on the offensive. Blockading strategies were thought to be the best form of defence, but Hitler's forces commenced the Blitzkrieg by crossing the Belgian border. Forward elements of the British Expeditionary Forces were cut off and others were pushed back. The British tried to launch counter-attacks but to no avail. Lord Gort could see that the Channel ports were threatened on the French coast and ordered the retreat to Dunkirk where the evacuation was to begin to save the lives of the Allied forces.

Now that the War had started in earnest people at home listened to the frequent news bulletins on their wireless sets, anxious for the safety of their loved ones. On the home front the news at Westborough Hall could not have been worse. Mary had succumbed to an infection for she had not healed properly after the birth of little Maudie, as she had since been named. The infection had spread and nothing could be done for her. When she could, Thea stayed with the Countess holding her hand trying to instil some strength into her fading life; but eventually Mary died in her sleep in the middle of May.

Both Thea and Clarissa were senseless with grief for the waste of a life; a life that had hardly been lived in recent years. There were also the two little girls who had never properly known a mother and now never would. As for their father, he was too far away fighting a war which was a threat to freedom. A telegram had been sent to Piers's unit but nobody was really sure about the state of chaos that existed in northern France and Belgium, and no reply had been received from him. The news bulletins had reported on the state of both British and French forces, as well as the casualties and prisoners of war. The bulldog spirit of Britain rallied to the defence of its own as the little boats as well as the larger vessels sailed across the English Channel, bringing home over two hundred thousand survivors, some of whom were French and Belgian, to the safety of these shores.

Mary Devine, Countess of Westborough, was buried on a bright, sunny day at the end of May. There were few mourners in the old church for there were few people who had known her in her brief marriage to the Earl. The dowager Countess sitting erect in her seat looked straight ahead of her with a dignity she could always muster on such occasions. Surrounding her were Minty and Diana, who had both travelled alone from their respective homes, and Thea whose eyes were red rimmed as she wept for the waste of a life, for the friend she had nearly lost through trivial arguments, and for the two motherless little girls who would never know a mother's love. Her hand felt the growing bump and she vowed to be the best mother in the world to her child and also to Piers's daughters. Mary's mortal remains were taken to lie in the Mausoleum alongside long-dead members of the Devine family. The sense of futility of such a young woman's untimely death hung heavily in the air as the last prayers were uttered and the door into the dark interior of her last resting place was firmly locked against the intrusion of the outer world. There was nothing to be done but to return to Westborough Hall, where a small gathering would unite in their grief and lack of understanding at the cruel world all around them.

By 4th of June the evacuation of Dunkirk was complete and there was no news of the whereabouts of Piers or many of his comrades in arms. Another sense of gloom descended on the occupants of the Hall as they waited with bated breath to hear from any of the sources who would provide some news on the matter. How could people endure such sadness in this topsy-turvey world, Thea thought, as the days passed; but the indomitable human spirit seemed to soldier on despite everything that was happening. Just days later a brown envelope addressed to the Countess was delivered to the Hall on a bright summer morning which would defy the trepidation in the hearts of so many. It had been Thea who had opened the front door to the telegram boy, whose face was flushed from the exertion of peddling so far to deliver the news. Thea, hands trembling and heart tumbling in her chest, gave the boy sixpence for his trouble and closed the door on him. The boy grinned gratefully at such generosity before returning at a much slower pace to consider how he would spend the money. There was no Countess to open the envelope but, out of courtesy, Thea went to find Clarissa, who was writing letters in the privacy of the small sitting room.

'Clarissa, there is a telegram for Mary,' Thea said, her voice full of trepidation. Clarissa looked up from her letter writing and took the envelope from Thea. Her face showed no emotion as she steadily took her paper knife and slit open the seal. Taking her time she unfolded the piece of paper very slowly as if she was keeping the news at bay for as long as she could. Thea could feel herself on the edge of tears as she wanted to know the contents. Finally the Countess looked up with rheumy eyes and uttered the words, 'Missing in action.'

'It doesn't mean that he is dead,' Thea said, trying to be as positive as she could be. 'We have all heard the news of the chaos out there. He could have been taken as a prisoner of war.' Clarissa's eyes watered as she took the hand of this girl who had come to mean so much to her, perhaps at times more than her own daughters, who did not visit too often now that they had families of their own.

'Yes, that could be the case,' she said, clinging to any vestige of hope that was thrown her way. Both women fell into each other's arms and remained that way until they heard footsteps and infant chatter which heralded the advance of young Jane, who gripped tightly onto the hand of Nanny who had brought her to see her grandmother. Silently Clarissa wondered whether this child was already an orphan and what the future would hold for her and her sister Maudie. Thea slipped away, allowing grandmother and child to have time together while she tried to make sense of her broken heart. This reality was what she had feared most since Piers' departure. She knew that other women shared her dread but, strangely, that did not make her heartache any easier to bear. Silently she prayed that Piers was alive somewhere and would come back to them one day. Hope was something to hold onto. There was no proof that he was dead.

Despite the sombre atmosphere at Westborough Hall the days flew past at a feverish pace. Thea had masked her unhappiness by keeping herself busy to allow her mind to concentrate on the immediate and not the events that had filled their thoughts in recent weeks. It was during this time that she suddenly became aware of feeling pains that she had not experienced before. When she had visited the doctor he had laughed at her, telling her that her body was becoming ready for the birth and would arrive sooner rather than later. He had been fully aware of the distress the Devine family was experiencing, as was the local area who loved the family that had been part of the lives of families for centuries. Thea was now very large and cumbersome. The early July heat did not help the situation either. All she wanted was the birth of her child to be over so that some normality could return to life at the Hall. There was just too much for her to do when she should be shouldering the responsibility for the estate. As it was it all hung too heavily on Clarissa's stoic shoulders. But on the other hand she wanted to be able to hold this child in her arms and give it a mother's love that was so denied to Mary's infant daughters.

After the news of Piers missing in action, Jack had arrived at the Hall unexpectedly. He had been granted a thirty-six hour leave before his regiment was leaving for an undisclosed destination. He had hoped that the impending birth was over so that he could see his child before his departure, but instead he had found a very subdued wife. Thea had tried her best to give her husband the attention he deserved but the atmosphere at the Hall was melancholy to say the least. The hours they spent together did not lighten the gloom which shrouded them. As it was Jack and Thea did not know when they would see each other again and any joy that should have been theirs at such a reunion evaporated as Thea knew that the arrival of the baby was imminent. There was just too much happening. When the time came for Jack to leave there was an air of resignation about them, a relief that the suspense caused by the chain of events surrounding life at the Hall would release them both from having to pretend that everything was all right.

'I love you,' Jack said as he took his wife into his arms for the last time.

Thea, anxious to send Jack away with a feeling of love and tenderness, submitted to his embrace feeling tremendous guilt at the way events had been between them.

'Keep safe for us Jack. I love you too.'

'Write to me,' he said almost desperately as he kissed her passionately.

'I will and as soon as this one arrives you will be the first to know,' Thea said, placing her hand over her extended stomach. Jack placed his large hand over hers and together they felt the child kick as they were all united in the flesh. He did not voice his fears but only hoped that he would at some time in the future see the baby that he had helped create. They took one last lingering kiss that would have to last them until the next meeting, where and whenever that would be. It was a very uncertain world as they all knew. The car containing precious petrol drew away, taking Jack to Worcester to catch his train without Thea going to send him on his way. It was just too risky with the imminent birth. He sat looking through the back window of the vehicle watching Thea grow smaller and smaller until she was out of sight. And then it was that he wept for the little family that he had wanted so badly and, deep in his heart, he felt that he would never see again.

Chapter 49

A week after Jack's departure life carried on in much the same way as before except for one thing. A visitor came driving up to the front door of the Hall. He cut a dashing figure in his fashionable suit and the trilby which was placed at a jaunty angle on his head. Even in these times of thrift and rationing anyone could see that he oozed wealth; his sporty Bentley was the icing on the cake. He strode around looking at the property here and there, his eyes gleaming at what he saw. He was in no hurry to knock at the door for he was drinking in every facet of the old building. Just at that moment the family car came around the side of the building and pulled alongside the vehicle of the visitor. The old chauffeur, Perkins, opened the car door, removing his peaked cap of which he was so proud.

'May I help you sir?' he enquired politely, but not liking the arrogant display of behaviour that he witnessed. The visitor looked as if he owned the place; there was a cockiness about his demeanour which puzzled the old man. Before the stranger could answer the front door opened and the dignified upright figure of the dowager Countess appeared, followed by the more ungainly figure of Thea who had come to see Clarissa off on her brief journey into Worcester, to attend some pressing business.

'Who are you?' the old woman asked, straight to the point and not liking visitors who came unannounced.

'I'll deal with this,' Thea cut in, not wishing Clarissa to be late for her appointment.

'Are you sure? I don't like the look of him. He looks too flashy for our world.' Thea could not suppress a smile for Clarissa, still retained a snobbish side. It was too ingrained into her character for she was of the old school. 'No, I will deal with it. I don't want you to be late for your appointment.'

She kissed the old woman on her furry cheek and watched her descend the steps to the awaiting car where the door was opened for her to sit in the rear of the vehicle. She had not given their visitor another glance. Thea waved until they had reached far into the distance and then turned her attention once more to their visitor, whom she found looking her up and down but his expression was inscrutable. Thea remained where she was wondering what all this was about. The visitor, however, had seen a very attractive young woman who was heavily pregnant; but his thoughts did not end there, for he wondered if the information he had been given was incorrect and his visit had been in vain.

'How can I help you?' Thea asked at last, giving the man her undivided attention.

'My name is Neil Devine. May I come inside please?' Thea looked doubtful but was curious, for the man had the same surname as the family.

'I won't eat you I promise, but I do feel that I do need to speak to someone here.' Throwing caution to the winds Thea retraced her steps inside leading the way into the small sitting room where a fire still blazed even on this warm summer's day. Indicating a seat she rang the bell pull which summoned Polly from the kitchen. After ordering afternoon tea, Thea dropped exhausted into a high-backed armchair, feeling that she might never get up again.

'What can we do for you?' she asked, her curiosity now aroused. Neil Devine was not sure how to broach the subject to this young woman whose identity escaped him. He assumed that she must be the young Countess and the rumours that he had heard were after all untrue. But if he did not take the bull by the horns, he would not know either.

'Are you the Countess?' he asked bluntly. Just at that moment Polly entered with a heavily laden tray which she placed on a low occasional table next to Thea.

'Thank you Polly,' she said.

'Shall I pour for you madam? You look done in if you don't mind me saying.'

Thea was tempted by the offer but felt that she would have to rouse herself for she wanted this man gone before Clarissa's return, but she was also curious to know the man's business.

'Thank you Polly but that will be all,' she said. Once the drawing room door had been closed she transferred her attention to her unwanted guest.

'No, I am not the Countess,' she said and heard a sigh emanate from the man. 'Can you tell me your business here please?' She was far from happy.

'I am Neil Devine and I believe that I am the next heir, after my father Matthew, to the title and the estate. With what I have heard I could even be the new Earl. Can you tell me who you are?' he asked rather insolently. Thea was not pleased by what she had heard but she was determined to put this man straight on many of the facts. 'I am Thea Carson, the half-sister of the Earl. The old lady you saw is the Earl's mother the dowager Countess. The Countess has passed away in childbirth just a few weeks ago. As for the Earl he is not dead, just missing in action. Now then, I want to know who gave you such information.' Neil Devine smiled at Thea, making her feel uncomfortable. For all they knew Piers could be dead and suddenly they would be without a home.

'I am not at liberty to divulge such information, but I am told that my branch of the Devine family should inherit if the present Earl is deceased and has not managed to produce a son so far. My lawyer has contact with the family lawyer of this branch of the family. I believe his name to be Fellowes.' At this revelation a shiver ran down Thea's back. Silently she prayed that Piers was truly in the land of the living for many reasons. 'And how far back do you have to go to show that you are the true heir? My father, the previous Earl, had no siblings.'

Neil Devine looked at Thea with contempt. 'Our branch of the family has always been aware of our closeness to the title for the current earls have held tentatively to the title without many heirs to fall back on. I think it is our right to know what is happening.'

Thea summoned her greatest measure of dignity when she replied, 'And I think you should be someone who respects the fact that this is a house of mourning after the death of the Countess and the current Earl has not been declared dead. And now if you would not mind leaving I am sure you will be informed if there is any news pertinent to your position. As you will expect, we hope the news will be good for the sake of our family.' Heaving her bulky body from the chair with considerable difficulty, Thea's face was flushed by the exertions she had made, coupled with the heat from the blazing fire. She indicated that the conversation was at an end. The tea that she had failed to pour was going cold in the pot while she once more rang for Polly to show the gentleman out. Neil Devine knew that he had started something here this day and, like a dog with a bone, he was not going to give up without a fight until he heard that his cousin several times removed had been declared alive.

'I won't let this go, you know,' Neil Devine spluttered. 'We will be told the truth and then we will claim our true inheritance.'

'We all want the truth Mr Devine. I want to know that my brother is alive and well. Until that day you have no claim on Westborough. I am sure the family lawyers will keep us all informed of events. Now I will say good day to you.'

Thea turned her back on the man allowing Polly to show him to the front door. She did not want him to see the tears that were beginning to well in her eyes. He had touched a raw spot with his business and the intrusion into their lives, one of mourning on possibly two accounts.

'Good afternoon sir,' Polly said sweetly, closing the front door swiftly on the back of the retreating man who mumbled under his breath at the treatment he had received. Polly knew where her loyalties lay. Several hours later Thea had related the conversation to Clarissa who, in her stoical way, had decided that she would telephone Earnest Fellowes the following day to get to the bottom of the matter. And that was precisely what she did. Earnest Fellowes was reluctant to discuss the matter over the telephone but had agreed to travel to Westborough Hall at the convenience of the dowager Countess. It was not a great problem to leave his legal practice for a day as he was amply financially rewarded by this wealthy family for his trouble. After clearing his diary three days later he arrived at the Hall immaculately dressed in his city suit complete with leather briefcase, walking cane and a trilby to complete the ensemble. He was directed to the library where he was received by the dowager Countess and Thea. He noticed a marked change in the Countess since their last meeting after the death of her husband. Despite the fact that she had aged slightly, her upright stature as usual was almost regal, a trait of the upper classes, but her demeanour had softened making her almost human. He wondered if the humiliation that James Devine had wrought on his wife had been the cause, little suspecting that the young woman sitting by her side had been a major factor in this transformation. That was also a huge surprise that the younger daughter of Beatrice Cavendish should look so at ease in this establishment.

'Well, I must now tell you that the Earl visited me in my chambers just before he left with his regiment,' Earnest Fellowes intoned in his rather nasal voice, making the people who listened to him flinch slightly before they became used to his delivery. 'He wanted everything to be legally settled so that there would be no disputes of any kind in case of his death. He did not wish to inflict such thoughts upon you but he knew he had to be practical for war is so unpredictable. Before I give you the facts I have been in touch with the firm of solicitors of Neil and Matthew Devine complaining that the gentleman in question had no business coming to the Hall to upset you all. I have requested that he leaves the business side of affairs to the lawyers to communicate if there is ever a need.' Clarissa shuffled her chair annoyed at the audacity of Neil Devine, but equally feeling angry with her own son who had not kept faith with his family by revealing all the facts. Thea just awaited the news that was to be delivered. She knew that Piers had revealed some of his concerns to her before his departure to the front. Fellowes cleared his throat before continuing.

'As you now know Matthew Devine is the heir to the earldom. Of course his lordship was hoping for the new baby to be his heir but that was not to be. In such circumstances he knew that he had to make arrangements for the welfare of his family who would have to leave the Hall. At the moment we don't know about the Earl's whereabouts but I do not see that it would hurt to tell you his wishes. I believe that you have all suffered enough emotional difficulties as it is.' He paused for a moment drinking deeply from his glass of Malvern water before continuing.

'He has removed the dower house from the estate and placed it in Miss Cavendish's name.' He glanced up and looked directly at Thea and then promptly went red noticing for the first time the huge bump denoting her pregnancy. Thea noted his discomfort and saved him further trouble.

'I'm Mrs Carson now.'

'Quite so,' he said, moving on with his information. 'Your ladyship will live with her and his children. He would like Mrs Carson to be their guardian until they reach their majority. There are sufficient funds to finance such proceedings.' The lawyer replaced his papers in his briefcase, took another sip of his water and waited for a response. It was not long coming.

'And if Piers returns?' Clarissa said.

'Well things will remain the same as they are now. Mr Devine will not be bothering you again unless the circumstances change. I will let you know, of course, how things stand should the present situation change.' He did not want to wait for questions for he had delivered all the facts. 'And now, dear ladies, if you will excuse me I have to catch my train, but please do not hesitate to contact me if other problems arise.' Fellowes was eager to be gone. The whole business was too sensitive to linger too long. He did not wish to mention the death of the Earl again. These were difficult times when the news was beginning to be full of casualties in the war zones. He rose to his feet which made Thea stand rather unsteadily as she made her way to the bell pull to summon Polly.

'Thank you Mr Fellowes, for putting our minds at rest,' Thea said. He smiled his goodbyes, casting one last glance at Clarissa who was still deep in thought. Thea followed him to the library door where she saw Polly waiting with the lawyer's cane and trilby hat. The girl opened the front door and he had gone, leaving Thea to return to Clarissa so that they could discuss this news further.

Chapter 50

At the beginning of July Doctor Brown was proved to be correct. Thea had experienced an exhausting day in the fields overseeing the Land Girls and their activities; this was much against Clarissa's advice. Thea was feeling vulnerable. Mary's death from childbirth had been on her mind a lot lately; she was not fanciful by nature but she was now feeling pains in her lower back. The pain stopped her in her tracks and all she wanted to do was to lie down, but there was nowhere near by except for the great horse-drawn wagon. Freya, one of the Land Girls, saw Thea's problem and ran to her to help. She was the oldest of seven children and, as she grew older, she had come to recognize the onset of childbirth.

'Come on Thea to the wagon. Have your pains started? You should not have come today,' she admonished in a caring way, helping her charge to sit on the end of the old cart. It had not struck Thea initially that it could be the start of her labour, but she took the good-natured help gratefully wondering how she would return to the Hall in her condition. Perhaps she would deliver the baby in the fields like some native in foreign parts. The thought almost made her laugh, but another pain came making her gasp. Yet she need not have panicked for Freya had the situation in hand. She had organized for the cart to be driven as far as it could go and then someone would run for help from the Hall. Thea witnessed these proceedings but could not quite understand what was happening as the pains gathered momentum. As the wagon slowly joined the road which led to the Hall Freya, young and fit, ran ahead to warn everybody about what was happening. Clarissa came out of the library to see what all the commotion was about, only to be shouted at that she had to ring for the doctor.

'But why?' she asked rather stupidly until someone mentioned Thea's name and her predicament. Clarissa shouted at Polly who was passing. She had remembered the old bath chair that had been used years ago by an elderly relative of the family. Polly ran to find it stuck in the corner of the conservatory. It was dilapidated and covered in cobwebs but it would do the job. At last Thea was bundled into the Great Hall where she lay in considerable pain on one of the sofas. Eventually she was helped upstairs to her bedroom while Nanny, fully cognizant of the situation, went into active mode to organize the whole proceedings. Betty Drew was no longer available to help for she had moved to a new position after the demise of the Countess. Clarissa wasted no time in telephoning the doctor, but it was the midwife who answered as the doctor was out on a call. She assured Clarissa that she would be straight over but would like to see Thea in bed when she arrived.

Dropping the telephone back into its cradle Clarissa turned to Thea, 'You have to go to bed my dear. Polly will help you.' Thea looked into the kind eyes of Piers's mother just as Nanny had descended the stairs. Between them the two women supported Thea up the stairs and into her bedroom. The pains were coming more frequently now but Penny Jordan, the midwife, had arrived. She had ridden like the wind along the country lanes to be there in time. Parking her ancient bicycle against the front wall of the Hall she stood for a moment to try and regain her breath. The afternoon was hot and her face was red from the exertion of her ride from the village. Clarissa opened the front door to the young woman and gave directions to find Thea's room. Taking two steps at a time in her haste, she was met by Nanny at the head of the stairs.

'I think that the baby will be here very soon despite it being a first baby. Thea is a very fit young woman.' She paused checking what she was going to say next, but it was not her business to make comparisons between Thea and the Countess. Penny Jordan entered Thea's bedroom, placed her medical bag on a chair and went to examine the mother-to-be, who was anxious for the whole ordeal to be over and done with. She had no time to linger in bed, knowing that she had too much to do.

'Be patient, just relax. Your baby is well on the way Thea. You are doing fine.' Downstairs in the sitting room Clarissa sat waiting for the news. She knew deep down that Thea would be all right but after the problems that the Countess had experienced, there was always that niggle of doubt. But Thea was made of sterner stuff. It was almost that she possessed Clarissa's genes for stoicism, but of course that was nonsense the old woman rebuked herself. Only a few hours later Scarlett Mary Carson entered the world crying lustily at the indignity of the whole carry-on. Thea, exhausted but triumphant, held her daughter to her breast, proudly thanking the Almighty for her safe delivery.

'You did well,' Penny Jordan said, grinning at a tired Thea. 'Time for a rest, my girl,' she said. Thea smiled sleepily in response and turned her head into the pillow, drifting into an exhausting sleep, promising herself that tomorrow she would start getting to know her daughter and write to Jack to tell him that he was a father at last. The following morning Doctor Brown drove up to the Hall to see his patient. Penny Jordan had given him all the details of the birth and how well their patient had done. He had been feeling lately that his reputation might be damaged after the catastrophe of the Countess's death, but she had not reacted well at either of the births of her daughters whereas Thea Carson was a strong young woman as had just been proved. His heart had been far lighter on this journey than on the previous occasions he had recently visited the Hall. Now, as he looked at mother and child, he smiled. 'You have done well Mrs Carson,' he encouraged, 'a quick birth does not weaken you too much, but I would stay in bed for a few more days to gather your full strength and then gradually rise for short periods of time. This will also help you bond with your daughter. I know how busy you all are here at the Hall. A lot seems to be falling on your young shoulders.'

'I already love my daughter Doctor Brown, but we are no busier than the rest of the country,' she said, thinking how the war effort had claimed everybody in some way or another. Doctor Brown thought otherwise, knowing how short staffed the Hall was. This was a stalwart young lady, he mused, and the Devines were lucky to have her in their midst; but he was determined that she would have her quota of rest before she started back to her duties. 'I'll be back to see you in a day or two,' he said.

He made his farewells but could not but be affected by a newborn baby cradled in its mother's arms. Even after all the years that he had given to his profession he was almost moved to tears by the arrival of a new life and the wonders of nature. Life threw many things at him, but this was the best.

Two days later, Thea sat up in bed thwarted by the level of inactivity that tied her to her room. Young Scarlett had been removed to the nursery at night to give her mother a good night's sleep, but during the day she slept in her crib by Thea's bedside where she could gaze, eyes wide with wonder, watching every movement and listening to every sound that the infant made. She was so grateful for the safe delivery of her daughter and felt how blessed she had been, while others like Mary had had such a difficult time. On her bedside table lay an envelope addressed to Jack Carson. She had taken her time to write the few lines that lay on the page. They had been words of pure joy but what lay behind such thoughts was the fact that she could barely conjure up Jack's face in her mind's eye. He had only been present in her life but a few weeks before, but they had had such little time together in their brief union as husband and wife that she felt that Scarlett was hers alone. But he was a man faced with the uncertainty of war and so she had run the full emotional gambit as a loving, dutiful wife, in order to help him to face the unknown. In truth it was Piers who truly held her heart.

She had written:

My darling Jack,

How much I miss you and pray for your safety every day. Now I write to tell you of the birth of your beautiful daughter Scarlett Mary, named after Scarlett O'Hara in 'Gone with the Wind'. That was the best film that I ever saw, one more little fact that you did not know about me, dearest Jack.

I hope this finds you safe and well and you can come home to us soon where we will be waiting for you.

Love and kisses from us both.

Your loving Thea and Scarlett

Thea had certainly been emotional when she had written the words as she thought about the brave doing their duty for their homeland, but she was guilt-ridden as she thought more deeply about her relationship with Jack. She wanted him to be safe but did not know whether she could live with him once the War was over. How strange and difficult life could be.

Chapter 51

As the late summer turned into autumn and the hues of the leaves changed into a radiance of colour, Thea was fully fit again after the birth of young Scarlett. She had returned to the full-time occupation of seeing to the running of the estate with only the limited workforce that was left to them. The Land Girls had become a blessing. They had worked for long hours bringing in crops and hay through the late summer weeks making full use of the double summer time. Their banter and good humour was infectious and they had drawn everybody onto their side; even Clarissa was good humoured whenever she was in their company, albeit a rare occurrence. They had been billeted out to the tenant farmers who occasionally had to disregard some of the girls' antics and rich language, but their hearts were always in the right place. The tenant farms were run by the older generation or sons who were not old enough to go to war, but there were also still the fully fit sons who were left on the land if a family could send others in their place. It was a case of everybody pulling together, to help each other out when times were difficult and there were plenty of those occasions. Thea had found that she had to keep some distance between herself and the Land Girls now that she had taken charge in Piers's absence. Her speedy recovery had allowed her to return to work quite quickly, but she knew that Doctor Brown had been correct to make her rest and regain her strength. The time had allowed her to bond with Scarlett, who was a lovely baby but with a character of her own despite her tender age. The nursery was constantly a hive of industry with three very young children to administer to. Jane was now the difficult one for she was running about boisterously while the babies slept. Thea, with her limited time, tried to mother the two little girls, giving them love; but her tender heart was tugged in the direction of her own daughter. It had been weeks after her short letter to Jack when a reply came, expressing his delight at becoming a father for the first time and wished he could see them both. It had now been revealed that he was in North Africa with his unit, but their true destination was secret. Yet he was safe, which happened to be the most important thing. The not knowing whether Piers was dead or alive had left a feeling of insecurity and despondency over the Hall despite the fact that life went on as normally as possible with a country at war. Clarissa was doing her best to be stoical as was her nature. Her relationship with Thea was still growing closer as she witnessed what the girl had done to keep the Hall and estate running as efficiently as it did, with all the limitations that war would allow. She had become a surrogate daughter in the absence of Minty and Diana.

At the end of September Thea received a letter from Beatrice desiring to see her granddaughter. Clarissa had changed so much over the past few years, but the sudden appearance of Thea's mother at the Hall would never be acceptable, so other plans had to be made. It was difficult for Thea to leave the Hall for a length of time so a visit to Devon was out of the question. To take a small child on a train which would be packed to capacity with military personnel was unthinkable, so Beatrice decided to travel to Worcester to see her daughter and granddaughter. She was going to stay overnight. It had all been arranged. Thea would be driven to Worcester by Perkins and take the nursery maid with her. All this had been a difficult decision, for petrol rationing restricted movement, but to justify the use of the petrol they were to do business for the estate in the city. It was so like military manoeuvres that sometimes Thea wondered if it was worth all the problems that it entailed. However, like everyone else they had to play their part. Thea stood at the bottom of the steps that led up to Foregate Street Station awaiting the arrival of her mother, who was to stay in the Swan Inn in the city. As Beatrice walked down the steps carrying a brown leather suitcase, Thea could not help but notice how well her mother looked. Her face was lightly tanned after spending the summer in the seaside air of Devon, but there was something else that Thea could not quite explain. There was certainly a radiance, a happiness about her which had not been apparent since her father had been alive; she was also fashionably attired despite the effects of clothes rationing. Falling into each other's arms they held on tightly for a few moments, knowing that they were so happy to see each other after so long. Since James Devine's death they had spent more time apart than together. Belle, the nursery maid, stood a little distance away holding the sleeping Scarlett. Thea stretched out her arms to take her daughter, carrying the beautiful child to her mother. Beatrice pulled back the shawl to look at the face of the sleeping infant before planting a kiss on the peachy skin of her cheek.

'She's beautiful, Thea,' Beatrice said in enraptured tones. Thea, like any young mother, smiled at the compliment and another surge of love swept through her. 'She is beautiful. I love her so much.' Beatrice noticed the healthy glow which coloured her daughter's cheeks. She had never seen Thea look so happy in a long time.

'You have not told me about Jack,' she said.

'There is not much to tell, really. We have not had a lot of time together, but he is a good man. He is thrilled by Scarlett's arrival.'

'He must be. It is so hard for them too, to be away from their loved ones, not knowing their children. If only this war was over then.' There was nothing more to say. It was a thought uttered across the land. A little while later, having found a tearoom where they could talk, they discussed family and personal matters. The baby lay fast asleep in Beatrice's arms as mother and daughter relished this rare time together.

'You are happy, Mama,' Thea observed reverting back to her childhood name for her mother.

'I am, Thea. I wanted to tell you personally that I have met someone, someone very special.' Their heads bent closer together over their half-filled cups of tea and tray of cakes.

'Who is he?' Thea asked, her curiosity fully aroused.

'He is a local farmer who is older than myself, a widower and he wants to marry me. His name is Michael Fullerton.'

'And you are going to marry him?'

'Yes,' said Beatrice happily, 'I love him.'

'But you loved Daddy,' Thea said not unkindly.

'Yes and I still do, but you can love two people in totally different ways.'

'Yes,' said Thea, 'I suppose you can.' The statement had made her think about her own situation, but she said nothing. Taking hold of her mother's hand she said, 'I am so happy for you, Mama. I never wanted you to be lonely once Sabine and I left home. Anyway, tell me about Michael Fullerton.' Beatrice shifted in her seat as Scarlett briefly opened her eyes, yawned and stretched her limbs before drifting back to sleep. Beatrice smiled at the infant, thinking what a beautiful child she was; but then returned her attention to Thea, who was patiently waiting.

'Well where do I begin?' Beatrice said. 'Michael is a gentleman farmer, quite wealthy and a widower.' She heard Thea sigh. 'Is everything all right?'

'I'm just relieved really. I thought he might be after your money.' Beatrice put out her hand and squeezed that of her daughter. 'I know you mean well by thinking that, but Michael is not like that at all. He does not know that I am a woman of means. Anyway, where was I? Ah yes. He is a friend of my cousin Esme's husband Tom. Almost a member of the family, you might say. I met him several times at Esme's for dinner and finally he asked if I would dine with him, just the two of us, and we have walked out ever since. Last week he asked me to marry him and I accepted. He wants to meet you and Sabine soon. He knows all there is to know about your father and the fact that we never married. Nothing in my past worries him but, most of all Thea, we love each other.'

'When are you getting married?' Thea wanted to know.

'Very soon, just before Christmas. There will only be a few of us at the wedding. He has no family to speak of and he so much envies me my two wonderful daughters and grandchildren. Honestly Thea, be happy for me.'

'Of course I am happy for you. You deserve to be happy again after Daddy's death. And he will make an honest woman of you and put a ring on your finger.' Thea wondered if she had gone too far with that comment, but Beatrice made no reference to it. They held hands briefly, sharing the love that they felt for each other.

'And Sabine, does she know too?'

'Not yet, but she will do soon for I am travelling to see her and my other grandchild.'

Thea smiled. 'How lovely,' she said, 'please give her my love.' They continued to talk about their lives, past and present. They laughed at happy memories and shed tears about events which had shaped their lives in more recent years; neither of them was anxious to leave. However, Scarlett was becoming fractious and began to whimper. 'I think that I must go. There is Perkins with the car,' Thea said, reluctantly.

'We must do this again,' Beatrice said. 'And you will come to the wedding?'

'Nothing would stop me Mama. All I want is your happiness.'

'And I yours, Thea. Always, and this young lady's.' Rising from their seats they kissed each other. Belle took young Scarlett into her arms and walked out of the tearooms to the car where Perkins had opened the rear door. Mother and daughter hugged one last time before Thea drove off to return to Westborough Hall. Beatrice watched them disappear before picking up her own suitcase to make her way to her hotel in the centre of the city. She was happy that Thea had accepted her news of the impending wedding in only a few weeks' time. Children, even adult ones, could sometimes be unhappy by a parent remarrying.

The return to Westborough Hall proved to be a joyous occasion. Thea was met by Clarissa, who had been waiting expectantly for her return. The old woman's face was a picture of radiance, a sight that was rarely seen these days with all the doom and gloom that had invaded their lives over recent months. The nursery maid had returned Scarlett to Nanny's domain, while the dowager Countess waited for Thea to follow her to the small drawing room with something of importance to divulge. The fire crackled welcomingly in the fireplace on this chilly late autumn afternoon. The remnants of afternoon tea still sat upon the occasional table and, beside it, lay a letter, the envelope of which had been torn open in haste. Normally the old woman would have used a paperknife for such an exercise but today was different. She lowered her tired body into her chair before passing the letter to Thea to peruse. Thea was not sure what the news would be but it could only be good by the reaction it had evoked in Clarissa. As she read and reread the news her own expression became joyous, too.

'Thank God; how wonderful.' She bent to kiss the Countess's cheek. The letter was from the Red Cross to inform the family that Piers Devine, Earl of Westborough was no longer missing in action. He was a prisoner of war. There were no details as yet of his specific whereabouts, but such information would be released to them later. Thea hugged Clarissa as they both shed tears of relief and happiness. Hopefully, Piers would be safe for the duration of the War, however long that might be.

The following morning Thea had returned to her responsibilities on the estate. She was about to go round the side of the Hall to enter by a side entrance. Her boots were dirty and there were few enough members of staff to administer to cleaning up mud through thoughtless behaviour. She noticed the same car which had been parked on the forecourt of the Hall only a few weeks before. Her temper flared, knowing to whom it belonged. As she reached the side entrance she encountered Neil Devine. He seemed casual in his demeanour and smiled nonchalantly at her, noting her newly slim figure which showed no sign of the effects of childbirth.

'What are you back for?' she asked rudely, not caring how she sounded. 'Everything is to be sorted through solicitors.' The man smirked at her. 'Let them get on with their conversation. I believe in action.' Thea hated the man on sight and then she smiled malevolently. The news of Piers being alive and well would wipe the smile from his face.

'You are trespassing on private property so I would suggest that you should leave immediately,' she said, looking him straight in the face.

'You won't be saying that soon when we claim what will rightfully be ours,' he smirked at her. Suddenly she laughed from pure happiness. 'We were informed recently that my brother, Piers Devine, is a prisoner of war. That means that he is alive and will return to us as soon as the War is over.' She stood, arms akimbo, waiting for a reaction, which came as the smirk vanished from his face leaving him speechless.

'And I expect on his return he will remarry and produce an heir of his own. Now get out of here.' Her face was a picture of pure triumph. She had shocked herself by behaving in such a fashion, but she could not help but laugh as she watched the man disappear quickly to his vehicle now that he knew the full implications of the news she had imparted.

Chapter 52

Thea's world had been transformed since the news of Piers's safety. Officially there had still been no news of his whereabouts but there was little doubt that the information would come at some time. War was not a straightforward business with all the uncertainties and chaos that ensued. There was also the matter of her mother's wedding to Michael Fullerton. Thea was pleased for her mother but she wished that she knew more about the man who was to become her stepfather. It was not often that Thea was secretive, but she had taken it upon herself to telephone Sabine. Neither could help the other on the matter, for Beatrice had only given them a thumbnail of detail on the matter. However, before long both daughters had received a letter informing them of the details of the forthcoming nuptials. It was to be a very small affair at the beginning of December. Sabine was to attend on her own, leaving her young child in the care of Nanny. Thea had decided to do the same, knowing that Scarlett was too young to be taken halfway across the country. She had told Clarissa about her mother, but the Countess had remained as tight-lipped as ever regarding the subject of her husband's mistress. It was enough that she had taken the woman's two daughters to her heart, but there was still no place for the woman who had stolen her husband. Now that Clarissa was less traumatized about life she had seemed to have forgotten some of the finer details of her disastrous marriage to James Devine.

As the days grew nearer Thea knew that she had to find a suitable outfit to wear. She dressed very casually these days, much like the Land Girls in britches and one of Piers's old jumpers. It had become her daily uniform ever since Scarlett's birth. One did not wear finery to trail through mud and farmyards but there was the added ordeal of clothes rationing. Many women had their clothes revamped by altering the style of the dress, either by using their own sewing skills or by using a seamstress. However, Thea did not know a woman locally who could perform such tasks and the dowager Countess wore the same clothes that she had worn for the last twenty years. She was no longer an icon of fashion if she had ever been one all that time ago. Thea regarded her clothes hanging in the wardrobe and suddenly she remembered the new clothes that Sabine had made her buy just before the outbreak of War. These clothes were stored in boxes in the closet. The items had been wrapped very carefully in tissue paper and had been sent down in trunks when she knew that she was returning to Westborough Hall. Suddenly relief engulfed her as she took out the clothes and found exactly what she wanted. As it would be cold on the day of the wedding, she could wear her fur coat that her father had bought her only a few months before his death. She also had a fur hat which, if worn at a jaunty angle, would just give her the *je ne sais quoi* factor that was necessary to make the ensemble that little bit more special. She knew that Sabine would be impressed by what she had done. As she hung up the garments in her wardrobe, she heard Polly's voice calling her urgently.

"Miss, miss there's a letter for you. Her ladyship said that it is important.'

'Thank you Polly,' Thea said, taking the letter from the maid before turning her back on her to return to the privacy of her bedroom. Unseen, she could hold the letter to her heart and allow the tears to fall unwitnessed by another human being. Having looked at the flourishing script written on the envelope she knew whom it was from. Tearing open the envelope, tears continued to blur her vision as she tried to read:

My darling Thea,

I think by now you will have been informed of my safety. I can reveal little of what has happened to me because of censorship but I am well looked after. There is sufficient to eat but the days are long and tedious with little to fill my mind. So I lie on my bunk and think of you all over there in England, where my heart yearns to be. I don't know how long that this futile war will last, but I hope you will be there waiting for me. I am saddened to hear of Mary's death and to know that our daughters are left motherless, but then I think of you darling Thea, that you will be mother and father to them during my absence. I look forward to your letters which will tell me all I need to know about home so that I can continue this dream. Just writing this makes me feel homesick for you all.

My love for ever darling girl,

Piers

Thea rested the letter in her lap as she looked through the fog of her tears. The letter said nothing, but it also said everything that she needed to know. But he was safe even if he could not be here in person and, for that, she was grateful.

What Thea and many other people on the home front did not know was the fact that Piers and his compatriots had been marched for three long weeks across France into the Ruhr in Germany, and were then transported by train to the prisoner of war camps throughout the country. As an officer Piers had received preferential treatment but many of the soldiers, below the rank of corporal, were sent to work in German industry and agriculture. The march had left many of the soldiers exhausted and rations were scarce. Some men had died en route, while the physically fit had fared much better. Piers was amongst these soldiers.

Thea went in pursuit of Clarissa, who was sitting in her habitual seat by the blazing log fire in the small drawing room. The November day was grey and cold, leaving a feeling of gloom and despondency that only such days could. Clarissa, spectacles perched on the bridge of her nose from her occupation of perusing *The Times* newspaper, looked up at the interruption to her solitude. She smiled at Thea as she regularly did and the hard contours of her craggy face softened in welcome. She was forever grateful of the girl's presence at the Hall and often wondered what she would have done without her. The mere thought of that left her with feelings of melancholia which, as always, she pushed away. There was no use pining for days gone by, for they could never be retrieved. Thea pulled up a chair beside the Countess and took the old woman's hands in her own, the newspaper falling to the floor in an untidy tangle of pages.

'Have you received any post today?' she asked, scanning the face of the old woman. There was no evidence of excitement in the wrinkled face.

'Why yes. There was a letter from my sister and one from...' Her sentence remained unfinished as she looked into the brightness of Thea's eyes. Her expression changed becoming one of expectation. 'Have you received one from Piers?'

'Yes,' Thea said, and handed the sheet of paper to Pier's mother. There was nothing of consequence to alert Clarissa's suspicions. Reading through the letter her eyes shone with love for this personal endorsement of her son's safety. She, too, was grateful that he would not need to fight again for the duration of the War. However, her ever abiding thought was that she wished to live long enough to see him again and that he could provide an heir for their dynasty. Hopefully God was on their side. She offered up a silent prayer as she often did for her son and the other British soldiers who fought so valiantly for their country. As the two women held each other there was no need for words. The love they bore each other had come a long way from the time when James Devine had died.

Chapter 53

It was a cold early December day when Thea stood in the nursery to kiss her young daughter before her departure for Devon. It was the first time that she had left her for any length of time, except for a few hours to work on estate duties.

'There is no need to fret. She will be well looked after,' Nanny said briskly. She did not need too many interruptions to nursery routine or sentiment for that matter. In her mind it made the children fractious. Thea smiled sheepishly to herself, knowing that Nanny had read her inner thoughts. Fundamentally Nanny was kind and looked after the children well, but she had never been a mother herself. Even Thea could not believe how she had changed since the birth of her daughter. The love she felt for Scarlett knew no bounds and this love had, over time, touched the lives of Mary's small daughters. Piers had been right when he wanted her to love his children. What amazed her most of all was how much love a human being could give. There was room for everybody to be so encompassed. The long journey to the West Country allowed Thea to reflect on events. She wanted to spend a little time with her mother and Sabine. It was so long since the three of them had been together, really since the death of her father. The fact that her mother was marrying for the first time despite the pretence of living with her father made her smile. Michael Fullerton was making an honest woman of her and the ring that he would place on her wedding finger could be shown to the world with pride. These were still times when women should not have children out of wedlock. She wondered if that would ever change but, for herself, it had meant a lot when Jack had placed her own wedding band on her finger. It somehow seemed to wash away the stigma of illegitimacy that she had felt ever since she had first learned that her parents were not married. She watched the drab winter scenery pass as the train seemed to gather momentum. Her thoughts turned to Piers and the letter that she had written him. There had been so many things to tell him so that he would be able to picture events as he read her words. The first words about his growing family would make him smile. Little Jane, nearing two, was a handful in the nursery. Although she was motherless she did not lack for love and attention. Thea knew that she had done her best to be mother and father to all the children. Maudie was growing quickly, turning into a placid and beautiful baby. Round and dimpled, she had the look of her mother while Jane had inherited the Devine features and temperament. It was easy for Thea to detect some traits of her own father, particularly in her determination to accomplish everything she attempted. There had been her own marriage to Jack to tell Piers and the subsequent birth of Scarlett. She had not wanted to do this to make him unhappy, but he did have a right to know just as she had a right to a life herself, for once Piers returned home he would remarry to produce an heir. This was what he had to do to continue the perpetuity of his inheritance. Beatrice was beside herself with happiness and excitement on two levels. The idea of marriage gave her an aura of respectability which she had never known during her adult life. She had never admitted it to herself before but her time with James Devine had left her feeling insecure, although she had trusted him implicitly. There had also been the subterfuge that they could not be seen freely in public because it would all cause a scandal in the papers, particularly as James was a member of the peerage. She also had to protect her children from scandal so that they could lead as normal a life as possible. This would all be different from now on. However, she was not marrying Michael Fullerton for the wrong reasons. She did love him just as she still loved James Devine, that would last a lifetime; but life went on and there was a lot of living still to do. Michael was a man who commanded respect; in fact he was a gentleman in every sense of the word although he did not have a title. He had been widowed for a long time and had never remarried, for he had not found a woman who could live up to his wife Cassandra until now. His pursuit of Beatrice, however, was quite different: he had fallen in love with her almost from the very first meeting. They had met through mutual friends and family and had been placed next to each other at dinner parties. They had found common areas of interest which seemed to bind them together, making them want to see more of each other as time went on. Eventually Beatrice had confided in him about her relationship with James and the subsequent birth of her two daughters. After that Beatrice had wondered why she had opened up on a subject which had been taboo for so long. Her thoughts were negative, as she believed the man would shun her as a scarlet woman; but Michael Fullerton was a man of the world and saw beyond the petty conventions that some people still harboured. His relentless pursuit of her had won her hand but, most of all, her love. Their courtship was only of six months duration, but they were very sure of their own minds.

'We are no longer children, Beatrice and we are not at an age where we need to prevaricate for long,' he had said. He was sixty years of age, more than a decade older than his future bride. The years and life in general had been kind to him for he did not look his age. As a gentleman farmer, he had not had to get his hands dirty as the workload was passed to others. His wealth meant that he could offer Beatrice the life of luxury that she had known with James but, he explained, the house and land would pass to his heir, his nephew Simon Fullerton on his demise. But Beatrice would be well looked after financially and there was a small house on the estate which would be her home for her lifetime, rather like a dower house but not quite on the same scale of magnitude. Beatrice was not avaricious in any way as she was wealthy in her own right, but she was touched that he had made provision for her future security. It touched her immensely that both the men she had loved had made sure that she would be well taken care of, after their days.

The wedding in the village church of Great Marston was small by many standards. Yet it was a moving ceremony for it was the family and friends who loved them both the best who attended on the cold winter's day. Thea and Sabine had met Michael for the first time on the eve of the wedding. The housekeeper, Mrs Dunn, had prepared a feast of a meal for the family, which included Simon Fullerton and his wife, Madge. It had been a delightful occasion full of warmth and good humour. The two sisters had loved Michael from the very beginning; firstly they could see how good and caring he was to their mother, but also because he was a gentle man full of humour and a very sharp wit. His nephew and his wife were much in the same mould, leaving Thea and Sabine in no doubt that their mother was in very good hands during the long absences that they spent apart. After the wedding, when it became time to depart, there should be no tears to shed, only laughter and promises to visit in the spring hoping that times would be easier and the War would be nearly over. However, tears were shed as any separation in wartime was tinged with wondering when they would see each other again even though promises were made. Sabine had decided to travel to Westborough Hall for a few days. She wanted to see her new niece and spend some time with Thea. They had had very little time together since Thea's sojourn in London before she had met Jack. On the train journey north the sisters had settled into their first class compartment away from the melee of bodies, particularly soldiers who were returning to their regiments. Thea had never minded travelling like sardines amongst the rest of society and now that there was a war on she felt only admiration for anyone who was doing 'their bit.' She felt that she was making a contribution herself with running the estate at Westborough Hall. She was like a farmer producing crops to fill the stomachs of people at home and possibly in the forces as well. She had looked at Sabine feeling a mixture of amusement and annoyance. Her sister was a fashion icon with a wonderful dressmaker who could remodel clothes into more stylish fashions of the moment. Even Sabine's hats had become works of art, making her into a fashion plate and, coupled with her great beauty, she could turn heads wherever she went. Everything had gone to Sabine's head, Thea thought, for she had become spoilt by her husband and now was quite snobbish as a result. Thea knew that her own feet were firmly planted on terra firma and that was not going to change any time soon. It was difficult to imagine Sabine standing in the mud on the farm wearing old clothes that had seen better days. Such was their lot in life, she mused, without any feeling of rancour. Suddenly Sabine's voice cut into her reverie. 'Thea, why did you call your daughter Scarlett?' There was an air of curiosity in her voice. 'Could you have not chosen something more traditional?' Thea burst out laughing, leaving Sabine with a perplexed expression on her face. Even the very snobbish dowager Countess of Westborough, who had mellowed beyond recognition, had never queried the choice of the name Scarlett.

'The name described her beautifully on the day she was born,' Thea trilled, filled with great mirth. 'She would often grow red from temper in the first few weeks.' Sabine was good natured enough to laugh at this too.

Part 5

Chapter 54

Summer 1942

Life had had its ups and downs as the War continued in Europe, North Africa and the Far East. Stories that were reported by war correspondents for the newspapers, the BBC and for Pathé news told of high numbers of casualties on both sides. Some accounts were more horrific than others. At home life went on much the same as before with the British population showing stoicism in the face of adversity and demonstrating their hatred of Adolf Hitler and his high-ranking generals. The newsreels and cartoons in the daily newspapers often poked fun at the activities of the German high command to lighten the load of the gruesome reports which filled the pages, recording the atrocities happening around the world. Thea knew that food rationing at Westborough Hall and the local area was not as intense as it was in the larger towns and cities, for they grew as much food as was possible as well as keeping the animals which had always been the mainstay of life on the estate. In season game was shot and found its way to the table of the affluent. There were always the poachers who shot game too, but rabbits were also caught and were eaten in the more humble of homes, so life was not as bad as it could have been. But as boys grew up into men, they left the land and went to war to play their part for home and country. As time progressed much of the work on the land was left to the young, women and the older generation to fill the gaps left by conscription. Even the part of the Hall that had been closed for the duration of the War and left under dust sheets for months had now been requisitioned by the military as a convalescent home for victims who had been injured in battle. There were burns victims and amputees who had to learn to cope with a world that was different from the one that they had known before the War. But most of all it was controlling the fears they faced coping with their injuries and the fact that they had been delivered a hard blow in life. Many wished they were dead. Thea, when she had time, would visit some of the injured in the west wing which had been taken over completely by the authorities. The medical staff and the patients treasured her presence, knowing how little time she had after running the estate and being both mother and father to the three very young children. As she talked to patients and staff about everyday events to keep some normality in their lives she became loved by all; they missed her if she could not find the time to visit them. Also she would read to patients who had lost their sight to help while away the long, tedious hours as they lay regaining their strength or learning to cope with their disabilities. The library at Westborough Hall had never been so well used for decades. Some of the officers who had been more fortunate in many ways and were making a good recovery were able to choose their own reading material and could be found talking to Clarissa and Thea. It was a situation that Clarissa had never experienced before but she had adapted well, offering her services where she could. The lives of the family at Westborough Hall were as busy as it could ever be.

The children in the nursery were growing up, each possessing a charm and character, so different from each other. Thea, much to Nanny's constant disapproval, would take the little girls to see some of the soldiers who were improving in health and would be ready to return home in the foreseeable future. It had been a happy interlude for the officers to spend time with the children, allowing them to look to the future to spend precious time with their own loved ones. But Thea did not frighten the little girls with the soldiers who had lost limbs and had become severely handicapped. They were not ready for that, but, now chattering and asking questions in her loud voice, Jane could sometimes hit a raw nerve with her childish observations. Thea, ever sensitive for the well-being of others, began to reduce the number of visits leaving the injured men missing the children's company, which had been an easy diversion for their suffering bodies and minds. Some of the men who had high rank would take up jobs in Whitehall if their injuries prevented them returning to their regiments. It was a constantly changing situation with newly injured men coming to convalesce. The nursing staff had taken up residence in the dower house and even some of the more seriously injured patients stayed there when they needed more specific care. And so it was that Thea spent her time consumed by all events at Westborough Hall. Letters from Piers arrived spasmodically, explaining the mundane regimentation of everyday life in the prison camp. He could give few details and there had been times when parts of his letters had been blacked out by the censor. He was not complaining for he knew that he was spared any future involvement in the War, but there were always the down times when the futility of the situation made the men think of home and their loved ones. Homesickness crept over them in waves and they lived for the days to receive letters giving news of home and their families. It was also a longing to witness the beauty of an English summer day; nostalgia was something they lived with on a daily basis. Piers wrote about his desire to see his children and his family but, in particular, Thea. He wrote telling her how much he still loved her and wanted to return to her. But again there was a futility there. Thea no longer showed these letters to Piers' mother for they had become too much of a personal nature, though occasionally she would read parts to Clarissa. However, Piers had not forgotten his mother and wrote to her whenever he could. The letters arrived haphazardly; sometimes there would be a number together or weeks could pass without hearing from him, but they knew he was safe. Piers had taken the news of Thea's marriage to Jack Carson in his stride. If he was honest there was a feeling of jealousy that the man could have Thea in a way that he never could, but he tried to ride above such thoughts. But there were also times when he lay on his bunk in the darkest hours of the night when he tried desperately to think of ways that he and Thea could be together after the War, but the answers were always the same. Deep inside him he knew that he had to let Thea go when he returned home. It was his duty to find a new wife to produce an heir for Westborough Hall. That should be the end of the matter, but the endless days of boredom allowed the usual thoughts to take up permanent residence in his mind. Thea heard from Jack now and then; he spoke of his great love for her and for the daughter he did not know. Thea replied with great affection but, in her heart, as time passed she found it difficult to visualize Jack's face and remember the brief time that they had spent together. She wondered if other wives felt the same and would relationships return to normal once the War was over? There had been news from the village of some wives having affairs, but it was the older generation who pointed the finger, forgetting how the world was changing for both men and women. She doubted if women would want to return to the kitchen sink once the mayhem was all over. Often she had to remind herself that both men and women in one way or another paid the price for the freedom that had always been taken for granted in their island fortress. The newsreels reported that the forces at the front fought valiantly for their country. But the experiences and sights could sometimes send men on a mental downward spiral as they watched the atrocities that surrounded them on a daily basis. In North Africa where Jack was fighting the situation was growing worse as the battles raged. At home the reports that were covered by Pathé news made people wonder what would happen next. Even Winston Churchill's stirring words of encouragement to the nation were not always enough to maintain the British bulldog spirit when wives, parents and even children witnessed the horrors that their loved ones had experienced; returning home they were sometimes blinded, maimed and burned in their service to their country.

Even Thea and Clarissa had seen evidence of this as men were sent heavily bandaged to begin their convalescence. They were not allowed mirrors until their mental scars were beginning to heal and they could look at their battered and damaged bodies without horrific thoughts.

Now in this summer of 1942 when the land was at its most beautiful, Thea's life was fulfilled with the joys of the children and her time with overseeing the responsibilities of the Hall and estate. There still were dark times when she would think back to the previous year and tears would fill her eyes as memories came flooding back. It had been a bolt out of the blue or a *coup de foudre* as the French called it; so totally unexpected when it came. The fact that Beatrice was no longer with them tugged at Thea's heartstrings. There were times when she felt inconsolable. Beatrice had promised her daughters after her wedding to Michael Fullerton that they would meet in the spring. Her marriage had lived up to everything that she had anticipated. He treated her well – no, treasured her beyond expectation. She felt a security which she had never experienced before and she put it down to the wedding band that she could display with pride and honesty on her marriage finger. She had been happy with James but he had legally always belonged to another, however tempestuous the marriage. But here in Devon she had Michael to herself, no longer having to share a lover, friend or husband with another woman and his family. Their union was based on friendship first of all and the letters that she wrote to her children reflected the happiness that she was experiencing. Their joy at this late flowering of romance in their mother's life knew no bounds.

Chapter 55

'Do you have to go up to London?' Michael asked. His large, kind eyes showed concern as he looked over the top of his half-moon spectacles at his wife. Beatrice was in the middle of drinking her second breakfast cup of tea. It was a leisurely start to the day as it was most days. Michael always said that now they were retired he was not prepared to race around as he had done as a much younger man. This had made Beatrice laugh uproariously for Michael left the house soon after breakfast on most days, making his way to meet his farm manager Ralph Wilks who had worked for the Fullertons for more than twenty years, in fact since he returned home from the Great War. He had worked his way up from being a farm labourer to his present position. He was Michael's trusted confidante in all respects pertaining to the running of the farm. Michael, although he was a gentleman farmer, had always been an outdoor kind of man and had no intention of changing the habits of a lifetime. Beatrice was happy about Michael's involvement with the farm, for it gave her freedom to run her new home and continue a life of independence as she had done with James' absences, all those years ago.

'Of course I need to go to London, darling,' she answered him. 'You know I have to sort out a lot of things that I have neglected for so long. The Devine town house should be returned to the Westborough Hall estate now that I no longer have need of it. James only sanctioned it for my lifetime to protect me after his death. He did not know that I would remarry.' Michael looked at her quizzically for a moment and then nodded his head in acquiescence. 'True,' he said. Beatrice had placed her empty cup once more into its saucer before rising from the table. She moved to stand by her husband's chair, putting her arms around his neck before kissing him on his stubbly cheek. He responded affectionately by kissing her back and smiling. He loved these spontaneous bouts of affection that he was subjected to. In fact he had not been as happy in a long time and the marriage had only increased the love that he felt. Suddenly, his face grew grave once more and he released her hand so that he could look at her.

'Sit down Bea. I need to talk to you.' Just at that minute Sylvie, the maid, entered the room to clear away the detritus of breakfast. Beatrice cringed as she listened to the heavy sounds of Sylvie's clumsiness with such expensive china. It was Royal Worcester china which she had brought with her to her new home. James had always insisted on patronizing the local businesses and this had been no exception. As the door closed behind the girl, Michael looked once more at his wife who had perched on one of the dining chairs, waiting for him to continue.

'As I was saying,' his hand reached out for hers in a moment of tenderness as he continued, 'I would rather you waited before you go to London. The Blitz is tearing the city apart. It can't last forever but it has gone on for quite a few months now. The papers are writing about casualties and the ambulance service and the hospitals are stretched to the limit.'

'You are a fusspot Michael. I will be gone one night. I have an urgent appointment to see Ernest Fellowes and I need to visit the house so that I can collect my papers and go through them here. I will be a day and a half at the most.' Michael knew that he could not stop her going but his concern was palpable. 'Well if you must,' he said, capitulating, but his face reflected the concern that he felt. 'Please do take care, darling. What time train are you taking?'

'I shall go straight after breakfast tomorrow so that will be the ten o'clock train. I will be back hopefully on the lunchtime train but at the very latest on the teatime train the day after. So don't worry. I will only need an overnight bag. By the way, I have invited the Timms in for drinks after dinner. You won't be an old cross patch when they are here will you.' She smiled at him, blowing a kiss which melted his heart.

'I won't be an old crosspatch, I promise, but you must come home to me safely.'

'Of course I will, you silly old thing,' Beatrice said affectionately. They kissed enjoying the closeness and peace of mind that their union had brought to their lives. It was something to be savoured at this time, when the world at large was in chaos.

March was appearing to be a beautiful month. The days were lengthening and the daffodils were in their full golden glory in gardens and hedgerows. Lambs followed their mothers in the sun-drenched fields and if the onlooker did not know that there were problems in the world at large, it would be difficult to believe it in the depths of the English countryside. Life seemed to continue much as it had done before the onset of war. Country people were up early and retired early, too. Beatrice had felt happy leaving Devon for a short sojourn in London. It was her home city after all and she rarely returned to it these days. She loved the buzz and the thrill of the city despite all that was happening there. Londoners were stoic in their resilience to the Blitz and the havoc that was going on all around them. They looked out for one another too, taking their community spirit to heart and retaining their sense of humour in adversity. It was leaving Michael that had tugged at Beatrice's heartstrings the most. After just such a short time they were so used to being together. They were joined at the hip, she would write to her daughters and friends and laughingly say it to Michael, too. He would smile with contentment as she had brought him so much happiness. These thoughts had been uppermost in his mind the previous day when he had tried to prevent her from returning to the capital. He had never been out to rule her life but her safety was paramount to him. He had watched her departure for the local railway station with a heavy heart but, as Beatrice had said, it was going to be such a fleeting visit and then life would return to normal. It had crossed Michael's mind that he should have gone with her but she was adamant that, as she was going to be away for such a short time, it was not worth his trouble. Beatrice had boarded the train, which was on time but she was amazed at the number of young servicemen who were filling the compartments to capacity. Then she admonished herself for there was a war on and the number of young service personnel would be travelling around the country to their bases or on leave. The corridors were crammed with them smoking or talking when there were no seats to be had. They looked as if they did not have a care in the world, but living life for the moment was a new philosophy which many of the young had adopted. Who knew what the future would bring? Beatrice had settled herself in a seat by the window of her carriage. A good-looking young man in the uniform of the RAF had helped her place her small piece of hand luggage on the rack above her head before he sat down on the seat opposite her.

'Thank you,' she said.

'That was my pleasure,' he smiled shyly at her. She noted how good looking he was. A uniform seemed to add that little extra polish to a young man, she thought, realizing that she was still staring at him. Inside her largish handbag she found what she had been looking for. It was Jane Austin's *Emma*, which she had taken out of Michael's library early that morning, just before she left the house. She had been told that delays were possible these days and boredom was something that she did not cope with very well. She had opened the book at the first chapter but her attention had been distracted by the number of seamen who were waiting on the opposite side platform for trains to take them further into the West Country to meet their ships. They hoisted their kitbags onto their shoulders as their train pulled up, obscuring them suddenly from view. Beatrice sighed as she settled down. The young man opposite smiled. 'It's a long journey ahead,' he said as a way of making conversation.

'Yes,' Beatrice said, not ready for conversation as she turned a page of her book, feigning concentration. Yet her mind was anywhere but thinking about Jane Austen's heroine.

Her thoughts were focused on her forthcoming meeting with Ernest Fellowes that afternoon, providing that the train was on time. She also wanted to return the town house to the Devine estate as she had told Michael. There was no way that she would live there again now that she resided in Devon. She was unaware that Piers had removed the house from the Devine estate, but Ernest Fellowes did not feel the need to inform her now that they knew Piers was still alive. Beatrice wished to make one last visit to the town house for sentimental reasons, but also to collect her personal possessions and documentation. She had changed her life since James's death, but it did not mean that she did not treasure the good times they had shared with their daughters. James had been a hugely significant part of her life emotionally and always would be. But Michael was the present and she owed him much, particularly because he had lifted her from loneliness for which she would always be grateful.

The train was taking an eternity to make its way to London. There had been several hold-ups but they were at last in sight of Paddington Station. If she moved swiftly she could make her way to Ernest Fellowes's chambers in plenty of time. As she left the station she felt that it would be quicker to walk rather than to take a taxi. She knew all the shortcuts to Ernest's offices. As she began her journey on foot she noticed many differences to the city which could only have happened over the winter period when the Luftwaffe had been bombing the capital relentlessly. Although the news bulletins on the wireless often read by Alvar Liddell had reported the constant bombardment of London, it was not until she had seen it for herself that it meant much to her or other people. It was the Londoners themselves who saw the full implications of the bombing day after day. There was evidence of craters in the road and great holes in the rows of terraced houses where there had been a hit, but the people just lived their daily lives around such events, keeping a strange normality. Somehow, Michael had been able to see far beyond her own blinkered eyes when he had been reluctant for her to return to the city.

Devon and the country had cushioned her from all this but, if she had remained in the city after James's death, this would have been part of her own daily existence too. Beatrice shivered as she continued to walk, barely recognizing streets that she had traversed for years in the past. Sandbags were piled everywhere, shielding doorways as well as they could. She thought about Sabine and Thea and their children, only too happy that they were well entrenched in the country to keep them all safe. It was no wonder that many London children had been evacuated. She had seen evidence of this in her own village.

Arriving at Larkin Street she climbed the number of steps that led into the building where the solicitor's offices were situated. Behind the reception area she heard the busy clacking of typewriter keys working away relentlessly in the typing pool. She looked around trying to think how long it had been since her last visit. It must have been years, for she had come with James once but, ever since then, Fellowes had come to see them. Ernest Fellowes suddenly appeared. There had been no indication that he had been informed of Beatrice's arrival, but there was a genuinely warm smile on his craggy face and he extended a hand for her to shake.

'Glad to see you Mrs Fullerton,' he said, using her newly acquired married name. 'Please come into my office.' Beatrice stepped over the threshold of Fellowes's sanctum of sanctums appraising its interior. Considering where she was it felt warm and inviting as if it had been designed by a woman's touch. Beatrice did not even know if he was married. The late March sunshine filtered through the windows, making the room much brighter than it really was. Fellowes indicated a chair across the great mahogany desk from his own. Before he said anything more a young woman wearing very drab attire manoeuvred a tray through the doorway and placed it on the large desk.

'Thank you Miss Jenkins,' he said without looking at her; she scuttled out like the mouse she was.

'Tea Mrs Fullerton?' he asked as he began to expertly pour for his visitor.

'Yes, please,' she said, removing her gloves to accept a proffered biscuit from the china plate.

'Now then Mrs Fullerton, I have all the papers in order for you to sign. It was very good of you to make the journey to London, for I know that the trains can be quite difficult with all the delays these days,' he rambled on, smiling at her.

'It was no trouble. I have other business to attend to while I'm here.'

'Quite so. If you sign here,' he indicated a place at the bottom of a large transcript. 'It states that you are content with the Devine town house being returned to the Westborough estate.' He looked over his half-moon spectacles, a frown creasing his rather large forehead. 'Heaven only knows when it will be used again with his lordship absent. I have arranged for it to be looked after for the foreseeable future unless Jerry decides to bomb it, too.'

Beatrice looked up at that moment at the unusual turn of phrase from the usually correct and pompous man that she had known for many years.

'I hope not,' she half smiled, hoping that he was joking, but his face had turned once more to being inscrutable. 'I will have to visit the property to collect my affects before I return to Devon,' she said.

'That is not a problem. There is a small staff there. They will be there to receive you.'

'Well I suppose that I must leave my keys with you, Mr Fellowes.' Here Beatrice's voice wobbled slightly as she handed over the keys for the last time. They had been in her possession for longer than she could remember. She took a sip from her cup of tea, but her untouched biscuit still lay on its plate. The next document was placed in front of her, which she signed with a flourish.

'Well, I imagine that must be all, Mr Fellowes.'

'Indeed, yes. I'm sorry that we will see such little of you from now on Mrs Fullerton. We have done business for so many years. I expect that I will hear about you from time to time through your daughters,' he said.

'Well, it was so much easier to transfer everything to Michael's solicitor,' she said apologetically, 'now that I live full time in Devon.' Her voice quivered as she stood up, indicating that their business was concluded.

'Of course, dear lady, of course,' the solicitor intoned, rising from his chair to grip the hand of his now former client. 'It has been a pleasure attending to the needs of your business. I am sorry that we have to part company, but it all makes sense under the circumstances. Goodbye and good luck.' He smiled benignly at her before rounding his desk and heading for the door to his office. Opening it wide he escorted Beatrice to the top of the steps and shook her hand before she disappeared, into the street below.

Chapter 56

The rest of Beatrice's day was carefully planned. She had decided to do a little shopping before taking a taxi to the home of the O'Connors, a couple she had known for many years. They had invited her to stay the night; but before that they had arranged to have dinner and spend an evening at the theatre. James and Beatrice had known their friends for so long that they had trusted them implicitly to keep the secret of their liaison. Occasionally they had visited Seamus and Perdita O'Connor in Ireland at their small estate when they wished to escape the hustle and bustle of London and the fact that they might be seen as a couple causing tittle-tattle in the papers. In Ireland they could be themselves relaxing as any married couple might among friends of long standing. Perdita, who was English by birth, did enjoy spending part of the year in London amongst a civilized society, she often said, rather than being shut away in the depths of the country. They had readily offered their hospitality to Beatrice knowing that she would not wish to stay even one night in the town house which was no longer her home. They had not stretched their invitation as far as Michael whom they had not met, nor did they approve of the short courtship which had resulted in marriage. Beatrice had her suspicions on this subject but had not imparted such news to Michael, not wishing to upset him. She knew her friends were snobbish but now, with making the decision to leave London for good, she was not sure when she would see them again. Her life had taken a very different turn. It was her decision to leave her hosts early the next morning to take a taxi across London to pick up the documents before catching the return train to Devon. But there was much to do before then, thinking of the evening ahead.

Thea had received another letter from Piers. It was not his usual epistle of life in the camp, at least what he was allowed to say about it. It showed how restless he was at being incarcerated in the POW camp. It had been over a year since his capture. Without his saying so she could tell that he was kicking his heels at the inactivity and the futility of life in general. She knew that he was a man of action wanting to keep busy at all times, just as he had been in the past when he had sat in the Lords and run the estate. Sitting down to reply to his letter, she sat pen poised thinking about what had been happening on the estate recently so that he could feel involved in life at the Hall. There was much to describe before she began imparting the antics of the little girls for his amusement; the children that he did not know, she thought ironically. There was Jane the little madam of the nursery leading the others into mischief, making the nursery staff run around after them. She wanted to transport him back to a time before the War started, when life had been richer, before rationing; but life had changed so much with all the shortages and fewer people to help run the estate. Her praise of Clarissa would enable him to see his mother as she had been in his childhood; the parent who was always there for the children that she had loved unconditionally while his father was with his other family. She put her pen down momentarily thinking what it must have been like for Clarissa when James had shown preference for Beatrice, who he considered his true wife as far as love had been concerned, although she knew that he had loved all his children equally. She could not demean James Devine in the eyes of his only son, but she sometimes saw her father for what he had been however much she had loved him. She wrote about the return of the town house to the estate expressing her own feelings on this as her childhood home. It was also a place where she could remember the happiness of her childhood and her life in the city she loved, and would revisit when the War was at last over. All of these thoughts tumbled from her pen as she wrote to the man she would always love.

Michael Fullerton stood on the station platform to meet Beatrice's train. He kept glancing at his watch knowing that it was late but there was a war on. He had used the pony and trap to drive the short distance from the farm to the train station. The vehicle was only small but there would be just enough room inside to place Beatrice's overnight bag. It should not have been a surprise to him how much he had missed her in the short time she had been absent, but it was. She had filled his lonely days with her beauty and joy of life. The short time since their marriage had been the happiest months of his life. His face was one of expectancy as he waited. Johnson, the general factotum at the railway halt, bustled from his office with some knowledge that the train was approaching. He looked at Michael, tipping his peaked cap out of respect for the man who was liked in the local area.

'Morning Mr Fullerton,' he said, the Devon burr colouring his accent.

'Good morning Johnson. The train is coming at last I see, better late than never!' Michael's face was more relaxed now as he began to move further down the platform.

'Yes, indeed sir,' Johnson's could just be heard above the hissing of the steam engine, but was lost when the brakes ground to a halt acknowledging that the train was stopping. Michael could see that it was packed to capacity with service men on their journey further into the West Country. Doors opened and closed. People crowded and then thinned out as they made their way along the platform until they found the exit of the station. Michael looked along the line of the train but there was no sign of Beatrice. The whistle blew and then there was another hissing as the train began to snake its way out of the station into the distance. Standing at a loss for a few minutes, Michael wondered where Beatrice might be. She had telephoned the previous afternoon after she had arrived at the home of the O'Connors promising to be on this very train. There was always the possibility that she might have missed it if she had been delayed sorting out her affairs, but she had assured him that it would not take long. Michael, feeling uneasy, turned towards the exit and then stood in front of the ticket office where Johnson was engrossed in sorting out a few details of his paperwork. Suddenly conscious of somebody watching him, he looked up into the anxious face of Michael Fullerton.

'When is the next through train?' Michael asked, his voice brimming with the turmoil that was beginning to stir inside him. Johnson took off his cap and scratched his head where very little hair grew. 'In two hours Mr Fullerton, unless there is a hold-up. Are you expecting your wife, sir?' Johnson had remembered Beatrice's departure the previous day. It was just one of those things that happened in a small place when you knew most people.

'Yes. I expect she will arrive on the next train.'

'More than likely, sir; these ladies do like to shop even if there is rationing,' he laughed at his little joke before his attention drifted back to the job in hand. Michael walked out of the station towards the pony and trap, deciding that he would meet the next train. It was his thinking that Beatrice would have left a message for him at home telling him that her arrival was imminent. Michael had walked through the front door of the farm house expectantly. The boy who helped around the farm had taken the pony and trap from him until it was required later.

'Has there been a telephone message, Valerie?' he asked his housekeeper. 'My wife for instance?'

'No, Mr Fullerton, there have been no messages.'

'Thank you Valerie.' The housekeeper walked away wondering what was going on. They had both been expecting Mrs Fullerton on that train. Michael walked into his small study. His desk stood in the large, bay window. For a few minutes he stood looking out at the garden which was showing that spring was on its way after a drab winter. His newspapers were spread out as usual across the top of the desk. Picking up the *Daily Telegraph* the headlines shouted at him about the bombing over the capital. It sent a shiver down his spine but he was too restless to read on about events that he did not want to contemplate. The mantelpiece clock chimed the hour. Pacing the floor for a few minutes he eventually heard Valerie sound the gong in the hall announcing that luncheon was ready. He walked to the small dining room which was easier to heat with the restrictions of war. There he noticed that the table was set for one although Valerie had been told that Beatrice would be home. Sitting in his usual place, Valerie placed the food in front of him, but he only moved it around his plate, knowing that he could not eat until he had heard from his wife.

'You should eat, sir. Mrs Fullerton will be on the next train, you will see.'

'Yes of course,' he said feeling guilty at leaving food that was badly needed in time of war. 'Thank you and sorry.' He flashed a half-smile at her as she began to clear away the dishes. Valerie said no more for she knew her employer well. It was common knowledge that he did not cope with a lot of stress since his late wife had died.

Later that afternoon Michael returned to the station in time to meet the next train which hissed and spat as it drew alongside the platform. It was a case of déjà vu as there was no sighting of Beatrice. Michael was at his wits' end now, convinced that something was terribly wrong. As he returned home his mind was on overdrive wondering what he should do. He knew nobody in London who could help him. It was not a city that he knew well, having only visited on a handful of occasions. He had always disliked the buzz and noise of city life, being a country man at heart. Open spaces and peace and quiet were more his style. He had often wondered how Beatrice had adapted to country living after having lived in the city all her life.

Chapter 57

Sabine had returned home after an afternoon of meetings. She was tired and frustrated about having to deal with a lot of bureaucracy. She was wearing her WRVS uniform, but she took off her hat which she threw down on the telephone table in the hall in a pique of temper. She had never had to join the organization for she was married with children, but the thought of what Thea was doing at Westborough Hall had made her feel guilty about the idleness of her existence; thus making her join and feel that she was doing 'her bit'. What had really surprised her was the fact that for most of the time she enjoyed it, but this was just one of those days. Everyone had them, she knew. There was the camaraderie for one thing, which she enjoyed, and the feeling of being useful guiding women of all ages to do what they could for 'our boys' at the front. She knew that she was naturally bossy, bringing out leadership skills that she had never known that she possessed. In some ways this new life of hers was far more fulfilling than lunching with friends who could only grumble about the shortages of war and never cared that other people had to cope as well. Looking at her hair in the hall mirror, she tried to smooth the wisps which had escaped from her serious-looking bun that had been adopted for her new professional capacity. Peter often laughed at her saying that she looked like a headmistress, which made Sabine angry feeling that she was not being taken seriously enough. There were two pieces of paper lying next to the telephone; this was where messages were placed in the absence of Sabine or Peter. As she read them she found that they were both from Michael Fullerton requesting that she should return his call as it was a matter of some urgency. This surprised her as he never telephoned her, as it was usually her mother. She wondered if her mother was ill which would mean a long trek down to Devon. She had often wondered why they did not live much nearer town and there was Thea right out in rural Worcestershire. What was the matter with her family, she wondered, because they had always been townies for goodness sake? Sabine lived in the country in Essex but they also shared their time living in the London property and they could commute easily into Town instead of having to travel halfway across the country to go to the theatre or see friends.

The telephone was answered by Michael, who had been anticipating a call, wishing and hoping that it would be Beatrice. As it was he had spent the afternoon hoping that his wife might walk through the front door full of indignation that he had not been there to meet him.

'Hello Michael. How are you?' Sabine's cultured voice came down the line. 'Is something wrong? Mother perhaps?' Now that it was put like that Michael felt a little foolish, but he had not known what to do.

'Yes, it's your mother. She has not returned from her visit to London. She should have been here hours ago. I thought that she might have met you without telling me.' Sabine frowned at this disclosure. 'Sorry Michael, I did not know that she was up in town otherwise I would have tried to meet her. It is not like her not to keep to time, despite all the delays, or she would telephone.'

'Yes, that was exactly what I thought. Do you have the telephone number for the O'Connors?'

'Yes, I do. I will telephone them and ring you straight back,' Sabine said.

'Thank you Sabine. I am most grateful,' he said before replacing the receiver into its cradle. Sabine was puzzled by her mother's behaviour. It was just irresponsible and most unlike her mother. She walked into the study to her bureau where she found the O'Connors' number. Returning to the telephone she dialled the operator and waited to be put through to the London number. After a few moments she heard the operator say, 'I'm sorry my dear there is no connection unless the lines are down. I should try again later.'

Sabine stood with the telephone receiver in her hand. She was trying not to panic too. What on earth was happening?

Thea crossed the Great Hall at Westborough Hall dressed in her habitual attire of trousers which had belonged to Piers, rolled over several times at the ankles, topped by a grey ribbed jumper with holes at the elbow over a more feminine blouse. She did not often find time to put on a dress or a skirt for the occasion did not seem to arise these days. Gone were the days when they dressed for dinner in the evening unless a guest had been invited. Even Clarissa had dropped her standards without batting an eyelid as they sat companionably side by side in the basement kitchen, eating their supper. Afterwards, Thea climbed the stairs to the nursery floor to spend time with the children whilst they ate their supper. It was a time of day that she loved. The children would chatter away describing their exploits in their baby language while covered in sticky goo from their nursery tea. The nursery nurse hovered anxiously to mop up any spills which might arouse Nanny's ire. She did not approve of the disruption that Thea brought to the nursery, although she was full of admiration for what she was achieving at the Hall and on the estate. The children were bathed and then gowned in their night attire before Thea read them the nightly ritual of stories that they loved. The endless choice from among the Beatrix Potter stories were their favourites as they sucked thumbs as tiredness overcame them. They slept in the night nursery together with Nanny in the room next door. She would not have allowed anyone else to attend them should they awake in the night, now an infrequent occurrence. Usually after their supper, Thea sat with Clarissa in the cosiness of the library as the Dowager indulged herself in the nightly routine of a large brandy. Thea often wondered where all the brandy came from during this time of rationing. The well never seemed to run dry. Thea did not ask, for what she did not know she could not lie about if questions were ever asked. Sometimes the senior doctors from the convalescent unit would join them but it was a rare event, for by evening the two women were tired and wanted their bed. Thea needed no brandy to coax her to sleep for the travails of the day were enough to accomplish that for her. The telephone rang in the hall. Thea, by now ready for bed, rose from her chair by the log fire, her cheeks flushed red as the warmth had made her drowsy. The hands on the ormolu clock on the mantelpiece pointed to nine twenty-five.

'Hello,' Thea said wearily into the mouthpiece.

'Thea is that you?' Sabine could barely recognize her sister's voice.

'It is a bit late to be ringing at this time Sabby,' she scolded her sister, but something in Sabine's voice brought Thea back to full attention. Suddenly her weariness had dissipated.

'What is it?' she asked, uneasily.

After the call, Thea had sat down on the sofa in the Great Hall by the log fire. She felt cold and disorientated and did not wish to return to the library or Clarissa, but she knew that the Dowager would want to know what a telephone call so late into the evening was all about. It had taken all her wits to assimilate the news that Sabine had imparted. It was horrid, unthinkable and brutal. Clarissa had half listened to the conversation, what she could hear that was and she knew from the tone of Thea's voice that she had been correct. Opening the library door she looked down the Great Hall, seeing Thea with her head between her knees as if she was hyperventilating. Returning to the library where she found what she was looking for, she poured herself another brandy, medicinal in this case, and also a large one for Thea. It would warm her and help the shock that she was obviously suffering. Clarissa was not quite sure about what had happened, but she knew it could not be Jack because Thea would be informed officially. Piers was safe, which meant that it was either Sabine or Beatrice. Shuffling along the stone-flagged hallway she carried the two large brandy blooms carefully. The nectar was too precious to lose these days. Finally she set them down on a low coffee table in front of where Thea sat. Clarissa looked at the young woman who she had grown so fond of in recent times; taking her hand she sat down beside her and said, 'Thea dear, tell me what has happened. You should drink this first, though.' She placed one of the brandy glasses between Thea's hands, watching as the young woman lifted a tear-stained face to Piers's mother. In fact her face was ravaged by the news that she had received. Thea took a sip of the brandy bringing some colour to her pale face.

'Drink some more,' Clarissa instructed. Thea drained the glass of brandy, which was slowly reviving her.

'Now tell me,' Clarissa insisted.

'It's my mother. She was killed in the Blitz last night. She was staying with friends in London and they did not have time to make it to safety. They were on their way home but the bomb fell and their bodies were found on the street.' Clarissa, who had never felt any affection for Beatrice, could at least feel the anguish for her daughter. Knowing that this was the moment to bury the animosity which had lain between the two women, Clarissa took Thea's hands in her own once more.

'My dear, I am so sorry. What a terrible thing to happen. There is so much sadness filling the world right now. I should go to bed and try and sleep. Tomorrow we shall try and work out what has to be done.' Thea still lingered, feeling that nothing would induce sleep that night. It had been the worst twenty-four hours that Sabine could remember since the sudden death of her father. She had used what influence she could muster through Peter's associates in the city. It had been discovered that several people had been killed when a Stuka dive-bomber had emptied its payload of bombs before hoping to return safely to the Fatherland. Sabine had discovered that all the bodies had been taken to a makeshift mortuary in a church hall and, from personal possessions, their bodies had been identified. Eventually they were taken by ambulance to the mortuary at St Anne's Hospital where Michael was able to identify his wife and take her body back home to Devon. He was a broken man after only a few, short months of marriage, so deep had his love been for Beatrice.

It was a time when so many families had been decimated by war on the home front and in the line of fire. Again the thought *live for the moment* could not be far from people's thoughts. It had also given Sabine food for thought. Her acknowledgement that the countryside was a safer place made her think of the well-being of her own children and that perhaps it might be better for them to be evacuated to Westborough Hall. There were also other matters to be considered too now that the town house was to be returned to the Westborough estate. Michael had confided in Sabine that Beatrice was to collect her private papers on this journey up to Town, but fate had intervened before she could do so. They had to be retrieved as soon as possible before they should fall into the wrong hands, and Sabine knew that was a task that would fall on her shoulders. It was a salutary lesson to return to the city which had seen her own mother's death now that she was a parent herself. Beatrice was to be buried at her local village church, Saint Josephs. The vicar, the Reverand John Reed, had visited the house to see Michael. The two men had been friends for the whole time that John had ministered at the church. He came to bring comfort as a minister of the cloth who had married them only months before, but his visit was also personal as a close friend. Michael Fullerton had been almost inconsolable at the death of his wife, but at the time of the funeral he was more in control of his emotions. Thea and Sabine had arrived dry-eyed but looking gaunt after the death of their mother. It had been a week since the bombing in London and their lives, like Michael's, had been turned upside down. Beatrice was laid to rest in the corner of the churchyard close to other members of Michael's family. It was a cold, blustery March day that offered no comfort to the grieving relations. There was no reason for the two sisters to linger in Devon. They hardly knew their stepfather and the cousins who had become dear to Beatrice since James's death. It was a time when the sisters had each other as they had all of their lives, but now they had to move on as all families did after bereavement. Sabine could return to the loving arms of Peter but Thea had to soldier on, to be strong for herself, the children and Clarissa: but nothing prevented her wishing that Piers was with her, to give her strength and love.

Chapter 58

Ernest Fellowes had written to Sabine two weeks after Beatrice's death. After offering his most sincere condolences, he explained that her mother had transferred her business to a solicitor in Exeter but in his continued dealings with the Westborough estate it was his duty to transfer the town house back to the Devine family. However, it had come to his notice that Mrs Fullerton had left some of her own personal effects behind including papers which she had been going to collect at the tragic time of her death. Fellowes had taken the responsibility of collecting these items which he wished to hand over to the oldest daughter, for her to dispose of as she deemed fit. He could send them or she could collect them personally from his offices at her convenience. He felt that it was not necessary to send the items to the new solicitor, nor did they need to be sent to Michael, for they were all from the time before her recent marriage. He was unaware that Sabine had already been informed of the existence of these documents. Fellowes felt that once these personal affects had been passed on to the appropriate people, that chapter of the Devine family had been closed for good and he could concentrate on the affairs of the new Earl, as he still thought of Piers.

Sabine had returned home to Essex with a heavy heart after her mother's funeral. On the return train journey she had thought of Peter and her children, how they had become more precious to her than she could ever have imagined. The days of the flighty Sabine, only interested in clothes and fashion, had long gone. She had decided to work on her parenting skills as well as becoming a more dutiful wife to Peter. She had thought about Thea who had thrown herself into life at

Westborough Hall, a huge rambling place where she would never be mistress once Piers had returned and remarried for the sake of his dynasty. What would Thea's life be like when Jack Carson returned from the War? Sabine felt that she did not love him and had probably married him because she had become pregnant. The snobbish side of Sabine, a part that she found difficult to suppress, felt that he was a no-hoper without a penny to his name and she fervently hoped that Thea held tightly onto her inheritance from their father and now their mother. As she entered her own home, she felt grounded and blessed. She knew that her mother had been loved by Michael Fullerton and he had given her the best few months of her life in recent years, but now her mother had gone and life had to go on as the old adage said. She took off her hat and gloves before looking in the hall mirror. The past few days had played havoc with her complexion, making her look tired and wan. It was then that she noticed a pile of correspondence which sat on the silver salver on the hall table. She picked up the wad of envelopes and flicked through them. Most of the letters were for Peter but she picked out two that were addressed to herself, carrying them through to the study and closing the door behind her. The children had gone for a walk with Nanny so the house was quiet for once. She opened the first envelope only to find that it was from her school friend sending her bits of gossip about friends they had in common. The second letter looked official and on opening it she discovered that it was from the Devine solicitors. She sighed. There had been enough officialdom over the past few days with her mother's will still to be read, but she had no intention of travelling to Devon in the next few days. She read Ernest Fellowes' very precise language about her mother's affects. Was there no end to it all, she felt? She was tired and emotional about all that had happened and she wanted time to think before replying. She did not feel like making a journey up to London after what had happened. Her children needed her; a few days delay would not hurt.

Thea had returned to Westborough Hall as emotionally drained as Sabine, but as the days turned into weeks and the longer summer days were upon her, her zest for life was returning. There was just too much to do with the land and the children to sit and mope about the tragic death of her mother. As Clarissa said 'getting on with things' was the only way to combat the stress of her heartache and so right she had proved to be. Thea had been grateful to be so busy. She missed her mother considerably but it was the silence that she found distressing. There was no correspondence or the odd telephone call to chat about Scarlett or other family business. She had written long letters to her mother over the years about the little girls and their antics. All this had amused Beatrice and she would answer with tidbits from Sabine and Thea's childhood which would rise to the surface after having lain dormant for so long. All these little treasures would be meaningless to the outside world but, to Thea, they would be filed away to tell her own child in the future. The closeness that she had felt towards Clarissa had inevitably increased as the months passed after Beatrice's death. Although her sense of loss had not gone away, it was becoming more bearable and life was being lived to its fullest. In the long summer evenings of double summer time Clarissa and Thea had taken to sitting outside in the gardens until dusk came telling them that it was time for bed. They spoke of their current lives and the past. Thea talked openly about her mother now that there was no hostility or rancour left in Clarissa. She became more honest about the situation that had existed between James Devine's two families, allowing Thea to see her father in a more three-dimensional light and not entirely through the rose-tinted glasses that Beatrice had always portrayed of the man she had loved so passionately. Clarissa's bitterness too had fallen away regarding her husband. She was frank and honest, revealing his good points as well as his bad. She also said that it had been more of a marriage of convenience between them. Love had played such a small part in it and, as time passed, it had all turned to dislike and possibly hatred. Thea looked at Clarissa as if seeing her for the first time through different eyes. It struck her how life, good or bad, could change people for better or worse. Her father had found another woman while Clarissa had been left to raise her own three children and to try and keep her dignity intact. Was her father any different from other members of the aristocracy? She had no answer for that question, but her heart went out to the older woman believing that it had been a man's world. After all this disruption to life through war and casualties, could women take their true place in society alongside men? They were doing their part on the home front, in the fields and in the factories; others gave their lives like the men working undercover in France and, when it was all over, would they want to return to staying at home, rearing the children and making life easier for their husbands? What would happen to her life once Jack came home? As if reading her thoughts, Clarissa had suddenly asked out of the blue, 'You don't love Jack, do you?' The old woman had been gazing into space as there was a companionable interlude between snatches of conversation. Thea had looked at Clarissa wondering where that nugget of information had come from.

'No,' she replied honestly. 'Not really. He is a lovely person but I don't love him like I should. He gave me Scarlett and I should remain grateful. We will have to make decisions after the War. I can barely remember what he looks like. It has been so long.' Clarissa looked quizzically at Thea, 'I bet you can remember what Piers looks like,' she suddenly said.

Thea regarded the dowager Countess with astonishment, in fact she felt totally dumbfounded. Had Clarissa seen something between herself and Piers? She turned her face away knowing that a blush had swept over her face like a tidal wave. When her emotions were more in control she turned to face Clarissa who was in a benign mood. 'Oh my dear, as an old woman I am a great observer of life. I know you both love each other but not as brother and sister.' Thea sat in silence, gazing at the older woman. She thought that if anyone else heard this conversation they would believe that the Dowager had lost her mental faculties, but she was as astute as ever. She observed the smile sweep across Clarissa's face.

'Don't worry, your secret is safe with me. Nobody will ever find out.' She leant forward and took Thea's hand and stroked the soft young skin. Having found her voice Thea said as it was futile to deny it, 'Yes we love each other, but we have done nothing wrong. We know that it can never be.'

'Oh I know my dear, but it is hard to be so self-sacrificing. I cannot advise you but only hope that neither of you is hurt. Piers has to remarry to produce the heir and it would be better for you to have a life of your own with young Scarlett once this damned War is over.' Thea had never heard Clarissa swear before. She reached out to take the hand of the old woman to squeeze it, a gesture that said 'thank you' for not condemning the pair of them.

Sabine was still contemplating what to do as regards her mother's paperwork. The thought of going up to London after what had happened to her mother frightened her. She kept constantly thinking of her own children being motherless if anything happened to her. She knew that she was being irrational, but it was difficult to put the situation from her mind. And there was also Peter who worked in the city, a high ranking civil servant advising over the War effort. There were many nights when he could not return home staying at his club if his days were long and tedious. Eventually she wrote to Ernest Fellowes apologizing for the delay in replying to him but said that it was quite impossible for her to collect them in person, for she was heavily involved with the WRVS work and hoped that it would not be a great inconvenience for him to send the papers to her. After a short period of time a large brown envelope was delivered. Sabine, not the best at dealing with any documentation, took the parcel which she filed away to be dealt with at a later date, when it could be put off no longer.

At about the same time a letter arrived from the Devon solicitor for both Thea and Sabine. Their mother's estate was to be bequeathed in its entirety between them. This also included the capital which had been left to Beatrice at the time of James Devine's death. All of this had been agreed with

Michael only days before her untimely death. Michael had had no need of her money and so it seemed to be only fitting that her daughters inherited her wealth now, making them very wealthy young women in their own right. Thea had thought long and hard about how she would use her inheritance after the War. Eventually she knew that she would buy her own property in Worcestershire for herself and Scarlett to make a new life. Whether Jack would become part of that situation, if he survived the War, was yet to be seen. She hoped to remain near Piers but by then he would have remarried as Clarissa had said, and would be attempting to produce his heir. That would be the time for Thea and Scarlett to move on with their lives.

Chapter 59

As the year of 1941 progressed the news concerning the North African campaign was not good for Britain and her allies. Thea had not received a letter from Jack for a long time. Although she was certain that she no longer loved him she only wanted his safety, especially as he was Scarlett's father, but she felt that at some point in the future they would divorce. There were too many women in much the same predicament, living in the moment and becoming carried away feeling that they were in love, but time told a different story. Thea had spent more and more time in the convalescent wing of the house. The dower house was also being used as a rehabilitation centre before the soldiers returned to their units or were discharged back to civilian life. They were men of distinction and great courage to have experienced such injuries; some men would never have the full use of their bodies again, others were suffering from stress which had been diagnosed in the Great War as shell shock. They had to deal with their emotions on a daily basis, often reliving past experiences. It would take time to return to their former selves, if they ever did. The mental scars took far longer to heal.

It was at this time when 1941 was giving way to the new year of 1942 that Thea met Captain Lawrence Appleton. He had been badly injured having lost the use of his left arm, which hung loosely by his side. He would not be returning to his unit but there would be a desk job waiting for him when his doctors felt that he was mentally and physically ready. It had been Thea's idea to throw 'a bit of a do' for the fitter patients that New Year. It was to help the men to socialize and find new confidence before they were declared fit enough to face their future. Some of the local families had been invited and food rationing coupons had been pooled in order to provide a festive feast. Bottles of alcohol had been found, probably from the black market, but nobody asked any questions for it was a time when morale had to be raised for 'our boys'. Clarissa had retired to her bed with the excuse that she was not up to a party.

'Of course you are,' Thea had laughed at the elderly woman. 'You will be the life and soul of the evening.' But Clarissa had had her way and, after an early supper in the kitchen, she had made a very quick exit fortified with the brandy decanter (the liquid never seeming to reach the bottom) and a suspiciously large glass. Thea had not witnessed this for she had been supervising the food and drinks which had been set up in the small dining room. The Great Hall and the other rooms were still bedecked with green foliage from the estate which included holly and mistletoe, producing a wealth of berries that Christmas. The large Christmas tree, also from the estate, was trimmed with the efforts from the children. Clarissa had had a fine time helping with these activities as the festive season had approached. Log fires blazed in the grates in all the rooms. There was plenty of fallen wood and branches to be found on the estate and in the woodlands where poachers still trespassed. There was a homely ambiance to the Hall giving a feeling of nostalgia of Christmases past. Thea had been responsible for all this, remembering Christmases of her own childhood. The guests came mainly on foot, though some even used their small precious amounts of petrol to venture out in order to have fun. It was a time when people wanted to forget the doom and gloom of war. Sabine and Peter had arrived with their two small children and their nanny. The top-floor nursery was bursting to capacity. Thea had managed to disappear for a few minutes leaving Sabine and Peter to greet the first arrivals. She had disappeared to her room to search her wardrobe for something to wear wondering why she had not done this sooner, but she was always so busy these days. Taking out dress after dress she realized that none of these garments had seen the light of day since the onslaught of war and they were out of fashion. However, there was nothing that she could do and deciding on a red dress as she could feel it satiny to the touch. Over recent months she had allowed her hair to grow long over her shoulders. Usually she wore it spiralled onto her head, out of the way with no fuss. Suddenly she had an overwhelming desire to look beautiful, not for any man to see but entirely for herself. She had such little time for herself these days and suddenly she had a yearning for the past when life was simpler with far less responsibility. When she had finished tweaking and curling she wanted to show herself to Clarissa for her approval. The Dowager's self-imposed exile from the party had upset Thea and by going to see her she felt that she was including the old woman in the events of the evening. Knocking on Clarissa's bedroom door, she heard a mumbled 'come in'. Turning the handle and pushing open the door Thea saw the dowager Countess propped up in bed with a cosy old-fashioned jacket around her shoulders to keep the winter chill at bay. Cradled in her hands was the inevitable glass of brandy, which had obviously been refilled.

'You look truly beautiful Thea,' Clarissa said nodding her head in approval. 'It is a good job that Piers cannot see you now.' Thea went to the older woman to give her a hug. Tears appeared in the Countess's eyes, for it had been a long time since she had received so much affection.

'I love you,' Thea said meaning every word that escaped her lips. The Countess smiled happily through her tears, 'You are the best thing to have happened to me in a long time. God bless you.'

'Good night Clarissa. Sleep well,' she said as she closed the bedroom door behind her. Her thoughts were now on the forthcoming party. Voices could be heard as the front door opened and closed to new arrivals. Lawrence Appleton had already been at Westborough Hall for four months to convalesce, but the doctors' assessment of his condition saw a rapid improvement in his health which made them think that he could be discharged soon after New Year, whereby he could return to his parents' home for the rest of the time of his recuperation. He would then be found a desk job within the regimental headquarters of the Grenadier Guards. It had always been his intention to see action once more but, he was told, that would be completely out of the question and this he had reluctantly had to accept. Since Thea had become more involved with the men and their rehabilitation many of them had held a torch for her, finding her intriguing and full of admiration for what she had achieved during the Earl's prolonged absence. She had told them that she was married and her husband was in North Africa, but despite all that several of them felt a little in love with her. Thea remained completely unaware of their emotions and treated each individual as if they were special. However, she had developed a close bond with Captain Appleton who had been invited for a kitchen supper on several occasions. It had always been in Clarissa's presence. To Lawrence Appleton this friendship meant more than just that. It was a physical attraction on his part but they had many interests in common, too. Lawrence's parents were farmers and it was Thea's increasing love of the land and the changing seasons which performed its magic on the landscape that had drawn the pair together to have extended conversations. It was Lawrence who declared his love for her one night when Clarissa had made an early departure from the supper table. Thea had been taken off guard as Lawrence had reached across the table to take her hand with the only good one that he possessed. Not knowing what to say, Thea did not wish to hurt his feelings, but this change in friendship had never been her intention. Her own life was complicated as it was without considering a love affair. It had occurred to her that after the War she might remarry and have another child. She would have liked Scarlett to have a sibling. Her daughter was growing up quickly and already regarded Piers's two daughters as her sisters. There was going to be a time when Scarlett would have to know the truth when they went to live on their own. Now, on the night of the party, Lawrence was waiting for her hoping that he might be able to monopolize her company, albeit doubtful for she was also the hostess. The sight of Thea descending the stairs had made his heart turn somersaults. It was the first time he had seen her dressed in evening wear and his love for her was growing by the moment. Sabine, who stood in the Great Hall near the Christmas tree talking to a major in His Majesty's forces, witnessed the appearance of her sister. Heads turned in the appreciation of a beautiful woman and Sabine felt a twinge of jealousy that her sister did look truly beautiful, heightened by the healthy glow from her outdoor life. But Thea, radiant, remained quite unaware of the whole situation as she hastened to play her role as hostess. Sabine had felt a little indifferent to Thea in recent months, even though she had made it her business not to show it. Some of these strange emotions had come about after she had finally found the time to peruse her mother's papers. There were many documents that she filed away wondering if they might be useful in the future, but she had also made a discovery that had taken her breath away. She had not told Peter, but she had decided that she would reveal her secret over the festive season. Somehow, though, she did not have the courage of her convictions thinking that there might be another opportunity in the future. Now, watching Thea, she wondered if she would ever have the courage to reveal her secret. A little bit of knowledge was a dangerous thing, she thought tartly, turning away from the image of her sister hoping to find Peter before the evening advanced too quickly. Now she was not sure that it was the best thing to have accepted the invitation to the New Year's Eve party. Perhaps they should have stayed at home, to entertain their own friends and neighbours?

Chapter 60

Thea had discovered that Lawrence Appleton was to be discharged into the care of his family at the end of February. The doctors hoped that he could have gone sooner but there was a reluctance about him to return to the outside world. This was not an abnormal occurrence. Sometimes members of the armed forces lost confidence in themselves when they had been shielded from the problems that had institutionalized them in the first place. Psychiatrists were often on hand to talk to such military men, but in Lawrence's case it had been noticed that he seemed to hold a torch for Thea, though there was no evidence that she held him in any special affection other than the fact that he had become a friend. Yet that could also be said for many of the other officers as she regularly stopped to chat about their health or ask after their families. The men were lonely, sometimes afraid of the future ahead of them, but most of all they were reluctant to voice their innermost fears feeling that it was a sign of weakness or, perhaps more than that, it was the British bulldog spirit to keep the stiff upper lip. Lawrence, however, knowing that his time for departure was imminent, had found Thea out in the gardens of Westborough Hall one day after the party. In fact, he had been watching for her and knew her daily routine.

'Will you walk with me?' he asked her on this cold February morning. Both were bundled up against the elements, Lawrence in his greatcoat and Thea was attired in Piers' old clothes topped by a coat with a gaudy, multicoloured scarf wrapped around her neck. She looked in complete contrast to the night of the New Year's Eve party. She had not had the occasion to dress like that, since.

'Yes of course,' she said looking at him curiously, her stomach dipping as if she knew what was about to come. His declaration of love for her over Christmas had not been rejected because she had not wanted to hurt him; but it had not been encouraged either, for she was married to Jack. She had actually had words with one of the psychiatrists about it. He had said that such a situation was not unknown, but a huge rejection could lead to the patient having serious problems with their self-esteem, particularly those who had been injured badly and could not return to their regiments fully whole again. They also felt that nobody would love them in their circumstances, leading to great psychological problems. After this, Thea had not been as often to visit the men knowing that she could never allow such a situation to happen again. She had wondered, half amused, if Florence Nightingale had evoked such a reaction in the men she cared for. Lawrence hurried to keep up with Thea's pace. He did not look as vulnerable this morning with the cold wind blowing his hair off his forehead and whipping colour into his usually pale cheeks.

'I shall be leaving in two weeks,' he said sadly.

Thea smiled at him, already having been told the news. 'But isn't that good news? It means that you are much better now. After a short stay with your parents you will go back to a desk job with your regiment. That will be vital work. Just think how useful your experiences at the front will prove to be.'

They walked on in silence for a while. 'Will you write to me?' he asked. They stopped walking and turned towards each other, looking through fresh eyes at the other person.

'You know I will. You must leave me your address.'

'There is no real hope for me then?' he asked with a sad smile on his face.

'You know I am married with a child, Lawrence. But we will be friends and write as often as we can, and in time you will meet somebody and have a family of your own.' Again he smiled his sad smile. 'Will I be able to see you again before I go?' he said, leaning forward to kiss her cheek.

'You will see me before you go, I promise,' she said as they walked in the harsh cold of a winter morning.

The comings and goings of the convalescence wards continued but Thea had learned a harsh lesson of becoming too involved with the patients. As the year progressed she had heard from Lawrence several times and there came a subtle change in the tone of his letters. As his health improved so did his mental well-being and thus he gained in confidence. He had not enjoyed the three months that he spent with his parents, although they had been kind to a fault; but his mother fussed wanting to do everything for him. Whereas it was vital that he should become independent as much as he could. But after re-joining his regiment he had rediscovered the camaraderie of his fellow officers, who treated him normally knowing that they could end up in similar circumstances if their luck did not hold out. All this meant that life was looking better for him, giving him the vision to see that Thea had been correct in the reading of their situation. She had too many demands on her life without taking on somebody who would have been an even greater burden on her time. He was not bitter in the way he thought, but pragmatic. Now he had met Lucy who had all the time in the world and for the very first time in his life he knew that he was in love. He wrote to Thea mentioning his new love and she, in return, was thrilled that his life had taken a turn for the better during these dark days while there was so much uncertainty in the world. As Thea thought about this little ray of sunshine she wondered how Piers and other POWs would cope once they were repatriated when the War finally reached its conclusion. It was a chilling thought. There seemed no end to the War with little good news for Britain and her allies but, by October, the future was looking slightly brighter. Lieutenant-General Montgomery had taken charge of the British forces In North Africa. It had been in the papers and on Pathé news. Thea, whenever she had time, avidly scoured the papers for news of the War wondering like everybody else when it might end and whether there was an element of hope. She and Clarissa discussed it endlessly and any snippet of news that Thea missed during her long, busy days, the Countess would inform her of any new developments there might be. Sometimes they would gather round the wireless set in the library listening to Alvar Liddell's distinctive tones reading the news bulletins. The old woman's mind was as sharp as ever and her ultimate ambition was to see her son return home to produce an heir for Westborough Hall. Thea had not seen Sabine since the New Year's Eve party and the communication between them had been limited. They seemed to be moving in different directions. Thea could not account for the distance, that seemed to have widened further. It was often said that mothers held families together but Beatrice was no longer there to be the glue to keep everything in place, so the gap widened further. However, it could also be the way the world was at the moment. It just appeared that nothing was the same anymore and probably would never be, again.

The girls' relationship with Michael Fullerton had never had the opportunity to develop. He had been married to Beatrice for less than four months and after her death he had written to both Sabine and Thea, thanking them for their support over the funeral. They had both replied telling him how happy he had made their mother which made them grateful that there were such memories of her personal happiness. After that the lines of communication had been severed. Even at Christmas there had been no card, making that the end of the whole business.

Chapter 61

There was news from North Africa. Montgomery had led the Eighth Army into attacking the enemy forces at El Alamein. The battle followed heavy bombardment that had lasted 12 days with lots of casualties on both sides. Thea and Clarissa waited with bated breath. Winston Churchill was high on victory, the first for the allies during the course of the War. His rhetoric had given the nation hope during recent years. Now here was the reality. The news bulletins were telling the country that allied desert troops had captured thirty thousand prisoners of war from Germany and Italy. The Axis forces were now in full retreat and were chased across north Africa before finally surrendering to the combined British and American forces. Churchill could not express his feelings grandly enough about the victory for the nation he loved; he ordered bells to be rung throughout the land. Could this be a turning point in the War? Hope of bringing 'our boys' home? The mood of the nation was jubilant. The bells rang even in the local church. The reserved British could celebrate and be proud. This was a time for celebration.

But two weeks later a telegram arrived on a Saturday morning and Thea knew what it was before she had slit open the envelope. She had opened the door to the boy whose red face had told of the exertion he had made on his bicycle ride. She took the envelope and made for the place where she would find peace and quiet for a few moments. Her hands were visibly shaking as she closed the door on Piers' study. The grey autumn light mirrored the doom in her heart. The telegram told her the news that she had suspected. Jack had died in North Africa. The piece of paper fluttered to the floor as she sat reflecting on her feelings of guilt that she might end the marriage after the War, though she had never wished him harm. Suddenly, the time came flooding back when they had made love in the early days of their relationship. She was the wife that he had always wanted and then there had been Scarlett which had made them a family, a family which had been denied him after the death of his parents. Thea put her head in her hands and wept. They were tears of guilt, loss, frustration and the wasted years that could have been better. Some of her tears were also for the loss of her mother and the fact that she could never have Piers, and also the weariness which came with so much responsibility. When she could cry no longer, she sat for a long time trying to remember Jack. The thoughts of his last visit to Westborough Hall when there seemed such a distance between them kept returning to her thoughts. Perhaps it had been the War that had pushed them apart, but there was no need for feelings of guilt, she thought. She had written copious numbers of letters telling of her love for him to keep him buoyant in the face of adversity. There had been tales of Scarlett in the nursery to make him laugh. Her mind went round and round and then the tricks played by her mind saw him buried in the hot, dry sands of the North African desert.

Finally her tears were spent. There was still real life to cope with, the living needed her. Jack was no longer at war, he was at peace. These emotions, she strictly told herself, were a self-indulgence that she could not afford. Life went on despite the hardships that had to be endured. Everybody had a different story to tell but life saw them through no matter what. Clarissa had wondered where Thea was, but Westborough Hall and the estate was such a huge place. She had not been concerned by Thea's prolonged absence but when she came to supper in the kitchen Clarissa knew that something was wrong. It was not just the redness of Thea's eyes but her normal vivacity had gone, leaving her lethargic and monosyllabic.

'Oh my dear, tell me what's wrong,' Clarissa said, her gnarled hand stretching across the table to take that of the young woman. And thus it was that Thea told her tale of woe and guilt.

'Jack never knew of your lack of love for him,' Clarissa said pragmatically. 'You paid lip service to everything that a good wife does. He went to his grave believing that he was loved. You could not have done anything more. There will be many women who will feel just as you do. The men won't always return the same after the conflict and there will be divorces, too. So be brave. You have been dealt a double blow in such a short time but the little girls need you and so do I.' Thea looked at the older woman, shocked by what she had said. This was quite an admission from the older woman; it had not been easy for her to admit her frailties of spirit when she had suffered, too, over the long years from many quarters. They held each other's hand for a long time allowing their private thoughts to float freely through their minds, thinking about their private losses. Thea had had to find a way of living with her emotions of guilt and, as the Christmas season was almost upon them, there was no card to send to ease her conscience. There was also no party this year. The festive season was to be spent quietly with the little girls and Clarissa. There was also the silence from Sabine which had been strange but, as usual, Thea sent a Christmas card and presents for her sister's children. Sabine had not replied and it felt as if her family had deserted her in one way or another. But the children made Christmas festive and lively. They had been allowed to stay up later than usual to play with their toys. It had been a difficult time to find anything exciting to buy them with the shortages but they shared each other's. Living so closely together in the nursery Nanny had always made sure that they shared toys. There were no fights and the little girls were brought up to be polite, as their heritage demanded.

It was in the middle of January when the Christmas festivities were long over and now snow lay scattered like icing sugar over the countryside that Thea received a letter with an official stamp on the envelope. The afternoon light was beginning to fade and the second postal delivery was later than usual. She had heard the clatter of envelopes fall onto the tiles of the Great Hall as she sat by the log fire in the library reading a copy of Charlotte Bronte's *Shirley*. It was a welcome interlude in her busy life. Clarissa was tucked up in bed with a streaming cold and a stone hot water bottle which had been discovered sitting in one of the kitchen cupboards that was used for storing such antiquities. Thea pulled her cardigan closer around her slim form before opening the door of the library. Crossing the hall she then picked up the pile of envelopes but was intrigued by the one which had been sent by Jack's regiment. She knew the insignia well. Returning to the warmth of the library she took down the paperknife which lived these days on the mantelshelf. Using the implement she slit open the envelope and sat back in her chair to read the contents of the letter.

She read on stunned by the information. It had appeared that Jack Carson was a courageous man and had been recommended for a gallantry medal, the DSO, for outstanding bravery regardless of the risk to his own life. This had all taken place in the midst of fierce fighting when he had gone into the field to rescue two badly wounded fellow soldiers. He had dragged them back to safety but was mortally wounded in the process. Thea could not read the rest of the contents for her eyes blurred with tears. As the weeks had passed since Jack's death she had begun to feel better, and now she was so proud of him. She could hear Clarissa saying in the intervening weeks, 'You're only human my dear. We have all had thoughts and done deeds that we are not proud of.' How right she was. Thea brushed the tears from her eyes, returning her gaze once more to the piece of paper. Jack's recommendation for outstanding bravery had been approved and as his widow she was invited to regimental headquarters to receive the medal on Jack's behalf at a special ceremony. She would be informed of the day and date in due course. She sat and looked into the dancing flames of the fire, seeing things that were not there and feeling that she was not worthy enough to receive the medal of her brave husband, Jack Carson. She felt that she was not fit to lick his boots and wondered if she really had to go. She felt she was a sham, completely unworthy of him. But something deep down inside her remembered what her father had told her many years before when she was a child. He had spoken of the Great War and the brave exploits of very ordinary men and women. It was certain circumstances which brought out the good or bad in people. She knew that she was not a bad person, sometimes selfish like most people but she had given her whole life in recent years to the running of the Devine estate, while looking after the children and Clarissa. Jack had said in his last letter to her that he was proud of her self-sacrifice. She would never be perfect but perhaps it might have been possible to have made a go of their marriage. Now they would never know. And there was Scarlett, Jack's only child, who would one day want to know about the father that she had never known. She would go to the ceremony to collect the medal so that her daughter would have something of significance as a keepsake of her father's heroism. Again the tears flooded her eyes. Would the well ever run dry? Then she laughed. Just wait until she told Clarissa.

Part 6

Chapter 62

The End of the Conflict

It was the day everyone had been waiting for for nearly six years. Victory in Europe Day was welcomed in the streets throughout the country, but London had seen nothing like it for years. Winston Churchill, his own political career uncertain, stood shoulder to shoulder with King George V1 and Queen Elizabeth and the two young princesses. They waved from the balcony of Buckingham Palace as the crowds cheered, roared and clapped their approval. Where else would they go at such a time? Happiness radiated from the faces of the Prime Minister and the Royal Family as the newsreels captured the moment. The news to the nation had been broadcast at three p.m. declaring the end of the War in Europe. Thea was jubilant because Piers and thousands of POWs would be freed across Europe. The news was not so good in the Far East, but surely it could not be long now? As well as such feelings of intense happiness she still had doubts about future events. She wondered if Piers might have changed during his five years as a POW. He could not be the same man who had left British shores with the expeditionary forces. And what about herself and Scarlett? Where would their future lie? She knew that she would always have a home at Westborough Hall but she still dreamt of buying her own place, maybe a small farm nearby where Scarlett could see the girls, 'my sisters' as she called them. The three of them were joined at the hip, doing everything together. Thea could not help but smile as she thought of the children. She also hoped that Piers would be proud of his daughters. After the victory in North Africa Britain and her allies continued to win battles. The D-Day landings of the previous year had begun the liberation of Europe although the cost to all sides had been huge in casualties, the numbers of which was still uncertain. Looking back over the intervening years Thea was now so proud of Jack. She no longer felt the guilt that she had done at the time of his death. She had done what other wives and close relatives had proudly done on her visit to the regimental headquarters. She had received his award for courage and brought it home. She had shown it to Clarissa who had supported her so much over the years but now it was laid away, awaiting the day when she could show it to Scarlett so that she would be old enough to understand the true heroism of her father. The world was changing so fast now that peace was upon them. Clarissa was excited by the fact that her son would be home, but there was also an anxiety about the perplexing situation that lay between Thea and Sabine. Neither of the sister's had had any contact since the New Year's Eve party of three years before. Thea did not know why and she had waited for an olive branch from her sister, but none had come.

'Go and see her,' Clarissa said. 'If you telephone she can make excuses, but if you're there in person there is nothing that she can do but speak to you.'

Clarissa had turned a huge corner in her life since the days when she had hated Beatrice and her husband. Perhaps age had mellowed her, but war and what could happen to the people you loved had left her with the feeling that all the animosity in the world was never worth it. Nation against nation had left the world badly off and the cost to human life had been terrible.

'You think that I should go,' Thea had said. She was at a loss about the whole matter. She and Sabine had been so close through their childhood and their young adulthood. There had never been a quarrel that she was aware of. Taking Clarissa's advice to heart, Thea had packed a small overnight bag and had taken the train to London. It was still busy after the declaration of the end of the War but she took taxis wherever she went. Her first port of call had been Sabine and Peter's town house. It looked as if it had been closed for the duration of the War. Perhaps there was a shortage of money or people wishing to work in service. They had suffered that at the Hall. She rang the front door bell and waited. After a few minutes the door was opened by an elderly woman who looked surprised to find a visitor on the doorstep.

'Is Lady Sabine or Sir Peter at home?' she asked tentatively not knowing what to expect.

'No they are not. May I ask who is calling?' the woman asked.

'I'm Sabine's sister Thea,' she answered. The woman's face lit up in recognition of the name. 'Come in,' she said taking Thea's bag from her as she stepped back into the hallway. 'I have the kettle on if you don't mind coming into the kitchen.'

'Of course I don't mind,' Thea said, thinking about the amount of time that was spent in the kitchen at Westborough Hall. She followed the older woman along the long hallway and down the steps into the kitchen, which Sabine had had modernized just after her marriage.

'By the way, I'm Sarah,' the older woman said as she made her way to the large cooker where the kettle sang merrily. 'I have been cook here during the War but now I am rather like a caretaker.'

'A caretaker?' Thea echoed, rather puzzled.

'I look after things for the family. Sir Peter comes occasionally to check on the house but Lady Sabine has not been here for a long time. I think it was to do with the bombings and her mother dying like that.'

'Ah yes. Our mother was killed in the Blitz. It affected us both very badly.'

'Nasty thing that. There have been so many wasted lives.'

'Do you know how my sister is?' Thea said as she sipped her tea. 'That is why I have come in search of her.' Sarah regarded Thea for a moment. 'It is only gossip which I don't like to pass on, but I think that you have a right to know. It has been said that she has been rather reclusive in the last few years. There has been another baby, though. It makes three at the last count.' Thea was rather taken back by such family news and was puzzled why she had been denied the information. What on earth had gone wrong? What was the matter with the pair of them? What would their mother have said? But maybe it would never have happened if Beatrice had been alive. Perhaps Sabine had had some mental breakdown. It made Thea want answers to the questions. For a moment the two women drank their tea in silence before Sarah suddenly said, 'What will you do now?'

Thea smiled, 'Go to Essex, of course.'

'You could telephone her from here.'

'Thank you, but I think that I will surprise her,' Thea said, but her heart seemed to be beating too quickly as she contemplated her meeting with Sabine. She intended to reach the bottom of the matter before too long. 'Thank you for the tea and the information, and now I must go,' she said, rising from the kitchen table.

Thea had hoped that Sarah would not pass on the news of her visit to Sabine and Peter. There was much she had to find out without Sabine knowing that she was on a mission. Thea had telephoned Clarissa to check on the children and the retort had come back sharply to say that they were perfectly fine with an army in the nursery to look after them. Thea had smiled at the sharpness of the Countess' tongue but, knowing her so well now, she knew that she was being missed even on this short absence. Clarissa relied on her more than she was prepared to acknowledge but the process was reciprocal, for the Countess' wisdom of mind and experience in years had played a major part in the successful running of the Hall and estate. However, most of all Thea wished to explain the events that had occurred in London. She really wanted to tell her that she would be away longer than she had first intended but would keep her informed as much as she could. The day was bright and sunny for the end of May and, after Thea's telephone call, Clarissa had taken up her seat in the garden while the little girls played around her, giggling and enjoying themselves under the close scrutiny of their governess. She watched their antics with amusement, amazed at their energy. These days they tired her more than she liked to admit. Later Miss Bennet, who was sitting watching the children, would take them inside to do something quiet which would give Clarissa the opportunity to doze in the shade of the apple tree, still heavy with blossom. Clarissa through half-closed eyes observed the very plain Miss Bennett who sat primly, a sunhat covering her short, straight brown hair trying to prevent the freckles from appearing on her rather pert nose. She was a pleasant individual and had taught the children well. Thea had appointed Miss Bennett as governess to the little girls when Jane was ready to begin her education. However, as the children were so close in age it had been decided that they could begin together, whereas the younger girls would begin this important part of their lives more slowly. Thea and Clarissa had had an argument over the education of the children. It was only one of a handful of disagreements they had had during the time they had lived together. Thea had wanted the children to attend the local village school so that they were widening their social world but Clarissa, still steeped in the traditions of the aristocracy, was adamant that as the daughters of the Earl they should be educated at home. When there was an heir that would be a different proposition.

'You can do whatever you like about Scarlett,' the Countess had said huffily. She knew that she could not dictate the decisions to be made on Scarlett's future, but she had a feeling that Thea would capitulate in the end. And she had been correct. Thea had not grown up as the daughter of an Earl in society because her father had been known as Mr Cavendish to the people who formed their small circle of friends. Thea and Sabine too had had a governess, but the world was now changing, making the girls require an experience of a more equal world; but to split Scarlett from Maudie and Jane would be to do her a disservice. Neither Clarissa nor Thea had wished to lose face but Thea had gracefully accepted defeat. When Piers returned home he would of course make the ultimate decision, so now the children were under the tutelage of Sophia Bennett, a well-educated young woman in her own right. On this occasion Clarissa had been proved correct, but now that the War was over would the order of things change?

'Maudie leave that alone!' Sophia called out as the young tearaway was pulling at something in the flowerbed. Her charge did not heed the warning. Clarissa opened her eyes from her catnap and smiled, remembering the childhood of her own children. They had been mischievous too but what a long time ago that all seemed, now. Suddenly she wished to see her own daughters and their children again after the separations that the War had imposed, but even more she wished to see Piers and wondered how long it would be before he was totally free to come home. She had continued watching the children with immense pleasure, but eventually Sophia had taken then indoors to return to the school room for another hour before nursery tea. Clarissa raised herself stiffly from the garden seat and unsteadily made her way across the lawn towards the open French windows, which led into the small sitting room. She would ring for a pot of tea she had decided. It was the most refreshing drink there was in hot weather. Polly responded to the ring and the request. On her return, carrying a tray, she also brought the afternoon post with her. After setting the tray on the low table she placed the letters of indiscriminate size next to the tea before returning to the kitchen. Some days with such a shortage of staff the poor girl seemed to be rushed off her feet. Clarissa perused the pile of letters. There were several for Thea who was always such a prolific letter writer but there were two in the same handwriting. The Countess knew instantly that they were both from her son. One was addressed to Thea so she picked up the other and slit the envelope open. Pulling out the paper from the envelope she noticed how short and to the point the letter was but, as she read, on her wrinkled features turned into a smile. This news was just what she had been waiting for. Piers was on his way home. His camp had been liberated and after a debriefing they would be allowed to return to England. The one downside as a senior officer was that he had insisted on leaving with his men. But no matter what, he was coming home to them at last. Her face was a picture of great joy but her wish was that Thea had been with her, so they could celebrate together.

Chapter 63

Thea had found a small hotel near Oxford Street where she could stay overnight before taking the train the next morning to Essex. She was still reluctant to telephone Sabine and decided that she would have a very early breakfast before making the short journey. Sabine had not been a particularly early riser so she hoped that she would find her at home. It was important that there were answers to her questions. The next morning Thea had caught the eight o'clock train and arrived at the small station less than an hour later. She took a taxi giving instructions for the last part of her journey. It was only a short drive before the man stopped on the road near the entrance to Sabine's home. She had decided to walk the rest of the way in order to compose herself before her confrontation with her sister. She felt a little nervous, if she was truly honest with herself; but that was silly, she admonished herself for they were sisters after all. As she progressed up the driveway she saw that the house was beautiful but not as large or as grand as Westborough Hall. She guessed that the house had been built before the Great War in mellow, golden stonework and it had been set in lovely gardens which would look impressive for most of the year, but was now in a blaze of summer glory. Thea stood for a moment drinking in the whole of the grandeur before her wondering what Sabine's life had been like behind the façade of the building. Picking up her bag she walked slowly on to find the answers to her questions which she hoped would give her peace of mind. Thea knocked the lion's head created out of brass and waited. Eventually she heard hurried footsteps before the great door swung open. A young woman dressed in normal attire, not in a maid's uniform, as Thea might have expected, looked at her enquiringly.

'How may I help you?' she asked pertly, looking Thea up and down.

'Who is it Jenny?' a familiar voice called from the interior of the house.

Thea looked uncertainly for a moment. 'I'm Thea, Sabine's sister.'

'Well, you had better come in,' Jenny said, holding the door wider for Thea to enter. 'Leave your bag here.' She indicated a place before leading the way down the hallway. The interior of the house was smaller than Thea had imagined but it was beautifully proportioned and the hallway was lined with light oak panelling. Jenny led Thea into a small drawing room which overlooked the beautifully kept gardens at the rear of the property. Sabine sat in a high-backed chair with the morning paper laid to one side on a small table. As she glanced up to see the visitor, a strange look passed over her face.

'Hello Sabine.' Thea bent to kiss her sister's cheek. Sabine made no comment but then she turned to the young woman, 'Jenny do you think that you could leave us?' Jenny looked concerned but said nothing as she quietly closed the door behind her.

'How are you Thea?' Sabine asked without emotion as she regarded her sister. 'It has been a long time.'

'Well, considering everything,' she said, 'but puzzled why I have not heard from you for so long. I did try writing.' Her voice trailed off. Sabine looked thoughtful and remained silent for a few minutes.

'Yes, I'm sorry about that but I have not been well for quite some time. The doctor said that I had too many shocks and I needed quiet and plenty of rest in order to recover.'

'Peter could have written to me to let me know,' Thea said, allowing a peevish tone to enter her voice.'

'Yes, he could have done but he has been busy with the War and my being ill. Jenny is not a servant, by the way. She is my companion, my gaoler,' she laughed ruefully. 'Peter has said that I should not be alone until I am completely better. He spends much of his time in London but I suspect that he has a mistress there. He has not been near me since George's birth.' A silence fell between them. Thea felt quite shocked by the revelations that Sabine was making. Had her marriage truly sunk to such depths after an idealistic beginning?

'It was Mummy dying like that which began my mental decline. Then Fellowes sent me her papers from the London house. That sent me nearly over the edge. It was then that Peter forbade me seeing you because they were mostly concerning you.' Thea shuffled on her chair, suddenly feeling on edge and wondering where all this was leading, but she did not want to interrupt her sister's flow. The questions would come later.

'I fell pregnant with George,' Sabine continued. 'It was not an easy pregnancy and the birth was difficult. He lacked oxygen at birth and it has left him a little simple. Peter wants to put him into some form of care but I have refused. I suspect, though, that Peter will have his way in the end, as he does in most matters these days.' Thea could now see how the difficulties of life had worn Sabine down. Her face looked sallow and gaunt; she had far from fully recovered from the troubles that had afflicted her. But she thought of Peter and wondered at his lack of care. She felt that this was a situation where she might have to intervene, but that was not really a good idea between husband and wife. Thea rose from her chair and went to kneel by her sister, taking her hand.

'You should have told me this. What are sisters for? We have always been close, Sabby. I feel so bad that I did not come before.'

'But you had the responsibility of the Hall, the children.'

'You must come and stay with us. You will get better. But now tell me what Mama's papers disclosed? Why were they about me?' Sabine wrapped herself once more into a blanket of silence, looking at Thea but not properly seeing her.

'Sabine, tell me please.' Thea returned to the present. 'You are not going to like what I am about to tell you. Do you remember after Daddy died and we learned about our illegitimacy, we had been so angry about the deception? Mama could have told us then but the secrets were still there.'

Thea wondered what all this was about. There seemed little gained by hurrying Sabine.

'The truth is that we are not sisters Thea. There is no kind way of saying this. It would seem that your own mother, Mama's sister Ruth, had died giving birth to you. Mama and Daddy took you in as their own child. Your natural father was killed on the Western Front in 1915 just before you were born. You were an orphan.'

Thea gasped, reeling from the details of her personal history. She had never detected any difference in the way that Beatrice and James had treated her but the subterfuge was too much, particularly after the lies that were disclosed after her father's death. Sabine rose from her chair and walked to the bureau where the papers were filed after they came into her possession. She thumbed through them until she found a birth certificate. It stated Dorothea Sanderson, daughter of Ruth Sanderson née Cavendish and Rupert Sanderson (deceased). There was also her parents' marriage certificate to endorse the knowledge that she had now discovered. Anger, such an alien emotion to Thea, raged through her. There was anger at her adoptive parents for having kept such vital information to themselves. And there was anger towards Sabine for shielding the truth from her over the past few years. There was anger at the heartache that she and Piers had been forced to endure when it could have been different. It was all too much. She sat on the floor beside Sabine's chair and howled in her distress, tears running in a torrent down her cheeks. Sabine sat and watched the volcanic eruption that began to explode within Thea's psyche and it made her afraid for their close relationship, one that had existed through childhood and beyond. Sabine felt that Thea's tears were shed for many reasons, never suspecting that at the bottom of her heartache was the fact that Thea could have been Piers' wife all those years ago, without the subterfuge that ensued.

'Stay the night,' Sabine begged. But Thea had already risen from her chair.

'No, not now, after this. You should have told me before Sabine. I need time to think. I shall take these as I believe they are mine.' There was a sarcastic tone to her voice as she wafted the papers aloft. She left a tearful Sabine without any feelings of remorse. Thea collected her overnight bag from the hallway, pulling the front door behind her with a resounding bang. She knew it was childish and rather unkind to treat Sabine so badly after her illness, but her thoughts were not entirely rational until she had truly digested the facts. The sun shone warmly down but there was an intense coldness surrounding her heart as she began her walk to the station to return to London and then to catch her connection to Worcester. As she sat staring out of the carriage window at the ever changing landscape, Thea had time to reflect on her personal circumstances. The information she had received just a few hours ago would once have been the answer to her prayers. Now she was unsure of everything. Piers had not returned home yet and, even though his letters declared his love for her, the reality of their being together might say something different. It was easy to see the past through rose-tinted glasses. She did not wish to tell anybody of her discovery, not even Clarissa, for everything had become too much for her to assimilate at the moment. In reality she was not even the same person as the one who had arrived to see her sister that very morning. Her heart was full of vengeance as she contemplated the people who had not told her the truth about whom she really was. There was much to think about before she could confide in others. The War had finished but the one in her heart was only just beginning. If there was still a bond with Piers, their relationship had to run its course like any courtship. Whatever they had, had been clandestine, secret trysts away from public scrutiny. It was the uncertainty of everything which upset her. In the past she had realized that Piers was beyond reach, but now there were endless possibilities. However, the one certainty in her life was that her love for Piers Devine had never been stronger than it was now. On her return to Westborough Hall Clarissa was waiting for her, waving an envelope while her face told the full story, one which Thea was now dreading. The journey into the future was just about to begin and, for the first time in a long while, Thea was afraid.

Chapter 64

It was now nearly a month after Thea's visit to see Sabine. Neither of them had written to the other believing that there should be time for the dust to settle on the whole affair. Anger could be a destructive force and surely time would allow it to burn itself out so that they could build new bridges in the future. One night after Clarissa had retired to her bed Thea sat at the library table with pen and paper. She had decided to write to Ernest Fellowes to see if he could enlighten her further on her personal history. She was aware of some of her circumstances but there was a yawning chasm in her knowledge of her father, Rupert Sanderson. Composing the letter took more thought than she had at first realized. There were several crossings out but eventually she had written what seemed acceptable in her very strange circumstances. She did not expect an instant reply but she was not disappointed, for it came swiftly enough:

My dear Mrs. Carson,

I am sorry you have received such a shock as to your true identity. I have known about the circumstances of your birth from the very beginning, since I began working for the Earl and his Countess. My profession has silenced me but now that you are in possession of the legal documentation, I can give you the facts. Anything else you will have to discover for yourself. My work is about facts and the truth.

Your birth mother married your father while he was on leave in early 1915. Later that year Mrs. Sanderson discovered that she was pregnant. She resided in the same street as the Devine town house. She wished to remain near

her sister Beatrice Cavendish while her husband was away.
The Sandersons were a wealthy family from Hampshire. I do
believe that they owned several properties on the south coast.
Rupert Sanderson, your father, was their only son. He had
fallen out with them many years before but he was wealthy in
his own right, having inherited a legacy from his grandfather.
His family did not know that he had married. After his death
in 1915, Ruth Sanderson was left as a very young widow who
depended on her sister to help her through these very difficult
times. She had asked her sister to be your legal guardian
should anything happen to her.

Beatrice Cavendish, your aunt, did just that when your
mother died not long after your birth. She had no need to
adopt you and she brought you up as her own with her
daughter Sabine Cavendish. The Earl was quite happy with
the idea and, as they say, the rest is history. After that you
became their daughter and your name was legally changed to
Cavendish.

The paternal side of the family never knew of your
existence but if you wish to take matters further, there are
ways of doing so.

I wish you every success in what you might decide. Please
do not hesitate to contact me if you have need of my services.

With regards from your friend (yes I mean that!)

Ernest Fellowes

Thea reread the letter with tears in her eyes. She so
wanted to know more about her natural mother but there was
nobody left who could tell her. Beatrice had never wanted to
talk about Ruth, other than to say that she was beautiful and
had loved her dearly. Now she knew why she had been
reluctant to speak out. Thea felt angry with Beatrice on many
issues just lately but she had not failed her as a mother. She
had been loved and wanted just as much as Sabine. Thea
thought of her own daughter and vowed that when the time
was right, she would tell her about Jack Carson. She did not
know a lot but there was his medal of valour which would

always belong to Scarlett. The world seemed to have turned on its axis more in recent times than it had during the whole of the War, or so it seemed. She felt that she was on a quest to discover the real Thea Sanderson and, when the time was right, she and Scarlett would travel to Hampshire to find her father's family if they were still alive. But there was also a legacy, somewhere, which her father must have left to her mother, Ruth. Ernest Fellowes had not mentioned that part of the mystery. Something else to unravel, she felt; a legacy for Scarlett some time in the future.

News from the Far East had finally left the world at peace. There had been an unconditional surrender by Japan on 14th August after the dropping of the atomic bombs on Nagasaki and Hiroshima by the Americans. It was another chapter to celebrate by the Allies. There was a lightening of spirit by everyone now it was, finally, over.

August had brought some lovely warm weather, not hot but warm and balmy like a true English summer's day. Thea had thrown herself back into the work on the estate, for there was much to be done. She also wanted to spend time with the little girls now that Sophia Bennett had returned home to her family for the summer; they lived on the south coast. Meanwhile the nursery staff was busier than they had been since the children had begun their education. They also took it in turn to visit their own families. So life in general was busy for the late summer brought harvesting and the Land Girls were still hard at work. Thea wondered what would happen when the men finally returned home. That should not be too long, now. Would the old ways return? Thea thought not but it would be interesting to see. As for her life with Scarlett, it would never be the same in the future. Clarissa had known intuitively that Thea's world had changed since her return from her visit to Sabine. Her manner had been different and she had kept her own council over what had transpired, making her appear a little distant and unsettled. There were no bad feelings between the two women, but Clarissa was a little upset that Thea had not chosen to confide in her if there were problems. It was all so strange to have secrets when Thea had always been happy and open. She wondered if Thea was unsettled about her future now that Piers would soon return home. The world at large was jubilant about peace but individual lives were still topsy-turvy after changes to the normal order of everyday life. There would not be a family in the country that was not affected by what had happened. But perhaps time would put a different perspective on events.

On this tranquil Sunday afternoon Thea had chosen to give some quality time to the children and had been playing hide and seek on the front lawns of Westborough Hall. There were secret places to hide amongst the bushes and the trees making it an ideal place for such games. Shrieks of laughter could be heard as the children enjoyed their time playing. There had also been mumbles of complaint from Jane and Scarlett who felt that Maudie was a bit of a cheat. It was Maudie's time to seek and she was counting, 'One, two, three… eight, nine, ten, coming ready or not.'

The others had disappeared swiftly knowing that their sister was too impatient to count properly which did not usually give them enough time to hide. Maudie opened her eyes and looked around her, but she could not see any of them. They were well and truly hidden. As her eyes swept around the garden she became aware of something or somebody different which had changed the immediate landscape. Looking more closely she spied a stranger, an unfamiliar figure making her shiver with fear. Suddenly she screamed and screamed until she was red in the face from the effort and sobs shook her small frame. The figure moved, suddenly feeling awkward that he had caused the child such distress. That had not been his intention but he had enjoyed the scene before him. Thea was not far away; she was hiding around the corner of the old building on the west side of the house, but on hearing Maudie's screams she looked to see what was the cause of such a rumpus, believing the child to be hurt. Maudie was pointing in the direction of the driveway, but there was an expression of utter fear on her face. Thea turned her head to discover what had so upset the child. There she saw a man in crumpled clothing whom Thea thought was an old tramp. There were more of them about in the summertime, arriving at the kitchen door asking for food or a drink of water to quench their thirst. Squinting to see better against the strong rays of the sun, she also took a few steps forward to witness the scene, revealing her hiding place. But she knew by his stance, time could not erode such memories. But there was also something strange about him, something that she could not pinpoint.

'Hush Maudie it is all right,' she said, having moved closer to comfort the frightened child and put her arms around her; but she still cried even though she was no longer alone. The figure leant against a tree watching them, a smile curling his lips; and then he leant down to pick up a battered suitcase. His tie was loosened and he held his jacket on one finger slung over his shoulder in a casual manner; it was in a way that Thea had witnessed many times before. They walked towards each other slowly at first and then they quickened their pace. Suddenly Thea felt self-conscious about her appearance as her hair was falling down from its fastenings after the exertions of the game. She automatically tried tidying wisps of it away behind her ears, but to no affect. They had moved to within feet of each other, then stopped to look with such intensity into the other's eyes. The smile that lit up both faces spoke volumes that the years apart could not destroy. Love and desire were still there for all to see if there had been an audience to witness such events. Thea saw now what was strange about Piers. His face was gaunt and pale from his imprisonment and his severe military haircut did not enhance his appearance, but he smiled that lopsided smile which used to lighten her world so long ago. By now Maudie had stopped screaming and the two little girls, having appeared from their hiding places, stood in a line watching and wondering. They had been told never to speak to strangers and were intrigued by Thea's response to this unknown man. They met and Piers kissed her chastely on the cheek, but his pleasure at seeing her was palpable.

'Welcome home,' she said, her face hosting a broad grin, 'welcome home.' Piers placed an arm around her waist as they walked towards the children and the house. The girls gawped, open-mouthed at what they were witnessing.

'Say "hello" to your father,' Thea said, but they continued to stare. Scarlett hung back, knowing that this was not her own father. Her own was dead for Mummy had told her. Jane, the oldest of the trio, had a thought that lay beyond the wisdom of a child of her years. She felt that now this stranger had returned to live amongst this house of women that everything would change beyond measure. Her chin wobbled as she contemplated this thought, but remained stoic in her refusal to let the tears fall. That would not be the way to greet this strange man, her father, who had existed in her imagination for so long fuelled by tales from Thea and her grandmother. Piers was equally at a loss, not knowing his own children. He smiled at the girls but did not attempt to hug them. There were too many bridges to rebuild before they could all truly move on. Would the world right itself, he wondered? Just because the War was over in Europe and now the Far East, it had left many uncertainties in day-to-day life.

'Why did you not tell us that you were coming today?' Thea asked.

'I wanted to take my time, to savour my freedom and to look at what is mine. It has been over five years.'

'I know,' she said. 'It has been long for all of us, but I don't know how you have coped with imprisonment.' Piers smiled again, wishing to pull Thea into his arms and kiss her with a pent-up passion that had lived in his head for all of those years, but the frustration of not being able to do so was still there. 'I have been a lucky one when I could have been lying dead somewhere. I have returned to you and all this,' he said, looking at the magnificent façade of Westborough Hall. Thea looked at him, wondering how he could be without bitterness after such a long absence. Her own feelings would have been quite different, she thought, if she had suffered similar experiences. They walked on towards the house while the children dragged their feet in their wake, wondering what would happen next.

Piers suddenly stopped for a moment to just absorb the beauty of the building that was his. He had imagined this homecoming for years. He had dreamt of it and, now he was here, his eyes blurred with unshed tears. Would he be able to get on with life as he had before? He had to, but he did not know. He had become a different person, which was almost the case when different experiences moulded one into somebody else. His thoughts drifted towards his fellow comrades in arms, wondering if their worlds and relationships had also changed beyond recognition. He knew that he had to take back the responsibility for his home, the estate and for the family that he did not know; but there was an undying gratitude that he felt for Thea and his mother who had kept the place running during his absence.

They climbed the steps and entered the house. Again Piers gazed around him at the sumptuous interior of the Great Hall drinking in its beauty as he had done so often over the years. The small sitting room door suddenly opened and Clarissa emerged leaning heavily on two sticks. She was wondering what all the commotion had been about. 'I thought I heard voices...'she began then gasped as she saw her son. Her walking sticks clattered to the floor as her hands went unsteadily out to him. Her face was covered in tears of joy.

'My son,' she said, and Piers had never seen her cry before, this stoic figure of his childhood.

'Mama,' he said using the childhood title out of affection. They held each other for a very long time, while Thea shepherded the three little girls away to the nursery in order to give them a feeling of normality in this topsy-turvy world. The separation for all had been just too much to bear. The young had been impatient for victory while the old wondered whether they would ever see their children again. It had been a long and cruel war, of that there was no doubt.

Chapter 65

The months following Piers' return home had not been as euphoric as everyone had expected. As the New Year of 1946 approached Thea knew that she was not happy, but some of it was of her own making. Naively she had expected to fall back into an easy relationship with Piers. But his personality seemed to have changed to some degree. She had had whispered conversations with Clarissa who, after the initial return home, had found her son moody and morose or, on other occasions, he sought solitude and would wander off to avoid conversations. He had confessed to them at one point that he was not ready to return to his position in the Lords. Perhaps he would in time but, for now, he was relishing his freedom which they could understand after his loss of his liberty for so long. He often stayed out in all weathers coping with the problems of the estate. It became his solution to not want to be tied to anything or anyone. But it had profound effects on the women in his life, including the children. Some of the demobbed soldiers had returned to their jobs on the land. There was little else they could do for it was a life they had known before the War and it was with these men that Piers would fraternize, as they were kindred spirits who had experienced similar fates of war. It was a hard adjustment that they all had to make. None of these former soldiers would speak of their experiences to their womenfolk or growing sons. Everything became deeply buried as they began to move on with their lives. However, Piers had told them one thing about the War. He had not been required to return to Germany like many other POWs. At his debriefing he had been questioned about the treatment of himself and his fellow soldiers, but he knew that he had been fortunate in the fact that the Commandant had been an honourable, well-educated man, a lawyer in his civilian life. He had rigorously upheld the rules of the Geneva Convention and had surrendered the camp to Piers as the liberating army was approaching. Other camps had not been as fortunate and it was now documented that fifty escapees from Stalag Luft 3 had been massacred on Hitler's direct orders. Other senior officers had to return to Germany to answer questions about their own camps. These crimes had to be made answerable to. *Following orders* was the excuse given, but the aftermath was fast approaching when justice had to be done and seen to be done. Thea felt redundant now that Piers had picked up the reins of running the estate. She was beginning to feel that now was the time for her to move on, to start a new future together for herself and Scarlett. She had played her part to keep the Hall and estate running, but now was her time to put her future first and lavish time on her daughter.

'I can't go on the way we are,' she had confided to Clarissa. Clarissa looked away, unsure that she could cope with Thea's departure from the Hall. They had lived in harmony for all these years and she did not want to lose her. Life at the Hall would be inconceivable without Thea. She could not understand the son she loved so much. It had been in her thoughts to return to the dower house as a refuge from her son's moods. It would be quite easy to do that now that the house had been returned to the Devines.

'Please stay,' Clarissa had said. It was not usually in her nature to beg. It was at this point that Thea unburdened herself of the story that Sabine had told her regarding the truth of her birth. They were sitting near the log fire in the library on a rather bleak January day. Thea had sat with a book in her hands, paying scant attention to its contents while Clarissa had been dozing, gently snoring in the chair that she had made her own over time. Eventually the two women, over a welcome cup of tea, had discussed the tale that Thea had kept to herself for many months. Clarissa now knew why Thea had been so distant over time. The news was the old woman's answer to a prayer. Both women sat in silence for several minutes, deep in thought. Thea was reeling from the fact that she had finally confided in someone about her origins and, strangely enough, she felt as if a burden had been lifted from her shoulders, finally as if she had been set free. Clarissa was quite shocked at the revelations she had heard but, in one way, it opened up possibilities that she could never have imagined in the past. She had grown to love Thea as if she was her own daughter.

'Thea, my dear,' Clarissa began. 'I do believe that you should seek out your natural father's family. It will ground you. You will get to know who you truly are. There are parts of you which are missing. It will also benefit Scarlett, too.' Here the Countess paused looking at Thea, thoughtfully.

'And I do believe that you should tell Piers. It is time now that he took full control of his affairs, physically and emotionally.'

'I can't tell him,' Thea said nervously. 'I am not trying to trap him into marriage. He has not spoken of personal things since his return.'

'Then he is a fool.' Clarissa was always one to strike at the heart of the matter. 'He has made no attempt to get to know his daughters and we are all walking on eggshells around him as if he is the only man who has ever been to war. Others suffered far more than he did. Did we not witness that here with men who had lost limbs, had gone blind and were mental wrecks from what they had experienced? Piers was one of the lucky ones. He was treated well, but now we are made to be his whipping boy.' Clarissa had stood up unsteadily in her anger. This was the woman of old who was not prepared to put up with problems that had been inflicted by others. 'People have had to suffer at home with all the shortages and by making a contribution one way or another towards the War effort they came through, perhaps not unscathed but they got on with their lives and have made the best of what is left to them.' Thea, despite the emotional turmoil that she felt inside, could not help but smile but the reality was that Clarissa was correct in every way. Piers had been fortunate in many ways, if one could regard being a POW as such.

'I think that you should tell him,' Clarissa reiterated, then promptly sat down again gesturing for Thea to pour her a brandy. She no longer cared about the time of day for everything had just become too much for a woman of her advancing years. Thea sighed, feeling guilty at the thought that life had been far less complicated before Piers' return. As March turned into April with spring now fully upon them, nothing had been resolved at Westborough Hall. Clarissa had watched with bated breath to see how the tide might turn, but it did not. The two people who meant the most to her were avoiding each other. She knew that something had to be done and she was the only one who could do it. Not usually known for interfering, Clarissa felt that there were exceptions to every rule as she watched the unhappiness in their faces as they lived out their daily lives. It was time to make a difference as they could or would not do it for themselves. The Countess watched and waited, trying to find the appropriate moment when she had Piers' full and undivided attention. That moment eventually presented itself. Sabine had invited Thea to spend some quality time with her in Essex. It was a way of building bridges to re-establish the bond they had always possessed. They had both been shocked in their different ways by the revelations of Thea's birth. Over the intervening months they had written to each other regularly. Sabine's health had also made a dramatic improvement, as had her relationship with Peter. Baby George, having seen several specialists, was not feared to be as bad as it had first been thought, but he was never going to be as 'normal' as his siblings were. It was decided that he would not be sent away but would be looked after in the bosom of his family. This had greatly cheered Sabine and slowly the cloud of despair that had hung over her began to evaporate and, with this renewed happiness, Sabine had learned of her new pregnancy. She and Peter were in accord once more. It was decided that the two young women would take time to enjoy themselves in the capital where they had spent their youth. Sabine had no fear of London now that the War was over, but memories of her mother's sad end still haunted her. And so it was that Thea with Clarissa's blessing left Scarlett behind at Westborough Hall and escaped from Piers' gloomy persona. At dinner on the evening of Thea's departure, now taken more formally in the small dining room, Clarissa sat at the elegant table ready to be alone with her son. Piers arrived looking handsome and well-groomed after a day spent outside on the estate.

'Is Thea not here?' he asked somewhat mystified by her unfamiliar absence. Clarissa was ready to seize the moment at all costs. 'No, she has gone to stay with her cousin, Sabine,' she said, keeping the contours of her craggy face perfectly straight. It was difficult not to laugh out loud but life had made her theatrical at times. There was silence for a few moments while Piers digested what had been said. He knew his mother had aged considerably during his absence but he had thought that her mind was still razor sharp. He regarded her quizzically for a few moments before saying, as he poured them a glass each of rather fine wine which had survived the War from the depleted reserves in his cellar, 'You mean her sister, our sister, don't you Mother?'

Clarissa looked at him, her eyes not wavering from his face. She wondered what was going on behind the mask which he had adopted over time. Just at that moment Polly entered the room to serve them the first course. Silence had enveloped the room until the girl made her departure. Clarissa looked at her son once more and, not mincing her words, said:

'Piers you are a fool. You have treated the girl appallingly. She has kept this place running single-handedly waiting for your return. I am not such a stupid old woman who does not know what she has said. Thea has gone to visit her cousin Sabine. I know of your love for the girl. I am not blind to such things. Others might not have noticed but I am an observer of life, the onlooker sees most of the game as the saying goes: particularly of those who live in such close proximity to me. Thea never breathed a word of it.'

Piers pushed his plate of food away, all appetite having gone. In the months since his return he had gained weight and his hair had grown back, now flopping over his forehead making him look younger than his years. His face had lost its gauntness and the wan features had been replaced by the weatherbeaten complexion of a man who worked out of doors. In other words, he had become a picture of health. Although he had lost the pangs of his hunger, his aloofness of recent months had suddenly been replaced by a curiosity that Clarissa had painted, and he wanted to know more.

'Why are you calling Thea Sabine's cousin?' he asked. His mother regarded him with an infuriating smile on her face. 'Because that is exactly what she is. When Beatrice died the truth about Thea's parentage became known. Her birth name was Thea Sanderson. Her real mother was Beatrice's sister Ruth, who died when Thea was just days old. There is not a drop of Devine blood in her veins.' Clarissa was eating her meal with great relish while continuing to watch the reaction of her son. He was silent as he thought about the information that his mother had delivered. On the other hand Clarissa thought about the months when Piers had not treated his family kindly, almost as if he was punishing them for all the time he had spent in the POW camp. She had heard about people not always treating their nearest and dearest well when they had problems. Human nature was a complicated affair, she mused. Clarissa knew that she was always capable of holding her own corner. That would never change, not even with her advancing years. Piers rose from the table and walked towards the fireplace, resting his arm on the mantelshelf. Looking straight at his mother he asked, 'Why has she never told me?'

'Well you only have to look inwardly to answer that question,' she answered bluntly. Now was not the time to hold back on the truth. 'You have been difficult since your return. We all know that the War has changed people. We have given you time, perhaps you need longer; but we have all had to make sacrifices of some kind. But we can no longer pussyfoot around your moods for much longer for you are making us suffer as well. Anyway Thea is thinking about leaving the Hall to make a home with Scarlett. She has become a wealthy young woman in her own right.'

'I have always loved Thea, Mother. I spent hours in the camp trying to find a solution to the problem, but of course there was no sensible answer to be had. When I returned there she was as beautiful as ever but she could never be mine. I knew that I had to keep my distance from her otherwise I could not hold myself responsible for what I might do and then a scandal of some magnitude would erupt, filling the newspapers with gossip. I can see now how cold and thoughtless I have been, even to the children. I can see the fear in their eyes when they look at me. I don't know how to relate to them although I want to so badly.' Tears rose into Clarissa's eyes as she now knew the torment that filled her son's heart. 'If you still love her you have to tell her and also the children who have never known a father. We have done our best but there is no substitute for the real thing.'

'Oh Mama, what have I done?'

'Nothing that cannot be fixed providing you do not prevaricate for too long.' She forced a smile through her tears. 'Thea and the children are very forgiving but it is up to you my son to do the right thing by them all. They are lost souls waiting to be found.'

'And you Mama?' he asked.

'It has taken me a lifetime to learn the art of forgiveness Piers, but finally I believe that I have done it. Even your father might be a little bit proud if he was still with us.' Piers did not comment but came to his Mother's side thinking how wise she was, but perhaps that came with age. If that was the case he had a lot of learning to do.

'What can I do to win her back, Mama?'

'Take it slowly so that you win her trust. Woo her as if you have only just met and then tell her how much you love her. Cherish her, my son. It is all any woman wants.' Clarissa turned away from him thinking of her early days with James Devine. She had never been cherished but her strength of character told her that perhaps she had never been a woman to want such things, because she had possessed an independent spirit.

'I have to be up early in the morning,' Piers said before going to kiss his mother good night. She said nothing more, leaving him to depart as she remembered years gone by. She watched his departure but was not deceived for Piers Devine, Earl of Westborough, was going to bed early to cogitate upon her words. Had she not seen it all before? She just had a feeling that everything would now be all right. Sometimes it paid to interfere, she mused, but only for the right reasons.

Chapter 66

Thea had enjoyed her week in Essex with Sabine. They had delighted in each other's company just as they had as children. Nothing could destroy that bond they had rediscovered. Thea had also formed a rapport with Sabine's children, particularly with little George despite his problems; he had proved to be very endearing. So it was with some reluctance that Thea prepared to return to Westborough Hall and all the problems that ensued there. However, she felt that her absence was long enough for she did not wish to neglect Scarlett, although she had no doubt that she was well taken care of. During her stay with Sabine she had confided the story of her relationship with Piers and her hopes and fears for the future. Sabine had offered much the same advice as Clarissa but as Thea travelled home on the train to Worcester she became more than ever resolved to look for the home that she had been contemplating for long enough, but had not possessed the courage to do anything about. Her mind was consumed with Piers. Part of her could not entirely blame him for his behaviour for he was not aware of the full circumstances concerning her past. However, she could not forgive him for the way that he had treated his children and, if he was to remarry to produce an heir, how neglected would the little girls feel once she and Scarlett moved away from Westborough Hall? She was also resolved to seek out the family that she had never known in order to discover the true Thea Carson. Suddenly family had become very important to her. The return to Westborough Hall was more pleasant than she had anticipated. First of all there seemed to be a truce between Piers and his mother. There were pleasantries uttered, showing that the knives with barbs had been withdrawn. He had welcomed Thea home warmly, asking about her visit and after the health of her family. Clarissa had observed the new initiatives with pleasure but held her own council, noting that Rome had not been built in a day and the courtship that Piers was subtly engineering would take time and effort from both of them. After dinner each evening Clarissa would drink her brandy in the library as usual and then would make some feeble excuse as to why she could not stay any longer, thus leaving the young people alone together. At first Thea and Piers had felt awkward in each other's company. Thea had been left in ignorance of the fact that Piers was aware of her true origins. He did not attempt to touch her physically but his wooing of her began to pay dividends as they really began to get to know each other again. They talked endlessly about their personal aspirations for the future and about the children, who had shown less fear of their father in recent weeks. As time went on Piers would lay a hand of affection on Thea's arm or brush a lock of hair out of her eyes in a moment of tenderness. He loved the way that it tumbled about her shoulders, giving her an air of youth which they had long since left behind. And as this continued Thea did not flinch at the touch and there became a stirring of desire for both of them. Clarissa was an intense observer of the full romance that was developing between them and she felt a certain pride in the way that Piers had handled the whole affair, not rushing into anything to frighten Thea away; but she began to feel that the time had arrived for Piers to disclose his knowledge of Thea's personal history. Yet she knew that she had interfered enough already and had to sit and wait patiently for her son to complete the task. Patience was not one of Clarissa's many talents but wait she must, trusting the instincts of the couple. It had occurred to Thea that matters were different with Piers since her return from Essex and her suspicions deepened, as time went on, that Clarissa might have had a hand in furthering the process along and had revealed the truth to her son. The mere thought sent a delicious tingle down her spine at the anticipation of what might come, but she was prepared to play a waiting game. However, she was totally sure of her love for Piers; had always been but now everything was different and their love had grown further although neither of them had voiced the fact. Then one evening Thea played her game of chance as she appeared at dinner, wearing her best dress of pink satin. She had curled her hair which fell around her shoulders and she looked breathtakingly beautiful, radiant. Piers looked at her as she made her entrance to the room and his heart seemed to flip with the intensity of his love for her. He knew that he could not continue to play the game of charades any longer. He could now legally make her his own; the waiting game was now over. Clarissa smiled in welcome knowing, just by looking at the faces, that the time had come. Wistfully she felt that in her day she wished James had loved her too, but nobody could revisit the past and before she had realized it such thoughts were banished. Piers was impatient for the meal to be over. Each course seemed to be endless and the conversation stilted but, finally, the time had come.

'I feel particularly tired tonight,' Clarissa said as she rose unsteadily from the table. Piers smiled despite everything. His mother was a true accomplice in the love stakes. 'I should go straight to bed Mama, you do look rather tired. I'll send Polly up with your nightcap.'

'No. I'll take it up for you,' Thea said, half rising from the table in an attempt to fetch it from the library. But a large hand suddenly covered hers to prevent her leaving the table.

'Polly will take it up,' he said firmly before acknowledging his mother's 'Goodnight' as she left the room. As the dining room door closed behind his mother he removed his hand and picked up the crystal glass containing the remnants of his wine and swallowed the contents. Thea sat rigidly in her chair looking down into her lap, where her hands were plaited together, wondering what was to come.

'Thea, we must talk.'

'Yes,' she said, looking up shyly. Piers reached for a hand which was firmly locked with the other, but she released them allowing him to raise one to his lips to be kissed and then be held.

'Thea, by now you must have guessed that my mother has told me the truth about your birth.' She moved uncomfortably in her chair. 'Yes, I have guessed,' was all she said, waiting for what was to come.

'I want to explain my behaviour after my return home so that you will understand.'

'All right,' she said. Piers looked at her before plunging into his story. 'Home was where I always wanted to be during those long, dreary years of dreaming and waiting. Like most soldiers the return home was not as magical as the anticipation. We have had demons to exorcise from the sights that we witnessed and the adjustment to civilian life has not been easy. Then there was you, looking more beautiful than ever. But the thought that I still could not make you mine was sending me crazy until...' His voice stopped as he looked deeply into her eyes, still not quite believing his own words.

'Until my mother told me the truth. Since then I knew that I had to take my time to win your love. I owed you that after the way I had behaved. I love you Thea with all my heart and I want you now and forever. Would you ever think of becoming my wife? That is, if you can forgive me?'

Thea looked down at her hands again while tears filled her eyes and ran in tracks through her make-up. A sob emanated from her slight body, upsetting Piers who rose to take her in his arms, so much wanting her more than he ever had before.

'Hush,' he soothed as if she was a child as her hands curled round his neck, until he kissed her more passionately than he had done anyone before. He led her to the door which he opened and then picking her up carried her upstairs to make her his own. There had been no need for further conversation as their bodies entwined told each other what they needed to know. Clarissa heard the heavy tread on the stairs, followed by the opening and closing of Thea's bedroom door. She smiled to herself and poured another glass of the best brandy in the world.

'Cheers,' she said softly to herself, raising her glass to the future of the Devine dynasty.

Chapter 67

Thea could not believe the state of euphoria which had engulfed her since that night. They had both cried tears of happiness and thanked God that their prayers had been answered. They had not declared their union to an outside world, although they suspected that Clarissa knew as she beamed at them every time they entered her orbit. There was no need to rush as they had a lifetime ahead to enjoy the future. But when the time was right they told the Countess, who felt that she was right to have given them a nudge in the right direction. Then there were the children. Piers knew that the girls loved Thea and this should not prove to be a problem for she had been a mother figure to them in all but name since their birth. But they had not foreseen the problem that had reared its head. Sophia Bennett had become aware by chance of Scarlett's unhappiness in the schoolroom one afternoon. She had lingered, allowing Jane and Maudie to run on ahead. This was not like Scarlett who was often first out of the door, but she hung back tearful and clingy. Eventually she told Sophia her fears, which the governess tried to quell. After Scarlett returned to the nursery, Sophia went in search of Thea whom she found reading in the library by the fire, for the spring day was chilly. After their discussion, which had quite shocked Thea making her heart ache for her daughter, she had come to a decision. The following day Scarlett was exempt from the schoolroom while mother and daughter took some quality time together. Jane and Maudie had expressed their disapproval at having to do lessons while Scarlett had gone with her mother on an outing. Thea had made a picnic in the kitchens and then mother and daughter, wrapping themselves warmly against the chill which still lingered, walked towards the woods to view the wild flowers and to talk without unwanted ears listening. They walked through the fields, Scarlett clutching her mother's hand as if her life depended on it. They entered the woods listening to the scuttle of small animals in the undergrowth and birdsong high up in the branches. They found a fallen log where they sat to eat their impromptu picnic. In the silence that ensued as they lunched Thea could see the unhappiness etched on the child's face. When they had finished eating, they scattered some crusts on the nearby foliage for the birds to take when they had gone, but that would not be immediately because Thea had every intention of talking to her daughter to reassure her that life was not going to change dramatically. She cupped the child's chin in her hand and kissed her cheek.

'I have something special to tell you Scarlett. I want you to listen carefully to me and understand what I am saying.' A sob emanated from Scarlett's small body, twisting Thea's heart in concern and bringing to the fore her motherly instincts to protect this tortured child.

'There is no need to do that, Scarlett,' she said, hugging her daughter closely, her heart feeling as if it was about to break. 'Are you listening to me?'

'Yeth,' Scarlett lisped as she tried to stem the flow of tears.

'I am going to marry Piers and then he will be your daddy. Maudie and Jane will become your real sisters, not just pretend ones.' Thea found it difficult to explain the situation to a small child.'

'I have a real daddy but he is in Heaven,' Scarlett suddenly said, repeating what she had been told over the years.

'Yes, I know Scarlett. You have a real daddy but Piers is going to help take care of you because he wants to. Your real daddy will always be just that, you're real daddy. Nobody will ever try to change that and I will always be your mummy and it will not be any different from what it is now. We will always live together like we do now. Nothing is going to change very much. We will be one, big family.'

The child's arms wound their way around Thea's neck as she climbed onto her mother's lap. Together they sat like that for several precious moments just holding each other, savouring the great love, the bond which could never be severed between mother and child. As they eventually pulled apart Thea's hand touched the secret place in her stomach where a new life was growing. She knew that she would have to tell Piers soon. Thea had given Piers her permission to use his considerable influence and wealth to track down the unknown Sanderson family in Hampshire. Although her happiness was nearly complete there was still one piece of the jigsaw missing concerning Rupert Sanderson. Piers had written to Ernest Fellowes to set in motion the task of locating Thea's grandparents. It had not taken long to find that they had lived in a rural backwater on the edge of the New Forest. Their deaths had been registered as a few years previously in a railway accident while travelling in Italy before the War. That had been where they had been laid to rest, never knowing that they had a granddaughter or great-granddaughter in England. The details of the sadness of such events had touched Thea's heart as they must have been lonely without a family to turn to. Their only child, her father, had died long ago. Again Thea felt parts of her life could have been sad and difficult too if events had not turned out as they had; she was forever grateful to Beatrice and James for giving her a home and all the love in the world. Even Scarlett would have had few relatives to turn to, but now their future was tinged with happiness. She looked at Piers who had read out the facts from Ernest Fellowes' report. He was deep in thought as he put down the letter on the table in front of him.

'I've been thinking, Thea, that you could contest the contents of your grandparents' will. And there is also the legacy from your mother, Ruth that is. That has to be sorted out now that the facts are known.'

'No,' said Thea, 'I don't want any of it. There has been enough heartache in the world as it is. Let them all rest in peace. I have all the happiness I need right now. I am rich in so many ways.' She rose from her chair and went to him. He pulled her close and kissed her with all the passion that he had saved up during the War years. Eventually they pulled apart.

'You know Piers we love you very much,' she said laughing as her hand slid to the secret place. Piers' eyes followed the movement of her hand and then returned to her face, where she smiled the secret smile which had touched her eyes and mouth in recent days. His own face brightened as he placed his own hand over her own.

'When?' he said.

'A long time yet, perhaps six months.'

'Could it be an heir?' he asked, his eyes bright with expectancy.

'I suppose it could but we have to wait and see,' she teased. 'There will be plenty more opportunities to create an heir and lots of sons for Westborough.' Her mirth was infectious, but suddenly her face clouded as she thought of Mary.

'What is it?' Piers asked, suddenly anxious.

'I was thinking of Mary.'

'Don't. Mary was a tortured soul, but now she is at peace.'

'But Piers, it does not seem fair that we share this great happiness while Mary lies in that cold place.' Piers did not answer her as his mouth pressed down hungrily on her own. They had all suffered so much over the years; now was the time to move forward into a brighter future, leaving past events to take care of themselves.

Epilogue

'Why have you taken so long to make the arrangements?' Clarissa said, angrily having climbed onto her high horse and had sat there for at least an hour. 'This could be your heir, Piers. Really I don't know what has got into you. Are you not bothered about the future of the earldom? Do you want long lost relatives to inherit what should go to your legitimate heir? Why has it taken you so long to get around to this marriage? You love Thea don't you, and all this prevarication is not setting a good example to the children.' The tirade had gone on and on. Piers laughed. 'Hush mother. Everyone will hear you. Anyway it is all sorted for two weeks' time. I have just come off the telephone and it is to be held in the Chapel in Westminster. It is going to be a small affair with just the family present.' Clarissa was silent as she relaxed into her chair to absorb the news. 'About time too,' she said, determined to have the last word on the matter. Henry James Devine, to be known to the family as Harry, the heir to Westborough Hall, entered the world four months after the marriage of his parents in January 1947 just as the snow began to fall, heralding the worst winter on record. Piers was so proud to have an heir and could not thank his wife enough for the special gift she had given him. His mother had been in her element after the news had reached her ears and she, not a particularly religious woman, had offered prayers and thanks to the Almighty; but most of all she thanked the young woman who had captured her heart over the years of her son's absence and had become her daughter in spirit, long before she had married Piers.

'I love you more than words can say,' he said as he looked tenderly from his wife to his sleeping son.

'And I love you,' Thea said, her words coming from the heart as she regarded the child with such tenderness.

'I think little Harry might want a little brother before too long.' Piers tried to keep his face straight.

'In your dreams,' Thea replied, unable to suppress the smile on her face. But deep down, she knew that Piers was probably right. An heir and another brother might be the best idea to strengthen the Devine dynasty for the future. They were now a true family, Thea felt, and the cheerful noise of children would no doubt reverberate within the walls of Westborough Hall for many years to come.